Half Smile

—for Ann Smith, in memoriam

Half Smile

SJ

With his toothbrush in hand like a Moon Pie, Reece argued with Horace about taking the truck. "I can do it. At least let me try."

Horace pushed back in his recliner, still wearing his dirty garden shoes. Reece could see his thinning hair, all gray and black, the hearing aid in his ear. "Well, boy, I'm not giving you the keys, but I won't stop you."

Dora held a dish towel. Her black, graying hair was flat, ready for her regular Saturday appointment before church on Sunday. "What if you hit someone?"

"I won't hit anyone. Look, you want me to take care of Kristin, right? Well, that's what I'm going to do. I think her parents have her up in arms." He reached into the key bowl on top of the gas heater. "And I'll come back by ten. How's that?"

"I'll be worried the whole time," said Dora. "Horace, are you going to let him do this?"

Horace sighed. "Well, it looks like it. You be careful, though, son. And call us when you get there." He looked down at his shoes, dusted with red dirt.

"I will. I promise."

Reece went back to the bathroom and brushed his teeth. He needed to shower. He looked in the mirror and noted his receding hairline, touched the scars on his temples, and could only think of Emma. He made a pass at combing his short chestnut hair and took a deep breath.

Reece slowed and pulled into the steep driveway. The

light was on in Kristin's bedroom, but the porch light was off. He opened the creaky door of the battered F-150 and could hear Walter barking in the backyard. Walter was officially their dog. He dreaded small-talking with Edwin, which would be inevitable. Gert would ignore him and pace through the house. He rang the doorbell and waited. The door opened.

"Well, hey there, trouble," said Kristin. "You've been a bad boy, but how was driving?"

"Just like a charm. You okay?" He kissed her on the lips and let her give him a big hug.

In tight jeans and a loose blue scrub, she led him up the carpeted stairs. She'd taken out her contacts and worn her glasses, which made her pretty green eyes look even larger.

Reece dreaded walking into the den to face Edwin in his recliner, hair neatly combed, a look of impatience on his face. And there he was.

"Hey," said Reece.

"Hello, Reece," said Edwin. He gripped the sides of his leather recliner. "Have a seat. Would you like a drink?"

"No, I'm fine." He saw Gert peek around the corner from the kitchen. "Hey."

Gert said, "Hey."

Reece plopped down beside Kristin, who curled into him. He put his arm around her and gave her a squeeze.

"Let me let Walter in." She opened the back door to the deck, and Walter wiggled in, switching his short stubby tail.

"Tell Daddy hello," said Kristin.

"Come here," said Reece. He patted Walter and

scratched his ears.

"He's such a good boy," said Kristin.

"And you're such a good girl," said Edwin. He clicked off the TV with the remote, followed by silence.

Reece focused on Walter and pulled him onto his lap. Walter drooled like a leaky faucet.

"Your day went okay?" asked Reece. He looked to Kristin for help. "Still taking care of the crazy lady?"

"Oh, Mrs. Dunlop, yeah, she thinks she's running the credit card receipts at Loveman's. You know that judge who was so rude to me? He died, coded on the floor."

"The final judgment," said Reece.

Edwin perked up. He had known the judge, exchanged small talk with him on occasion at City Hall. "That's terrible."

"That he was rude to me?" asked Kristin.

"No, Kristin. He was an old man. He always spoke to me." Edwin reached and touched the Bible on his TV tray. "He's in God's hands now. Not for us to judge."

Reece could feel the religion in Edwin's voice, his tone, the way he moved his hands. It was all so familiar but also newly strange. If anything, Ethiopia had been a sucker punch to his convictions. He rubbed Walter's head.

"There's an opening on night shift in ICU," said Kristin. "You could apply. We'd be neighbors."

Reece thought about that. "Is Sheila still the head nurse there?" He knew her from nursing school.

"Yep, and I said something to her. She seemed to think it was a good idea. If you're up for it. Have you had more dizzy spells?"

"Well, no seizures," said Reece. "I have another CT scan

scheduled, so that should be interesting, to see if my brains are still scrambled." He grinned and let Walter jump onto the floor. "Good dog."

"He's your little baby," said Kristin. She punched him in the arm.

An airplane flew over the house.

"Judges are special people," said Edwin. "I think they are called by God. It's a big responsibility. But God is the final judge. We have to remember that."

Reece sighed. "Is he fixed?"

Kristin laughed. "Who, the judge?"

"Kristin?" asked Edwin.

"No, Walter. Has he been neutralized yet?"

"He was fixed before I got him, but he's still a little man. He chases those squirrels. Don't you, buddy?" Walter rolled onto his back, Kristin's foot rubbing his belly.

"There's even a book of Judges in the Bible," said Edwin.

Reece thought back. His parents had taken him to church on Wednesday nights to be a part of the Royal Ambassadors, a club for boys and the venue of many Bible drills. He imagined that he could turn to Judges faster than Edwin. He knew each of the sixty-six books of the Old and New Testaments in order, a minor accomplishment.

"Even angels get tossed out of heaven on occasion," said Reece. His throat tightened.

At that, Edwin coughed, picked up the black Bible, and thumbed to find Judges. Gert was rattling pans in the kitchen, rearranging them in the cupboard. "God is a merciful God," said Edwin.

"He took the judge," said Reece.

"Reece," said Kristin. "Let's just let the judge go. Mrs. Dunlop is a hundred times more interesting."

"Is she a Christian?" asked Edwin.

"For Pete's sake," said Reece. "She's a schizophrenic woman who's had a massive heart attack. What does it matter if she's a Christian or not?"

"Reece," said Kristin. She put her hand on his leg and squeezed.

Gert appeared, holding a dishtowel with a trefoil pattern. "You don't want her to go to hell, do you?"

"She wouldn't know the difference," said Reece. "So, do all crazy people go to hell? And she's not crazy. Her reality just isn't ours." He leaned forward, elbows on his thighs. He wanted to roar into outer space strapped to a rocket.

"You guys, let's talk about something else," said Kristin.

"But this is important," said Edwin. "It's about everlasting life. She will still be held accountable for her sins regardless."

"At least she doesn't call me a jackass like the judge did. I think Reece is right. She's in a special category."

"He called you that?" asked Reece. He was making fists, opening and releasing. "What an asshole. No excuse for that."

"Maybe he wasn't in his right mind," said Edwin. He pushed on the lever of his recliner, bringing his feet to the carpet. He was still wearing his dress shoes.

"Or maybe his true colors were flying," said Reece. "I don't get your logic."

"God isn't logical," said Edwin. "He doesn't think like we do."

"Neither does Mrs. Dunlop. Maybe she's God in disguise," said Reece.

Edwin closed the Bible and placed it back on the TV tray, along with the remote. "What we have to remember is that God sent His only Son to forgive us of our sins. He is a forgiving God."

"That's just dandy," said Reece. "I need some fresh air."

Kristin watched Reece struggle to stand and arch his back. "We're going onto the deck," she said.

Edwin nodded, and Gert decided to sharpen the knives.

On the deck, Reece stood at the railing, looking into the purplish sky. A warm breeze blew. He gazed out over the back yard, partially covered in pine straw with a scattering of dandelions in full bloom. His body felt weak, but his mind was surging.

"I wonder what he would think if he were shot in the head, doing God's work."

"Reece, stop it. Take a breather and sit down. That's just the way he is. Dad just doesn't understand. His heart is good, though."

"Whatever." He pulled two folding chairs close.

"He gave you permission to marry me. Remember that."

"Uh huh," said Reece. "I suppose I'll need to go to seminary, though, so I'll be able to converse with him. Why does every conversation have to go back to the Bible with him?"

"It's just the way he is. You were making him mad, and you might need to apologize."

"Apologize? For what? It's like he's provoking me. I'm just not the same person I was. Ethiopia changed all of that..."

"I wish you'd never gone. I didn't want you to go." She gazed at Reece, his face tight, his eyes strained. "Has it changed the way you feel about us?"

Reece felt like crawling into a hole and dying.

The jeep stopped outside the gate. Craig had figured it was quicker to get to AK than to try for Addis Ababa. Terry would be in AK. He could fly Emma out as soon as possible. Her days in Godo were over. They'd ridden in silence for nearly two hours. There had been nothing he could do with the fat one holding the gun on him. He blew the horn, and the gate opened to the skinny guard with his rifle and welcoming smile. He motioned the jeep in and closed the gate.

Lisa was outside tending the lettuce in her small garden, wearing olive culottes with a sleeveless beige sweater and a rough straw hat to protect against the blistering sun. "Hey!" She watched Emma fall to her knees and bend over as if kissing the earth. She was wailing, crying. "Oh my God!" Lisa dropped her hoe and ran.

Craig was kneeling beside Emma, his hand on her back. Dirt creased her shirt, bits of dry grass in her hair.

"What happened?" Lisa went to her knees. "Honey, what's wrong? Can you come inside? Craig, what happened?" She searched his face.

Emma only balled tighter, heaving with tears.

Craig's eyes watered. "We were attacked. Three soldiers. One had a pistol. It's bad." He was squatting and lost his balance.

"Oh no," said Lisa. She draped herself over Emma and squeezed her. "Emma, Emma. Let me help you."

Alene came out of the dining hall. He glanced at the puzzled guard. "Mendeno?" The guard just shrugged and asked if she was the one who had jumped from the helicopter. Alene put his finger to his lips, even though the guard spoke in Amharic. Alene listened and looked studious as usual, but frowned a puzzled frown, wishing that his English was better.

Emma sobbed and dry heaved, bracing herself against the ground. "Fuck," she said, and dry heaved again.

Craig stood and watched Lisa protecting Emma, whispering to her, rubbing her neck. "Let's get her to my place," said Lisa.

"Fuck," said Emma. She sat up and screamed at the sky, eyes cast to the pebbly ground. "Fuck it! Fuck everything!" And then she broke down once more, weeping herself dry.

"Emma, let's stand and go to my place. Let me help you." She glanced at Craig. "It's what I think it is, right?"

Craig blanched and mumbled, "Yeah. They were brutal. I was helpless to stop them. I think they may be here in town."

"Mother of God," said Lisa. She helped Emma to stand. "Come with me, just walk, just you and me."

Emma moaned and walked. Her scraped knees bled, her hands bruised. "Goddamn it."

They slipped into Lisa's place, and the door closed. Lisa latched the door and then led Emma to the small bed she shared with Terry. "Here, sit down, rest."

Emma did as she was told, running her hands through her hair, forcing past the tangles, whimpering now, her eyes red and bloodshot. She looked into Lisa's dark brown eyes, almost black, and then focused on her long, dark hair, a single poofy braid. "You're beautiful. Thank you."

"What do I need to do right now? They raped you,

didn't they? We need to get you cleaned up."

Emma shook her head in disbelief. "Yes. I need to shower and bad. You have a shower."

"Yes, for sure," said Lisa. "Let me heat some water, make it a hot shower. I'll get Alene to bring some clean clothes from the warehouse. I'm going to take care of you. By God, we'll make them pay. Damn, you're such a good person. How could they—"

"I'm done," said Emma. "I'm going home. This would have never happened if Reece had been here. I just know it. Oh, God." She cried.

Lisa consoled her for another moment and then set about heating water and preparing the shower. She went outside, and the three men were still standing there as if frozen. She called Alene and asked him to bring some clothes for Emma: shemeez, sooree, kalsee. She knew there was no underwear, wust-lebs.

"Ishi," said Alene.

"She okay?" asked Craig. "I'm so sorry. I don't know what to say." He examined his hands, his smooth, hairless hands. "What can I do?"

"Nothing for now, except maybe you could cook something, maybe boil some potatoes, make a sauce for them. We have some fresh enjera to eat with it."

Alene was back in a hurry, carrying an armload of shirts, pants, and socks. "Thank you," said Lisa, and she hurried back to Emma. It was beginning to rain.

"Emma. I have clothes. The water is heating, takes longer with the altitude, but you know that."

Emma sat with her face in her hands, her dirty face streaked with red and dirt. "I bet they're at the hotel. Just down the road, probably celebrating with a bottle of wine. Motherfuckers...I'm sorry."

"No apologies from you, sister. If they're here tomorrow, I'll string them up personally. If Terry were here, he'd take the guard's gun and hunt them down."

"Where is he, Terry?"

"He's back in Addis, having some new parts installed on the copter."

Emma glanced at the large steel pressure cooker on the stove. "You got a pressure cooker."

"Yeah, boils faster and hotter. I'll mix it with some cold water, but try to keep it warm. We need to get you clean inside," said Lisa. "There's no douche, but we can improvise."

"Get me some saline and a sixty-cc catheter-tipped syringe. If you have it. I'd also like a vial of penicillin procaine. If you have it. And a ten-cc syringe and needle, eighteen-gauge."

"I'll find them, but it may take me a few minutes. I'll have to find it myself in the supplies. Alene doesn't really speak English." She checked the water and saw bubbles on the bottom of the pot.

Back outside, the rain had thickened and fell like rice on the ground. The three men were still standing around, but had drifted apart. Lisa yelled to Craig to help her with the supplies inside the dim warehouse. He hurried over.

"Can you find syringes and needles?" She went to a shelf with boxes of Icelandic IV fluids, looking for the saline. She ripped open a box and took two liters.

"Need a flashlight in here," said Craig. He looked helpless.

"You look there, and I'll look over here."

It took them a few minutes. "Oh, damn, penicillin. Here it is."

The word made Craig wince.

It took some rummaging, but with the supplies in a grain bag, Lisa hurried through the rain back to Emma. By now, it was a decent downpour. Inside, the spout on the cooker hissed steam. Emma was holding her hands over it.

"I got it," said Lisa. "In the bag. We have to go outside, in the rain. The shower is private, but no roof. There should be water in the barrel, and I'll add the hot, okay? Do you want to take the saline out there or do it in here? You tell me."

"Did I say how beautiful you are?" Emma's eyes welled with tears. "I feel drunk."

"I'll stand in the shower with you, okay? I can help. I'm here to help. You hold this bottle and I'll bring the hot water."

Emma held the bottle at her side like a football and followed Lisa outside and around the corner. Lisa pushed into the shower stall and pulled Emma in with her. The wind whipped against the metal sides. A quarter-barrel stood atop a rickety shelf made of poles and particleboard. The pot was heavy, and she lifted with two hands, burning one. She just grunted and dumped it in. A spigot with a three-foot piece of garden hose drooped down.

"There's no thunder," said Emma. "Why is there never thunder here?"

"Let's get you naked. Help me out. You'll be cold."

Emma stood naked and shivering as the stream of warm

water poured down her breasts. She closed her eyes and let Lisa rub her hair and face with a bar of yellow soap.

"Here, you do the rest, and I'll direct the water. The rain helps."

Emma ran the bar of soap over her body. She felt the tenderness of bruising on her shoulders, arms, and stomach. She washed and washed, outpacing the thin stream of shower water.

"You're doing great," said Lisa. "Take your time. I'll boil some more water if we need to."

"Maybe just turn around while I flush myself out," said Emma. Like she was in the clinic, she unstoppered a bottle of saline and drew up 60 ccs in the syringe. She squatted and then sat leaning back against the metal wall, but room was tight. "Hell, you're going to have to help me."

Lisa did as asked until both liters of saline were empty. Emma stood and raised her arms. "More soap."

It took another five minutes, but Emma endured the cold rain and tepid shower water. She didn't want the shower to end.

Without a towel, Lisa shielded Emma as they hurried back. She had forgotten to turn off the gas stove, and the flames fluttered with the incoming wind.

With the mood somewhat subdued and talk shifting to Reece's memories of the tornado at the hospital and tales from the clinic in Godo, Gert and Edwin excused themselves for bed at ten-thirty. Gert wanted Reece to leave, but knew that Edwin didn't have the balls to tell him, as she mentioned to him in their bedroom.

"Well, that was fun," said Reece.

"Reece, they're good people. You can be difficult, you know. They're not used to someone challenging them." Kristin nuzzled into him and took his hand in hers. She'd brushed her teeth, taken off her bra, and put on her Tony the Tiger pajamas.

"I suppose," said Reece. "You're pretty cute in your pajamas. I bet the doctor at Carraway, what's his name, Dr. Bozo, would kill to see you now." He drew her in closer.

"Lord. I can't even remember his name. Maybe I can sneak you into bed." She moved in for a kiss and pressed against him.

Reece melted into her, the stress of the evening passing, and let his tongue play with hers. He could see her nipples hard against Tony the Tiger's chest and leaned sideways, pushing her down on the small couch. Out of habit, he slid his hand beneath the cushion and came up with a hairbrush. "Found your hairbrush."

"Shut up and pay attention, buster."

"Buster, huh." Reece slid onto his side, mirroring her into the cushions, and tossed the hairbrush over his shoulder. He kissed her and then blew into her ear, tracing it with his tongue.

Kristin moaned and pressed into him. She could feel him down there, hard as a rock.

After an hour of making out, Reece excused himself to the bathroom. He hated the smell of semen in his underwear and wished that he and Kristin had a place where they could take it all the way, if she would. She had flat out told him she was saving herself for the marriage bed, but he wondered. He had felt the same way before Ethiopia, but things had changed, and time was no longer a non-entity. Time was ever present, a pressure that forced the matter of his mind into new forms, new directions. He had fantasies of taking Kristin to a strip club and then to a cheap motel with a broken TV. He flushed the toilet, and Kristin was there waiting for him.

"Did you flush your little children?" She touched his crotch.

Reece felt hot. "I guess. Is that like murder?"

"Yes, a murderer, a naughty boy. I like the bad boys. But I have to get in bed. I'll never wake up, you know, seven to three."

"Yeah, and Mrs. Dunlop needs you. Tell her I said hey." He kissed her and grabbed her butt cheeks.

Kristin laughed. "Stop. You'll wake the old folks." She pointed at their bedroom door.

"Let's not wake the pilgrims," said Reece.

"Shush," said Kristin. "Go. You have to go before I eat you."

"Oh, baby," said Reece. "Okay, I have to drive. I feel kind of tipsy."

"You should. Go." She followed him to the door.

Outside, Reece looked at the moon. In Ethiopia, the sun was rising.

The next morning, back at the lake, Dora examined Reece in his blue shorts and running t-shirt. "Boy, you look whooped."

"Feel whooped." Reece sat in her recliner. Horace had been up for an hour and was walking the property, as he said.

"So, how is Miss Kristin? Healthy as a peach? She's a pretty girl. You want grits for breakfast?"

"Good and good. Need to get a shower before breakfast."

"She reminds me of my sister Earline when I was your age." She took a copper-bottomed pot and added three cups of water.

"Nice," said Reece. "So, I'm dating your younger sister?" He laughed.

"Shut up with that. You know what I mean." She pulled down the bag of white grits and measured out a cup. "Make some eggs, too."

The phone rang, and Reece jumped and then yawned.

Dora answered, and it was the prayer chain from church. She listened and nodded.

"Who was that?" asked Reece.

"That was Doreen McKindreck. Her mother is in the hospital with walking pneumonia." She took a grocery list notepad and wrote it down.

"Walking pneumonia. That's like the damn walking catfish."

"Reece, watch your mouth. Let me call Maybell and let her know." She retrieved an address book and thumbed through the pages, looking for Maybell.

"I'll do the grits," said Reece. He looked at the water in the pot, pouring in grits. He grabbed the butter from the fridge and added two tablespoons. "Where's the dingdang salt?" He looked around, found the shaker, and shook.

Horace burst in through the back door, carrying three bass on a stringer.

"What the hey?" asked Reece. He put the grits on the electric eye.

"Free food," said Horace. "Old Elbert was up early and caught these on a plastic worm." Elbert Sykes was Maybell's husband in the house next door and Horace's gardening buddy. The Sykes went to the Methodist Church, but that was okay, even though it was a cult, according to the Baptists.

Dora put her hand over the phone. "Horace, get out of here with them slimy things. Don't mess up my kitchen."

Horace frowned and grabbed a long knife from the wooden holder. "Free food," he said, and left the way he came. He'd survived the Great Depression.

Reece got the grits going, and Dora finished up her prayer chain phone call. "That was Maybell. She said Elbert brought those fish in, and she told him to get out and give them to hungry folks."

Reece smiled. "I got the grits going."

"Okay, you git out. That's my job," said Dora.

Reece put the spoon down and went outside. Horace was at the picnic table, cleaning the fish. Reece felt a little wobbly and leaned against a pine tree, sixty feet straight up. Horace didn't hear him, and Reece eased beside the house toward the road. The sun blazed toward the high nineties. A red pickup truck crept down the road, and it was Mr. Cargill coming out to fish off his lot. He had a unique pier made of aluminum airplane parts. Reece waved. Mr. Cargill waved and slowed, the window down.

"Hey, boy! You back from China? I heard you went crazy and went on over."

"Yeah, in the flesh. Ethiopia, Africa. I was in Africa." He stood a foot away from the truck, breathing in the exhaust.

"Well, hell, I thought it was China. I heard about your accident. Got tangled up with the police?"

Reece chuckled. "Not exactly, but I did get shot. Right through the brain. What about them apples?"

Mr. Cargill whistled. "And you're walking around. You're dang lucky, boy."

"I guess I am." He wanted to tell him about the clinic, about Emma, about the flat-topped mountains, about the spicy food, about the toucan he had seen.

"You take care, you hear? I'm out in the boat today. Can't beat it with a stick."

"You know it," said Reece. He waved as the truck jolted into first gear.

Reece crossed the road and walked beside Horace's garden, the corn ripe and ready to pick. He passed a small thorn tree and noticed a tiny snake impaled there. He walked across a patch of dusty red dirt and stepped around a red anthill. He'd mowed over them a hundred times, but they always came back. It was seventy feet to the lake through ankle-high grass. Off to his left, a killdee shrieked and ran from him, pretending to have a broken wing. There was a rock nest on the ground with eggs near-by, but he couldn't spot it. And then there was the lake, warm in the morning air, bleeding its rank mossy smell. The pier was T-shaped with a bench. He'd helped Horace build it years ago, during a summer when his parents were still alive. A five-foot-thick band of cattails lined the bank.

Reece stepped onto the pier and watched a two-pound bass whisk away in a surge. Minnows played in the shallows near the cattails. He felt invisible but like lead and walked the pier, his bare feet pressing the weathered wood. He had to pee and cursed. All around him, water bugs walked. A turtle was floating, its nose in the air. Farther out were circles where bream had poked their fins. Above were swallows, flitting and crying. He felt like screaming and putting a gun into his mouth.

Emma slept with Lisa, snoring and moaning. She awoke with a pounding headache and felt sore in her stomach and chest. It had been real. Everything was real. She turned over, and Lisa was staring at her.

"You okay?" asked Lisa. Her eyes were puffy. She hadn't been able to sleep.

"No," said Emma. "I don't think I am. Is my breath bad?"

"What? Oh no. Mine's probably worse, morning mouth." She reached and hugged Emma, but Emma pulled back.

"Sorry," said Emma. "I should get up. Thanks for helping me last night, especially with the shower. I know you got soaked."

Lisa threw back the blankets and stood. "I would have done anything for you last night. I still can't believe it. We have to go into town and see if they're at the hotel. I know the town administrator. Terry has given him rides upcountry and to Addis."

Emma shuddered at the thought of seeing them again. "Do you have a gun? I don't think I could do it without shooting them. They're the last people I want to see. Damn animals."

"Here, I'll make some tea. Let's just focus on that. I don't want to stress you out. We'll do what you think is best. How's that?" She had slept in a pullover dress and slipped into a sweater. "I need to go to the john, so just stay put. Okay?"

"Yeah," said Emma. "At least the penicillin is working

on me. I want to do another injection today. Bastards." She rolled out of bed in baggy corduroys, a soft polyester sweater, and two pairs of socks. The nights were chilly at seven thousand feet.

Emma watched Lisa go and stretched her arms over her head, wincing at the soreness. Her knuckles were scratched and a dull blue. She thought about her mother, and a pang of sadness and rage flashed through her. Her dad had beaten her and maybe worse. Men sucked and were vile creatures in general, but then there was Reece, Dr. Guthrie, and Afewerki. The feeling of helplessness from the day before washed over her, and she squatted to keep from falling. She felt nauseous and hammered the cement floor with her fist. "Damn!"

Fresh from the shintabet, Lisa knocked on the guestroom door. There was no answer. She walked around to the dining room, and the door was open.

"Hey," said Craig. He nursed a cup of hot coffee. He wasn't wearing his hairpiece and looked like a cartoon. "Yeah, it's me. How's Emma? I can drive her back to Addis today, ASAP, unless Terry can fly her? What do you think? Coffee?"

"I don't drink coffee, thanks," said Lisa. "She's okay, still freaked out. She's been through so much, and this is just unbelievable. I'll ask her what she wants to do. I imagine she wants to get out of here, out of the country as fast as she can. I would."

"I just don't get it. Do they think they can just get away with it? The whole scenario is jacked. I guess they could have just killed us, too."

"Don't say that," said Lisa. She shuddered. "Let me get

back with Emma. I'll get back with you. Do you think we should report this to the administrator? I think we should."

"I think as many people as possible should know. Does he speak English?"

"None as far as I can tell. If Daniachew were here, he could interpret. There's a teacher in town who could help us. We'll try him. Damn, though, what's today? It's Sunday." Lisa bit her lip. "Ah! Sorry, bit my lip."

"Yeah, that could be a problem, the English," said Craig. He scratched his smooth, bald head.

"We'll figure it out. Let me check on her."

"Sure," said Craig.

Lisa waved at the guard and pushed the door open. Emma was looking into a small mirror hanging over a washbowl.

"Hey," said Lisa.

"I still look the same, except for these red marks on my forehead. You know I got a full hand of hair on one of them and made him scream. I hope I yanked his brains out."

Lisa put water on to boil for tea. "Can I ask if it was more than one?"

Emma swallowed. "Yeah, the two of them. One was puny. The other guy had to help hold me down, the motherfucker. All I could do was scream and spit. Sorry about my language."

"Scum of the earth," said Lisa. "I'm so so sorry."

"So am I. It would have been best if I had been able to jump out of the helicopter sooner, but Terry was too quick."

"No, don't say that, Emma. You've endured enough stressful situations for a dozen good people. Do you think it's time to go home? I know I'm ready for a break." She added tea bags and sugar to the beat-up pot.

"Damn straight," said Emma. "I guess I should have never come. This is not my land, not my people. I'm just an interloper. I felt, though, that God led me here, but for this? Am I supposed to learn something? That men are slime. That God let this happen?"

"Emma, I'm not religious. Terry and I are the pagans around here. You know that. But it makes me wonder. Most people here have been so gracious, so humble."

"Yeah, I've met some people who have lived like animals their entire lives and are as nice as can be. I sometimes felt that I had saved a life here and there, and that I was appreciated. That damn Hyena, though, has been a thorn in my flesh. And then he freakin' shot Reece. And he's still stirring up trouble. Yeah, I guess it's time to pack my bags."

Lisa poured two cups of sugary tea into orange plastic cups. "What do you want to do now? Craig says he'll drive you back today. Maybe Terry comes back today, but it could be tomorrow."

"Thank you." Emma let the tea steam her face. Back home, she loved cold, sweet tea. The restaurant where her mother worked made it best. "Thank you for everything. I'd like to walk into town and take care of this myself, but I don't think I can do it. I don't have the energy. As much as I want them to pay, I should just walk away. If Reece were here..." Tears pushed and welled.

"Come sit at the table," said Lisa. "You had something special with him, didn't you? You guys were an impressive pair in the clinic. It must have been hard to have him just yanked away like that. Have you heard from him? I heard he was out of the hospital, but that's all."

Emma sipped her tea, letting it coat her mouth before she swallowed. "Poof, gone...I talked with him while I was in Addis. He's walking already. He'd jumped into the lake and been attacked by leeches, the dumdum." She laughed. "He's with his grandparents."

Lisa cleared her throat. "So, can I ask if he's still engaged?" She leaned forward, expecting Emma to whisper.

"I told him I loved him, and he didn't say it back. If that's what you want to hear." She felt angry at everything, at everyone. "I talked to him twice. The first time, Kristin was there, and she told me to get lost and leave him alone."

"Wow. That's heavy," said Lisa. "I don't mean to pry."

"I'm pretty sure he doesn't love her, but he's made this commitment, and he's afraid to hurt her feelings. Maybe I should be angry at him. But maybe I'm the problem." She shook her head. "I'm just at my wits' end. I don't know what to do." She sank into the hard chair.

"We have to take care of you. I'll go back with you and Craig today if you want. Or we'll go into town and report this. But it's Sunday, and we may have trouble finding the administrator. I think it's best if we get you out of here. We'll have your stuff from Godo flown back to you."

Emma tasted the tea. "Yeah, but I need to at least say goodbye to everyone. I can't just disappear. I feel like such a coward."

"That's the last thing you are," said Lisa. "I've always admired your tack and tact. The Mission was so lucky to have you. The people, too."

"So, how's Craig? I didn't even think to ask if he was

hurt or okay. The fat soldier held him at gunpoint, I think. I just remember jumping into the jeep and yelling at him."

"Yeah, he's fine. He's sorry about what happened and feels terrible. He said he'll go into town with me if that's what we decide to do. But, the more I think about it, we just need to get you back to Addis and see if the Mission can file a report."

"That would be pointless," said Emma. "Apparently, soldiers can do as they please."

"We have to try, for your sake, right?" She leaned over to brush the hair from Emma's eyes. "They have to be punished."

"I suppose God will punish them. That may be the best I can hope for." Tears wet her eyes. "Those poor women in Godo being raped by the Hyena and his thugs."

"He's the devil."

"So many devils, so many angels." Tears slid down Emma's face, and she gave Lisa her lopsided smile.

"You want more tea?"

"No."

"You want to eat something? I can scramble some eggs?"

"No. Not hungry. I have a headache. Can you get me some water?"

"You want some Paracetamol for your headache?"

"No, just water." The tears were wetting her hands now. She looked around the small room, at the unmade bed, the tiny stove, the used syringe and needle on the little round table. A kind of wind seemed to be surging through her, a storm. "God, I just want to vomit."

Lisa filled a clean cup with water.

Emma drank it all, and a resolve coursed through her.

"Here's what we have to do. We're going into town and confronting them at the hotel. Then, Craig is driving me to Godo. Terry can come in a day or so and fly me out. That way I can say my goodbyes."

"Emma. No. That's just too harsh, don't you think, on yourself?"

"Can it get any worse?" She tapped the empty cup on her leg.

At the last minute, Kristin went in to pull an extra three-to-eleven shift. Reece had spent Saturday evening calling his friends. A few had visited him in the hospital, and they were curious about how he was doing. He felt that his world was constrained to Kristin and passed on invites to have dinner, but he did ask his buddy Keith out to the lake the next night. They had met at the community college while Reece was in nursing school, both being members of the Baptist Student Union. They had been on a mission trip to Indiana, of all places, and liked to take in the occasional movie. Keith had invited him to church, but Reece said he was going with his grandparents, the first time back in church since he'd returned.

Sunday morning, Dora and Horace were up early, getting ready. Dora made a big breakfast of eggs, toast, bacon, and oatmeal. Reece picked out the raisins as usual, but then ate them all in one bite.

"Get your shower, son," said Horace. "Get yourself pretty for church." He adjusted the volume on his hearing aid, which was squealing.

"I won't do Sunday School," said Reece. "But I'll make the service. I don't have time to get ready, plus I don't feel up for it. Kind of tired."

"Backing out now," said Dora. "Everybody wants to see you. The preacher wants you to give a talk, too. They gave you money to go over there, if you remember."

Reece frowned. "Yeah, they did. Let me just ease back into it, though. Just going to the service has me nervous for some reason. We going out to the Sizzler after? I'll let Kristin know."

"We'll go wherever you want, son," said Horace. "Need to get some flesh back on your frame. How much weight you reckon you lost?"

Reece had weighed himself in the bathroom. "About twenty-five pounds at least. Weighed one-thirty-five this morning."

"You do look awful thin," said Dora. She headed into the bathroom to spray her hair again.

"Well, just lying in bed for a month took a few pounds off. You're feeding me, so don't worry." He popped the foot on Dora's recliner. His eyes roamed the warm, familiar room, the big console TV, the kitchen table, the gas heater, the window AC unit. He thought about Kristin, her warm body through her clothes. He thought about Emma, her lopsided smile. He thought about how he was grateful for the hot shower in the bathroom.

Half an hour later, Horace and Dora left. Reece had an hour before church started and decided to call Kristin. She was sleeping in after her evening shift, and Reece asked Edwin to let her know they were going to the Sizzler after church. He took his time getting ready and headed out to the F-150.

He drove past the pool that belonged to lake residents and wound his way on back roads to the Baptist church in Palmerdale. They had held a special dedication ceremony for him before he'd left for Ethiopia and had routinely lifted him up in prayer at the services, especially after he'd been shot. He drove past a large sprawling pasture with a large pond at the bottom of the slope. The day was perfect, blue and sunny. An acquaintance of his had been killed in a car wreck just there. Pine trees lined the road with the occasional house. Crossing the train tracks, the red brick church with the handicap ramp up the side was to the left. He shifted into low and pulled into the gravel lot across the road. The walk to the church seemed to him miles in distance, and he floated there absorbing the details: the faded parking stripes, car hoods still creaking with heat, the ragged flap of a busted blue balloon. To his left and right, he nodded and smiled, feeling hands on his back and hearing words meant for him. Up the ramp he went, and there were deacons handing out bulletins, which were good for ten percent off at the Jack's down the road. He shook hands, smiled, and looked to see that his shoes were attached to the ground. Inside the double sanctuary doors, he looked for Horace. Dora would be in the choir, wearing a maroon robe that matched the pew cushions. Approaching Horace, he nodded and waved. Horace was unwrapping a peppermint and sliding it into his mouth. His hair was neat and trim along his neck, and Reece slipped in to sit beside him.

"Well, hey, boy!" An elderly lady turned and reached toward him, as if she were grabbing a doughnut.

"Hey," said Reece.

"We are so glad you are back!" Her name was Wanda. Mrs. Daniels. A widow. Reece had known her husband. It seemed that all of the women outlived their husbands, that there was a uniformity in the whiteness of their hair, that they lived secret, lonely lives without their life partners.

Reece smiled, nodded, and folded his hands in his lap.

Horace was talking to a middle-aged man on the same pew. Reece couldn't remember his name. He was shaking hands with him over Horace. The man was speaking, and Reece just said, "Thank you. Good to see you."

The pastor walked in and stood beside the pew. Reece gazed at him, the age spots on his temples, his thinning hair, his large teeth, and tried to stand, sat, and then stood. The preacher's eyes were watery and sincere, awash with untold burdens. The preacher gripped Reece's forearm, and Reece felt that he was wrestling him. He moved on to the next pew, and Reece felt himself lowered onto the thin pew cushion, the hard oak against his back. He glanced at the piano, and there was Patricia, whom he had dated for a month or so. She didn't seem to see him. The organ player was on her bench, an older woman whose husband was an alcoholic. She was ghost-playing, getting warmed up for the service, the sound of the wooden petals beneath her shoes like distant taps and thuds.

The choir entered and filled the loft, Dora in the second row, looking dignified and regal. The choir director followed, Brother Macguffin, robust and portly, his belly preceding his chest and narrow shoulders. Reece wondered if Kristin was awake yet. He wondered what Emma was doing. It would already be dark in Godo. Perhaps she was reading letters by candlelight or taking a sponge bath from a pan of warm water. He realized that the two places were connected by what, a vacuum, a sphere, a cylinder, or maybe just words? The service had started, and he noticed everyone was standing, holding their hymnals. Brother Macguffin was behind the pulpit, leading them in song. Reece stood, and a flash of black ran through his head.

He put his hand on the pew in front until his vision re-emerged. Horace was holding the hymnal so that he could see it. It was page 212. "Love Lifted Me."

"I was sinking deep in sin, far from the peaceful shore…"

Reece sang the words by heart, but with his eyes glued to the stanzas. The boisterous chorus. He tried to lift his voice to match the mood of the song. In Godo, the dogs had begun to fight and tear each other apart. The Hyena was drinking katikala, already high on qat. Isaac, Mariam, Barra, and Afewerki were telling jokes about the Russians in Amharic. The stars were so thick in the black sky that it looked like a spilled milkshake. The first bullet had missed him, but the second…Emma had saved his life.

The song ended, and everyone took their seats. Reece touched the pew to make sure he was sitting as well. The preacher was talking and saying his name, and then he was praying, or was he just bowing his head? Horace nudged him and told him that the preacher had asked Reece to pray.

Reece felt like he was lifting to the white vaulted ceiling. Standing, he could hear words coming from his mouth. He bowed his head and focused, giving thanks for the church and its people. He lifted up those who were sick and asked God to forgive them for their sins. And then he was sitting again, breathless, it seemed, filled with oxygen that didn't quite know where to go.

There was another song, this time sitting down, and recognition of any visitors in the congregation. There were little white cards and golf pencils for them to use, to leave their names and addresses and phone numbers. There was an offering, and Reece had nothing to give and passed the plate to Horace, who dropped in a small envelope with a ten-dollar bill inside. They sang another song. Reece wondered what it was like to drop acid. Why was it drop acid and not take acid? He wondered why he'd never tried marijuana, and vowed to himself that he would take up drinking alcohol, maybe vodka, maybe whiskey. He thought about all the things he'd never done. He'd never had sex, intercourse. He was freaking twenty-one years old, no twenty-two. He'd turned twenty-two in the hospital at UAB. His eyes gravitated to an object on the shiny floor. It was a girl's beret. It was green. Green Beret. A pressure built in his chest. He needed to laugh and hard. He panicked and stifled himself as if holding back a tremendous cough. He gripped his thighs, imagining that he looked insane, and focused on what the preacher was saying. Like a tire deflating, he came to himself and stared at the pulpit, gathering himself in. Maybe he would just start with beer.

The sermon lasted forty-five minutes, and Reece had no idea what had been said. With a creeping dread, he waited for the final song of the day, the invitational. Lost souls were invited to come home, come home. "Ye who are weary come home." Reece fought an urge to run down the aisle and grab the preacher and confess that he was damned, that he was forever changed, that all was not as it appeared to be. Perhaps there was life on other planets. Nothing was impossible.

There were no takers for the invitational, and Harold Spraggs ended the service with a long prayer, asking those present to remember the sick and those serving overseas in the armed forces. Reece held his eyes closed, imagining the smells of the clinic, the peroxide bubbling in infected ears, wounds swimming in pus, goiters as big as footballs, diarrhea, tapeworms, scabies, eyes clouded white with blindness. And the flies! The damn flies crawling up your nose and into your ears.

"Amen."

Emma would not be dissuaded, and she threatened to go into town by herself. Lisa managed to delay her for an hour, reminding her that it was Sunday and a day of rest.

Emma sat in the dining shack with Craig. She'd had tea and now coffee with Craig and was feeling revved up. Craig had put his hairpiece back on, but it was askew, giving him the look of a young boy. Lisa was getting ready.

Craig tapped his fingers on the indoor picnic table. "I'm worried about Eve. She'll be upset that I'm not home on time." He checked his large watch.

"You're certainly welcome to go ahead and go," said Emma. She pushed her orange cup back and forth.

"No, I need to be here. I can't let you get hurt again. Not that it'll do much good."

Emma realized that Craig didn't have eyelashes either. "I'm going to let folks know what they did. They won't be so brave with people around." Her hips hurt from the penicillin injections.

"They could be gone, maybe just passed through."

"I bet their Rover is at the hotel. Probably celebrated last night with whiskey and then slept with a prostitute... The bar should be open by now to serve lunch. Maybe we'll get to have lunch with them. Ha!"

Craig flinched. "I'll be honest. I'm dreading this. I suppose it has to be done, but things could get out of hand."

"Yeah. Anything can happen." Emma examined her clean pants and wondered who they'd belonged to, what country they were from. Same for the gray jersey she wore, which just read "Titans." She'd showered again using cold water and antiseptic cleanser. She felt sore and strong, but as if the floor was about to give way beneath her.

Lisa came in through the screen door, her thick hair still wet. "I'm ready. You guys ready? Emma, you sure you want to do this? We'll do it for you, and you can stay here."

"Heck no. I'm not sending you to do my dirty work. This way it'll be three on three." Her throat tightened, and her mouth felt dry and tasted like coffee. "And let's walk into town instead of driving. I need to get limbered up."

Lisa nodded. "Okay. We'll stop at the schoolteacher's house to see if he can interpret for us. He might balk, though, when he hears soldiers are involved."

"I'll use body language," said Emma. "You might have to hold me back." She wanted to say, "Cocksuckers."

"Emma, listen," said Craig. "We can't stir up trouble. We just need to report this. I think it's a bad idea to have any contact with those guys. They're rotten to the core."

"Let's go," said Emma. "We'll figure it out when we get there."

Outside, thin streaks of cloud striped the sky's pink pig belly. It was a bit gray, and puddles of water stood from the night's rain. The usual stiff wind poured up and over the cliff line that ran on the other side of the road. Beyond was a vast distance, the river valley, and then Godo, invisible from AK, twenty-six miles by twisting road. Emma shivered.

Beyond the compound, they walked on the rutted road. It was only about half a mile to the hotel. They passed a vast empty field scattered with untold numbers of fist-sized rocks. Even so, the locals played soccer there, using homemade balls, sometimes just straw sewn into cloth. They passed a weather station set inside high fencing with a lock on the gate. And so they walked, soon reaching the roundabout on the edge of town. And now there were single-story shacks and closed shops, all leaning one way or the other. Emma's heart pounded in her chest, and she felt short of breath.

"Ferenj!" A child in a grimy dress grinning in a doorway.

Lisa waved, and Emma tried to smile. Two old men draped in shammas nodded.

"Dehna aderu," said Craig. The old men nodded again, each holding a walking stick.

They passed a low-slung building, the government health clinic, then a gas station with hand pumps, the administrative compound with the jail, and then a water project with six spigots, five of which were broken. Up ahead were trees that surrounded the hotel. Emma felt like she was going to throw up.

Lisa stopped. "We have to pass the hotel to get to the schoolteacher's house. Okay?" They nodded.

Emma looked at the rocky, yellow dirt of the road. She kept her eyes down until she sensed she was beside the hotel. Craig had stopped.

"Damn," said Craig.

Emma couldn't bear to look, but knew that the Rover was there. They walked on for five minutes and turned into a small alley. Lisa took the lead and rapped on the sheet metal door. The door opened, and Ato Shimellis looked surprised, a wisp of smoke behind him. He smiled and stepped outside.

"Ah, Dr. Lisa." He called all the ferenji doctors. He looked at Craig. He looked at Emma. "What is it today? Shall you come inside? We will drink coffee, no?"

Lisa spoke. "We need your help to interpret for us. We have some business with the administrator."

"Yes, of course." He walked to the shanty next to his and banged on the wall. "One moment."

"Abet?" came a voice from inside.

Shimellis yelled for the woman to prepare coffee for the doctors and turned back. "Come."

Inside, the four of them cramped the room. There was a quintal of teff against the wall and a single chair, but there were two low stools with leather-strap seats. On a table, incense was burning, a strong smell of sweet perfume. They each took a seat, and Shimellis sat on the huge bag of grain. He was all smiles. "There is no food, but you will eat at the hotel, no? My sister will bring the coffee."

"Thank you," said Lisa.

Craig nodded.

Emma's heart was pounding, and she worried she wouldn't be able to face the soldiers. She would have to tell Shimellis about the rape. And then he would tell the administrator. What would happen then? Would he just laugh and say, "Tsk, tsk, tsk?" She remembered the ladies and children at the shelter in Godo and felt bad that she was not there to check on them. Without the guard and his gun, those women would be raped as well.

Shimellis dropped his smile and folded his hands. "What is this problem today?" He wore neat knit pants and a long-sleeve buttoned shirt. His jaw was nearly square.

No one answered.

Craig cleared his throat. Lisa nudged him with her dark eyes. "Um, yesterday, on the road, three soldiers attacked us. They're at the hotel."

Shimellis frowned. "Oh, that is very bad. Do they take your money?"

"No, but—"

"They raped me," said Emma, sitting on a low stool. She felt hot, dizzy. "Two did. There's a fat one, too. He has a pistol."

"Oh my goodness," said Shimellis. He knew precisely who the fat soldier was, the one called Nikita. "Ah, he is a bad man. Very dangerous. We must be careful."

"Could they be arrested? If we report this?" asked Lisa. "You have to help us decide what to do." She toyed with her long ponytail, pulling it from side to side.

"Ah, he will shoot me," said Shimellis. "It is very bad, this thing."

"Does the administrator work today?" asked Craig.

"No, no. It is Ihud, the Sunday. He will be at his home, or he may have his food at the hotel. He has no wife and is divorc-ed."

"We have to report this," said Emma. "They can't get away with this."

"The fat one will deny this thing," said Shimellis, standing over all of them. "We must be careful. I think this must happen in Addis Ababa. I am powerless to accuse him."

Emma tried not to choke. She felt her throat was closing, her heart beating there. "I will accuse him then. They're at the hotel. If the administrator can't do anything, then I will." She wanted to rip out her hair and scream.

There was a light knock on the door, and a voice just

above a whisper. A young woman in a loose dress of gray fabric entered, carrying a tray with cups and a bowl of sugar. Following her was a little boy of five, with just a handful of puffy hair on the top of his head. He carried the clay pot of coffee like a golden chalice.

"Let us drink," said Shimellis.

His sister carried the tray around, and everyone took a small, white porcelain cup. She placed the tray on the floor and took the bowl, doling out spoonfuls of sugar. She did not speak, but took in deep whooshy breaths to acknowledge them. She then took the coffee and, without spilling a drop, filled each cup.

"Amenseganolo," said Emma, and the others thanked her as well.

With wide eyes, the little boy placed the pot in a straw holder, the bottom of the pot being round, and hurried to a corner where he squatted with eager but shy eyes.

"Bataam taruno," said Lisa to the boy, who smiled and murmured.

Emma sipped her strong coffee. She didn't need more caffeine, but there was no alternative.

"So, what to do?" asked Craig. "I say we cut our losses, and I take Emma back to Addis today."

"Cut our losses?" asked Emma. She drank more coffee. "What does that mean? You mean that *I* need to cut my losses?"

Craig tried not to stand. A lone fly buzzed him, drunk from the incense. "No, I didn't mean it that way. I mean, what can we do? Sounds like these soldiers are untouchable."

Emma grunted.

Lisa held Emma's hand. "Emma, it won't do any good to confront them here." She looked at Shimellis. "They could hurt Shimellis if he gets involved. We'll need to get Dr. Guthrie to help us figure this out."

Emma made an animal noise. "I'm not leaving without confronting them. They will pay. By God." She felt strong, then weak, then angry. "Shimellis doesn't have to get involved. I get it. But doing nothing is just wrong."

Shimellis shifted from foot to foot, looking to Lisa for support.

"I don't think it would be wise to confront them. What good would it do? You need to heal. Just seeing them again could be awful."

"Hell, what if I'm pregnant?"

"Emma, I'm sorry," said Lisa. "I just want to protect you, that's all."

Craig felt compelled to speak. "We just need to cut our losses." He grimaced at his words.

Emma looked at him like he were a crazy man and finished her coffee.

"Shimellis, thank you. I know you have to be careful," said Lisa. "We'll report this in Addis. Dr. Guthrie will help us. Emma?"

"Yeah, just like he did with the damn Hyena who shot Reece in the head. He'll never be charged or accused or whatever. I guess I just give up, tuck my tail, and run back home."

"Emma, you're a brave woman, but think. More people could be hurt."

Emma stood. She steadied herself against the wall. "Fine then, let's go. No sense wasting time." She dropped her cup, and it broke on the rough cement floor.

Kristin walked into the Sizzler, crowded with Sunday churchgoers. She walked the main dining area that swaddled a long salad bar, and saw Reece and his grandparents in an adjacent dining room.

Reece saw Kristin, wearing tight jeans and a short-sleeved shirt. She looked fresh and alive, and he waved her over. "Hey, want me to stand in line with you?"

"Hey, y'all," said Kristin. She smiled wide, happy to see them.

Horace put his fork down. He was eating a salad of lettuce and tomatoes. "You sure do look pretty, girl. Good to see you."

"Did you work today?" asked Dora. "You got your jeans on."

"No," said Kristin. "Worked yesterday, the evening shift, but slept in late. You know."

"I'm going to stand in line with her." Reece took her elbow and guided her through the swarm of people. "You look great."

Kristin punched him in the arm. "What did you order?"

"Just a steak and fries with the salad bar."

They got in a long line that snaked through a roped barrier like an amusement park.

"Sirloin?"

"Yeah, sirloin," said Reece. "Went to church this morning with the old folks."

"And how was that? You look good in your dress pants."

Reece squeezed her elbow. "It was very strange, almost

like a dream. I couldn't believe that I was alive, back there, experiencing the same thing as before I left. It's like time was standing still."

Already, there were six newcomers behind them, the line backed up to the bathrooms.

Kristin was careful of the boy in front of her, trying not to step on his shoe. "You need to come to my church again. It's more exciting."

"Yeah, sure, sometime soon."

The line moved forward in six-inch increments. After ten minutes, Kristin took her tray and ordered a sweet tea.

"What're you having?" asked Reece.

"The sirloin tips with a baked potato," said Kristin.

"Sirloin tips with a baked potato," said Reece to the cashier.

"Butter or sour cream," said the cashier. A wisp of hair hung across her face.

"Just butter," said Kristin. "Let me pay, silly."

"I guess you'll have to. I only have a couple of ones."

Kristin pulled out a twenty and paid. "You can carry my tray."

"My pleasure."

They maneuvered back to the table and sat next to each other. Reece looked around at the humanity, wondering at the collective Sunday appetite, thinking about how much food would wind up in the garbage. Sitting in church took little energy, and there were quite a few fatties in the crowd.

"Well, you do look pretty," said Dora.

"Sure do," said Horace.

"Thank you. Y'all hungry?" Kristin put her cloth napkin

on her lap. She recognized several people around them.

"Like a starved chicken," said Horace. He forked in a mouthful of salad, dripping with orange French dressing. "Could have got ten percent off at Jack's, though."

"Don't be so cheap," said Dora, "and enjoy your dinner."

They bantered back and forth, and soon their meals came, stopping the conversation. And then there was dessert: banana pudding, soft serve ice cream, and apple cobbler.

"Kristin, you should come to church tonight," said Dora.

"I think I'll go to my church tonight. I was hoping Reece could come with me. There are more people there our age."

"No old folks at your church?" asked Horace. He fiddled with his hearing aid.

"I didn't mean that," said Kristin. "Sure, we have older members, but we also have a lot of younger people."

"I guess we're the old folks," said Dora. "Have you gained weight, Kristin? Looks like you have."

Reece grinned and could tell that Kristin was a bit flummoxed. "She's put on thirty pounds." He laughed.

Kristin reached over and pinched him through his dress shirt.

"Ow!" Reece dropped his spoon on the floor. "Well, heck. That hurt."

"Don't be such a baby," said Kristin. "Do you think I look fat?"

"No, no," said Reece. "I was just playing along."

"Well, evidently I've put on weight." Her eyes were wide

and accusing.

"How much weight have you put on?" asked Horace. He was getting about half of the conversation.

"Horace," said Dora. "Don't make her mad."

"I'm not mad," said Kristin. She took a bite of banana pudding, mostly pudding, just like she liked it.

"So, anyway, how about the price of cod in Denmark?" asked Reece. "I hear it's through the roof."

Kristin frowned. "Knock knock."

"Who's there?" asked Reece.

"It's gigantic, fat Kristin." She pushed away her bowl of banana pudding.

"God, you're as skinny as a rail," said Reece. "No harm done."

"I'm sorry if I offended you, Kristin," said Dora. "It just looked like you put on some weight. You need it, though, to round out those angles."

"Oh Lord," said Reece. Kristin was nudging his leg with her leg, probably meaning that she wanted to leave. "So, maybe Kristin can give me a ride home?"

"Sure," said Kristin. "You ready to go? It's been great seeing you guys."

"Well, don't go off mad," said Dora.

"Granny?" asked Reece. He made "let it be" eyes at her.

"I'm not mad," said Kristin. Her chest was flushing, making her neck red. She could feel the heat there. She stood. "Come on."

"Yeah, right," said Reece. He finished his iced tea, stood, and put his two ones on the table to add to the tip. "Guess I'll see y'all back at the house."

Horace's hearing aid squealed. "Y'all leaving? Not gonna eat your food?"

"Yes, Horace. They're leaving. Pay attention," said Dora.

"Okay, we're gone. See you back at the house." He led Kristin toward the exit, glad that was over with.

"I can't believe she thinks I'm fat."

The sun was out in full force as if sanitizing the Sunday afternoon.

"Just let it go. She just speaks too plain sometimes. Both you and I could stand to gain some weight." He followed her to her Toyota.

Kristin frowned and opened the doors. A whoosh of hot air hit her in the face.

They wound up going to the zoo, feeling sorry for the animals, then back to the lake, where Reece changed clothes. He followed Kristin to her house to go with her to church. He'd forgotten his Bible, which he usually carried. He hadn't cracked it since coming back to the States, though.

They had just enough time to make grilled cheese sandwiches and follow Edwin and Gert to church, nondenominational and nondescript. Inside, the wooden pews and woodwork sheened like honey. There was no baptismal behind the choir loft, no stained glass, just a tall angled ceiling, a beige carpeted stage with a simple amber-colored pulpit, and a microphone. Reece had been once before.

He gazed around at the self-gathering people, lots of twenties and thirties, young families, most of them. Gert and Edwin sat on the back row on the other side of the aisle. A man introduced himself and shook Reece's hand. Reece forgot his name within seconds, focusing on the man's purple shirt, Burt, Curt.

"What was his name?" asked Reece.

"Patrick," said Kristin. "He's the pastor. He's married to the woman up front with the cat-eye glasses. She's pretty cool. Her name is Rhonda, and she's also the church secretary."

"Makes sense," said Reece. "Might as well get the whole family on the payroll."

"Reece, shush." She moved in close to him, thigh to thigh. "Didn't you write and tell me that you led Bible study with the workers back in Godo?"

He put his arm behind her on the pew. The cushions were turquoise. "Yeah, but no. Maybe a couple of times. They were far more religious than I was. They liked to sing hymns after dinner, which was okay. I recognized most of the songs."

It was just about seven, and the congregation found their seats, a light hubbub in the air. Reece noted that the acoustics were excellent. A young couple three rows ahead of them whispered, but he could tell they were talking about what they would eat after church was over. He gathered that they decided on Wendy's, but would just get ice cream and not food.

Pastor Patrick and another man mounted the stage. Patrick sat, and the choir director took the pulpit, but there was no choir. The song was on the back of the bulletin, which Kristin held. Reece had never encountered the song before and had trouble mouthing the words. There was no offertory or recognition of visitors in the audience. Pastor Patrick was ready to get down to business.

"It's a good crowd tonight," said Patrick.

His voice made Reece think of a bowl of limes. He liked

how casual it was.

"As you know, we have an urgent point of business this evening regarding our brother, James Pernoy. I'd first like to read from Matthew, chapter 18, verses 15 through 20." The scripture detailed a short process for excommunicating a church member.

Reece frowned. He glanced at Kristin. "What's going on?"

She put her hand on his thigh and squeezed, meaning for him to be quiet.

"We all know of the infidelity of Brother Pernoy. He has refused our efforts on three occasions, and it has become our duty to take Biblical action on behalf of his wife and child. Is there any discussion?"

"What the?" asked Reece.

No one spoke.

"Brother Pernoy has passed on this chance to ask for forgiveness publicly, and thus we are compelled by God to sever ties with him and offer our full support to his Becky and Melissa."

Pastor Patrick continued to speak, but Reece didn't hear. His blood was boiling. He looked back at Gert and Edwin. They looked stone-cold serious.

"Let's go," said Reece. He stood and walked out, not waiting for Kristin. The air outside seemed dry and large, like walking into a closet that is bigger than you expect. He spat on the pavement. "Damn."

Kristin followed at a distance. "Reece, that's so embarrassing, walking out like that. What are you thinking?"

"Hell, they're kicking somebody out of the church. Is that how you help people? That just sucks." His hands shook.

"Reece, it's just what they do. Why are you so mad?"

"That's just the cherry on top." He walked toward her car, opened the door, and slid in.

Kristin closed her door. "My parents are going to be so ticked off with you."

"So, that's the church. Brotherly love, the whole shebang. That just takes the whole damn cake." He laughed.

"Reece, it's biblical."

"So is stoning. Would Jesus have tossed him out like that? Maybe that guy's wife was a bitch. Maybe she ran him off. Who knows? Just the idea, in church no less. Jesus Christ." He punched the dashboard, careful, like it was a ripe peach. "Maybe if he'd raped someone, but still you wouldn't make a public spectacle out of it. That's just wrong."

"He cheated on his wife. You heard Pastor Patrick. He betrayed his wife."

"Or so the Germans would have you believe," said Reece. "Let's just go. This day has gone to hell. Just drive. Get the hell away from here."

"Reece, please. This just gets harder every day. I don't know if you're the same person anymore. You're so touchy."

"Touchy? Kids are dying from diarrhea, and all this dingbat Patrick can think of is how to humiliate someone in public. Damn. And, yeah, maybe I've changed, but for the better as far as I can tell."

"Oh brother. We need to see the counselor again."

"Good luck with that, unless you want to go by yourself."

Deep silence, the sound of a key sliding into the ignition, the car starting, windows rolling down.

Reece looked at the sky, a dulling purple-blue. There was nothing up there to indicate a problem. It was a perfect sky with swallows flitting, eating mosquitoes and gnats.

"Reece Myers, do you love me for who I am?"

With Emma following, Lisa and Craig walked past the hotel, where a black Range Rover was parked in the courtyard, surrounded by eucalyptus trees. Lisa glanced back.

"Emma!"

Emma marched up to the Rover and glanced inside the tinted windows. She spied the outdoor tables and a young man sitting there, drinking a St. George beer. The door into the bar yawned in front of her like a giant black eye. She could hear voices behind her and walked inside. At first, it was too dim to see, but soon the room came into view. The barmaid was behind the counter, a big smile on her face. And there he was, Nikita, the fat soldier with his pistol. Emma charged him, feeling a hand on her shoulder.

"You dirty bastard!" Emma shook. "Where are your soldier friends, drunk?"

Nikita truly looked shocked, but then a smile crept across his broad face. He put his finger in the whiskey in front of him and put his finger into his mouth. He said something in a tone of speaking to an ashamed dog.

Lisa put herself between Emma and the soldier. She'd never seen him before, but he looked pretty damned official in his neat uniform. She turned and pressed against Emma. "Emma, no. It's no good."

Craig stood in the doorway like a shadow.

"He held the gun on Craig, while they raped me, for God's sake!" She pressed against Lisa, causing her to stumble. "If I had a hand grenade, I'd shove it down his throat!"

The barmaid had run through the back into the kitchen, peering out from the doorway. She couldn't afford to be shot. She had six children.

Lisa regained her balance and hugged Emma as tight as she could. "Emma, no."

"Where are they! Your friends! I'll break every last bone in their sick bodies." Emma felt exhilarated and then defeated. She sank into Lisa's embrace. "They have to pay. Oh, God, they have to pay."

Nikita downed his whiskey and stood to leave. He looked toward the back door into the kitchen and saw daylight. "Fucking bitch," he said in English. He hitched his green trousers and walked that way.

Emma surged, and Lisa held on. "Emma, listen! Don't do it. We have to go."

Emma was weeping, tears warming her cheeks. She relaxed and let Lisa turn her toward the door, a bright rectangle of light. She was there and then outside, Lisa's arm around her. The man drinking beer looked away.

"They're in one of the rooms," said Emma. "I'll find the bastards."

Craig maneuvered into position. "Emma, listen to Lisa. We have to cut our losses." He grimaced.

Emma growled like a bear and wiped the tears from her eyes. She let Lisa guide her away from the hotel and onto the rocky dirt road. The sky seemed endless, and it was. Craig and Lisa framed Emma as they walked back to the compound.

"I need food," said Emma.

A small stall had opened, and Lisa bought a box of vanilla crème cookies made in Yemen. "Here, eat these. I'll make lunch when we get back." She handed Emma two cookies and held the box out for Craig, who passed.

"Can it get any worse?" asked Emma. "Can it get any worse?"

Craig thought it could, but didn't say it.

Lisa nibbled a cookie. "You want me to make a pizza? I can make a mean pizza from famine food." She relaxed her hold on Emma, just holding her hand.

"Ferenj!" came the familiar cry, and a little boy wearing only a short dress ran and grabbed Emma's free hand.

"Oh, mamoosh," she said, overwhelmed with a different kind of desperation. "Cookie?" She took a cookie from Lisa and handed it to the little boy.

"Kuki!" said the little boy. He held the joy of the world in his smile.

Another and then another soon skirted them, holding out their hands. Lisa gave them all away within seconds. Emma noticed one whose eyelashes had begun to turn inward. "We have to get some ointment for her eyes." She went from feeling flat and dead to particularly alive.

"Sure," said Lisa. "Nah," she told the little girl. "Come." The little girl beamed, flies caking the corners of her eyes. She wore a leather amulet around her neck on a tattered string, her feet and legs dusty.

Emma took the little girl's hand, a lopsided smile on her face. "We have to wash your eyes, see. And put some ointment there." She squeezed the tiny, strong hand, and it squeezed back.

At the Mission compound, Emma located the tetracycline ointment and took three tubes. Alene was there, and Lisa sent him back into town with simple instructions of "in the eye, ain, three, sost, times a day." Alene nodded and led the little girl away, her hands full of famine biscuits.

Craig went to his room, and Lisa and Emma entered the dining facility, which had a tiny kitchen, to make a pizza.

"See, we have the flour and oil from the States, tomato paste from Italy, the canned cheese from Australia, salt and garlic from the market, and just enough of this salami." Lisa arranged the items on one of the indoor picnic tables. "You chop the garlic. You like garlic?"

"I didn't use to, but I do now." Emma felt like a freshly turned potato, half in the dirt, half in the sun. "Just chop it up?"

"Yeah, peel it and chop it."

Emma busied herself. Lisa took flour and mixed it with baking powder and salt. There was no yeast. Soon, they had a somewhat round pizza crust, and Emma smeared on diluted tomato paste. The soft yellow cheese had to be cut into small pieces by hand, and then Emma sprinkled on the garlic. Lisa placed rounds of salami thick with morsels of fat. She didn't have a pizza pan, so she used a small cookie sheet, which she slid into the tiny hot oven.

"There," said Lisa. "Lunch. Take a seat, rest. I can't believe you stood that fat soldier down. He was terrified."

Emma tried to smile. "Thank you. You really are a beautiful person. Thanks for not letting me get killed."

"No worries, sweetie. We'll get this reported in Addis. Let's just focus on the good, all the good things you're doing here."

"Yeah, but they're shutting us down. The end."

"Not the end, just a new start, a new beginning," said Lisa.

"Well, that sounds corny," said Emma.

Lisa smiled. "But, it's true, right?"

"Maybe."

"You scared Craig out of his mind back there. He was sure you'd be shot."

"Me and Reece, shot. I doubt if I would have felt it. I was so mad."

"Now, do you think that Reece would want you hurt like that? Hell no."

Emma smiled. "He was a tough nut."

"Yeah, like you no doubt."

Emma thought about the time difference. "He's asleep about now, maybe dreaming about this place."

Craig raved about the pizza, wanting more than one slice. He was eager to get back to his wife in Meranya. Instead of waiting another day, he and Emma decided to tackle the rough and tumble drive to Godo. The trip was relatively quiet, with the only excitement coming from a farmer who demanded a ride. He'd jumped in front of the jeep, waving his arms.

The jeep trounced up the steep hill into Godo, the afternoon waning into evening. Craig parked beside the warehouse compound, and they walked up to living quarters. He would have to spend the night and worried about his wife, Eve.

"Emma!" said Ketow, welcoming them inside. He shouted for the others.

Isaac, Barra, and Mariam came from their rooms, welcoming Emma. Barra broke into song, singing in English, "This is the day, this is the day, this is the day that the Lord hath made, that the Lord hath made…"

Emma joined in. "We shall rejoice, we shall rejoice, we shall rejoice and be glad in it, and be glad in it…"

They stood there in a knot, all smiles.

"You are well, Mr. Craig?" asked Isaac. His words slurred naturally, and his s's became z's. He wore his trademark mechanic's jumpsuit.

Craig looked weary, the drama, the driving. "Yes, but there has been some trouble." He waited for Emma to pick up the story.

"The news is that this feeding station and clinic will be closed soon. I'm going home," said Emma.

"No, what iz thiz?" asked Isaac.

Mariam took a deep breathy inhale, and Barra whistled, shaking his head. "This is bad news," said Barra. "What we are to do? You will have many things, but we will have nothing." The whites of his eyes flashed.

"Don't assume you'll lose your jobs. No one said that. I'm sure the Mission will find other work for you if possible. Right, Craig?"

"It's not my call. I don't want to guess. With the famine winding down, many people will become unemployed, even me."

"We are missing you," said Mariam. He pulled sunglasses from his pocket and put them on.

Barra clicked his tongue. "When is closing? Today? Tomorrow?" He told Ketow, and Ketow groaned, scratching his head.

"No, not today or tomorrow. But I will be leaving soon. A bad thing happened yesterday, and it's time for me to go, but the station is closing regardless, according to Dr.

Guthrie."

"The other stations are closing too, Meranya, Rabel, Gundo Meskel. Not just here. We have to cut our losses," said Craig.

"Hmm, what does it mean?" asked Barra. "This cutting? Someone is cutting?"

Emma laughed. "It's just what he says when he's nervous. Right?"

Craig frowned. "Well, we should quit while we're ahead. Does that sound better?"

Barra looked puzzled. He spoke to Isaac and Mariam in Amharic. They nodded. "Is joking, no?"

Emma tried to sort it out for them, but got to the point. "I was attacked by soldiers yesterday. They had a gun and threatened to shoot Craig. This is the second time I've been attacked here. I need to leave before I'm shot, like Reece."

"Thiz terrible news," said Isaac. "We are sorry to learn thiz."

"You are okay?" asked Barra.

Emma's chest tightened, thinking about it. "No, they hurt me. I could be pregnant."

All three took deep gulps of air. They understood now.

"It iz very bad. We must to shoot them," said Isaac.

There was a knock at the gate, and Ketow ran there. He opened it for Afewerki, who had been told of the jeep's arrival. "Hallo!" he said, grinning. "How is Misrak? Her children are missing her."

Emma blanched, having forgotten about Misrak. "She is very, very sick, in the hospital in Addis. She will be there for many days."

Barra mumbled to Afewerki.

Afewerki's face went dead. He looked at Craig and then at Emma. "What shall we do?"

Emma felt exposed and suddenly lifeless and arched her back. Was she telling them she'd been raped? She was.

Craig spoke. "We're going to speak to the police in Addis. Nothing can be done here."

"Yeah, I doubt if the Hyena would care," said Emma.

"Yes, he will celebrate," said Afewerki. "He is full with hate for us."

"Thieving murderer," said Emma. "I need to go inside and lie down. Sorry." She was glad it was Sunday, but she would need to visit the shelter before dinner to make sure everyone was okay. The women and children depended on them for protection, as well as food and shelter.

Craig stood there, wondering where he would sleep. He watched Ketow unlock the door to Emma's house, and Emma disappeared inside.

The team huddled closer to Craig.

"She has been rap-ed?" asked Barra. He whistled low.

"Yeah," said Craig. He put his hands in his pockets.

"She was alone?" asked Afewerki.

Craig blushed. "No, I was with her. The fat soldier held a pistol to my chest and said he would shoot me. There were two others..."

"There was fighting, no?" asked Barra. "You are hurt?"

"Emma was hurt, and not me. Dear God. I was powerless to stop it." He looked pasty and sick, his neck red from the sun. He was worried about his wife, Eve. They had to cut their losses while there was still time. He was sure of it. There was a time and place for everything, but the time to leave had come. "It's the writing on the wall," he said.

"There iz writing?" asked Isaac. "On the wall?"

"It's just a saying." Craig sighed. He could only think in clichés. He hadn't slept the night before, and his eyes felt like lead. Eve would make him French onion soup with crusty bread. She understood him better than anyone. He backed away from the group, feeling pressed.

"Ah, you are feeling sick," said Barra. "You must take a rest, to sit, please, inside." He pointed to the dining hut.

"Thank you," said Craig. "I'm beat."

They looked at him, puzzled.

"Yes, rest, that's good. I'll go inside there and rest for a while. Thank you. Will dinner be soon?" The pizza had been delicious, but had left him hungry.

"Ow, soon," said Mariam. He looked official in his shades.

Craig stooped and disappeared beyond the plastic flap.

The team talked in hushed tones among themselves. What would happen next?

The ride to Kristin's house seemed like a silent caterpillar walking on the edge of a jagged leaf. Reece anticipated each turn, marveling at the homes and stores. He enjoyed not having to talk, listening to the hum of the engine, the automatic transmission, the swell of the brakes, more a song than a sound.

"So, you don't love me for who I am?" asked Kristin. She pulled in the left turn lane and stopped behind a miniature cement truck. The light was red.

"Maybe we should buy motorcycles and ride across the country." He slouched in his seat, wildly comfortable.

"Why do you say that? You want me dead? I would never ever buy a motorcycle, and you know it." She turned on her blinker.

"You might like it," said Reece. "Don't knock it till you try it."

"Didn't you get hit by a school bus when you were in high school?"

Reece perked up. "Yeah, nearly went under the back wheels, bounced, hit a curb, and flew over the handlebars. Did a perfect flip and landed on my butt. Those were the days, Killeen, Texas. The town my parents were murdered in."

A chill shot through Kristin. "Reece, that's horrible. I'm sorry. It must have been awful."

"Well, my parents never even tried to track that school bus down. Just let it go, like it was nothing. I was nearly dead meat. The bus passed me while I was trying to turn.

Could've been attempted manslaughter. Damn bus just took off. I was too shocked to do anything."

"Reece, it makes me feel so bad when you talk about your parents like that. I wouldn't wish your childhood on anyone. But they didn't deserve to be shot like that."

Reece slouched again. "No, they didn't. That freak who shot them is dead. I wish he were still alive, rotting in jail. This one guy, a doctor, I think, tried to help him after he drove through the glass. Thought he was hurt. That bastard just shot him in the chest. Luby's…"

"I'm sorry." Kristin took the left turn, passing a McDonald's and a Lowe's. The freshly paved road was coal black with wasp-yellow stripes.

Reece felt unwell, manipulative, dirty, and lucky. "They found a Steely Dan tape in his cassette player. He'd just bought it five minutes earlier. I remember hearing music, and that's where it was coming from, from inside his little truck. It was as if the music would protect me, like that's what happened. The people who lived heard the damn music. My parents never listened to the radio. They had some old records, but never listened to them. One shot each to the head. Dead without hearing the music. The night I was shot…"

"Reece, no. Don't talk about it. I nearly lost you. Just don't, please." The winding road was smooth, the tires silent. She turned on the radio, Carly Simon singing.

"Ex-communi-cation is making me wait," sang Reece. He sat up straight, his lower back aching, a muscle knotting.

"Oh, stop it." She drove with two hands, her lips pursed. "It's what the church does, has to do. Otherwise, what would happen? Everybody would just do what they wanted to. Think about his poor wife and child. It was for them."

"Hell," said Reece. "Maybe he found true love."

"I can't believe you said that." Kristin gripped the wheel. "Did you find true love in Africa? Is that what you mean?"

"Are we destined to argue about every little thing?"

"Little? I'm going to Food World for some ice cream. Little thing, really? Is our love just a little thing to you?"

"We're still at it."

Instead of turning right, she kept going straight toward the grocery store.

"They don't have ice cream in Ethiopia, but they have these little Italian pastry shops, pasticerrias. Little cakes, real pretty. Always smelled like milk in there. Reminded me of a dairy in Germany, when I was in first grade over there." He put his fist to the small of his back.

"Well, that's swell," said Kristin. "I guess you want to go back and eat some cakes with Emma."

"Can you just get off that train? For about five seconds? Jesus Christ."

"You never answer my questions. You just start rambling. What am I supposed to think?" They came into Roebuck proper, and she turned toward Food World.

"We worked well together, that's all. It's like we were partners, like we'd known each other forever, that's all. That's just the way it was. Ask God your questions and not me."

Kristin grumbled and turned off the radio as if that would settle things. She parked in the vast lot.

"I know someone who's worked here for at least twenty

years, and he's still a cashier. He's as gay as the day is long, but would never admit it. Bernard. Maybe he's working tonight. Can I go with you, or are you on a solo quest for ice cream?" He opened his door.

"Do what you want. You probably don't even have any money."

"I have a nickel and two dimes. Will that buy me some forgiveness?"

He stood on one side of the car and she on the other, looking across the rooftop.

She remembered her purse, grabbed it, and slammed her door. Reece fell in behind her and followed her into the store. He looked for Bernard but didn't see him. He slowed and let her break away for the frozen foods. At the end of the aisle was a display of pork and beans. His mother had served them often. There was a sliver of pork fat on top inside each can. That way, they could call it pork and beans. He put his back to the cans and looked around at the humanity. He watched an old woman pulling a bedraggled teen girl behind her. The girl looked slow and had a face like a fried egg. He wanted to tell the woman to quit dragging the poor soul. They passed and slipped into the aisle with toilet paper.

Kristin opened the freezer door and took a half-gallon of Rocky Road. With her ice cream, she retraced her steps and saw Reece. She ignored him and went to stand in the express lane.

Reece saw her seeing him and walked up. "Okay, I'm sorry. I know it must be serious if you have to buy ice cream. You know, you're very distinctive, your hair, your chin, the way you glide."

Kristin said, "Distinctive? Does that mean pretty?"

"Yes, of course," said Reece. He wanted to dig himself out of the hole. "You just have your own look. I like it."

Kristin stepped back and joined him. "Well, that's better, country boy. You remind me of a country boy who's come to the city with big eyes and big plans."

"Okay," said Reece. "That's a new one. I'll take it as a compliment."

Kristin pulled into the driveway beside the F-150. Reece carried the ice cream.

"You might not want to be here when my parents get home." She fetched two bowls and two spoons. "You want some, right?"

"Yeah, I need to gain some weight." He realized his error.

"And I don't?"

"Lord, look, let's call it even. That whole excommunication thing just freaked me out."

"Maybe not even. But I guess you're out of the doghouse. Can you let Walter in?"

Reece opened the back door, and Walter wiggled in. His whole behind shook, his stubby tail wagging. He looked at Reece and barked.

"He loves his daddy," said Kristin. "That's a good sign at least. Animals know. You know?" She scooped the ice cream sprinkled with marshmallow and bits of nuts. "Here you go, bucko."

"Thanks," said Reece. He sat on the couch, and Kristin joined him. "How long do I have? Maybe thirty minutes before the Bible thumpers get home?"

Kristin moaned. "That was uncalled for. Are you just trying to get me to dump you?"

Reece sighed and touched the spoon in his bowl. "They are a bit extreme. I mean, there's more to life than church."

"Reece, you would have never said that before you went to Africa."

"I went to Ethiopia, a country in Africa. Mr. Cargill thought I went to China."

Kristin had to laugh. "He's the guy who likes to fish, the metal pier?"

"Yeah. So, are we okay here? Before I have to leave?"

"Maybe a tiny apology, and tell me you love me for who I am, not for who you want me to be."

Reece twisted, the knot in his lower back clenching. "Okay, I'm sorry, but for what, I'm not sure, and I love you for being who you are."

"That was mediocre, but I guess I forgive you." She savored a bite of the cold ice cream, licking the spoon.

"Excellent," said Reece.

"Do you even still believe in God? Can I ask that?"

The million-dollar question. "I've been shot in the head. How do you know what I have to say about that is even sensible? I've been thinking about that, you know. I'm not a bad person, and then that happens. My parents died in front of me. Little kids are going blind because of black flies. People go to bed hungry, and we're eating ice cream. Dying from hunger, no less. What am I supposed to think?"

"God has a plan for everyone. It's not for us to judge. God's will is God's will."

"And a tire is round and goes flat when a nail punctures

it. Is it still a tire?"

"You and your word games. Of course, it's still a tire. It can be fixed."

"God needs fixing?"

"You need fixing. You'd better just go."

Inside her tiny house of mud and poles, Emma sat on the single wooden chair. The legs wobbled. She gazed at her little propane stove and fridge. There was her shelf with a few cans: tomato paste and cheese. White sheets of plastic covered the walls, the rafters made of poles holding up the corrugated tin roof. Beside her cot was the oversized table, which held candles, a flashlight, matches, a Bible, her devotional, a pen, and a notebook. She thought about her bedroom back at her mom's house in Hueytown. It was as big as this little house and filled with stuff, which seemed like treasure from so far away.

She needed water and topped off a cup from her water filter. She thought about the advice to count one's blessings. And then the sickly soldier was on top of her, forcing himself inside her, grabbing her breasts, choking her, pounding down her shoulders. He had smelled like the inside of a dirty oven, and she could feel his grease still inside her. Could that be an answered prayer, that two men had raped her instead of three? Should that be a blessing to hold next to one's heart? She dry heaved and spat sticky phlegm onto the cement floor.

Outside, the others convinced Afewerki that he should check on Emma. He approached the metal door and knocked. "Emma?" He listened and knocked once more. He turned to the others and shrugged.

Emma heard the knocking and went to her bed. She sat on the edge and pulled the pillow onto her lap. Several flies buzzed the room, sticking to the walls. The pillow smelled like unwashed hair, and she buried her face into it. She thought about Misrak in the hospital. She thought about the women at the shelter and collapsed into herself, closing her eyes. She had to check on them. She'd heard the guard was sleeping with some of them, paying them. He was such an old man, and she found it hard to believe. She had to pick her battles, and it seemed that the incidents were consensual.

Emma fought the urge to sleep. It took a minute, but she stood and put on a light jacket. It was always windy at the shelter, and the afternoon was cooling down. She opened her door, metal scraping the cement floor. She looked out over the green courtyard, smoke coming from the cookhouse. She called out to Afewerki.

"Abet!" Afewerki jogged over. He was wearing his Exxon ballcap and a pair of beat-up hiking boots.

"Hey, man, will you go to the shelter with me? Check on the ladies?"

"Of course," said Afewerki. "Shall we go there?"

"You look like a little boy with your hat." Her burden lightened just a bit.

"What is it? My hat? Shall I take it off?"

Emma laughed. "No way. It was a compliment. I like it."

"Oh," said Afewerki. "It is good, the hat."

"Yes. Let's go."

They walked through the gate and turned left into the lane wide enough for four. "I'll be saying goodbye soon," said Emma. "It could even be tomorrow."

"That is terrible." He greeted others on the path and shook the hand of one man who had been drinking.

The path narrowed and wound up left to the Orthodox

church. Emma reached into her pocket and put a birr in the locked collection box outside.

"The priest will appreciate," said Afewerki.

"I wish I had come to more of the services." The wind quickened, the land there devoid of trees or bushes, leading up to the exposed shelter.

Within a minute, they were there. Emma smelled cook smoke and feces. Thin women holding babies huddled in the doorways of the two long shelters that reminded Emma of chicken houses. She zipped her jacket.

The old guard stood ready with his rifle. He greeted them with his toothless smile. He wore baggy tattered shorts and a patched shirt of heavy green cloth.

"Any problems?" asked Emma.

Little boys and girls circled and drew close, reaching out to touch her like ghosts. One little girl with braids took her hand. Snot caked her nose. She was barefoot and dirty. Emma reached down and picked her up, cradling her on her hip. The little girl whispered and buried her head into Emma's shoulder.

Afewerki listened to the old man, nodding and frowning. The old man spoke for several minutes, gesturing with his hands.

"The Hyena has been here today. He gives trouble with the ladies."

"What?" Emma rocked the little girl. "What did he do?"

Afewerki frowned. "He is telling some ladies here to come and cook for him. To wash his clothes. He will hurt them."

"That's outrageous. Who does he think he is? They're not his slaves."

"He has ordered them to do these things."

"Hell," said Emma. She kissed the little girl and set her down. "Did they go with him? I want to talk to him."

"They are at his house. He was using his gun."

Emma focused. A rage. "Okay, we have to go to his house, the bastard."

"Emma, there are many other problems," said Afewerki. "He will to shoot you."

"What other problems?"

"The ladies are complaining of scabies, and the fleas are in the house. They are itching and scratching."

Emma felt like vomiting. "Ugh and damn. Let's talk to the ladies, and then we have to go to the Hyena's house. I could spend the rest of my life just..."

Afewerki walked down to the shelter. One woman came forward. She was in her thirties and had four children. Her husband had stepped on a nail and died. She had lost their single ox paying for the funeral, and she had not been able to plow or pay someone to plow for her. Her little house in Aferbiny had begun to collapse, and there was no food. The goiter on her throat bobbed when she talked.

"Look," said Afewerki.

The woman pulled up her dress, exposing herself. Her groin was littered with hundreds of flea bites. She scratched for emphasis. Everyone was suffering, she told Afewerki.

"This sucks. We need to treat them with Permethrin. Tell her we will come tomorrow."

"Yes, but we must treat the shelter. The fleas are living there in the mattresses." By mattresses, he meant the large pads made from grain sacks stuffed with corn shucks."

"Does the guard have fleas?"

Afewerki asked him.

"Yes, he has the fleas in his pubic hair," said Afewerki.

"I thought so. Tell him, we will treat him tomorrow…Oh hell, let's do it now. Why wait?"

"Dinner will be soon," said Afewerki.

Emma thought. "Yeah, and I want to confront the Hyena. So, tomorrow we will come with medicine. Do we have the Permethrin in the little cans, to paint the mattresses?"

"We can buy," said Afewerki. "But, we should not visit the Hyena. He will cause trouble."

"He's already causing trouble. I can't let those women be near him. He's bad news. Afewerki, promise me that you'll help these women after I leave."

"Emma, they will go. I cannot feed them."

Emma knew he was right, but what to do? "Okay, but we have to go and let those women come back here. Their children need them, not the Hyena."

"He will be angry," said Afewerki. "You must not."

"He will rape them. You know that. We're going." She looked at the little children around her, all of them asking for caramella, candy. "I want to buy a goat for them to eat tomorrow. Who should I give the money to?"

"You must give to the guard. He will buy and slaughter. The women will cook. It will be a special thing for them."

"So how much?"

"Perhaps forty birr for the large goat."

Emma pulled forty birr from her pocket, and Afewerki explained to the old guard. He laughed, nodded, and folded the birr into his elaborate draping that kept him warm.

He thanked them.

"Okay, let's go," said Emma.

"Ishi," said Afewerki. "Dinner will be soon, no?"

"But, we have one place to visit, right? Take me there, but I know where he lives."

"Emma, it is bad to do this thing. He will anger and shoot."

"Let him shoot."

"No, no."

"Look, I'll go without you."

"Emma, you cannot do that thing."

"Come with me or go to the compound. It's your choice, but I need you to interpret."

Afewerki looked defeated. "Okay, but we must hurry. The darkness will be soon." He put his hands in his pockets. The wind whipped his shirt.

Instead of leaving and avoiding the wrath of Edwin and Gert, Reece pulled Kristin close and kissed her. They soon wound up embracing on the couch.

"Scratch my back in the middle," said Reece. His back was his major pleasure zone.

Kristin ran her hands beneath his shirt and raked her nails. "You are so weird."

"God, that feels so good." He groaned.

Kristin kept raking. "I'm going to make you bleed."

"Do it."

They rubbed and scratched, kissing in bliss. Reece opened his mouth wide and took in her tongue, searching her mouth. He pulled away, his jaw slightly out of kilter. "Oh."

"What's wrong?"

"I think my jaw is out of whack." He tried to touch his teeth together, and they didn't quite match up. "A kissing injury, you devil."

"I'll be your devil if you keep kissing me," said Kristin.

"Sounds good to me." Reece felt that his left ear needed to pop and pushed on top of her.

"Oh, baby."

Neither heard the Impala pull into the driveway. Reece ran his hands down the length of her leg and then to her chest. Through her blouse and chemise, he felt for her small breasts. Kristin inhaled, her hand over his erection.

The front door opened, and they scrambled.

"Hello!" said Edwin, coming up the stairs.

"Reece!" Kristin straightened her blouse.

Reece sat up, drunk with near sex. He smoothed out his short-sleeve shirt. He even felt that the hair on his arms was out of place, guilty, and he rubbed them. A surge of anger, he felt like some lame teenager,

Reece and Kristin sat like statues on the couch.

Gert just passed through the living room into the kitchen, but Edwin walked into the den with his large floppy Bible, the red ribbon marker marking the scripture that delineated excommunication.

"Well, I didn't expect you to be here," said Edwin. He needed to pee, but sat in his recliner. He reclined, then put his feet back on the carpet.

"Oh, Daddy," said Kristin.

"I wonder where your sister is?"

"That Robyn. Probably at Wendy's," said Kristin. Robyn went to a different church, the mega-church off I-459.

Reece twiddled his thumbs, waiting for the inevitable. "Well, I should probably be going." He glanced at Kristin. He wondered if he had lipstick on his face.

"Y'all left early. I was hoping you'd stay for the sermon," said Edwin.

"Yeah." Reece could hear Gert shuffling things in the kitchen, probably putting the dishes away.

"Marriage is a serious boat to float in," said Edwin. He wanted to buy a bass boat for his days off, but Gert had said, "No way."

"Daddy," said Kristin.

"I guess that guy was guilty as charged." Reece's mouth felt dry, and his erection was fading. He looked up at Kristin, standing in the middle of the room, like she was going to catch some valuable object from falling over.

"He betrayed his family and would not repent," said Edwin.

Reece crossed his legs and folded his hands on his lap. "No one died, right?"

Edwin looked blank. "Christ died for our sins, if that's what you mean."

"Not really."

"The church is God on Earth. We have to uphold the Bible, the holy word." Edwin peered at Reece through his bifocals.

"That's nice. But what about forgiveness? I guess God never forgave Adam and Eve."

"Reece," said Kristin. She sat next to him and took his hand. "You're still in Africa."

"You mean Ethiopia," said Reece. "Africa is a freaking continent with fifty countries or more."

"Whatever," said Kristin. "You know what I mean."

"Maybe," said Reece.

"God commands it," said Edwin. "If we didn't do it, who would?"

"I guess you could have called the FBI on him." Reece was energized, ready to fight until the death.

"Man's rule has no place in sin," said Edwin.

"So, he shouldn't go to jail for cheating on his wife?"

"No, sheep can't care for the sheep."

"If Christ is the shepherd, then who are the sheep. Isn't the FBI just one big sheep?" Reece yawned, feeling feisty and illogical.

It took another half hour, but nothing was resolved. Reece excused himself and said goodnight to Kristin at the top of the stairs.

"I love you," said Kristin, kissing him on the cheek.

"I love you, too."

Monday morning, Reece was up early enough to eat with Horace and Dora. He was telling them about the excommunication.

"The poor guy wasn't even there to defend himself. But I don't blame him. I would have done the same thing."

"Sounds like a bunch of kooks," said Horace. "Are they holy rollers?"

"No, they don't wear helmets and jump the pews," said Reece.

"Ever'body's got their way of doing things," said Dora. "You want more grits?"

"I guess I should run it by the church first."

"Run what?" asked Dora.

"The grits, whether or not I'm allowed to have more."

"Now that's just plain silly."

"That's what I'm saying," said Reece.

"Well, you don't have to go back," said Horace. He cut a sausage link in half with his fork and dragged it through syrup.

"Don't worry," said Reece.

"What if Kristin wants to get married there?" Dora pushed her rolling chair next to the stove and took the pot of grits.

"I guess, she'll be there by herself." Reece stopped chewing his sausage and watched a big ladle of cheese grits ooze onto his plate. "Thanks, neighbor."

"Neighbor?" asked Dora.

"You're sitting next to me. You're my neighbor." Reece laughed.

"Sounds like you don't want to get married," said Horace. "I wouldn't rush it. You're still young. There's plenty of fish in the pond."

"Kristin is a sweet girl, though. Just her parents are funny. Although she could be friendlier," said Dora.

"Did I tell you about the old monk I met who was digging a church into the rock, in the side of a cliff with a pick, a chisel, and a hammer? I walked there with Emma one day."

"Here comes that Emma," said Dora. "I'd like to see her picture."

"She's white, right?" asked Horace.

Reece chuckled and took a sip of orange juice. "You ever heard of a black Southern Baptist missionary? They don't exist."

"Well, she could've been one of them blacks you were working with," said Horace.

"She wasn't from Ethiopia. She's from Hueytown."

"Yeah, that's right," said Horace. "I forget sometimes. So what about the old man?" He cornered some grits with a biscuit and pushed them onto his fork.

"He wore a yellow outfit and a little skullcap, a monk of some sort."

"Was he a Christian?" asked Dora.

"Yeah, a Christian, Orthodox, the church there in Ethiopia. He lives by himself and just digs away six days a week. The room he had carved out was as big as this house."

"Did he wear gloves?" asked Horace.

"No gloves," said Reece.

"Well, that's kind of crazy, don't you think? He wasn't being punished, was he? Some of them priests are a little light in their loafers," said Dora.

"Don't talk about that," said Horace.

"I don't think he liked little boys, if that's what you mean."

"Did he have a wheelbarrow?" asked Horace.

"Yeah," said Reece. "One with an old iron wheel on it. Looked ancient."

"Well, I guess he sounds like a nice, hard-working fellow," said Horace.

"I'd say so. Anyway, he wouldn't let Emma come inside because women weren't allowed. She was pissed and then went back by herself to see if she could bribe her way in. The Hyena and his guys attacked her while she was walking."

"Oh my word," said Dora. "What did she do?"

"Well, she tried to fight them off, and then the old monk appeared and yelled at them to leave her alone."

"Did she get hurt?" asked Horace.

"Tore her clothes, I think."

"Why are men so nasty sometimes?" asked Dora. "It's a wonder she wasn't killed over there like you almost were."

"And that Hyena is the one who shot you?" asked Horace.

"That's what everyone thinks, but we can't prove it."

"I'd like to shoot him," said Horace. "Sounds like a real dog to me."

"For sure," said Reece. He scooped some grits with his spoon.

"So, what about that excommunication?" asked Dora.

"You let that slip."

"It was the dumbest thing I've ever seen. I got up and left, and Kristin followed me. Pissed off her parents."

"What did the fella do that got him kicked out?" Horace pushed back from the table and patted his round belly.

"I gathered he cheated on his wife."

"Well, that's breaking the Ten Commandments," said Dora.

"Maybe so, but what authority do they imagine they have? What about forgiveness? What about just 'Hey dude, you're not welcome here anymore' and leave it at that? Why put on the big show unless you just want to humiliate him? The guy probably fixes mufflers for a living or works in a bank. It's not like he's a criminal."

"To each his own," said Horace. He stood and brushed crumbs from his shirt onto the table. "That sure was good. I've got some wood to saw up, son. Maybe you can help me."

The phone rang, and Reece jumped. For a brief instant, he wondered if it could be Emma, but she was supposed to have left for Godo. "Hello?" It was the prayer chain from church. "Prayer chain," and he handed the phone to Dora. The cord was too short, and she made Reece move so she could take his chair.

Reece and Horace stood there, waiting to hear.

Dora covered the receiver. "It's that McKorkle lady. Her husband committed suicide, hung himself."

Reece winced at such gruesome news on a Monday morning. Everybody knew that the husband was a drunk. He'd once come to a Wednesday night prayer meeting and started speaking in tongues, brandishing himself as a lunatic.

"We got to get that wood before we cut it up," said Horace. "Just down the road. They gutted the house and threw out some fine old boards and paneling."

Reece followed him outside into the warm sun filtering through the pines. "What you gonna use it for?"

"Might build me a tool shed on the back of the garage. It's getting so cluttered in there, I can't work." He had built the two-car garage, added an extension onto the house, framed in the front porch, which was Reece's bedroom, and poured the driveway. He was always on one project or the other. There was already a large pile of boards beneath the shell of an old van behind the garage.

"You ready to go now?" asked Horace. "Or you need to polish your toenails first."

"Do I get paid more if they're polished?"

"Maybe not, but get some shoes on. You'll need those."

"Oh yeah, shoes."

It took them an hour or so to load the wood and return. Horace backed the truck into the driveway.

"I'll unload, and you stack it."

Reece nodded. He waited for the maelstrom of wood to begin. Gentle, Horace was not, and soon the first board, a two-by-six with a thin film of cement, came flying his way. "Try not to kill me," said Reece.

"Just mind your body," said Horace, and he tossed a ten-foot two-by-four spiked with nails.

"Jump to Jesus, don't crucify me." Reece started a new pile for two-by-fours. "Remember when that Taylor boy threw a dart in my arm?"

"Plugged you good. Said it was an accident." He wrestled a half-sheet of three-quarter plywood.

"Yeah, what he says and what he did," said Reece. "Funny thing is, it didn't hurt, but I was afraid to take it out. Hurt the next day, though."

"I remember when you stepped on a nail at that house I was building in Palmerdale. You wouldn't pull that out either. Had to wrestle you."

"That one hurt like hell." Reece laughed and watched another two-by-four sail his way. "Got me sweating, old man." He wiped water from his forehead.

"Sweat equity. I should be a rich man," said Horace. He'd worked for thirty years as a carpenter at a pipe shop, sometimes working seven days a week, month after month. He was the first of his family to venture out from the farm.

"What's this job pay instead of cheese grits and sausage?"

Horace laughed. "How about a pillow, a blanket, a roof, and a hot shower?"

"You know, that's what I missed most over there, a hot shower. Had to bathe with a little pan of cold water most times."

"More than you missed Kristin?" Horace dragged out two heavy boards nailed together. "Need your help with this one. You get that end."

"I guess not, just missed material things." He hoisted the heavy load to his shoulder, and Horace wrestled the other end. "She wrote me just about every day, and I talked to her when I was in Addis."

"Yeah, you got a big responsibility headed your way, son. I'd think long and hard. I was twenty-seven before I married."

"Robbed the cradle," said Reece.

They dropped the board.

"Got lucky. First saw her sitting up under the school-house stoop when she was twelve. She sure was a pretty girl. So, are you dead set on this marrying?"

Reece pulled a two-by-two from the pile in the back of the truck. "This'd be good for staking beans in the garden." He threw it like a javelin.

Horace went to the next board, pulled it, and looked down the length, checking the straightness.

"I'm just getting antsy, is all. Her parents definitely don't like me. They think I'm some kind of devil, I think."

"Well, you do marry the family, son. No getting around that, unless you haul her off to China." He stood a long, thick board on end and let it fall toward Reece.

Reece had paused, staring into the pines. The board caught him across the bridge of his nose and knocked him down. "Hell!" He looked for his glasses and touched his face. "Damn."

"You all right?"

Reece held out his crooked glasses. "Maybe, but not these."

"Got a lump there, son."

Reece bent the frame back and tried them on. "A little wampus."

"You need to rest?"

"No, I'm good." He took a deep breath. "I got a question. You ever drink alcohol? I've never seen you take a drink. There's that wine in the cupboard."

Horace wiped his face on his shirt sleeve. "In the Army, I drank a little beer. Never had a taste for it. Why?"

"I think maybe I developed a taste for it over there."

Horace swung a short section of four-by-four post, and it thudded on the pine straw. "Well, a drink here and there never hurt nobody. Just don't tell your granny."

"Right," said Reece. "Or Kristin. That would ice the cake."

Emma walked faster than usual with Afewerki struggling to keep up. They passed his parents' compound, trotted through the market area, and made for the bar. The Hyena lived just beyond in a square house of two rooms with a metal roof. A tall fence surrounded his home, and a grizzly, yellow dog skulked in the courtyard. It growled and bared its teeth behind the gate.

"What should we do now?" Emma was whispering.

"We should leave. This is very bad. The dog will bite, so we cannot go inside."

Emma banged on the gate made of corrugated metal. A faint tin of music came from the house, the door ajar.

"Emma!"

"I'll get those women if it kills me."

"Maybe they have gone. We do not know."

"You have to help me, right?" She fisted the gate again. "Dammit!"

The door opened, a woman, but someone pulled her back inside. Dusk was falling, making it hard for Emma to see. "I saw her. They're in there by God. Dammit, the door closed."

A man and his wife had stopped, watching them. Soon, along came a farmer with his plow on his shoulder, waiting for something to happen.

Emma picked up a rock and threw it, hitting the roof.

"Emma, no." Afewerki grabbed her arm, but let it go.

She threw another rock and hit the crooked metal door square on with a loud crack.

Inside, two women huddled in the corner behind a small fire of hot coals. They had washed all the Hyena's clothes and were preparing his dinner. Both knew what would follow. He would make them drink katikala and chew qat.

The Hyena, not quite drunk yet, cursed. He checked his Makarov to make sure a bullet was in the chamber and opened the door, peering out. Another rock hit the roof, and he flinched. One woman yelled out, and he screamed for her to shut up.

"It's him," said Emma. "I saw him." She banged on the gate and kicked it with her foot. The dog lunged and gnashed its teeth, growling like the devil. "Hey! I know you're in there!" She turned to Afewerki, who was whispering to the small gathering crowd. "What's the word for come out?"

"Nah," said Afewerki. He put his hands in his pockets and shrugged. "It is not wise."

Emma threw another rock and yelled, "Nah! You coward!"

Puzzled and rattled, the Hyena worked out the impossibility in his mind. The crazy ferenj was throwing rocks at his house and yelling for him. He coughed and spat, losing some of the qat packed into his lip. He went to his rickety table and took a swallow of katikala. *Bang!* Another rock hit the roof.

"He's coming out," said Emma. She watched the Hyena emerge from the shadows. "Nah! You bastard!" She felt a hand on her shoulder, but ignored it. "Afewerki, tell him to let those ladies go. Now."

"Oh, what is it?" asked the Hyena. His voice quavered

a bit. He walked halfway to the fence and saw the crowd there. He would have to be careful not to shoot them. "Crazy bitch ferenj. What do you want?"

"Afewerki, what did he say? Tell him to let the women go. Do it."

Arms folded, Afewerki spoke as gently as possible. He told the Hyena that Emma was there for the women, if they were inside. He coughed and held his breath.

"They're not your property," said Emma through her teeth. "Let them go!" She turned, expecting Afewerki to translate.

"The pretty ladies are cooking my dinner. They want to drink with me tonight. Perhaps you can join us." The Hyena laughed.

A titter went through crowd, gradually understanding the situation.

"If that damn wusha wasn't there, I'd get them myself," said Emma to everyone.

"Maybe she wants to feed the wusha with her pretty skin," said the Hyena. He tried to discern if any of his minions were in the crowd that moved back as he approached. He forced a smile.

Afewerki spoke. "She will go if the ladies can go. Their children are calling them."

The Hyena moved to within an arm's length of the gate, his eyes perhaps too wide. "Come and drink with me. I will let them go."

Emma saw the pistol at his waist. "What did he say?"

"He wants for us to come and drink with him. Then he will let them go."

"Ha!" said Emma. "Yeah, I'll drink with him if he ties up

his dog. Not a problem. Be glad to. Maybe he'll get drunk and show me his other asshole."

"What she is saying?" asked the Hyena.

Afewerki shivered and put his hands back in his pockets. The last thing on earth he wanted to do was drink with the Hyena. He turned and looked at the crowd, all frozen with the drama. He relayed half of what Emma had said. Perhaps it was the quickest and safest way.

The Hyena took a step back, just a bit wobbly. "That is good news. I will hold the wusha, and you will go inside. No? Maybe the ferenj will get drunk and apologize. First, though, she must apologize to the people for creating trouble, for throwing the stones to my house. I must knock the stone from her shoulder."

Afewerki translated. Before she could say anything, he turned and told the crowd that she was sorry for throwing the stones and that she would go now and drink with the Hyena who had forgiven her.

"What are you saying?" asked Emma.

"We must let him knock the stone from your shoulder. It is a custom. Then we can go inside."

"Oh, so I'm going to get on my knees and apologize is what you're saying."

"Please, Emma. Think of the ladies. It is the only way."

"Dammit. Okay, but out here, not in there with that damn dog."

Afewerki asked the Hyena to come outside the gate. The Hyena chuckled and kicked the dog, which slunk away growling. The gate opened, and he was there.

"Onto your knees, bitch," he said.

Afewerki winced. He wasn't sure if Emma knew the

word for bitch or not. "You will pick a stone and put it onto your shoulder. He will knock it."

The crowd was paralyzed.

Emma went to her knees and chose a smooth stone. She placed it on her left shoulder.

"No, the right is better," said Afewerki.

"Hell," said Emma. She could smell the dirt. The sky looked like home, and she moved the stone.

The Hyena mumbled to himself and pulled the pistol from its holster. A collective gasp from the crowd. Emma stared up at the Hyena, striving to crawl into his eyes. With the barrel, he reached down and tipped the stone. "I should shoot you, but now let us drink. We will celebrate, no?" He shot once into the air, scattering the people.

"Dear God," said Afewerki.

"Very impressive," said Emma. She stood and swiped the dirt from her jeans. "After you, kind sir."

The Hyena, smiling, walked through the gate and grabbed the dog by its neck. "Come," he said in English and motioned toward the house, a darkening square in the dimming light.

Afewerki led the way, and Emma followed. She passed him, though, and entered the house and saw the two women huddled in the corner, terrified. "It's okay," she said. "Nah," she told them.

They looked at one another.

"He will not let them go until we drink," said Afewerki. He'd never been inside the Hyena's house and expected to see human skulls and bowls of blood.

"Well, at least they don't have to squat on the floor. Tell them to sit on the bed or on the stools. I can stand."

The Hyena was inside and closing the door. Scraps of waning daylight came through the closed windows, bathing the interior in shadows. He went to his table and picked up the bottle, which was only half full. He ordered Afewerki to go and fetch a fresh bottle, areke this time, flavored with garlic. Afewerki told Emma, and she told him to go.

Emma motioned again for the ladies to take the stools, and with big eyes, they did, murmuring like small birds. Emma took one of the wooden office chairs. She looked around the otherwise bare room. There were pages from a magazine plastered to the wall, blond women, an ad for Icelandic Airlines. There was an AK-47 in the corner and a can of soybean oil, no doubt stolen from the warehouse. The bed was made of poles, laced with strips of leather. The room smelled of smoke and vaguely of farts.

"So, the American princess would like to drink, no?" He brought down two orange cups from a crooked shelf made of particleboard, scavenged from airdrops of grain early in the famine. He emptied the bottle with two pours. "We shall not waste the drink on these two whores." He laughed and handed Emma a cup.

Emma smirked, smelling the smoky liquor. "Ugh," and she took a sip.

"Bataam taruno!" he said, taking a hefty swig, navigating the liquid past the qat in his mouth. He would gradually swallow the leaves, giving himself an ecstatic high with the alcohol, knowing that he would vomit. Maybe the ferenj bitch would lick it from his face?

After unloading the wood, Reece took a shower and headed out to Palmerdale to the convenience store. He filled up the F-150 with the twenty Horace gave him and bought a six-pack of Coors Light. He had no beer savvy, but liked the can.

Back at the lake, he walked in with his contraband. Dora was there, already working on lunch.

"What you got?" asked Dora.

Reece looked guilty. "Beer. It's good for you."

"Beer? Not in my house, young man. What's gotten into you? You take that right back outside and bury it." She looked around for Horace, but he was watering the garden.

"Granny, look. I was shot in the head. I nearly died. I think I have to experience life before it's gone. It's just beer, not whiskey, or even wine." The six-pack weighed a ton in his hands, and he felt as bad as Eve with her damn apple.

"Not in my house. Why do you need beer? Pretty soon, it'll be moonshine. My daddy used to sneak out in the barn, made him all teary-eyed and slurring his words." She looked imposing, holding a dishtowel with a diamond pattern.

"What if I keep it in the garage? It'll stay cool there."

"Look, boy, as long as you're under my roof, that can't come in the house. What would Kristin think? She'd tie a knot in your tail."

"Have you ever tasted beer? It's not so bad. Refreshing."

"Don't try to pull my leg. No is no. Now go and make

that disappear, before I get a switch like my momma used to with me."

Reece blushed at her wrath but couldn't help laughing.

"What's so funny, boy?"

"I don't know. You're just so mad, is all. Horace said you would be."

"He told you it was okay? Why I'll—"

"No, no, he just said you wouldn't let me bring it in here. Can't blame me for trying, though."

"Git, just git out and get rid of that." She dipped a spoon into a jar of mayonnaise.

Reece couldn't stop laughing. "Okay, okay." He turned and went outside with his paper bag of beer. The mail lady in her dirty white Explorer pulled up to the mailbox. Reece waved. She waved. He thought about hiding the beer in the RV, but then had a better idea. He would go down to the pier and drink all six. They'd be gone, right? He figured he had two hours before lunch and walked across the road. He saw Horace on the far side of the garden beneath the black walnut tree, talking with his buddy Elbert from next door. The gasoline pump was on, gushing lake water into rows of late tomatoes.

Reece stepped onto the pier, the pump vibrating the whole shebang. He walked to the end and sat on the hard wooden bench. Should he pace himself, or should he just drink them? He popped the tab on one, and it foamed and pooled on top. He sipped and then chugged the first one, feeling thirsty. The sun came out from behind a pillowy cloud, and the heat felt good on his skin. No one was out on the lake that he could see, and he popped another one.

Kristin skipped lunch but drank a can of chocolate Ensure from Mrs. Dunlop's room. Her other patient was Chastity, the young woman in the car wreck. She'd continued to have episodes of ventricular tachycardia due to her chest trauma, but her chest tube had been removed over the weekend, her lung fully reinflated. Kristin peeked in at Chastity and then walked into Dunlop's room.

"Mrs. Dunlop, we're going to get you up in the chair, okay?"

"Okay." The word took a while to form, and she enunciated with great care.

Kristin stepped out of the room and saw Winston. "Hey, can you help me get her into the chair?"

"Sure." Winston was tall and skinny, scrub pants bunched around his waist.

Emma put a blue pad in the chair, untied the wrist restraints, and lowered the bed rail. "Up in the chair. Here we go."

"I need a dol-lar," said Mrs. Dunlop.

"What you need a dollar for?" asked Winston. He raised up the head of the bed.

"I have to buy some but-ter. I like but-ter sandwiches."

Kristin took her legs and pulled them sideways while Winston handled her upper body. "Sounds yummy for your tummy."

"Yummy for your tummy," said Mrs. Dunlop.

Each taking a side, Kristin counted to three, and up came Mrs. Dunlop and then into the chair with a soft plop. Her hand went to the feeding tube in her nose, and Emma caught it just in time.

"Thanks," said Kristin.

"No problem," said Winston.

Emma tied the wrist restraints and tilted the chair back, raising the foot. "Mrs. Dunlop, where are you today?"

"I'm at home. This is Thursday. I don't work on Thursday. I need a dol-lar."

"You're not in the hospital?"

"I am at home. I need some but-ter for a sandwich."

"You're on a liquid diet, so we can't have a sandwich today. Maybe tomorrow."

"Okay." Mrs. Dunlop looked like a fat baby bird.

Kristin took a white blanket and arranged it on her lap. "You warm enough?"

"I am cold."

"Okay, here." Kristin pulled the blanket over her arms and shoulders. "That should do it. Okay?"

"Yes. I run the credit card receipts at Loveman's."

"And you do a great job," said Kristin. She looked out and saw Brad on the unit. He was Dunlop's resident. "Okay, I'll check on you soon. You just relax there."

"I will relax here." She smacked her lips as if they were dry.

"Hey," said Brad. "How's the crazy lady today?" He wore his white jacket and a pair of dress shoes with thick heels.

"Don't say that. She is so sweet. I wish everyone were as easy as she is, crazy or not. When can we take out the feeding tube and let her eat?"

"Today, if you'll grab coffee with me sometime." He scribbled in a chart.

"Ha, that's funny. But, really, can we start her on soft food and work up?"

Brad shook his head. "Sure, whatever you say. I'll

write the order. However, we need to ensure she's getting enough calories and plenty of fluids. More work for you."

"Great. She wants to eat a butter sandwich. Maybe write that today?"

"Butter sandwich? That's a new one." He drummed his fingers on the black desktop. "How's your fiancée, your other patient?"

"Don't call him that. He's driving now, a real miracle. He's going to apply for a position in ICU, so you'll get to see he's real and not just..."

Another doctor joined them, Dr. Joiner. He was married but was known for his wild parties. "What's shaking?"

Brad patted him on the shoulder. "Just taking orders from this gorgeous nurse."

Kristin rolled her eyes and grabbed Mrs. Dunlop's chart. "Here, write me that order you promised." She watched him do it.

"See what I mean?" asked Brad.

"I see. Say, I'm having a cigar party at the pad tonight. Drinks and cigars. Ladies welcome. You two should come over, around eight."

"Ooh la la," said Brad. "What do you say?" He put his hand on Kristin's shoulder, but she shrugged it away.

"I don't drink, and I definitely don't smoke cigars," said Kristin.

"Well, what do you do?" asked Joiner. He knew that Brad was desperate.

"I've got work to do," said Kristin.

"Hold up," said Brad. "You could just drop in. I'll bring some soda, some ginger ale, whatever you like, and cigars are optional. Right?"

Joiner laughed. "Everything's optional. My wife will be there. She always complains that I never invite ladies over. I think you'd like her. You'd be doing me a favor."

Kristin looked at them looking at her. She gazed around the unit, and others were watching, she could tell. She saw Debbie give her a thumbs up before heading into a room. Debbie had said she was crazy not to give Brad a try. Kristin thought about Reece, what he would say. Maybe it would wake him up if she went to one of these parties.

"Let me think about it. I want to get that feeding tube out." Feeling watched, Kristin walked to Chastity's room to check on her first.

"Way to go," said Brad. "I'm totally shocked."

"Slow and steady wins the race," said Joiner. He grinned.

"Thanks, man. This could be the turning point." He seemed to be short of breath.

Reece was on his third beer when the pump engine stopped, out of gas. He stood and looked to see if Horace wanted him to start it back up. He waved and stumbled, catching himself. Horace wasn't looking his way, so he headed to the gas can beside the overturned boat, carrying his beer with him. A red-winged blackbird swooped and grabbed onto a cattail, holding itself sideways. Reece watched the bird, forgetting what he was doing. The bird took flight, squawking. Reece realized he was holding the beer can and placed it on the pier.

The metal gas can was half full. The pump engine was a Briggs & Stratton, 2.5 horsepower. He unscrewed the gas cap and dropped it into the water.

"Dammit."

He watched it sink into the mossy muck. He squatted and then lay on his belly, reaching into the water. He scooted out farther until he could touch the bottom with the tips of his fingers. He could see his wavy reflection and cursed. He was unbalanced and scooted back, scraping his stomach on the wood.

"Hell."

Standing, he lifted the gas can and poured, spilling some onto his shoes.

"Perfect."

He turned and kicked his can of beer over, and the liquid glugged out.

"What the?"

The only way he could get the cap would be to get in the water, so he pulled off his shoes without unlacing them. He sat on the pier and eased down into the water. He worried about leeches, but what could he do? He reached in and swirled his hand, coming up with nothing. It took him a good five minutes of hunting, but he found the cap and hauled himself back onto the pier, realizing he had to pee like a racehorse. He'd done it before, so he stepped off the pier and waded in among the cattails. Then, back at the pump, he screwed on the cap and yanked the cord. The engine roared to life, and the siphon jerked, pulling up the green water.

"Finally." He stared into the lake, lost in his thoughts.

"Hey! I saw you peeing in the cattails."

Reece jumped and turned. He saw a young blonde woman wearing shorts and a tube top held up by a skinny string. It took him a second.

"Oh, hey, Cindy." She was Elbert's granddaughter, and

he'd had a crush on her, but she was five years his junior. "Good to see you." He had to speak above the engine racket.

"You too, lake boy. Do you just pee when you get the urge?" She unfolded her arms, revealing what Reece considered to be an ample bosom.

"Ha, sorry about that. You want a beer? It's the beer."

"Hell yeah." She stepped onto the pier. "Watering the corn and the cattails."

At the end of the pier, Reece peeled out a can and handed it her.

"Coors Light."

"Yeah."

"Okay."

"What you been up to?" He wondered if his fly was zipped.

"Not much. Just working at the dealership, running the reception desk." She sat close beside him on the bench.

"Cool. Hadn't seen you in a while." She smelled like coconut. "How's your brother?"

"He's not so good these days. So damned depressed. He hates his job." A pack of cigarettes magically appeared. "Want one?"

Reece hadn't smoked since he was a kid, hiding and sneaking around to do it. "Uh, sure. Cigarettes go with beer, right?"

"Damn straight," said Cindy. She held out the pack and lighter to him. "You're looking good. I expected you to be a train wreck, considering what happened." She examined the scars on his temples. "Can I touch it? Damn."

"Yeah, getting shot is more than it's cracked up to be."

He felt her fingers on his face. "Uh, you're looking good, healthy."

"As a horse?" She laughed. "So, what was it like over there? I've been to Florida, and that's about it. I can't imagine going to Africa. What country was it, Nigeria?"

"Ethiopia. Yeah, it was a trip, a real mind bender. I think about it all the time. All the nonsense left me over there. Like someone held me by my ankles and everything I knew just came out in one big lump." He could see that her nipples were hard beneath her yellow tube top and took a big puff of Camel.

"Must have been exciting. I need something like that. Maybe I'd grow up."

Reece sipped his beer. "Yeah, I guess that's what I did, grow up. It's hard to see people so nice but so screwed by life. But most everyone seemed happy despite the hardships. No electricity, no running water. Houses with straw roofs and dirt floors."

"What did you miss most?" She finished her beer with a large gulp and blew smoke all in one motion.

He wanted to say Kristin. "Well, I guess a hot shower."

"Yeah, a cold shower sucks. You still engaged? My granny said maybe you weren't."

"She said that? I wonder why? Her name is Kristin, and she's a nurse, too. I don't think you've ever met her. Good Lord, that pump is loud."

"Don't know her. What did she think about you going to Nigeria?"

"Ethiopia. Well, she wasn't too happy about it. But I got shot and came home early, so maybe that's been a good thing for her."

"Getting shot was a good thing, or coming home early?" She lit another cigarette.

"Coming home early. Getting shot not so good. She came to see me in the hospital over there. I don't really remember, though." He looked at Cindy's tan legs. She was a natural blonde with neat bangs. Sometimes she wore glasses but had her contacts in.

"Remember that tape you made my brother? You called it Maison du Poulet."

Reece laughed. "Yeah, Black Sabbath, ARS. House of Chicken. It was kind of an inside joke."

"Maison du Poulet." She laughed and took a drag.

"You want this last beer?"

"Nah, it's warm. You look like you need it. You're skinnier than I remember," said Cindy.

"Yeah, well you too. I mean you look trim, look good." He knew he shouldn't drink the last beer, but he was a little rattled having Cindy with him. He could see every curve.

"We should hang out sometime," said Cindy. "I didn't realize you drank and smoked."

"Well, I didn't until now. Good Christian boy you know. I figured it was time. Yeah, maybe we could grab lunch or something sometime." He wanted to shoot himself for saying such a thing. Kristin would kill him.

Afewerki returned with the areke and nearly dropped the bottle. The two women sat on stools, hugging their knees, and Emma sat on the Hyena's bed with him standing over her, singing a bawdy war song.

"Ah, the son of Christ has returned," said the Hyena. His red eyes flashed, then went dull. "Hurry with that bottle. We are thirsty, no?"

Emma took a small sip of what she had. "Tell him to let the women go. He wanted me to drink with him, and I've had enough." She took another sip of the warm liquor, and it burned all the way down.

Afewerki handed the bottle to the Hyena and told him what she had said.

"Oh, no, no, no," he said. "We must drink this bottle first. Their children can wait for momma's titty." He roared at his own speech.

"He says we must drink the bottle first."

Emma frowned. "Maybe if we get him drunk, he'll shoot himself."

"What she is saying? What she is saying?" He unstoppered the bottle and poured in two fingers of the spicy areke.

Afewerki told him that Emma had said she was not thirsty.

"You liar. You are lying for the white devil. She must drink more." He held out the bottle, and Emma pulled her cup back. "You must drink!"

Emma frowned. "I haven't finished this one yet, tell

him." She took another sip. "Afewerki, will you help us drink the bottle?"

"I do not like, but I will help."

"Give him a cup," said Emma to the Hyena.

Afewerki translated. The Hyena snorted and pulled down a thick glass, filling it halfway. "Here you go, Christ child. Drink to Mengistu!" He wobbled and sat beside Emma on the bed, which sank toward the middle.

"Jesus," said Emma. She scooted to the edge of the bed. "What would his mother think about him making these women work for him and probably worse?"

Hearing the question, the Hyena laughed. "My mother died giving birth to me. How do you like that!" He gulped from his cup, gripping the bottle with his other hand.

"Well, that's sad," said Emma. "What about his dad? Is he alive?"

The Hyena thought and muttered.

"He says that his father has died by twenty years from an accident," said Afewerki. "He is having seven older brothers and sisters, and he is the youngest."

"Hard life," said Emma. "Look, I'm going to finish this cup," and she did, wincing. "Can we all go now?"

The Hyena ignored Afewerki and launched into a story from his childhood. After his father died, he was sent to live with an uncle in Gojjam. The uncle was a very bad man. His wife was very young, and he beat her because she could not have a child. The uncle beat him as well because he ate his food and drank his water. Afewerki picked up the story. "By six months, he had run away back to Addis Ababa and was living near the dump for three years. He learned to eat garbage, but soon joined the army and was sent to the north to fight the Eritreans." Afewerki paused. "He has killed many men, but never a man that he drank with."

The Hyena reached the bottle out toward Emma's cup. She held it there and let him pour. She could smell the garlic infusion and gagged. The Hyena laughed. The bottle was half empty, and darkness was falling. He barked at the women in the corner to light a candle so the ferenj could see. Everyone knew that ferenji had weak eyes. One woman stood and lit a candle from a coal in the fire. The candle flame wavered, adding little light and large shadows.

Emma sipped her areke. "God, that burns and tastes awful." She wanted to stuff cotton in her stomach to absorb the foul liquid.

Afewerki sipped his as well, making a face.

The Hyena laughed and coughed. "It is good for the man's special bone, no! To make it very hard like the stone." He cheered himself and took a drink, raising his glass to Emma.

"Just keep drinking, brother," said Emma.

"What?" asked the Hyena.

Afewerki said, "She says she will drink until the bottle is empty."

"Bataam taruno!" said the Hyena. He made Emma show him her cup, but it was still a quarter full.

The women in the corner had gone from terrified to trying not to fall asleep. This would be a great story, though, to tell back at the shelter. This ferenj was drinking to save them.

Emma took a small sip. "Afewerki, ask him if he's ever

killed a woman. We know he's raped them."

The Hyena narrowed his eyes as if seeing something unclean. "Have I not been a soldier? Of course, I have killed a woman. Many women are soldiers in the north. They have guns and grenades and will kill a man just like any man. I am no fool. I am alive."

"Ugh," said Emma. "What did he think of the Icelandic nurses who were here before we came?"

The Hyena reared up and tilted backward. Emma caught his shoulders and pushed him forward. He laughed.

"Oh, the pretty nurses from Iceland," said the Hyena. "Yes, one is Eydis, and one is Svana. I remember them in my heart. They are great people and liked to drink areke and tejj. They were sleeping in tents and treating the people for many things. They give to me many things—blankets and medicines. They have returned to their country." He looked wistful.

"So, why don't you like me?" asked Emma.

Afewerki shook his head, no and more no.

"Ask him. I'm curious."

The Hyena listened to the question and grew silent, taking a deep breath. "Because you do not share with me. The people are seeing this thing and wondering why you are not sharing with their leader. It is hurtful, and so I steal from you. And you shout at me and refuse to shake my hand. This is not the way of the Habasha." He held out the bottle, and Emma let him pour.

Emma could smell him, an odor of unwashed hair, garlic, and alcohol. Sitting beside her he seemed small, not the size of a killer or rapist. But, he shot Reece in the head!

She felt a slow buzz coming on.

"So, I apologize if I have seemed rude or selfish," said Emma. "But you make me so angry, interfering at the clinic and bothering women. Don't you think killing people and bragging about it makes people nervous? Plus, your nickname is the Hyena!"

"Oh oh," and he laughed. "Yes, I do not like that name. My name is Emanuel, and the people spread many rumors."

Emma took a hefty swig. "Aw, that's a pretty name for a guy. Emanuel. Afewerki, why didn't you ever tell me his real name?" She poked Emanuel in the arm.

"What is it? She is to hit me?" He laughed. Emma laughed.

Afewerki shook his head and shrugged. He was taking tiny sips and drifting toward the closed door. A mouse with a long nose ran across the floor and disappeared through a crack in the wall. Afewerki wanted to be that mouse, to be gone. With the door closed, he felt very warm from the fire and the body heat.

Emma drained her cup and winced. She motioned Afewerki over for a refill. "One more shot, brother!"

Afewerki shook his head no.

Emanuel thrust his cup at him. "No! You must drink. You are not a little boy on his mother's tit. Come!" The qat stuffed in his lower lip spilled out onto his lap. "Tebeda," he said. "Fuck." He brushed the gooey wad onto the floor and put his boot over it. "One more for us all! Who is first?"

"Afewerki, you need one more. I can't drink much more. I feel kinda sick."

Emanuel portioned out the remaining liquor into the

cups and glass. "See, I am sharing? No? You must share with me and respect me. I am the town administrator, and the people are watching."

Emma heard what he was saying, but was steadying herself against the areke. "Yeah, what he said." She held her breath and took a swallow. She felt like she would vomit, and there was half an inch left in the cup. Emma let her cup come to rest on the thin blanket and flicked her wrist, spilling most of it. She brought the cup to her lips and drank what was left. "Bucka! Enough!"

"You are finished," said Afewerki. "Thanks to God." He steadied himself and downed his drink, screwing his face into a knot. "Xavier meskin."

Emanuel laughed and slammed the bottle on the floor. "Shall we play checkers? I have the board and bottle caps for the pieces."

"No, no," said Afewerki. "You promised, and we must leave with the ladies."

The two women stood, looking at the floor. Both wore dirty long dresses and no shoes.

"I command it!" said Emanuel, becoming the Hyena. "The Icelanders played with me. Why not you?"

"Look, we have to go." Emma put her hand on his bony shoulder. "You must keep your word. Maybe we can play another day?"

Emanuel melted under her touch. "Okay, okay, perhaps tomorrow, no?"

"Maybe," said Emma. She stood, went dizzy, and sat back on the bed. "Ooh." She wondered if there were bedbugs.

Afewerki extended his hand to her, but she brushed it

away and stood. "I'm okay. I think. Tell the ladies we're going." She turned to Emanuel. "Good night, sir." She held out her hand, and he shook it with an enormous smile, showing his gold teeth.

The two ladies were out the door in a hurry, headed to the gate, forgetting about the dog. One screamed as the dog bared its fangs and growled from its belly. It circled them, licking its yellow teeth.

Afewerki yelled for the Hyena to come. The Hyena staggered to the door and called out. "Wusha!" The dog sat but then lunged, biting one on the ankle.

"Dammit!" said Emma. She rushed toward them, ignoring the dog that was slinking now, expecting a beating.

"Wusha!" The Hyena kicked it in the ribs and fell down. "No problem," he said, wiping his scraped hands on his pants.

Everyone was out of the gate in record time, and Afewerki closed the raspy door. "Praise to God. We are finished," he said.

"Hell, not yet," said Emma. "We need to get this one to the clinic and clean that bite right now."

Afewerki sighed and explained, and the woman took a deep breathy inhale, nodding with wide eyes. He told the other woman to hurry back to the shelter, and she took off like a rabbit, hopping between stones on the path.

Cindy went up to visit her grandmother and write down the number Reece gave her. She kind of looked and walked like a model, one with attitude.

Reece watched her go between the gardens and stop to speak with Horace and Elbert. He took his beer and sat on the edge of the pier, his toes dangling in the green water. Should he still be attracted to every good-looking woman he saw? Maybe it was a character flaw, or maybe he had some sort of spin on a gift, the ability to appreciate beauty. He thought about his own gift of mercy and wondered if Kristin would spare him some of hers if needed. Damn, life was short.

Reece drank the beer slow and watched the Jesus bugs skitter on the water. A foot-long bass swam close and then darted off, making a *bloop*. The sun was hot on his head and face but he felt good. The humidity of the lake swallowed him, giving him a slick of sweat down his spine.

He turned and saw Horace moving the irrigation hose to a row of corn, which they would harvest soon. He preferred to cut it from the cob and freeze it, which made a royal mess. Reece downed the beer and belched and had to pee again. "Dammit." He stood and wavered, his vision going blank for a few seconds. He walked toward the garden, wondering if he looked drunk. He felt drunk.

"Hey," said Reece.

"Hey, boy," said Horace. "We gonna gather this corn tomorrow?"

"Oh yeah, get the corn," said Reece, "then let the stalks

dry in between the rows and burn 'em. That's really why I came back, to help you with corn." He laughed.

Horace eyeballed him. "You okay, son?" He saw the plastic bag with cans in it. "You been drinking? Oh Lord. Don't you let on to Dora. She'll skin you alive."

"Just a few beers. Cindy drank one. Replenish my bodily fluids." He felt that his face was flushed, and it was.

Horace kicked the black PVC pipe into the row bottom.

"Yeah, just beer. No liquor. I did have my first liquor over there. Kind of like vodka."

"You weren't drinking on the job were you?" Horace leaned on his hoe. "Get killed that way."

"No, just at night, after dinner. Everybody over there drinks it, but it's all homemade." Reece wanted a hoe to lean on. He could see Cindy sitting in a hammock across the road, talking to her grandmother. He focused on the tall pines. They just shot up, straight into the air, sixty feet, seventy feet. The tops swayed beneath blue sky, and he began to sway with them.

"Get a hold of yourself, boy," said Horace. "Maybe you need to walk around the garden a few times before you head to the house."

"Gotta pee," said Reece.

"Go behind the garage. Just don't let Dora see you."

"Right. Will do." He walked toward Elbert's garden. Elbert was in the rows hoeing weeds from his tomatoes. Reece waved. Elbert waved and said, "Hey, boy!"

Reece walked around the gardens and soon finished one lap. He didn't feel any better and decided to walk down the road to the swimming pool and back, and then around the circle. There was a racket and what sounded like screaming, and two dogs burst from the woods chasing something. They had it up against the fence, barking to high heavens and lunging. The animal was throwing itself against the fence.

Reece began to trot and then to run. He felt like he was floating. It was a young deer with white spots. Slobber hung from its mouth, and its eyes blared. Reece yelled at the dogs, and they stopped for a few seconds, puzzled. The deer kept dashing its head against the fence and making desperate cries for its mother. Without thinking, Reece plowed into the deer and grabbed its torso. The deer fought him, and the dogs went crazy again. He had it in his arms, thrashing, and he yelled at the dogs. Now what? Reece stood there in the gravel parking lot holding the deer. It probably weighed fifty pounds and was bleeding from its hindquarter, a gunshot. "Hell."

With the dogs circling and yapping, Reece walked up the road, intent on reaching the woods and letting the deer go, realizing it would probably die. The deer hyperventilated and grunted like a baby. It took all his strength, and he mustered as the hill steepened. He passed two houses and, at the bend of the circle, stumbled into the woods. His arms burned, and his legs felt like lead as he pushed his way past brambles and vines. Beneath his feet, the pine straw was several inches thick, and he felt like he was wading through mud. Finally, without any strength left, he dropped the deer and waited. He turned to yell at the dogs, and the deer shot off like a rocket into the pine thicket. "Hell and damnation."

For good measure, he picked up a rock and threw it at the dogs, confused and growling, sniffing the ground and the air.

Reece bent over to catch his breath and began the walk around the circle back to the house. He felt like he'd run a marathon and climbed a hundred-foot rope. He wondered who had shot the deer and then wondered what the CT scan would show of his brain. Had he just imagined the scene with the deer? He felt sick and dry heaved. Dora was outside with a broom, watching him come down the hill.

"Hey," said Reece. "Someone shot a deer...and dogs were trying to kill it." He stopped to catch his breath.

"My Lord," said Dora. "You look whooped. You know you don't need to be straining yourself like that. Go sit in the swing, and I'll get you some ice water. Of all things."

Reece thought that was a good idea and plopped onto the metal swing. He would have a good story to tell Kristin. She was always rescuing animals, squirrels, turtles, and birds. Sweat soaked his shirt.

"Here you go, boy," said Dora. "Drink this and then finish sweeping off that driveway for me. You okay? You don't look normal."

Reece remembered the bag of beer cans and thought that he still had it in his hand. He panicked but then realized he must have dropped it at the pool. He breathed in and then out. He took the amber glass of water and sipped, awakening his urge to pee. He glanced at his crotch just to make sure. "Thanks."

"You got to take care of yourself, boy. Ain't no deer worth you dying over. Now rest and sweep that driveway before I get mad."

Reece laughed and then laughed some more. He had a

headache. He had to pee. "Not a problem. Whatever you say, Granny." He relaxed and realized he was barefoot. The bottoms of his feet felt numb and swollen. "Left my shoes at the pier."

"Catching a deer barefoot. My, my. You beat all, boy."

"Okay, I'm fine. Just give me another minute."

Dora clucked her tongue, *tsk tsk,* and went back inside.

Kristin finished her shift, giving Mrs. Dunlop a Tylenol suppository for a spiked fever and emptied yet another giant bowel movement from Chastity. As she finished giving report to the oncoming nurses, she saw Brad waiting on her.

"Coming tonight? Dr. Joiner, I mean Steve, lives in a loft on Third Street. I've got the address here." He handed her a prescription blank with the address on the back.

"And what time is this party?"

"I don't know, but come around seven. I'll be there. Plenty of parking on the street, but don't park in the pawn shop lot. You'll get towed."

Kristin examined the paper like it was a moss-covered stone. "Yeah, okay Mr. Persistent. But just for an hour, maybe."

"You need my number?" asked Brad.

"No, and you don't need mine," said Kristin.

Brad laughed. "So, see you there. I've got to run next door and see a patient. Had his throat cut by a steel cable."

"Ugh," said Kristin. "Yeah, well, see you there."

"Perfect," and he walked through the double doors that led to ICU.

Kristin went to the break room and changed into her

street shoes. Eudora, the unit clerk, was taking a break, reading *The Birmingham News*.

"Dang, that Dr. Phillips has the hots for you, honey." She wore dark blue pants and a white top. She kind of looked like a sailor with her short, jet-black hair.

Kristin blushed. "Well, he can hold his horses as far as I'm concerned. I keep telling him I'm engaged, but he won't give up."

Eudora laughed and peered at the comics. "Be careful at them parties, though."

"Oh God," said Kristin. "I'm just going to pop in and straight out. That's it."

"He's a real looker."

"Shorter than me, I think." She tied her shoes and put her work shoes in the tiny locker.

"Not short on cash, though, from what I hear. Drives that fancy car."

"I guess cars make the man, right?" asked Kristin. She rolled her eyes.

Debbie walked in carrying a bag of O-negative. She held it between her hands to warm it. "Lucky lady."

Kristin frowned and brushed her curls back. "I don't think I can take much more of this talk. You guys are awful. I'm engaged, for God's sake."

"I like Reece. Don't get me wrong," said Debbie. "He's a great guy. I nearly cried when I heard what happened."

"Yeah, well, I did cry," said Kristin.

"Nice young man," said Eudora. "I always liked the way he took care of his patients."

"Yeah," said Kristin. "Well, I'm outta here. See you tomorrow." She gathered her things and left, wondering what she would wear.

In the dark clinic, lit by two small candles, Emma poured peroxide over the dog bite. The wound frothed with foam, and she could hear the bubbles. "Give me a four-by-four." She felt unsteady from the alcohol.

Afewerki opened a package and held it out for her. Emma dabbed the wound. The woman looked on in silence, sucking her teeth.

"Some ointment and another four-by-four." She dressed the wound and pressed down the silk tape. "Done. But we need to give her a big dose of penicillin, just in case."

Afewerki explained, and the woman nodded. Emma drew up sterile water and injected it into the vial of powder, shook it, and drew up 10 ccs into a syringe capped with an 18-gauge needle. "Here we go." Afewerki had the woman stand, and Emma pushed the plunger. The woman let escape a small whine. "Okay," said Emma. "Let's get the H out of here."

"Ishi," said Afewerki, leading the woman by the elbow.

Together, they trudged to the top of the steep hill and, with the woman between them, escorted her back to the shelter and the rank odor of human feces.

"Tomorrow, we take care of the fleas," said Emma.

The woman thanked them, tears in her eyes, and disappeared into the long, low building. Afewerki spoke to the guard, and then they headed back to the compound.

"What a strange night," said Afewerki. He shivered in his short-sleeved shirt.

"I'm hungry. You hungry?" asked Emma. "Plus, I have a

headache."

"Oh, yes, very hungry. We are late for dinner. The alcohol is to blame for your headache."

"But it was worth it, right? I would have never guessed that the Hyena's real name is Emanuel. Did you know that?"

"I didn't know," said Afewerki. "It means 'God is with us.'"

Emma laughed. "What a hoot."

"What does it mean?" asked Afewerki.

"Hoot means, uh, I guess it means what a joke, but that's not what I really mean."

They came to the gate, and Afewerki knocked for Ketow to let them in.

"Abet?"

The gate opened, and they plodded inside. Afewerki told Ketow to bring what was left over. Isaac and Mariam were outside, and Afewerki filled them in on the happenings before heading to the dining hut. He ducked under the flap and held it for Emma. There was a kerosene lantern on the table, and he fumbled, looking for matches. It took a minute or two, but soon a red-tinged light and hiss filled the small room.

"Thank you," said Emma. "I couldn't do it without you."

"Chicorilla," said Afewerki. He adjusted his Exxon ballcap.

"I'm serious," said Emma. "You're a lifesaver. So patient. Thanks for drinking that areke. I was about to vomit." She felt alive, needed, as if it had been a dream.

Afewerki smiled and laughed. "The taste is terrible. I do not like. You shake his hand and drink with him. He may cause some trouble."

"I get it," said Emma. "He's almost likable. His parents dying and being raised by his uncle would make someone desperate, maybe even mean."

"You must ask him his birthday to buy him a present." He laughed.

Emma smiled. Inside the hut, she felt safe and warm with Afewerki. "Oh, here's dinner."

Ketow placed a platter of cold enjera topped with shurowot, spicy lentils.

"Amenseganolo," said Emma.

"Yiqirta," said Ketow. He bowed and pushed back outside to his post by the gate.

"*Mmm,* that's good when you're hungry," said Emma.

"Yes, very good." Rarely was Afewerki ever completely alone with Emma. Between bites, he glanced at her face, her hands. He wore a stony look, as if constipated.

"You look worried," said Emma. "What's on your mind?"

"My mind?" He stumbled his words a bit. Had she not said more than once that she loved him? That she could not do without him? "It is nothing." He put a wad of enjera and wot into his mouth. He wondered if he should give her the gursha, a small bite offered from his hand to her mouth, a practice among close friends. But she was a she and not a he. His father had warned him away from becoming involved with Emma, as she had a strong will and could not be tamed. His mother, though, often spoke of the possibility with glee. What if they were married? The entire village would celebrate.

He swallowed his bites with some difficulty. His voice quavered when he asked her to accept the gursha.

"Yeah, sure. The guys are always doing it."

Afewerki tore off a piece of enjera and folded it around the cold wot. His hand shook in the gaslight as he brought the gursha to her mouth. She laughed, and her lips touched his fingers. He waited for her to return the favor, as was customary. Ideally, he should offer her three gurshas, so he offered another one, this one larger.

"Okay," said Emma. She took the bite into her mouth, wondering if she should reciprocate. Why not? "Okay, a gursha for you. Right hand only, just in case you were wondering." She packaged the wot in the enjera and held it up to his mouth.

"Thank you," he said. Chill bumps scooted across his arms and back. "One more for you, the Trinity."

Emma was tired of the game, but took the third gursha, which filled her mouth. "I'm full. Thank you."

"Ah, then you are to say 'tagabjallo,' but very quietly, as if you are in pain from eating so much foods."

"Okay, tagabyellow."

Afewerki laughed, "No, tagabjallo."

"Tagabjallo," she whispered in a pained manner.

"Oh, perfecto. Very good. You are becoming Habasha, no?"

"Feels like it," said Emma. "Drinking and eating. Do you feel better now that you've eaten? My head feels better." She could hear dogs fighting in the distance.

"Yes. It was necessary to eat after drinking the areke. It is very foul." He made a face. He looked down, and his shoe was touching her shoe, and she was not moving her foot. The others would mock him, though, accuse him of trying to gain her favor.

"You're different, Afewerki. You don't like the hard liquor, and you don't have a girlfriend. Or do you?"

A cloud of grasshoppers buzzed inside his chest. What to say? "No, no, it is bad with the village women. They only want to have the children. Many are divorc-ed here. The men do not like a bossy wife. But...you are different, I think." He swallowed his saliva and shivered.

Emma pushed her chair back and yawned. "I'm sleepy? Are you sleepy?"

What does it mean? "Well, you must sleep. And I must sleep."

"How about some chamomile tea before bed? Have I made that for you?" Reece had bought the flowery tea at the Victory store in Addis.

"Yes, that is very nice," said Afewerki. He stood and then sat back down.

"I'll make Irigit a cup of regular tea, too. Helps him stay awake." She stood and wiped crumbs from her lap.

"He will be happy," and Afewerki stood. He mimicked Emma, wiping his lap of crumbs, but there were none there.

Outside, the sky swirled with stars, illuminating the compound. Candles flooded each of the team's rooms. Irigit, sitting on a stool outside the cookhouse, had replaced Ketow. He saw them leave and went to take away the platter. He then watched Afewerki follow Emma into her little house, the light of candles seeping through the cracks around the door and the window.

"Have a seat," said Emma.

Afewerki took the chair. He took off his ballcap and bent the brim back and forth. He watched Emma fill a pot with water and place it on the gas stove. It would take at least ten minutes for it to boil.

"You will go, soon, no?" asked Afewerki.

Emma had to stop and think. "Yes, very soon, I think. I expect to see the helicopter tomorrow." She prepared three orange cups, dropping chamomile bags into two.

"So, you may leave tomorrow?" His voice rose.

"I haven't really thought about it today, but that could be the case. I can't stay after what happened. It seems like a lifetime has passed. I need to get back home and do what I'm not sure."

Afewerki sighed. "The others will be very surprised."

"Do they even know what happened?"

"Yes, everyone is knowing."

Emma lifted the lid and checked the pot. No bubbles yet. Everything in Ethiopia was harder, even boiling water. She opened the fridge and couldn't see inside clearly. She closed the door.

"There's that dang mouse in the wall, behind my bed."

"Yes, I can hear it. Shall I kill it?"

"No," said Emma. "I guess it has to live somewhere."

"Emma?" Afewerki cleared his throat.

"Yes?" She dreaded what might come from his mouth. He was her protector in Godo, especially since Reece had been flown out.

"I have been wanting to ask you." He put his cap back on and folded his hands.

Emma checked the pot again. "Ask what?"

"Oh, it is a dream."

"A dream?" She braced herself. He was the kindest man in the world, but she was not attracted to him. Had she led him on?

Afewerki cleared his throat. "I am dreaming to come to US and study there."

Emma could feel her heart beating. "Really?"

"Yes." He bowed his head.

"Well, that would be super. How would you do it?" She remembered the sugar for Irigit and heaped in three tablespoons.

"It is necessary to have a sponsor." He pinched his thigh through his jeans.

"Like a person, or maybe a church?"

"Yes. That is my only hope. It is very difficult to leave this country unless you die."

"Hmm. Maybe I could talk to my pastor back home and see what's involved." One candle died and she re-lit it.

It was as if he did not hear her. But then he said, "Really?" He had learned that word from the Icelandic nurses. "It would be a dream, of course."

There were bubbles at the bottom of the pot. She held out one cup and poured and handed it to him, then poured for Irigit. She opened the door and called out.

"Abet!"

"Chai!"

Irigit trotted in and took the steaming cup with two hands. "Thank you," he said in broken English with a wide grin. He would live and die in this small place.

"Yiqirta," said Emma. She closed the door against a stiff, cold breeze.

Reece stayed in the swing, breathing off the alcohol, waiting to be called in for lunch. He remembered the driveway and grabbed the broom. With a definite headache and his bladder nearly bursting, he swept down the middle with bold back-and-forth strokes. The pine straw was sticky on the rough concrete and required multiple swipes. He worked his way to the end and then turned, sweeping to the left. He reached the end, turned, and swept to the left until the driveway looked new. Having worked up a sweat, he peed behind the garage, trying to delay encountering Dora again until the last possible moment. He felt he reeked of beer.

While he was peeing, Cindy came through the backdoor from next door and saw him. Reece turned the other way. "Dammit." He turned to look, and she was coming his way.

"That's the second time I've caught you peeing outside," she said.

Reece cut his stream and zipped.

"What are you, a mountain man?"

Reece laughed. "Yeah, maybe so. Sorry about that."

"Everybody has to pee," said Cindy. She held a piece of paper in her hand. "Got my number here. La Maison du Poulet." She laughed and handed it to him. The number didn't have an area code, but he knew it was 205.

"Oh yeah, thanks." She looked fresher than ever in her tube top and shorts. She was barefoot and avoiding the pinecones. "I can't remember. Did we decide to do something in particular?"

"No. Maybe play some pool, get a drink, with the permission of Kristin, of course." She stretched her arms over her head. Her armpits looked shaved and smooth.

Reece tried to laugh, but he chortled instead. "Great. Yeah, I'll have to run it by her, I suppose. Being engaged and all. Thanks for understanding. Otherwise, I'd just say yes." He shut his eyes and opened them. She was still there.

"I got a new pistol. You know anything about shooting? Maybe we could shoot some tomatoes in the garden, let you teach me."

Reece felt a thrill in his pants and tried to make it go away. "Uh, sure, maybe after lunch. Granny'll be calling me pretty soon. He looked up to the sky, and the hot sun was directly overhead. He looked a little bit too long, making his eyes water.

"What's for lunch? My granny's cooking salmon patties. You could eat with us."

"Not sure, let's go check." He walked to the driveway, and Cindy followed to the back door. "We're both barefoot." He remembered the deer and turned to tell her the story, but she was right on his heels. "Come on in."

"Hey, Granny. Look who's here. Cindy."

Dora stood at the stove with her spatula, turning the fried okra, Reece's favorite. "Well, I declare. You sure have grown." She looked Reece in the eyes.

"Hey, Mrs. Myers. Good to see you. I'm just out visiting the folks on my day off." She walked past Reece and gave Dora a side hug. "I just invited Reece for lunch, but we needed to check with you first."

Dora narrowed her eyes. "Well, I got his favorite here with some pork chops."

"Yum, fried okra." Cindy walked into the attached den and looked around. "Been a while since I've been inside."

"You're welcome to eat with us," said Reece.

Dora turned the pork chops with a fork. "You're more than welcome, girl. I got enough. Got some cornbread in the oven, too. Just let your granny know."

"Can I call her?"

Reece noticed her great posture. "Yeah, phone's right there." He pointed to the black phone on the wall.

Cindy dialed the number, but got a busy signal. "She's on the phone with her card-playing buddy. Let me walk over and tell her."

"How long?" asked Reece.

"About ten minutes," said Dora. "Run down and let your granddaddy know."

Reece said okay, and he and Cindy headed back outside.

"Be back in a few," said Cindy.

Reece watched her walk away between the house and the garage and headed down to the garden.

The party was at seven, and Reece still hadn't called, which steeled her resolve to go. Kristin ate dinner and then showered. She told her sister Robyn about the party and asked her to go with her, to "protect her from Brad." Robyn had laughed and said, "No way." She had a Monday night Bible study, but told Kristin to be careful.

"Where do you think you're going?" asked Gert. She had washed the dishes and put them away.

Kristin wondered if she should tell the truth. "Just a work party I was invited to."

"You going to call Reece?"

"No. He hasn't called me, has he?"

"Well, the phone rang earlier, but I didn't get to it."

That made Kristin pause. Maybe she should call him. "No, he can always call again if he wants me." She went to the bathroom to put on makeup and looked at herself in the mirror, adjusting her curls. She thought about Reece not calling and shook her head.

"Be back in an hour or so!" Kristin heard Edwin and Gert say okay and headed outside into the warm, still air, holding the address of the loft in her hand.

She remembered not to park in the pawnshop lot, but had trouble finding a spot on the street. She drove around and settled for a space about two blocks away on Third Street. She found the door to the lofts, but the door was locked. She held the button next to "Joiner," and the door lock buzzed. She hesitated, and the door was still locked. She pressed the buzzer again and opened the door. The foyer looked industrial with large blank walls. There was an elevator and a set of black steel stairs.

By the time she rang the doorbell, it was seven-thirty.

"Hey, welcome!" said Joiner. Techno music was playing, and the vast room was filled with smoke, cigar smoke.

Kristin stood there like a baby bird waiting for its mother. "Hey," and she giggled, overwhelmed.

"Don't just stand there, come in. Hey, everybody, Kristin is here!" A low cheer from a few in the crowd at the other end of the huge loft.

Kristin walked in and felt like a moth drawn to a bright

light. There were people she didn't know, and she just kept walking across the long open room, gazing at the tall ceiling. She realized that Joiner had her by the elbow, leading her to what looked like a bar. A woman in a red miniskirt and hoop earrings was there.

"Drink?" asked Joiner.

"Water is fine," said Kristin. She saw Brad coming toward her.

"Water?" asked Joiner. He laughed. "Misty, make her the house special. We call it Leave 'em Dead."

"I don't really drink," said Kristin. She realized she had brought her purse and wondered if she should put it somewhere. "Alcohol that is."

"Hey," said Brad. "Remember me? The evil Dr. Phillips." He put his hand on her shoulder. He watched Misty hand her a martini glass. "Yeah, house special. Good choice. Come with me. We're watching these crazy videos."

Kristin tucked her purse, glanced at Misty, and held her glass with two hands. The liquid was dull red and cold. She looked around for other women, and there seemed to only be Misty at the bar. Her throat tightened.

"Hey guys, this is Kristin. She's a nurse at Carraway."

There was a large projection TV playing a video of Brazilian jiu-jitsu highlights. A half-dozen guys on couches turned and nodded, smiling.

Kristin only recognized an intern. "Hey," she said, as if into a deep well. The room was cold, three ceiling fans spinning at full speed. A large plant that looked like marijuana sat in the corner near the wall of windows.

"Kill his ass!" said a short stocky guy with sideburns, wearing a turtleneck. He slammed the couch arm. The others were oohing and aahing with the heavy metal of the video. Most were smoking cigars.

Kristin could see over Brad's shoulder. He was still in his blue scrubs and tennis shoes. She wondered what to do. Watch the video?

"Son of a cock!" said Brad. He turned and Kristin was right there, his face to hers.

"What is this?" asked Kristin.

"Just hanging with the guys," said Brad. "I'm glad you made it. Usually, we play poker and get a little shit-faced but Joiner has these videos."

Kristin smelled her drink. It smelled like alcohol.

"Have a sip. It's tasty. Loosen you up. You look great by the way." He edged away from the couches.

"Thank you, but maybe not. What's in it?"

"Vodka and cranberry juice, mostly vodka. Good for your kidneys, right?"

"Why aren't you drinking one?" asked Kristin.

"I've already had a couple. Can't you tell?" He smiled, and Kristin could nearly see down his throat.

"Motherfuck, did you see that!"

Brad turned to see what he had missed.

"Split his head open. Oh my God!"

"I don't want to watch this," said Kristin. "I thought this was going to be a party of some sort. I can't stay long, regardless."

Brad turned his attention back to her. "You look great, and this is a party. But maybe I'm being dense. Misty's not interested either."

"Is Misty someone's girlfriend?"

"No, she's Joiner's wife, lucky guy," said Brad. "Let's go

talk to her. She looks lonely. Gives me better odds, two on one." He winked at her.

A collective "Ohh!" and then "Busted his balls!" followed by clapping and foot stomping on the hardwood floors.

"Yeah, let's go talk to Misty," said Kristin. "She's gorgeous. Does she just stand there waiting to serve drinks?"

"I hadn't thought of it like that. She's not nailed to the floor, if that's what you mean." Brad laughed and took her by the elbow. "This way, hot stuff. Restroom's over there," and he pointed.

"Do you work tomorrow?" asked Kristin. She peered into a hundred-gallon saltwater aquarium at clown fish.

"Actually, I'm on call and work tomorrow."

"Shouldn't you be sleeping?" asked Kristin.

"Shouldn't you be drinking?" He laughed.

They passed the open kitchen, and there was Misty in her tight dress, sitting on a barstool, looking bored.

"Hey guys!" Her nails were impeccable, her arms toned, and her smile brilliant. "Another round?"

"Hit me," said Brad. "But tell Kristin here to give it a try. She's a little shy with her booze."

"Shy?" asked Kristin. She shrugged his hand from her elbow and, with two hands, took a sip and coughed. "Good Lord."

"Language!" said Brad, making Misty laugh.

There was a roar from the back of the room and more stomping and clapping.

Misty shook Brad's drink and dropped in a sliver of lemon peel. "Yeah, go for it, girl. I'll drink with you if that'll make you feel more comfortable. All these damn doctors with their fucking cigars. God help us."

"So, what do you do?" asked Kristin.

"What do I do? Pretty much just look good and pour booze. What do you do? You work with Brad?"

"Uh, yeah. Work at Carraway. I'm a nurse there." She took another sip and tasted the cranberry juice. "Why is it so cold in here? Is this your loft?"

"Yep," said Misty. "It's in the pre-nup. How do you like that? Dr. Joiner is used to working in the OR, so that's why. Freezes my ass off sometimes."

Kristin had no idea what she was talking about. "I like it, except for the smoke. It's so big, so open, just one big room." She could see the king-size bed across the way.

"You girls want to talk?" Brad looked impatient and drained half his drink. "Doesn't she look great?"

"I love her curls and green eyes," said Misty.

Kristin took another sip. "Thanks. Can I sit in the chair? I've been on my feet all day."

"Hell yeah," said Brad. "Take a load off. I mean rest your weary soul. I'll check on you in a few." He downed his drink, winked, and walked back to the guys.

"How long have you known Brad?" asked Misty.

"About six months, I guess."

"You guys dating?" Misty spun her glass around on the granite bar.

Kristin choked. "No, no. I'm actually engaged. He was so insistent that I thought I would just see what he was up to, out of curiosity. I guess maybe we're friends." She sipped the drink and sat down.

"I do think he's mentioned you, come to think of it. Tall, thin, perky boobs. That's you, right? I can imagine you in a scrub top."

"That could be anybody, really, right? This drink is growing on me."

"No, it's you. He likes you, I can tell. He would never invite just anyone over here. I mean, you're not a guy, right?" Misty poured herself a shot of vodka and tossed it back.

"Well, I'd be a guy with boobs," and she laughed. "How long have you been married?"

"Going on seven months. It's not so bad. I get bored, though. He's only home maybe one night a week, but that's okay. He pays the bills and then some, plus he has that beefcake factor. I like you."

Kristin sipped. "Well, thanky, I mean, thanks. God, I hope I don't have to call my sister to drive me home. Is one of these enough to get you drunk?"

Misty laughed. "God no. Maybe three or four for a novice. Oh, here comes Brutus for a refill." It was the short stocky guy with sideburns.

"You ladies look lovely tonight. Hit me, baby, one more time." He started to sing.

"Cut the funky town," said Misty. "I'm the only one allowed to perform here." She poured ice into the shaker. "Straight up, Doc?"

"Straight up!" Brutus laughed and stumbled. His cigar touched Kristin's arm, spilling ash onto the floor. He didn't notice.

"You sleeping on the couch tonight?" asked Misty. She shook the vodka, cranberry juice, and ice and poured it into a glass.

"Is there room in your bed?"

"Not tonight, big boy," said Misty. She tried to high-five

Kristin, but she missed, or did Kristin miss?

"Shit, then the couch it is!" He stumbled away, back to the video of guys pounding and breaking each other.

"Why are all of these doctors so damn short?" asked Misty.

"Yeah," said Kristin. "What's up with that?" She finished her drink, feeling warm and safe with Misty. "I can't believe I drank that. Never had vodka before."

"You need a break?" She poured herself another shot.

Kristin turned at the sound of hooting from the back. Brad was waving at her, giving her a thumbs up. She waved back. "Hit me," she said. "Just one more."

After Afewerki left, Emma thought about what she had promised him. She wondered if she'd made a mistake. Maybe it would have been better if he'd hit on her and she'd had to reject him. It would make for a cleaner departure. Too tired to undress, she pulled the blanket tight, a thrill of coming home in her bones.

The next morning, while washing with a pot of warm water, Emma heard the helicopter, the vibrations against her eardrums. She hurried to dress and then opened the door. Everyone had already left for the warehouse and clinic compound, and she smiled at Irigit on her way through the gate. She could tell that the helicopter had not yet landed, and picked up her pace. She stepped on a stone and twisted her ankle as a little boy grabbed for her hand.

"Fudge!" She apologized to the startled boy, hopped for a few feet, tripped, and kept going. All she could think was that Dr. Guthrie had come to save her, to take her away to the safety of Alabama. She pulled back, going down the steep hill, her ankle throbbing. Already, there was a line of twenty beside the fence, waiting for her arrival. The helicopter flew over and then circled back. She waved as if for dear life, the weight of the last two years bearing down on her, the rape overwhelming everything. Outside the gate, she found herself panting for breath and shaking.

The helicopter landed and powered down as Dr. Guthrie emerged and trotted toward the clinic. Emma greeted him, surrounded by the team. Afewerki bounded through the gate and joined them.

Dr. Guthrie looked grim. He shook hands with everyone and then gave Emma a tremendous side hug. Without warning, Emma shuddered and began to weep, gasping between breaths. She tried to speak, looking around at the bewildered faces.

"Emma, let's get inside." He walked her to the warehouse. "Emma, I came as quick as I could. You're done here. You got that. I'm taking you out today."

The team stood outside murmuring, Emma and Guthrie standing in a shaft of light beside piles of bagged grain. Barra made an effort to start up a round of "This is the day" but it fell flat after the first "that the Lord hath made."

Emma squatted, leaning back against the grain, sobbing. A charge of deep experience throbbed through her, and she forced herself to take deep breaths, gradually regaining herself. It seemed as if she was dying, and her life was flashing before her eyes. She heard the shots and saw Reece collapse. She saw the fat soldier with his pistol, the other two with grim, leering grins. The children calling "Ferenj!"

"Emma," said Guthrie. "Just take your time. No hurry. We're gonna take care of you."

Emma looked up and tried to laugh. He was wearing his trademark tight short-sleeved shirt that seemed two sizes too small. "Oh, God," was all she could muster, and gradually her tears stopped, and she regained control of her breathing. "Thank you, thank you," she whispered.

"Yiqirta," said Guthrie, and he helped her to stand.

"Oh, God," said Emma. "I can't leave. The clinic, and there are fleas in the shelter." She wiped her eyes with her hands. "Afewerki!"

"Abet?" Afewerki came to her side.

"The fleas in the shelter. You have to treat the building and air out those nasty mattresses. Then treat the women and children with Permethrin." She hiccupped.

"Yes, Emma," said Afewerki. He wore his ballcap backwards.

"See, these guys will get it done. They'll still be here for a while after you leave. But the clinic will have to close," said Guthrie.

"The people will be sad," said Afewerki.

"We'll be sad, too. But there's still the government clinic here."

"They are using the needle many times," said Afewerki.

Guthrie frowned. "I'll send a letter to Atakabura there. The last thing he wants to do is re-use needles."

"What a hell," said Afewerki.

Emma laughed at that. She felt unhinged in a way. What next? "So, when do we need to leave?"

Terry walked in. He came over, hands in pockets, and put his arm around her. He wore a tan flight suit with hiking boots. "Good to see you. Sorry, I wasn't there this weekend."

"Yeah, we survived," said Emma. "You smell good."

"Thanks. Good to know."

"How about we leave after lunch?" asked Guthrie. "Give you a chance to have one last meal with the guys and get your stuff together."

"I need to see the folks in line, too. I can't just send them away."

"Well, you'll need to call it early, though," said Guthrie.

Emma nodded. "Afewerki, can you skip breakfast and get started in the clinic with me? We can eat some famine biscuits."

"Yes, Emma." He turned his ballcap around.

Everyone walked out of the warehouse into the dull, hard sun. Emma then asked Barra, Mariam, and Isaac to treat the shelter for fleas and provide Permethrin lotion to the women and children with scabies and flea bites. They were stunned to hear that she would leave that day.

"We are missing you already," said Barra. "I wanted to invite you my home, to meet my mother. I have promised this to her."

Mariam was silent with enormous eyes and his large shirt pocket.

"We have been lucky you have been here," said Isaac. "You muzt write many letters."

Emma felt a knot in her throat, realizing that maybe the crying had just begun. "Thanks." A few hot tears, and she blinked them away. She felt the wind in her hair, and it felt like the wind of a strange land. "And what're you guys gonna do in the meantime?"

"I brought some ivermectin," said Guthrie. "Terry can help me. We can do a cattle clinic in the market. Word will spread pretty quick. Don't worry, I know how to stay busy. Hopefully, the Hyena will mind his own business."

"Did you know his name is Emanuel?"

"Who?" asked Terry.

"The Hyena. He told me that his name is Emanuel."

Isaac was unlocking the clinic door with his key on a string. The door scraped open. Emma tried to see the clinic as a whole, but could only see a slice through the door.

"Huh," said Guthrie. "Well, we'll let you get to work." He patted her on the back. "Super Emma."

Emma stepped up and went into the supply room for a case of Permethrin. "Here you go, Isaac. This is for the skin. You'll need to buy the Permethrin concentrate for the building itself."

"Yes, we have already," said Isaac. "We will use the paintbrush. It is very strong."

"Okay, just don't want them to get mixed up."

"Ishi," said Isaac, and he departed with Barra and Mariam.

"Afewerki, call in the first two," said Emma.

Afewerki was eating a famine biscuit. "Ishi." He went to the clinic door and let eight people into the compound. The first two were older women, perhaps fifty, sisters. They were weavers and reputed to have the evil eye. Afewerki avoided eye contact with them and led them inside.

"Mendeno?" asked Emma to the first one, who took a seat on the bench. Her dress must have been pink or red at one time, but was so faded and patched that she seemed to be wearing scraps held together with magic glue. Emma's heart went out to her, more so than usual. She would treat this woman and then never see her again.

With her sister nodding her approval, the woman told her story. She had been circumcised as a young girl along with her sister. Did Emma want to see?

"No, no," said Emma. "Just tell her to finish the story."

The woman nodded. Since then, she'd had low energy and had found that foreign foods gave her the best energy. She wanted a can of Nido powder to mix and drink. Her sister wanted one too. To Emma, the Nido mixed with water tasted like a vanilla milkshake. The sister then proceeded to pull up her dress and part her legs. Afewerki looked away.

"Yikes, here it comes," said Emma.

The outer labia had been trimmed away along with her clitoris. Emma just stared. "I suppose a can of Nido powder is warranted. We don't have many, so can they share a can? Heck, what am I saying. Let's give them each a can."

Afewerki clucked his tongue. "The others will be jealous. Many people will come for the same."

"Well, let them come until it's gone is what I say. Right?"

"It is your wish," said Afewerki. He stepped into the supply room, and there were only three cans left.

The women's eyes lit at the sight, and they each took a can, holding it like a fat chicken.

"Maybe get grain bags so the others don't see what they have," said Emma.

Afewerki ran for the grain bags and soon returned.

"Do they have any other problems?" asked Emma.

Afewerki asked. "They are saying that life is very hard, and what should they do?"

Emma frowned. What to say? "Tell them that I am sorry, that I will pray for them? Oh, let's give them some vitamins too. For energy."

"They will sell in the market."

"Maybe not."

And so it went for another three hours and forty-five minutes until twenty-five patients had been seen, and the clinic door closed. There were still twenty-one patients outside, waiting, even though they had been told the clinic was closed. Emma had brought out two grain bags filled with famine biscuits and had Afewerki distribute them. She trudged uphill, heavy with the need of the people and feeling guilty that she was leaving.

"Let's check in at the shelter," said Emma. "Before we eat lunch."

"Yes, today I am very hungry, but as you wish." He took the lead, shooing away children with their filthy hands and faces covered with snot and flies.

"Ferenj!"

Emma laughed and made a silly face, scaring a little girl.

Afewerki led the way past the church and up to the shelter. The old guard was outside the cookhouse, taking in the smells of lunch and watching the topless women stir pots and make fresh teff enjera.

"Bataam taruno," said Emma, seeing the corn husk mattresses out in the sun, the women mingling, the children playing. Both Isaac and Mariam emerged, holding small cans of Permethrin and worn paintbrushes. She peered into the cookhouse and greeted the women there.

"It is good, no?" asked Isaac. He was sweating in a thick mauve sweater.

"Very good," said Emma. "Be careful and don't get fleas yourself."

"Yes, we are worried, but God will protect us," said Isaac. Mariam nodded. "Barra has left to fear the fleas."

Emma just let it go. Barra was peculiar at times, but he was right to fear the fleas. A nasty case of scabies was miserable. "You will have a special crown in heaven," said Emma. She felt an upwelling of sadness and choked it back.

"You are okay?" asked Isaac. "God is watching. He will take care."

"Yeah," said Emma. "We were just checking in. Are you able to stop for lunch?"

"Ah, yes," said Mariam.

"Yes, thank you," said Isaac. "We shall come, no?"

"Well, put those cans away so the kids don't get into them," said Emma.

Afewerki had to translate.

"Ishi," said Isaac.

The mothers had gathered into a group, giggling and murmuring, with the children running and playing. Emma watched them and took a snapshot in her mind. She turned away and began the walk downhill, followed by Afewerki, Isaac, and Mariam. It would be her last meal with the team.

Reece ate his lightly breaded, fried pork chop with his fingers. Cindy was using a fork and knife.

"You not married yet, girl?" asked Dora. She watched Horace spoon out the last of the fried okra, mostly just brown bits and cornmeal crumbs.

Cindy frowned. "Well, I just graduated high school last year. I don't think I would make a very good wife. Not being a cook and all."

Reece laughed, gnawing at his t-shaped bone.

"I married Horace here when I was seventeen. Had to or starve to death."

"Well, I'm pretty well fed," said Cindy. "Especially with food like this. This is super." She picked up her pork chop bone to finish it off.

"You know I could never wear one of them halter tops like you got on. Shows too much skin." Dora sipped her tea.

"I like it," said Reece.

Cindy reached over and punched him in the arm.

"Ow," said Reece.

"I guess maybe my bosom is not as big as yours," said Cindy. "Not as much to show."

Horace grunted and looked out the window.

"Well, I had two children, and they helped," said Dora.

Cindy laughed. "My granny, though, has the biggest boobs of all. They're absolutely huge." She wiped her fingers on a plain paper napkin.

Dora's eyes twinkled. "I reckon she beats us all."

Reece shook his head, thinking about Kristin's small breasts. "Does it make you more of a woman to have big ones?"

Horace coughed. "I think this conversation has strayed a bit. Pass me the salt, if you don't mind." He took the salt from Cindy and shook it like hell on his pork chop, half going onto the table and half onto his lap.

"You want some meat in your salt?" asked Dora. "You know that's not good for you."

"I'm as healthy as a horse," said Horace. It was Dora who was being treated for high blood pressure and not him.

"I guess I married a horse," said Dora.

Reece and Cindy laughed, and Horace lost his false teeth for a few seconds. After lunch, Cindy helped Dora with the dishes, and then she and Reece went out to the swing.

"I need a cigarette. You mind?" asked Cindy.

"No. I'll have one with you."

A pack of Camels magically appeared from her shorts. She lit one and then handed Reece the pack.

"So, is your fiancée at work?"

"Yeah." Reece noticed they were both pushing the swing with their feet. "At Carraway. That's where we met. She was a student nurse in CCU, and then she hired on."

"Is she a blonde? I'm thinking she's a blonde."

"No, dark brown curly hair."

"Oh," said Cindy. She inhaled and blew smoke. "Would she be jealous that we're hanging out?"

"Yep," said Reece. "She would. Ha."

"I'm an old family friend, right?"

"That's a good way to put it." He puffed and blew smoke. "She's tenacious."

Cindy shook her head. "What does that mean?"

Reece thought. "She's loyal, I guess."

"That's scarce these days. I'm seeing an older guy, a motorcycle mechanic, but it's not like we're stitched together. You know?"

"Yeah." Reece felt perplexed. Was she coming on to him? If he hadn't been engaged, he would ask her out in a second.

"So, what did you learn in Ethiopia? Did you miss her?"

"Yeah. But she was always asking me to come home, so I could never really get settled in. You know?"

"Sounds kind of clingy to me."

"Or maybe it's true love, if there's such a thing." Her arm was touching his, and his manhood was responding. He squirmed in the swing, trying to think of something awful. "You know what we probably treated the most in the clinic?"

"Who's we?"

"This other nurse named Emma. She was there for a few months before I got there. Tapeworms and roundworms. Kosa and wosfat, the Amharic words." The words made him sad.

"Gross," said Cindy. "I couldn't deal with that. So, did you get along with Emma?"

"Yeah. We were a team, seeing up to a hundred patients per day. It was wild." He felt his heart beat faster.

"Did you have the hots for her?"

"I wouldn't say that. She was pretty, you know. And ballsy, too."

"Sounds like a character."

"She's from Hueytown, so that was neat." He hung his head a bit, looking at his crotch. Was she moving closer to him?

"I need some floss to get this pork chop out of my teeth."

"Yeah, me too. We ate a lot of sheep and goat over there."

"What about pork chops?"

"Heck no. Pork was forbidden. Didn't see a pig ever," said Reece.

"Huh. Want to go down to the lake? Got any more beer?" She stubbed her cigarette and held it.

"Sure. No more beer, though." Reece wondered if he should call Kristin at work. What would he do, ask her if he could drink more beer with Cindy?

"I can get some from pawpaw. He drinks Old Milwaukee. Not bad. Let's go over."

"Okay."

"Come on." She stood and offered her hand to him, and he stood with a grunt. "I need to get a job. I feel bad lazing around while everyone else is working."

Cindy laughed. "Hell, you've been shot in the, excuse my language, the fucking head. Take it easy, soldier, while you can."

Reece considered that. He had been shot in the fucking head and had lived. Maybe there was a God. But then why had he been shot in the first place? To make this little rendezvous with Cindy possible? He stood and bent over dizzy.

"You okay?"

"Just dizzy when I stand. Probably from being shot in the effing head." He grinned and followed her between the house and the garage, past the propane tank that fed the heater, and then across the line of monkey grass into the Sykes' yard.

"Come on in." She held the screen door for him.

Reece walked into the tiny, paneled den. There was a strong smell of hot grease and old cigarette smoke. He let Cindy pass and followed her into the living room that ran into the kitchen.

"Hey, mawmaw, look what the cat drug in."

Maybell was at the sink, banging a skillet with a dish sponge. She turned and blinked. "Well, hey there, boy."

"Hey, Mrs. Sykes," said Reece.

"I seen you walking around. You should come over and say hey."

"Just getting my bearings back," said Reece. "It's good to be home."

"I guess China was a shock to your system, that and being shot and all." She rinsed the skillet that she'd fried the salmon in. "You hungry? You look like you done lost some weight." She was still wearing her housecoat, a long shift made of yellow cotton. Her eyes loomed large behind her bifocals.

"Nope, we just ate," said Cindy. "Pork chops and okra."

"Yeah," said Reece. He felt meat between his back teeth and ran his tongue there.

"Mind if we grab a couple of beers? Reece here is a great conversationalist."

"Lord, don't get him hooked on beer," said Maybell. She knew how Dora was about alcohol.

"I reckon he's a big boy," said Cindy. "Thanks." She leaned over and rummaged in the fridge and extracted two cold cans.

Reece put his hands in his pockets. "I guess a beer never hurt anybody."

"You was a missionary, boy. That don't mix does it?" She dragged a wet rag from the sink and wiped it around on the stove, knocking crumbs onto the floor.

"I guess I was a missionary, until I was shot. Now I'm just me."

Maybell nodded as if a great truth had been revealed.

"Okay, mawmaw," said Cindy. "Come on, Reece."

Reece followed Cindy through the open door onto the carport and back into the sunshine. Cicadas trilled in the woods, rising and falling. Her shorts were really short, and he imagined her naked.

"She's a good woman," said Cindy.

"Solid as a rock," said Reece, holding his Old Milwaukee. He felt free and wild and breathless.

They walked across the yard and passed between the gardens. Elbert was in the back of the garden where grew a long row of tangled blackberry briars.

"Hey, pawpaw!" said Cindy.

Elbert looked up and waved. Reece waved.

Reece followed Cindy onto the Sykes' pier, which had a railing and a boathouse. The electric water pump hummed, much quieter than Horace's gas pump.

There was a wood bench, and Reece sat next to her. The water was calm, the hot sun overhead, leaning toward the other side of the lake.

"God, this makes me want to get naked," said Cindy.

"What?" asked Reece.

"It's just so damn pretty out here. Right? I could just

jump in, if it weren't for all that damn moss."

"Yeah," said Reece. "Makes you feel alive."

"So, what is it about your fiancée? Why is she the one?" asked Cindy.

Reece sipped his beer. "I don't really know, to be honest. I mean, it was just a feeling. I had planned on going to Ethiopia before I met her. And then I went."

"You mean you felt bad about going?"

"We just had this connection, you know. It's hard to explain."

"You felt guilty about leaving her, didn't you?"

"Heck yeah, I did. It was hard to leave, and I, well, you know, wanted her to know that I really cared about her."

"So, you asked her to marry you?"

"I guess I did."

"Was that the right thing, though? Sounds a little fishy to me."

Reece didn't know what to say. He sipped and glanced at her, and then into the green water. There was a Christmas tree on the bottom, just a few feet out.

"Sounds like you got guilted," said Cindy. She pulled out her cigarettes and lighter.

"Maybe it sounds like it. But it was just this strong feeling, like I owed her something for her..."

"For her what?"

"I don't know, just because it was the right thing to do."

Cindy offered him the pack, and he declined. "If you hadn't gone over there, would you have asked her to marry you?"

"Jesus, are you a psychiatrist?"

"Could be," said Cindy. "But would you have?"

Reece squeezed the aluminum can. "I really can't say. I don't know. Maybe not as quick as I did."

"You mind if I get some sun?"

"What do you mean?"

"This." Cindy pulled her tube top down and exposed her breasts. Reece witnessed her large maroon nipples, which transfixed him.

"Turn you on?"

Reece spluttered. "Well, yeah. My God."

"Feels so fucking good. It's hard to go around always covering up."

Reece crossed his legs and leaned forward, nearly falling over.

"Got you rattled, huh? I do have great boobs. You know you want to look."

Reece wanted to do more than look.

"Want to go in the boathouse, in the boat? It's kind of a fantasy of mine. Lots of spiders in there."

Reece closed his eyes, seeing red streaks on black. "In the boathouse?"

Cindy pulled up her tube top. "Yeah, in the boathouse."

Lunch was a fiery kiyawot with chicken and hard eggs stained a dull red. Emma sweated it out as usual, drinking a liter of cold water from her fridge. She had one package of chocolate morsels left from home and shared it with everyone, getting *oohs* and *aahs*. Guthrie and Terry were still out treating cattle for worms.

The team was murmuring, eating, glancing at Emma as if she would disappear in a poof of white smoke. Barra spoke up.

"You are to take home your boots for hiking, no?" He made an effort to laugh.

Afewerki groaned. "We have shoes," he said.

"Yes, but the boots are special."

Emma was caught off guard. "Who needs them the most? I'd certainly be glad to give them away. I have a small foot."

"Perhaps it will fit my foot," said Barra. He smiled.

Emma kept a straight face. "If Misrak was here, I'd give them to her. But maybe Zenebek could use them. She has no shoes."

Barra spoke. "The women are used to this thing." He prepared for her the gursha and brought it to her lips. "For you."

Emma's blood boiled at the thought of Barra needing the boots more than Zenebek. She pondered what to do other than yell at him. She opened her mouth and took the food.

"This idea may work," said Afewerki. "We choose the

name from pieces of paper."

"Oh," said Emma. "Like drawing names from a hat?"

Barra looked displeased.

"Ow," said Afewerki. "But no one is having a hat."

Emma thought about all the things in her tiny house that she should leave for others: flashlight, candles, Bible, pillow, blanket, Kool-Aid powder, a small radio she rarely used, and clothes. A random drawing seemed like a good way to go, and hadn't Guthrie's wife suggested it too, or was it Teresa, except she was giving the boots to Zenebek regardless.

"I have some paper in the house," said Emma. She ducked out of the dining hut.

Isaac, Mariam, and Afewerki scolded Barra about the boots.

"She must give freely," said Isaac. "She is generous person."

"What a hell," said Afewerki. "We shall never see her again, like the Icelanders." He shook his head and swallowed back a lump in his throat.

"She is good worker," said Mariam. He stroked his thin beard.

Emma pushed through the flap with two pieces of paper and a pen. "Afewerki, you can make pieces with names on them. Make sure Zenebek is on there too and Irigit and Ketow."

"They are just the guards," said Barra.

Mariam kicked him under the table, and Barra grunted.

Soon, Afewerki had seven slips of folded paper. Isaac took the enjera platter and yelled for Irigit. With the papers in the middle of the table, Emma said, "This is for the boots. I'm drawing." She stirred the papers, closed her eyes, and chose one. "Ah, Zenebek!"

Everyone laughed except for Barra. He only smiled. "Shall we look the paper?"

"No!" said Afewerki.

"Next is for my little blue radio." She picked. "Oh, for Barra!"

Barra laughed. "Is good to have a radio, no? I will like it. Thank you."

Emma thought about what would be good for Irigit to have. His hat was a shambles, and she had a nice ballcap and toboggan he could wear. She went through the motions and drew. "Irigit gets my hats." She laughed, and the others laughed with her.

Just then, Irigit poked his head inside. "Abet?"

Isaac handed him the empty platter and told him about the hats. Irigit took off his tattered hat, held it over his heart, and murmured his thanks.

"Next is for my pillow and blanket." She drew. "The Hyena! I mean Emanuel!"

No one laughed at first, but then they did.

"Just kidding. Looks like Afewerki gets those."

"Thank you, Emma."

"Not a problem. It's an expensive pillow from the States. Duck feathers."

Barra looked a little jealous.

Emma knew that Mariam was the most religious, although Barra was the most pious, and the Bible went to Mariam. He nodded his thanks. "Xavier meskin."

Emma then drew for the flashlight and candles. "Isaac!"

"Thank you," said Isaac, smiling.

"Let's see, I have a couple of things left. I'm going to leave my clothes for the ladies in the shelter."

"Oh, they will fight," said Afewerki.

Emma reconsidered. "Yeah, it would only be for three or four. Maybe your mother would like them?"

"Yes," said Afewerki. "She will like."

"Great," said Emma. "I have some packs of Kool-Aid. Maybe I'll just divide those up."

"Thank you," said Isaac. "We will like it."

"That's it, I think. I feel lighter already. I need to brush my teeth and get this chicken out of my teeth."

"You are having some American toothpaste?" asked Barra.

Emma thought and then stirred the papers again. "Ketow! I'll give Ketow my socks and fingernail clippers too."

Everyone laughed except Barra.

"Is there anything else?" asked Emma. She looked at them sitting in their folding chairs and felt a pang of sadness. They were truly her friends, even Barra, who at times seemed to be at odds with the Christian imperative.

"You have given enough," said Afewerki. "We are happy."

At that, Emma put her face in her hands and could not hold back tears. "You guys...are the best in the world. I'm really going to miss you. I have to go home, though. It's time." Her cheeks glistened as she smiled at them. "I can't thank you enough for being my friends."

Mariam's eyes welled with tears, and he coughed. The others looked sad, especially Afewerki.

"My camera! I forgot about my camera. I don't have any

film, but you can buy it in Addis. This is for the big bucks." She stirred the papers for a full minute. She could feel the tension and said a brief prayer that it would go to the one who needed it most. "Afewerki!"

"My goodness," said Afewerki. "I will take photographs and send to you every month. Amenseganolo!"

"That would be super, but you don't have to. That could get expensive. Well, that's it, I think, unless someone wants my underwear."

No one said anything. Emma laughed.

Irigit was calling from the gate.

Afewerki stood and stepped outside. He peered back inside. "It is the Hyena. He is wanting Emma."

The color drained from Emma's face. The Hyena had attacked her on her visit to the church in the rock. He had most likely shot Reece. He had hired thieves to steal from the warehouse, and he was a known rapist in the village. And she had recently learned that his name was Emanuel.

"Emma," said Isaac. "He will go. We shall wait."

Emma stood. "No, let's see what he wants."

She stepped into the bright sunlight and saw him there at the gate alone, without his minions, and he was not wearing his pistol. She walked that way.

"He wants to give you some presents," said Afewerki. He looked displeased, with his arms folded.

The Hyena was grinning and holding a chicken and a bottle.

Emma drew closer and nodded.

"He is bringing to you this chicken and some katikala. He has heard that you are leaving. You must give the katikala to your father."

Emma stepped closer and took the bottle. She would never give her father anything, especially alcohol. The Hyena, Emanuel, held out his hand, and she shook it, saying thank you. Emanuel grinned, somewhat sober, dressed in his military fatigues.

"Thank you for drinking with me," said Emanuel. "You are good woman, no?"

Afewerki translated.

Emma wondered if he would ever confess to shooting Reece. She looked at his worn face and his neat clothes. He was just her height, shorter than most men in Godo. "And are you a good man?"

Afewerki hesitated but asked him.

Emanuel seemed to grow even shorter. With a studied look, he said, "Even the hyena must eat and drink," and left it at that. He smiled, handed the chicken upside-down to Afewerki, turned with a single tear in each eye, and hurried away.

"Well, that was something," said Emma. "Maybe give the chicken to Zenebek or Irigit, okay?

"Ishi," said Afewerki.

Just then, Terry and Dr. Guthrie appeared.

With his heart pounding in his throat, Reece unlatched the boathouse door. He looked back at Cindy, standing there in all of her glorious youth. "Me first?"

"Yeah, get in before pawpaw comes."

Reece squatted and pulled the bass boat closer with a rope and stepped into the boat crowded with oars, life vests, and fishing poles. "Holy cow."

Cindy did the same, and they both stood hunched over. Water lapped against the boat as it moved from side to side.

"Here," said Cindy. "Sit in the chair by the motor."

Feeling like a remote-controlled turtle, he inched his way there.

"I'll get this going." She pulled down her tube top, her breasts swaying in the dim light. "This is exciting."

"Yeah," said Reece. He was thinking of Emma, the night he was shot, her breasts.

She was unbuttoning his short pants, and then she was pulling down his underwear. "Ooh, tidy whities."

"Oh God," said Reece. "I'm engaged. I can't do this." He looked at his stiff member, throbbing like a steam train.

"Just relax." She moved in.

Reece stood and slammed his head into the top of the boathouse. "Shit!"

"Shit!" said Cindy.

"Oh God," said Reece. "I can't, sorry. I just can't." He didn't want to tell her that he was a virgin, that he'd never been given a blowjob. He pulled up his underwear and pants and sat.

Cindy looked hurt. "You want to kiss first?"

"Yeah, I mean no. So much has happened."

Cindy took a seat. "I need a cigarette for sure." She pulled up her top. "That's new."

"I'm sorry," said Reece, and he was. He remembered that life was short and wondered if he was making a mistake, missing out. He watched her scramble onto the deck. He heard Mr. Sykes and panicked.

"Y'all going fishing?" asked Elbert.

Reece froze.

"Just killing some spiders is all," he heard Cindy say.

He gathered himself, his heart racing, and crawled out. "Hey there." He saw Cindy's hand reaching out to him, and he took it, stepping onto the pier. He worried that his fly was down, but didn't look. He turned away and walked to the end of the pier and sat on the bench, looking out over the lake.

Elbert turned off the pump, grunted, and walked back to the garden.

Cindy joined Reece on the bench. She thumped the cigarette pack in her palm and took out two. "Here."

Reece took the Camel she lit off hers. "Kind of like a movie."

"Yeah. You must love her."

Reece said, "Yeah."

Brad loaded Kristin into his Porsche. She fell into the leather seat. He had no idea where she lived.

"Kristin? You have to give me directions." He cranked up, turned off the radio, and headed toward the interstate.

He knew she lived north of town.

As soon as the car started moving so did Kristin's stomach. She wretched, holding it back. "Stop!"

Brad pulled over, ran around, and opened the door. Kristin fell out, vomiting onto his shoes. She vomited again and then again.

"Fuck. Are you through? Are you okay?"

Kristin was crying. "Take me home, please! Oh God."

Brad closed her door. A group of three teenagers was approaching, holding a boom box. He hurried back to his side and gunned it, turned, realized he was going the wrong way, and did a U-turn, squealing his wheels. The on-ramp was just ahead.

"Kristin, look at me. You have to help me here. Is it the Roebuck exit?"

The inside of the car was swimming. "Yes."

It took ten minutes, and he exited. "Left? Right?"

Kristin groaned and tried to make sense of her surroundings. "Left, then right. Oh, what is wrong with me?"

Brad gunned it, then slowed and took the right. With a couple of wrong turns, he finally approached the house, creeping along until Kristin said, "There." All of the lights were on in the house. He pulled into the steep driveway, hoping he wouldn't have to meet her parents. He struggled out and went to her side. The front door was opening.

"Fuck."

He opened her door, but it swung back.

"Goddamn. Kristin, help me. We're here. I'll walk you. Just stand." He glanced at the door, and her parents were on the small porch. "Hell."

Kristin stood and moaned. She bent over and dry

heaved. "I have to work tomorrow. Oh God."

"Babydoll?" It was Edwin, trotting down the stairs. "Who are you? What's happened?" He took Kristin from Brad and struggled to hold her up.

"I think it'll take us both to get her up the stairs. I'm Brad. We work together."

Each on a side, they walked her up the brick steps. Gert backed away from the door, her hand over her mouth.

"Come on. We got you," said Brad.

They reached the door. "I've got it from here," said Edwin. "Come on, baby, inside."

"I'm sorry," said Brad. "Really. She just drank too much." He held the door, locked eyes with Gert, and nearly fell backward off the steps. He turned and trotted back to his car.

"What happened?" asked Gert.

"Just get me to bed," said Kristin. She looked up and saw Robyn at the top of the stairs, staring at her with wide eyes.

"You know you can't drink, honey," said Edwin. He got her to the top of the stairs. "You need some water."

"No," said Kristin. "Bed. Just the bed."

He walked her to her bed. "Robyn, can you help?"

Robyn pulled back the comforter and sheets, and Edwin let her sprawl there. They pulled up the covers, and that was that.

The next morning, Kristin's alarm sounded at five. She struggled to make sense of the noise and tried to figure out where she was. Her mouth was dry, and she was wet with sweat. She remembered the night before, then remembered that she had to be at work at six-thirty. She pounded the mattress with her fist and cursed Brad and the house special.

In the shower, she slipped and fell, hitting her head on the shower tile, landing on her knees. "Aaagh!" Why had she let her guard down at the party that wasn't even a party, just a bunch of drunk guys smoking cigars watching a video? And why hadn't Reece called her? He could have gone with her and should have, but maybe she'd wanted to see what it felt like to be out with Brad.

"You okay in there?" Gert knocked on the bathroom door.

"Yeah!"

Kristin hurried through her shower and rushed to get ready for work. She wanted to call Reece before she left and see where the heck he'd been. She doubted if he'd even care if she went to a party with a bunch of men. The blow dryer screamed wind.

"You want some oatmeal?" asked Gert.

Kristin wore white scrubs, ready to go. "Thanks, Mom. In a minute. I need a big glass of orange juice too."

"You gonna be able to work today? You looked awful last night. I didn't sleep a wink, worried you would quit breathing."

Edwin walked into the den, working his tie. "You've never done that before, baby. That Brad seemed like a nice guy, but did he give you the alcohol?"

Kristin just shook her head. "I drank it of my own accord, and I need to call Reece. Did he ever call while I was gone last night?"

"No, honey, he didn't," said Edwin. "I'm sorry."

"This would have never happened if he'd just be there for me," said Kristin. "Oh, what am I saying!" She grabbed the phone and dialed.

The phone rang a few times, and Horace answered. She almost hung up. "Hey, it's Kristin. Is Reece up?"

Horace cleared his throat and adjusted his squealing hearing aid. "Hey there. He's still asleep. You want me to wake him up?"

Kristin thought. "Yes...please."

"Hold on." Horace fumbled the phone into the wastebasket beside his recliner. "Dammit." He retrieved it by the cord. "Reece!" He leaned forward and stood. "Hey, boy! Hey!"

Reece heard his name and opened his eyes. "Yeah?"

"Kristin needs you on the phone. Maybe something bad happened."

Reece sat up and threw his legs over. He scratched his head, trying to understand what Horace was saying. "Kristin?"

"Yeah, son, Kristin, on the phone. Hurry up."

"Okay." He grabbed his shorts from the floor and, shirtless, went to the phone. His mind raced, but was more or less blank, still asleep. He sat in Dora's recliner. "Hello? Kristin?"

"Reece, you awake?" asked Kristin.

"Am now, what's up?" He scratched his chest. Dora stood at the stove, all ears, and Horace was in the bathroom.

"You never called yesterday. Why?" Kristin dragged the cord to the kitchen table and sat.

Reece thought about Cindy, her large, soft breasts in

the boathouse. His pants coming down.

"Reece?"

"Yeah, right. I don't know why. I should have. I'm sorry...I don't want to seem clingy, I guess."

"Well, maybe I want you to be clingy. I need you, Reece. I almost lost you. I can't go through that again." She wrapped the cord around her hand and pulled it tight.

Reece scratched his thigh, a scab there, and made it bleed. He thought about cling peaches in a can with syrup. "Nobody's losing anybody. You want me to come by for lunch? What's a good time?"

"Of course, I want you to come for lunch. Let's try 11:15. Promise you'll come?"

"Well, yeah. If I say I'll be there, I'll be there. You know that." He slumped in the chair. Should he tell her about Cindy. No way. "In the cafeteria?"

"That's easiest. But really, I need to hear from you every day, and seeing you would be even better...I did a bad thing last night."

Reece sat up. "A bad thing. What?" Did she sleep with a doctor, with that guy Brad?

"I went to a lame party, a bunch of doctors from work at a loft downtown. I didn't want to go, but was feeling lonely and Brad practically begged me. So, I went." She went to the sink for a glass of water and mouthed orange juice to Gert.

Reece raised his eyebrows. This was curious. "What happened? Did something happen?"

"I drank alcohol, Reece, three of these drinks with vodka in it. I've never had liquor my entire life."

"Were you able to drive home? You okay now?"

"No, my car is still on the street. Dad's going to drive me down there. I have a huge headache and feel beat up like I fell down some stairs." Kristin gulped her lukewarm water.

"Did you pass out?" He was squeezing his knees together.

"I don't know, maybe when I fell on my bed. Robyn said my eyes looked like cracked glass."

"Wow, you going to work?"

"I can't let this make me take a sick day. That would really make me feel bad."

Reece wondered again if he should tell her about Cindy. "That's strange because yesterday I bought some beer and drank five on the pier. Granny was mad that I bought it."

"Reece, be careful. The last thing you need is alcohol."

"Well, it made me feel pretty good, drinking it in the hot sun. No harm in beer. Vodka might be a different story."

"So, I'm the bad guy?" Kristin pounded the rest of the water and took the juice glass from her mother, pushing it back and forth on the table.

"No," said Reece. "Maybe Brad is the bad guy, luring you to his Hobbit hole."

"For Pete's sake. Hobbit hole, really? The loft belonged to Dr. Joiner. God, my head hurts."

"Take some Tylenol?" Reece imagined two white tablets, chalky, kind of hard to swallow. He swallowed in sympathy.

"Yeah, I mean no, or not yet." She held the phone to her chest. "Mom, can you get me some Tylenol?" Gert nodded.

Edwin popped in. He put his hand on her shoulder and

touched her hair. "We need to go, honey."

"Say, I've got to finish getting ready for work, so will see you at 11:15, right? Come by the unit. People ask about you all the time."

"Yeah, I'll see you there. Maybe they'll have that gooey cheese cornbread." He laughed. Kristin laughed. And all seemed relatively well.

Dr. Guthrie gave a booming hello to everyone gathered at the gate, and Terry waved. Guthrie placed his bag of instruments in the tall grass.

Emma felt a thrill at seeing Guthrie and Terry. They were there to whisk her away like magic. She imagined a soldier having fought and then returning home, how joyous that would be. But it seemed like only yesterday when she arrived.

"Yo ho ho," said Emma. She felt that her feet were lifting from the ground and hugged Guthrie and then Terry, thanking them.

"Oh, she is pirate," said Afewerki.

Everyone laughed.

"Yes, I know this thing," said Afewerki, smiling.

"You need some time to pack?" asked Guthrie.

Barra said, "She is giving away many things. To Afewerki goes the camera!" He grinned. "I am getting small radio."

Emma coughed. "He's right about the giving away part. I'll just have a small bag to take on the plane, although I have a painting I want to take back." She imagined Reece meeting her at the airport, what a miracle that would be.

"She is very generous, no?" asked Isaac. Mariam nodded and inspired.

"Yiqirta," said Emma. "I wish I had more stuff to give away. Next time I'll bring a big bag of tweezers to give to everyone."

Barra perked up. "Oh, you have this thing? The tweezers?"

Emma laughed. "You want them? You can have them. No problem."

"Thanks to God," said Barra.

"So, yeah," said Guthrie. "Pack your stuff and we'll say our goodbyes."

"We are to say goodbye?" asked Isaac. He looked worried.

"No, not you guys, not yet. But I need to talk with you about how we'll close the clinic. We'll announce it thirty days in advance. In the meantime, you can empty the warehouse and distribute what's left. We've been more or less ordered out by the RRC. Everything has to go, except leftover medical supplies. We need to bring those back to Addis for traveling clinics. That's our next step." When Guthrie spoke, he put his thumbs in his pants pockets. "Beautiful day anyway."

"Yes, thanks to God," said Afewerki. Murmurs of approval.

Emma hugged Isaac. "I'll miss you, soul brother." She turned to Barra and stopped herself from offering him a handshake. She opened her arms, and he came to her. "You are the best singer in all of Ethiopia." Barra beamed and thanked her. Mariam stood back, looking at his shoes. "Mariam," said Emma, and that was all. She hugged him tight and laughed, thinking about the huge pocket on his shirt that could hold a football. "Oh, and there's this devil, Afewerki." Afewerki smiled. "No, no. Not to say such things. We will miss you, Emma." They embraced for what seemed to him an eternity, and he blushed.

"You guys are the best. I'll never forget you, and I will write. I promise." Tears slid from her eyes to her cheeks, feeling hot.

Emma went to her little house and looked around. The house was her tiny piece of comfort, but there were the bullet holes in the back wall. She opened the fridge and wondered if she should turn it off, extinguish the pilot light. There were six bottles of cold filtered water in Icelandic IV bottles. She left it running for the guys to use as long as the propane held out, and the same for the stove. The crude shelves held cans of tomato paste and cheese. A towel dried on the back of the chair, which she would leave. She only needed a change of clothes to pack into a small tote bag. Should she leave the photos of her family? At the last minute, she picked up the mini album and a few loose pictures to take back home. She would not light the candle beside her bed ever again, and that made a few more tears. She turned, and Irigit was there, wearing his church ballcap, holding the remnants of a broom that he used to sweep her floor every morning. He looked terribly sad. She went to hug him, and he laughed a loud laugh and patted her back.

"I'll miss you, Irigit."

Irigit took his cap off, held it over his heart, and wished her a safe journey to her home so far away, a place he could barely imagine. He swept, stirring up dust, and Emma stepped out.

"Hey, Dr. Guthrie," said Emma. "I need to clear the line of patients at the clinic and then visit the shelter one more time."

"Emma, we don't have time for that. Maybe let Afewerki treat what he can while you're at the shelter. That work?"

"I can do this," said Afewerki. "If someone is very sick, I

will wait for you to come, but most will come with worms and fleas."

"And the lice," said Isaac. He scratched his body and laughed. "The lice, they are coming every day. What we should do now wiz-out Emma? Afewerki must take care, no?"

Guthrie weighed in. "We can let Afewerki run the clinic for another thirty days and take care of the minor stuff."

"He's earned his stripes," said Terry. And then he had to explain what he meant.

"Heck, he knows as much as I do," said Emma.

"But no dispensing of antibiotics or pain meds or starting IVs. We need to have qualified personnel on site for that," said Guthrie. "All right, so Emma, go, and Afewerki, go. We'll meet up at the clinic in half an hour."

"I need an interpreter for the shelter. Isaac, can you come with me?"

Isaac stood a little straighter. "Yes, Emma. I am coming." He pushed his wire-framed glasses up on his nose.

They passed the church and came to the shelter on the hillside. The shelters smelled of concentrated Permethrin, a sharp chemical smell Otherwise, it was feces and urine from the open toilets. A small group of ragged children circled them, giggling and flashing smiles.

"Promise me, Isaac, that you'll help to find these women a way home. Will you visit every day that you are still here?" Emma took the hand of a thin little girl and told her that she was so pretty. She had butter in her glistening rows of braided hair. The guard had stood and walked their way with his rifle on his shoulder.

"Yes, to you I will promise this thing. No problem. Perhaps some will want to stay."

"That would be totally fine as long as they have food and water. It just breaks my heart to leave. Should we tell them? I think we should."

"Yes, I will tell," said Isaac. He greeted the guard and told him the news. The guard's watery bloodshot eyes widened a bit. A brown hat sat flat on his head. The wind ruffled his worn shirt and shorts.

"He looks so sad." Emma held out her hand and received the old guard's hand into her own. "Amenseganolo. Isaac, tell him to take good care of the ladies and give him the food in my house."

The old guard nodded and said that he would, but wondered what would become of him, his job, his duty. Like Irigit, he took his hat, held it over his heart, and mumbled. That made Emma remember Ketow.

"Isaac, I didn't leave anything for Ketow. Damn." She fished in her pocket and pulled out twenty birr. "Give this to him."

"Yes, Emma."

"Okay, let's tell the ladies." She now had a boy holding one hand, the girl the other. Snot and flies crusted the boy's upper lip.

Isaac called out, looked into the shelter, and called out again. Soon, fifteen women, young mothers and a few old ladies, gathered in a huddle. All Emma could think of was what if someone tossed a grenade in their midst. They would all be killed. The women stood with somber faces, and even the children slowed their play as if a crocodile had appeared and was waddling their way.

Isaac told them Emma was leaving, and an even greater

hush ensued. One young mother with her three-year-old son on her back fell to her knees at Emma's feet, the bells on the leather carrier jingling, and began to cry. The other women murmured and put hands over mouths shaped like Os. "Who will bring us food?" one asked. "Who will protect us?" asked another. Isaac translated in monotone for Emma.

Emma sank, knowing in her heart that she was somehow betraying these women to the caprices of chance and hardship. She choked and tried to speak. Within a few days, she would be on a plane headed back to Alabama. These women would still be here, scratching out their lives from day to day.

"God," said Emma. "Tell them I'm sorry and that they will be taken care of for another month." She let tears trickle down her flushed cheeks and opened her arms.

A woman with a bright red scarf on her head came forward. Then another, all smelling of the familiar smoke, milk, and sweat, until there were hugs all around. "God, I will miss them." Emma stumbled back a few steps and felt the weight of the world on her shoulders.

"It iz okay," said Isaac. "God will help them."

"Well, He better," said Emma. She let her head fall and turned away. Isaac followed.

At the clinic, Terry was in the copter going through preflight. Emma stepped up into the clinic for the last time. There were a dozen left in line. The guard was to turn away newcomers. Afewerki was there, pouring peroxide on a leg wound, what looked to be a deep tropical ulcer with a gooey yellow center.

"Jesus Christ," said Emma. "Tell him, he needs a dose of

penicillin." She went to the shelf for the vial, sterile water, needle, and syringe.

The young man's eyes brightened at the mention of a murphy, the injection, and he stood, nearly letting his pants drop to the floor. He grunted when the needle went in, feeling the pressure of the milky 10 ccs in his buttock.

"Done," said Emma.

"Bucka," said Afewerki.

The man nodded and limped out.

"What's left?" asked Emma.

Guthrie poked his head in, assessing the situation.

"I can treat all. You may go, Emma," said Afewerki in a hush.

"Are you sure? I just had to give an injection. I know you're not supposed to, but if you had to give an injection, do it in the upper outer corner of the buttock. Never in the middle. Okay? Oh, Jesus, it makes me insane to think I'm leaving you with this work. Are you angry?"

Afewerki summoned the next patient, an old woman with a large, tattooed goiter. "No, Emma. I am not angry. I could not be." He paused. "You will help me to come to US? It is my dream."

Emma wondered at what she had promised. "Yes, I will. I will do my best. You deserve it. Who knows? Maybe you'll become a doctor and come back to Godo."

Afewerki smiled at that, and there was a commotion at the gate, shouting.

"The Hyena," said Emma.

"No, no, it is something else," said Afewerki.

They both stepped out of the clinic, and a man with bulging forearm muscles walked toward them carrying something with legs. Emma's stomach dropped, and Dr. Guthrie said, "Shit."

Reece parked in the aged parking deck and walked into Carraway Hospital. It had been what, four or five months since he had been there? He noticed the clean smell, almost fruity. He passed a barbershop and wound his way to the elevator up to CCU on two.

He took a left off the elevator and looked into the break room. Winston was there, smoking a cigarette.

"Oh my God," said Winston. "Lookie here." Winston drove a vintage white Trans Am with a black phoenix decal on the front hood.

Reece shook his hand. "Good to see you, man."

"You too. You look good from what I've heard."

"Yeah, hard row to hoe being shot in the head." Reece laughed.

"You here for Kristin. I can get her for you." He snubbed his cigarette.

"Going to lunch and have some gooey cornbread. You look good. Still skinny, I see."

Winston laughed. "Just bones, but hey, just come on in. No need to make you wait."

"Thanks," and Reece followed Winston through the automatic double doors into a very bright unit. Right away, he smelled the smell, a mixture of iodine and baby powder. He stopped, stunned somewhat at being back in this place. He gazed at the twelve rooms arranged in a horseshoe, and there was Kristin at the long desk, writing in a chart. She seemed a thousand miles away.

"Hey!" said Debbie, rushing past with an IV bag. "You're

back!" She didn't stop.

Reece recognized most everyone, except a couple of new interns. He could see Eudora, the unit clerk, tapping away on her keyboard. Kristin looked up and saw him, smiling for a second, then finishing her charting in a flurry.

"You're here!"

"Heck yeah." Reece waved at Kirksy on the other end of the unit. She was so tiny and never wore a bra.

Reece met Kristin halfway and hugged her. "Let me say hey to Eudora."

"Do that and let me suction an ET tube. Be right back." Kristin hurried into number six, a young woman who had aspirated vegetable soup and developed SARS.

Reece walked around to Eudora and surprised her. "Hey!"

Eudora looked up, startled. "Well, hey, boy!" She tried to stand, but fell back into her rolling chair. Behind her sat Leslie in her purple scrubs. She turned and stood, glancing back at the bank of heart monitors.

"Hell, boy. You're a ghost. Dear God, we prayed for you. You know that, right?" asked Eudora.

Reece walked around and gave her a hug, and then hugged Leslie. Someone tapped him on the shoulder, and it was Kirksy.

"For Pete's sake," said Reece. "It's like a family reunion."

"Good God, boy, we thought you were done for," said Eudora.

"Damn right," said Kirksy. Her hand went to his temples, tracing the scars there. "You are one lucky cracker, boy."

Reece could only smile. He felt overwhelmed and choked for a second on his saliva. "You guys are great. It's great to see you."

"We know Kristin is sure glad to see you," said Eudora.

"Glad to be back is all I can say. Although I'm missing out. You know what I mean?"

No one knew what he meant.

"I'm here to have lunch with Kristin." Reece looked, and there was Dr. Phillips at the long desk. Reece somehow knew. Phillips looked so neat and clean.

"Yeah, you better be," said Kirksy. She raised her eyebrows at Reece.

Reece didn't know what to say. "Getting some of that gooey cornbread."

"Gross," said Leslie.

Reece saw Kristin come out of six, wadding a paper towel in her hands. He watched Phillips watching her and felt a pressure behind his eyes.

Kristin joined the little party. "He looks great, doesn't he?"

"Better than I thought he would," said Kirksy. "Hold him tight this time. Boy, your traveling days are over. You got that?"

Reece laughed. "Not even Gulf Shores?"

"Maybe Gulf Shores, but Africa is off the list." Kirksy brushed back her short hair, which looked like a boy's.

"No argument here," said Reece.

"That's what I want to hear," said Kristin. "Let's do lunch. I only have about twenty minutes."

In the elevator going down was an old woman with a flabby face in a wheelchair. She was headed back to her room from dialysis and looked like she'd been beaten. Reece smiled at her, and the doors opened.

The cafeteria was abuzz with visitors and scrubs. They had the gooey cornbread, and Reece ordered that along with collard greens, black-eyed peas, and a flimsy piece of fried whitefish. Kristin had macaroni and cheese and banana pudding. There was nowhere to sit, and they hovered until a table opened up.

"Loud in here," said Reece. He tasted his cornbread. "Mmm, got the jalapenos in there." He examined the people walking past him, recognizing quite a few.

"And you ran off and left that behind. You know you love this place, this cornbread," said Kristin.

"I didn't run off. I just took a job that was far away."

"Don't quibble the details." She sipped her sweet tea.

Reece ate, thinking. "Tell me about that party."

"I've only got twenty minutes or so. Let's talk about something else."

"Still have a headache?"

"No. I don't."

"Was he hitting on you, that Brad, your knight in shining white coat?"

"He's always hitting on me."

"I mean, at the party, was he aggressive, encouraging you to drink?"

"Maybe he asked me to have a drink. The guys were all watching some martial arts video. The loft belonged to Dr. Joiner, and I talked mostly to his wife."

"And he had to drive you home? I can't imagine that."

Kristin waved at a respiratory therapist, Wayne, with the long sideburns. "So, where were we? You were going to tell me what you did yesterday, right?" She laughed.

"No, we were talking about you." He wanted to say, "Honey pie," but figured she would get mad.

"And now we're talking about you."

Reece told her about Cindy, letting the cards fall where they may. "I don't know if I've ever mentioned her, but I saw Cindy yesterday. She was visiting the Sykes next door, her grandparents."

"Really? Is she hot?" He had her attention.

"Well, she dresses to show, if you know what I mean."

"To show what?"

Reece finished a mouthful of greens and cornbread, washed it down with sweet, iced tea. "To show her body. She's a great person, though, kind of an old friend, although mostly I hung out with her brother in the summertime." He tapped his fork on his white plate.

"So, you like her body? Did she come onto you?"

Reece took his time with a bite of peas. "It was unexpected. I was on the pier and she came down, just talking, and...she pulled her tube top down to get some sun." He cringed and felt breathless, looking away.

"Reece, really? You're kidding? What did you do? Did you look?"

"Of course I looked, but didn't stare. What else could I do? I didn't know what to say."

"That's just ridiculous. Everywhere you go, there's some bird after you. Is this how it's gonna be when we get married?"

"Anyway, the water pump was on. She pulled her tube top up, so that's that."

Kristin had stopped eating. "So that was it? She flashed

you and then just disappeared?"

Reece finished his iced tea even though he didn't want to. He toyed with his cornbread. "Well, sort of. She, uh, wanted to go in the boathouse, but I said no."

"God, Reece. In the boathouse? To do what, play doctor?" She pushed back from the table and folded her arms.

"I think she intended, uh, wicked things, if you know what I mean. But luckily, Mr. Sykes came down to the pier, and nothing happened." He realized his mistake right away.

"What do you mean, 'luckily'? If he hadn't come down, you would have had sex with her in the boathouse? Oh brother, that beats all."

"Hey, don't get in a tizzy. Nothing happened. We had lunch, that's all." He tapped his tea glass, pushed his plate, leaned back in his chair.

"Reece Myers. You had the gall to eat with her after that? You wanted her is all I can say." She folded her paper napkin and put it on the tray.

"No, no, Granny invited her, I think. We had pork chops. That's it, totally."

"I'd like to give her a piece of my mind. I would never just sit down and pull my shirt off like that. And to top it off, you're engaged!"

"She didn't know that. Hadn't seen her for a couple years. So, what happened in the car with you and Dr. Brad? Or can you remember?" He took a bite of the soggy fish and chewed with effort.

"You're just terrible. I'm leaving." She stared at him like he was a goldfish on a wet paper towel.

"No, don't go like that. Finish your lunch. The macaroni

and cheese here is legend, like the cornbread. I'm sorry, but at least I'm being honest." He reached out to touch her elbow, and she let him. "I'm sorry it happened."

Kristin's shoulders slumped. "Are you still a Christian? I mean, you've really changed. That would have never happened before."

Reece coughed. He wasn't sure what or who he was anymore. When he was unable to move in the hospital, he'd had vivid images of hell, had pondered long and hard his situation. His entire world had come undone and was lying in pieces inside his head. He stared at his plate.

"Reece? Mom and Dad say you've changed, too, and that they're not surprised. They're worried that you're going to hurt me, and I'm worried too...Say something. Reece?"

Reece felt dizzy, grabbed at the table, and toppled out of his chair.

The young girl moaned, her face pink and oozing, her clothes burned, a smell of charred flesh. The man, her father, laid her on the ground and stared.

"IV fluids," said Guthrie.

Emma ran inside, and Afewerki asked the father what happened. "She has been burned with the kerosene from the lamp. She has dropped it into the fire and then to fall in."

Terry had run over, couldn't look, and turned away, headed back to the helicopter. Even he knew this would be an evacuation. The girl looked dead but was wheezing, having inhaled the fire. Bloody fluid trickled from her mouth. Barra turned away, gagging. Isaac and Mariam looked on, mumbling to one another.

Guthrie checked the carotids on her scorched neck. The girl tried to scream, and he went for her femoral artery instead. "Tachycardia, but regular. I'm afraid she's going to suffocate."

Emma was back outside in less than a minute with the supplies. She squatted, then kneeled with the IV, going for a neck vein, but the skin was too severely damaged, and she had to settle for the left arm. Within seconds, dark blood poured from the IV, and with Afewerki's help, she plugged in the fluids, taping it down in a hurry.

"What a hell," said Afewerki. He shook his head, watching Emma work.

"Any ET tubes here?" asked Guthrie. "Her airway is constricted, and I can see it closing down."

"Damn, none," said Emma. "We're taking her with us, right? We have to. She'll die otherwise."

Guthrie frowned and coughed. "Yeah, we need to get out of here as fast as possible. You got all your stuff?"

"Yeah," said Emma, hearing the helicopter's twin engines begin to whine. "Afewerki, is this her father?"

"Yes."

Just then, a woman, carrying a naked baby in her arms, ran into the compound screaming. She stopped and stared at her daughter on the ground, who was struggling to breathe. She wailed and shouted, and the father took her and held her.

"Tell them, she's going to Addis with us," said Guthrie. "It's no good if they come with us. We'll get her to the hospital as fast as possible."

Afewerki told them. The man nodded, holding his wife and baby, trying to keep her from collapsing.

"It's not the way you imagined you would leave, but let's get going," said Guthrie. "Afewerki, get me a scalpel, some iodine swabs, and a ten-cc syringe."

"Ishi," and he ran inside.

The girl's wheezes began to sound like squeals, and her eyes rolled up and down, her lungs struggling for air.

"Silvadene, I'll get Silvadene," said Emma. "What's her name?"

"Abebe," said Afewerki. Another flower.

"More IV fluids and kits, too," said Guthrie.

Emma bumped into Afewerki on his way out and ran inside, stuffing supplies into her pockets. She grabbed three liters of saline and rushed back out with her arms full. She felt heavy raindrops hit her arms.

Guthrie had the father and Afewerki carry the girl to the copter and lay her on the floor behind Terry. Guthrie wrenched a headrest from a passenger chair and tossed it to Afewerki, who put it under the girl's head. The mother staggered toward the helicopter, and Isaac grabbed her and led her back to the clinic as she screamed for her daughter's life.

Before turning away for the last time, Emma said her last words to Isaac, Barra, and Mariam. "I'm going to miss you. Thank you for everything that you've done. God bless you."

They closed in around her with baffled looks and then parted and watched her run to the helicopter.

"Can Afewerki go?" shouted Emma.

"Depends on fuel." He put on a headset and asked Terry, who turned and gave a thumbs down.

Afewerki hopped out with what seemed to be fear and heartbreak in his eyes. He stood stooped over, the rotor wash beating his clothes. He felt Emma hug him, but could not hear her words. Without a sound, he jogged back to the group, watching from the clinic door. It began to rain, then poured.

Guthrie closed the doors and took the IV bottle from Emma. Emma got on the floor and propped the girl in her lap, making it easier for her to breathe. The hard door pressed into her back, and Emma cried, wiping the tears away as they came. She saw Guthrie with a headset and felt it slip over her head. There was nowhere to hang the IV bottle, so he sat and held it at chest level.

Terry could see they weren't buckled but gunned it anyway, with visibility less than ten feet. "Hold on!"

Emma kept her eyes on the girl's chest and straightened her arm with the IV. Before the girl's dress could dry into the burned flesh, she peeled away strips of the charred cloth from her chest, cutting with scissors she'd jammed in her scrub pocket. The girl's eyes went wild, but she barely moved. It took ten minutes, but soon the burned area emerged, which reached from her navel to her forehead, face, and ears. The girl looked up at Guthrie, shivering. Afewerki had thought to throw in a wool blanket, and Emma pulled it over her.

Within twenty minutes, in a driving rain, they passed over Alem Ketema, heading straight for Addis Ababa.

"She gonna make it?" asked Terry, followed by a shot of static.

"I'm praying," said Guthrie.

Emma couldn't reach her talk button, but nodded. Her time in Ethiopia couldn't possibly end with the death of a young girl, and the helicopter throbbed, passing in and out of clouds and rain, buffeted back and forth. Fifteen minutes outside of Addis, Terry radioed the old airport at Lideta, requesting an emergency landing for the burn patient. Usually, he landed at the new airport, but it was farther from Black Lion Hospital. There would be no ambulance, and a taxi would be the best they could hope for.

Terry descended below cloud cover to roughly eight hundred feet and navigated toward the landing area marked with a large white circle. The Polish Army base was at the southeastern end of the airport. There would be no time for checking papers or chatting with Kapitan Jozef or the other soldiers, just a quick evacuation to South Africa Street.

Emma's heart dropped as the helicopter descended. Abebe's breaths had become spasmodic, and now she seemed to have quit breathing. Emma ripped off her headset and let Abebe's head onto the cramped floor. She yelled at Guthrie, but he was already on his knees, swaying as Terry circled back over the airport. Without pausing, he leaned in and tried mouth-to-mouth. His breath went nowhere, and the girl's chest did not rise.

"Airway occluded!" he shouted. He'd already taken off the nipple end of a syringe with his knife, making a temporary airway. He pulled the scalpel from the pile of supplies scattered across the floor. He looked for the iodine swabs, but they were out of reach, and he went in without hesitation, cutting a deep X into the girl's throat. Blood oozed and sputtered as Abebe fought to breathe. He took the syringe and forced it into the hole, releasing a gush of air, and Abebe was breathing on her own, but bleeding, bleeding.

No jeep came to meet them. Terry let the copter idle, and Emma and Guthrie extracted Abebe. A light mist fell, the sun behind the thick clouds. Emma smelled the city and the fuel and the weeping burned skin.

"Good work!" she shouted.

"Not out of the woods yet," said Guthrie. He held the IV bottle up high, and Emma clutched Abebe, who was sprawled across her lap, the air sucking in and out through the makeshift airway.

A jeep roared up, and it was Fidel with his driver. He motioned for them to get in. Emma and Guthrie struggled with the limp body. Her eyes were wild, and she was trying to scream. The jeep sped down the runway toward

South Africa Street and only paused at the gate, breaking into a heavy jam of traffic.

"They taking us to the hospital?" asked Emma.

"That's what seems to be happening," said Guthrie. He held on for dear life as the jeep lurched and crept between lanes, gathering stares from the crowded sidewalks and vendor stalls.

The jeep squeaked into the rotation at Mexico Square and headed up Aragay to Churchill and then Zambia Street. The IV bottle was about to run out.

Cars and taxis blocked the emergency room, and the driver stopped in traffic, waving for vehicles to go around. Emma couldn't believe she was back at the hospital again, and in they went, Guthrie with the torso and Emma with the legs. Inside, all of the city seemed to be there. Guthrie barked in his stilted Amharic, and a path emerged through the crowd, staring at the crazy ferenji and what appeared to be a dead body in their grip.

A nurse told them they couldn't pass.

"Bullshit," said Emma, and she backed into the door, pushing it open. It was less crowded, and Guthrie took the lead, heading for an empty stretcher with a thin black pad. They placed her like a feather, and Guthrie shouted for help in Amharic, Italian, and English.

For three minutes, Reece seized on the floor, his eyes rolling back in his head. Kristin stayed there with him, turning his head to the side, watching his respirations. A crowd had gathered, including several doctors. He trembled from head to foot like bacon simmering in a skillet. By the time a crash cart arrived, he lay still, breathing deep, in and out.

"Reece?" asked Kristin. "Answer me, Reece!" She put her hand on his sweaty forehead.

Reece looked around at legs and then up at faces and folded arms. He had regurgitated, and he swallowed the bitterness in his mouth. "Shit on toast," he said.

"What? Reece? Can you sit up? You look a little blue. I'm sorry..."

Reece's first thought was to run to the truck and drive away as fast as possible. "Hey." He sat up with her help, and a small round of applause erupted. He looked beneath the tables and remembered the day his parents had been in Luby's, trying to hide. "Damn, what happened?" He struggled to remember and could only think of gooey cornbread.

"Had a seizure, another one," said Kristin.

A hospital liaison had arrived, a Mrs. Padgett. "We have to get him to the ER for an evaluation. Are you his wife?"

"No," said Kristin, "his fiancée."

"I don't need the ER," said Reece. He turned to his knees and was able to stand.

"Just to be safe, sir," said Padgett. "You work here?"

"He used to work in CCU," said Kristin.

Reece found himself between two doctors in white coats. "Walk slowly," said one. "Here comes a wheelchair," said the other.

"Just wheel me to the parking deck. I'm fine, really." And then he was in the wheelchair, being pushed through the crowded dining room.

"Reece, you have to go."

Reece gripped the arms of the wheelchair and put his feet down. "No, I'm fine. I can drive."

The doctors and the liaison tried to talk sense into him.

Reece stood, fell back in the chair, and then stood again. "No, just let me rest. Kristin will take care of me. She's my fiancée." To prove his point, he stepped over the wheelchair legs and walked a few steps, the doctors at his side. "I'm fine, really. Just been shot in the head is all. No worries." He raised his elbows to make space. He looked around the dining room, all eyes on him as if he'd been accused of a great crime, as if he was walking to his execution.

"Reece," said Kristin. "Let's just do the ER to be safe." She maneuvered in front of him, looking into his greenish-brown eyes.

"I said no. I'm going to the parking deck. I'll sit in the car for a while and then go. You need to get back to work, right?"

"Oh, Lord," said Kristin. "I'm sorry, but he wants to leave."

The doctors melted back a few steps, but Padgett did not. There could be a lawsuit. "Please, sir, just come with us."

"I said and mean no," said Reece. "Get the hell away

from me." He felt his blood pressure rise, his face flush. "I survived an F-5 tornado!"

Kristin saw that it was futile. "He won't go, so let me push him to the deck. Reece, will you do that? Let me push you to the deck?"

Reece was looking at his feet, his old Clarks with the heels worn down. "Yeah, let's do that." He sat in the wheelchair and waited.

"Will you sign this waiver?" asked Padgett. She held a clipboard with forms on it.

"Sure," and he took her pen and struggled to sign his name. "There, let's get out of here."

Kristin unlocked the brakes and pushed him through the tables and into the hallway. "Reece, you should have gone to the ER."

"Maybe, but I feel fine." He slumped in the chair, arms folded across his chest.

"Can I call your grandparents to come get you?" She headed to the exit to the parking deck.

"No, I'm fine. I don't know how to say it otherwise." He put his head in his hands. "Damn."

"Okay, but you have to call me when you get home. Promise?"

"Yeah, no problem."

"What level are you on in the deck?"

"Three, I think. I always parked on three."

Kristin hit the automatic door button and pushed him into the warm air. It took a minute, but she found the beat-up F-150. Reece stood and stretched as if just waking up.

"Thanks, maybe I'll come over tonight? That okay?"

"That would be great, but maybe I should come and see

you. Let me come out there. Okay?"

"Yeah, okay." He opened the squeaky door. She was waiting for a kiss, and he turned and kissed her. "Thanks for understanding. You know I don't like doctors prodding me."

"I do now," said Kristin. "Drive safe, go slow."

"Right," and he climbed in.

Reece watched Kristin walk away in his side mirror. He was a little foggy and decided to wait a few minutes, listening to 99.5 Rock on the radio. Don Henley's "Boys of Summer" played. He liked the music video, but wanted something a bit harder, something to match his physical state, something like a bullet to the brain. Maybe some Black Sabbath. He turned it up anyway, the music sounding metallic inside the bare cockpit of the F-150.

He replayed the seizure in his mind. He'd thought he was in Ethiopia when he came to, that Emma was there, but then there was the air conditioning, the tight carpet, the undersides of tables, and faces he didn't know peering down at him. Seeing Kristin had jolted him back to reality. He cranked the truck.

The truck emerged into bright, bright sunshine, and he squinted. He forgot to push the clutch and ground the gears. "Dammit." He needed to be on Carraway Boulevard but had turned left instead of right. He couldn't decide what to do next, so he just drove straight, then pulled over into a parking space. He turned the radio down and forced himself to think. He needed to do what? Take a left and then what? Another left? He scratched his head and pulled out with his blinker on. It took another wrong turn and then two more correct turns before he was on the road to the interstate. He concentrated, glad that he had a lane to enter on without merging.

The truck's steering was a bit loose, and he concentrated on that, forgetting that he needed to exit at Tallapoosa Street until the last second and swerved, making it, but with a horn blaring behind him. "Easy now, country boy," he said. The truck seemed to be guiding itself and swung around for the drive through Tarrant City, where he'd lived as a small boy. His dad had worked at a grocery distribution center there, and he'd had his foot crushed beneath a pallet of canned vegetables. Thankfully, the four-lane was pretty straight, and he'd driven it so many times that he felt himself go into autopilot. He passed the motorcycle dealership, nodding to himself that he was doing okay, but everyone seemed to be passing him.

"Damn."

In second gear, doing thirty miles an hour, he brought it up to fifty in third. His mind wandered to Ethiopia. He wondered if Emma was in her little house, getting ready for bed, maybe praying for him. He was there in her room, watching himself lean over her, his hands slipping down into her scrub top. She wasn't wearing a bra. His mind stayed there.

Ten minutes passed, and he couldn't figure out how he'd driven the last few miles. A thought lodged in his head. There was a liquor store up ahead that he'd never been into. He wanted something substantial, and the image of Cindy's breasts hit him in the face. God, what if she were at the lake? She would have a drink with him. Nothing would happen, though. They had breached the void, but perhaps come to an understanding. He remembered the smoke and fire of the katikala. The taste was nothing to write home about, but he craved the dullness and buzz.

Reece pulled into the rinkydink strip mall and parked. He felt that maybe he was a man now and had earned the privilege of man things. A cowbell on the door jangled, and he nodded to the skinny man behind the counter. Before him lay a sea of bottles, and he had no idea what he was looking for.

"Help ya?" asked the man. He wore new overalls with a clean white t-shirt and had three days of gray stubble.

"Just browsing," said Reece. He stumbled. Without wasting time, he headed straight for a brown bottle with a fancy label. It was Drambuie, 750 ml, and he lifted it, feeling its weight. He figured it would do and, without pausing, headed to the register, his heart pounding as if he had stolen something.

"Twenty-four even," said the man.

Reece fished bills out of his pocket, took his change and the paper bag, said thank you, and passed back out into the brilliant heat. He was already on the pier, or maybe in the RV, having a sip. Imagining his small room, the candle, the Bible, the letters from Kristin, he skipped back to Godo. He could smell the cook smoke and feel the flies drilling into the corners of his eyes. But he had to get a job, get back in the hospital, and earn his keep. He asked himself why, but could only think of needing money to buy things, and that seemed a poor excuse. There was the CT scan in a few days. He wondered what the point was. What would it show that would do him good? Maybe he would need to take Dilantin for his seizures, but he was convinced that it was temporary. He would just cancel the appointment. He couldn't afford it anyway, and Horace had already paid his hospital bill, which he knew was enormous. Were things falling into place? He couldn't decide, and he missed his turn.

"Dammit."

The F-150 did a U-turn, and Reece was along for the ride, soon passing into Palmerdale and out to the lake. He drove, mesmerized by the tall pines and the rolling green hills blanketed in kudzu. There was more to life, a lot more, and he made a promise to find it in all its glory.

Back at the Mission, there was a late dinner at the Guthrie's. Emma spooned in a mouthful of cubed potatoes cooked in butter. Abebe was alive, but could easily die. While there, they'd seen Misrak. Emma had peeked beneath the bloody bandage and seen heavy stitches and three drains. There was no guarantee she would live.

"What a day," said Guthrie for the third time in a row. He was sweating.

Emma nodded and poked at a piece of fried tilapia from the freezer.

"You two need to get some rest," said Livvie. She stirred the potatoes in a brown bowl to keep a film from forming on top.

"I'll need to get with Ben to see about funds to pay for the bills for Misrak and the girl. This might call for a special requisition from headquarters in Virginia." He scratched his buzz cut.

"I could try and raise some money when I get back to the States," said Emma.

"It'll be in the thousands, perhaps fifteen or twenty." He sopped his fish in hot Merti ketchup. "Any money you can raise would be helpful. I imagine your church is going to want you to speak about your experiences here."

"So, when do I leave? I mean, what about the attack? I was raped."

Livvie nearly spat out her tea. "Oh my. So, it's true."

"Yeah, not that I want to talk about it. But something should happen to those soldiers. They'll do it again."

Emma felt lightheaded and distant from the room. The yellow light from the ceiling bulb made the wood paneling look like Graham crackers. The ranch-style house didn't belong there, seeming like a movie.

Guthrie pushed back from the table and crossed his legs. "I hate to be honest, but we'll likely never be able to identify them. I'd shoot them myself if the opportunity arose." His face turned red, and his sun squint was in full force.

"Maybe you should give us guns when we travel," said Emma.

Livvie was shaking her head no.

"Government won't allow it. That's big trouble if we're caught with guns of any kind. But we could start sending a guard along."

"Especially if there are women," said Livvie. She kept stirring the potatoes as if an unexpected guest might arrive.

"You're right, and I'm sorry that we've gotten kind of lax. Nothing like that has ever happened before," said Guthrie. "But still, if you can, I'd like to have a report of what happened to submit to the embassy here, to have it on record. Maybe you can do that tomorrow, just write down the facts, what you remember."

Emma frowned. "Right. But I don't know that I can do that right now. It might have to wait until I get back home."

"Well, that's fine," said Guthrie. He looked at the ceiling and yawned. "Damn kerosene. A kid shouldn't be handling kerosene, especially around a fire. My God."

"She looked horrible. Makes my situation seem kind of thin. At least I'm...alive." Emma shook her head and ate her last bite of fried fish. "Real good, Livvie. Hit the spot."

Livvie had been holding her breath and pressing her hands between her knees. She took a deep breath. "You're welcome. You want more? There's plenty."

"Tagabjallo," said Emma. "I am satisfied."

"I'm going to run over to Ben and Teresa's and then hit the hay," said Guthrie. "Emma, you want to go?"

"It's dark outside. You driving or walking?"

"I can drive if that suits you." He stood and went to get his jacket and keys.

"Yeah, that suits me," said Emma. It suddenly occurred to her that she could call home. She needed to call her mom, but wanted to call Reece. What would she tell him, that soldiers had raped her? How would he respond? Was he hoping for some pristine virgin like Kristin? "I'm ready when you are. Let me go pull on a sweatshirt, though. Livvie, can I help with the dishes? I hate to have to cook and wash dishes."

"No, no, for goodness' sake, go with Norbert. I've got this. It's my calling, one of my gifts, washing dishes."

Emma laughed. "Is that in the Bible, washing dishes?"

"I'd have to look it up, but my guess is no." She gathered the plates and silverware.

"Where's your concordance when you need it?" asked Emma. "Not in your pocket?"

Livvie laughed, seeming relieved. "You're a smart cookie, Emma, and we love you." She gave Emma a big hug.

"Thanks."

"Ready?" asked Guthrie. He wore a loose windbreaker.

Guthrie pulled the Toyota van onto the road, driving as slow as possible. Figures of men and women filled the bright headlights. He cut the lights according to custom and crept along, turning them on every few seconds and then off. At the Mission gate, he beeped, and the gate swung in, the guard wrapped in a shamma, shouldering his rifle.

They walked together to the Ashberrys. The door was open, and Guthrie knocked. Little Claude came storming up, stopped in front of the door, and made a low growling sound. Teresa, in a traditional Ethiopian dress with gold fringes, appeared in the dim light and opened the screen door.

"Well, hey!" She held her newborn Kimo in one arm. "Come in. Ben's eating by himself. Claude, step back, son." Claude ran and jumped onto a soft chair, making clawing motions with his hands like he was a tiger.

Guthrie walked ahead and met Ben in the dining room. He was picking at a whole roasted chicken cooked in a crockpot. They gave each other grim looks.

"Hey," said Emma. "Good to see you."

Ben stood as if expecting a hug, and Emma obliged. "You okay?" asked Ben. "We've been worried sick about you." His natural Florida tan looked yellow in the light from the single bulb. He wore thick glasses like Claude, and his eyes seemed to swim behind the lenses.

"You guys ate?" asked Teresa. "Chicken, just chicken and some enjera."

"Just ate," said Guthrie. "Had some surprises on the way." He told Ben about the little burned girl.

The group of four stood very close to each other, unsure of what to do, whether to sit or remain standing. Emma coughed and suggested they sit. "Good idea," said

Ben, and they gathered in the crowded living room.

Ben made small talk, and Teresa told them about a basket-weaving class she was taking with a local woman. Emma fidgeted, knowing they wanted to hear about the attack, the rape. There was silence, and wind soughed through the house. In the distance, a dog barked. Someone was shouting.

"We've got to talk about money to pay for the hospital bills," said Guthrie. His words fell flat.

"Yeah, we can figure that out," said Ben. He held Claude between his legs, squeezing him.

"So, when am I headed out?" asked Emma.

Everyone looked at everyone.

"I'll have Tesfaw arrange a ticket out," said Ben. "It could be tomorrow or a week from now, just depends."

Emma looked relieved. She felt guilty about wanting to get out as fast as possible. "No hurry."

"Right," said Ben.

Teresa excused herself to change so that she could feed Kimo.

"So—" said Ben.

"What do you think about these soldiers who attacked me?" asked Emma. "I suppose that's the elephant in the room. One held me while the other one raped me. Took turns...The fat one held a gun on Craig." She could see his smooth face, could feel the weight of the soldiers on top of her. One had smelled like vomit. "I smelled vomit. I wanted to vomit. I want to vomit right now." And she did feel sick talking about it.

Both Guthrie and Ben shook their heads.

"I feel awful for you," said Ben. "We'll do what we can.

But it's not guaranteed that anything will happen."

"That's a shame," said Emma. She felt her heart thudding in her neck and chest.

Silence reigned all around. Teresa emerged from the bedroom in jeans and a flannel shirt unbuttoned, little Kimo sucking madly at her exposed breast. Emma remembered the soldier doing the same to her and looked away.

"Why the sad faces?" asked Teresa. "Want to see the basket I'm working on?"

"Honey, Emma is telling us about the attack."

"Oh," said Teresa. "Should I leave?"

"No, but maybe we're not interested in your basket just now."

Teresa slumped and adjusted Kimo in her lap. "I'm sorry." She tried to make eye contact with Emma.

"Yeah, no biggie. I'm alive, right?" asked Emma, making fists.

"Maybe, she just needs to talk to me," said Teresa.

Ben and Guthrie looked at each other.

"I don't want to talk about it," said Emma. "That fucker raped me!" She stood and sat back down, a dry heave working its way from her feet to her head. "Dammit! My whole church is praying for me, and this happens! What's the point, even?" Tears wanted to flow, but seemed stuck behind her eyes.

"Emma," said Guthrie. "Get it out. Let it come out."

Kimo sucked and sucked, lost the nipple, hiccupped, and found it again.

"Dammit to hell," said Emma. "If Reece had been here...never would have happened. He would have protected me. Right? Gun or no gun. We were the perfect team." And then she broke down, sobbing into a throw cushion, gritting her teeth, and seething.

No one moved, and they let her misery pour like an angry flood.

"Why? Why?" and the sobs evened into soft whimpers. "God, I'm such a big baby! Is God testing me?"

Teresa had wanted to say that very thing.

"Well, I get a big fat F...What time is it?"

Teresa looked at her watch. "It's about ten."

That would be two in the afternoon back home.

"Can I use your phone?" asked Emma, wiping at her tears.

Reece pulled into the driveway behind the long Buick in the garage. He left the liquor in the truck and opened the squeaky door. Cindy's little Honda sat in the Sykes' driveway next door. The back screen door opened.

"Reece! It's that girl from Africa on the phone. Hurry!" said Dora.

Reece tripped and fell. He picked himself up and lumbered into the house. Horace was in his recliner, holding the phone like a banana.

Reece took the phone and its tangled cord and sat in Dora's recliner. The silence sounded far away. "Hello?" His pulse quickened.

Emma heard his voice. "Reece?"

"Hey, Emma." He felt a chill and shivered. "Yeah, it's me."

"Reece, I think I'm losing my mind, and I'm coming home, maybe tomorrow." Why was she whispering?

Reece strained to hear her. Had she said she was coming home? "Wow, back to Alabama?"

Emma perked up. "Well, that's home, right?"

"Of course, home. You calling from the Guthries?"

"No, I'm at Ben and Teresa's."

"So, you're in Addis. Are they closing the clinic?"

"In a month. The team is still there. How are you doing? It's so great to hear your voice." She sat on the unmade bed. The handset was heavy and black. The room smelled kind of like poop.

"Yeah, good to hear yours too. I can't believe you're

headed back."

"Reece, will you meet me at the airport? I need to see you."

Reece felt tingly, imagining her walking through the gate at the airport. "Sure, just let me know when."

"Will Kristin care?" She looked into the dark mirror and saw the wall behind her. Her bedroom at her mom's house was similar. Maybe she was already back in Alabama, and it would only take Reece about forty-five minutes to get there.

"Hmm, maybe not, considering everything that's happened." He felt his heart beating in his throat. Had he forgone sex with Cindy because of Kristin, or Emma?

"Reece, I was attacked on Saturday, driving from Addis. I was with Craig. These three soldiers were following us in a Land Rover."

"Jesus. Did you get hurt? You okay?"

"Yeah, they hurt me." She wanted to say that she needed him.

"Damn it all," said Reece. He wanted to ask if they had raped her. "I wish I had been there."

"We had stopped to pee. Some enormous boulders. One, a fat guy, had a pistol."

"No." Reece remembered stopping to pee when he rode with Craig to Alem Ketema, the huge boulders. He'd been there, knew what it looked like. He could see three soldiers, one fat and with a gun.

"I'm staying at the Guthrie's tonight. As soon as he heard, he flew up with Terry and said that I was done. I wasn't scared when they were doing it, but all of a sudden, I am now. What if something happens, and I can't leave? I feel like I have a bucket over my head."

"I know the feeling, or maybe I don't. Damn, that pisses me off. Any idea of whether or not they'll be caught?" He thought he knew the answer.

"No. Guthrie says no. They're soldiers and do as they damn well please. Can you promise to meet me at the airport? You can drive me to my mom's, and we'll surprise her. I want you to meet her."

"I promise." Reece saw his life spinning out before his eyes. Kristin. Emma. Cindy. Dora. Horace. Kristin's pet squirrel. He pinched his thigh, pushed his feet into the carpet.

"Oh, thank you, thank you. You're the only one who will ever understand. You know that, right?"

Reece could only think that she'd saved his life that night. Shouldn't that be enough for Kristin to understand? But she'd want to come along too if he told her. Maybe he wouldn't tell her, but then what?

"Reece? You there?" There were regular beeps on the line.

"Hey, yeah, here. Sorry. When will you know when you're coming back? I'm going to apply for a job, get back to nursing, as Granny says. Maybe this week."

A wave of sudden joy surged inside Emma. She choked. "Maybe, maybe tomorrow. Tesfaw will check on a ticket. I'll probably have an overnight layover, so it'll take me two days."

"Better than being evacuated in a Med-Jet, I guess." He tried to laugh but only wheezed.

Emma laughed. "Sorry. God, I'm jealous that you're there and I'm here. I kind of feel like the TV went haywire and there's nothing but static. I need to get out of here bad. I'd walk if it were quicker. This place is trying to kill me. Reece, I'm terrified I'll never see you again. That something bad will happen. I've never felt like this."

"You're a tough cookie. Just take a deep breath. Everything will work out."

"God, I hope you're right…" and the line went dead.

Emma sat with the receiver pressed to her ear. The dial tone. There was no dial tone. She hung up and listened. The phone was dead, and that happened just like the power going off several times a week. She dialed the operator anyway, but with no response. "Shit." She put the phone in its cradle and felt a wave of panic. Reece had said to take a deep breath, and so she did. Maybe he would call her back, but the phone was dead. Claude scratched at the door, pretending to be a three-toed sloth. He pushed open the door and walked in like a robot, sniffing the air with a tight face.

"What happened?" asked Dora. "She okay?" She stood in front of the sink drying the skillet with a dishtowel, the one with a plaid pattern.

Reece sat there looking at the phone, the dial tone humming. "Guess the phone went dead over there. She's coming home, probably this week."

Horace's hearing aid squealed. "What you say?"

Reece twisted toward him. "I said that Emma's leaving Ethiopia, coming home. This week."

"Who's Emma?" He took out his hearing aid in disgust and fiddled with it.

"Horace, she's that nurse who saved his life in Africa when he got shot. Lord, what will Kristin think? Reece, you gotta be careful with what you do. You hear?"

"I know, but she wants me to meet her at the airport and drive her home. I can't say no." He hung up the phone.

Dora frowned. "That might be what breaks the camel's back."

"Camels?" asked Horace. He wedged his hearing aid back in.

"For Pete's sake, Horace, listen." She put the skillet in the drawer beneath the stove. "Reece is engaged, and this Emma is wanting him to pick her up at the airport. She might have saved his life, but he's not engaged to her." She put her hands on her hips.

"Okay, okay, hold your horses," said Horace. "I got a hearing problem in case you forgot."

"I don't forget. I live with it every day!" She tackled the stainless-steel sink with her scrub pad and some Comet. "He just has to watch his p's and q's, that's all. Reece, are you listening?"

Reece leaned back in the recliner and popped up the footrest. "Loud and clear. I wonder if I'm up to run to the dam and back. I had another seizure at the hospital today. I think I need to exercise to get my brain back on track."

"What? No, certainly not," said Dora. "Horace, did you hear that? Another seizure, and he says he wants to run to the dam!"

"Boy, don't press your luck," said Horace.

"No, that's what I need. A good sweat. Get my heart running, clear the cobwebs. I used to run around the lake three times."

"It's the hottest part of the day, boy," said Horace.

"All the better," said Reece. "I'm doing it."

Dora shook her head and rinsed the sink. "One stubborn human being you are. What if we have to call an ambulance?"

"Well, call the cheap one." Reece laughed. He stood, felt woozy, and went to his bedroom to find his running shoes.

Laced up and wearing his favorite blue shorts and no shirt, Reece walked to the road in front of the house. He saw Cindy in the hammock next door, talking to her grandmother. He remembered the Drambuie in the truck and felt his groin tingle. He wished away an erection and started doing jumping jacks and bending over to stretch. Cindy was waving. He turned and checked the slight bulge in his shorts and cursed. He pretended like he didn't see her, but then gave up and walked over.

"Boy," said Mrs. Sykes. "You lost your shirt?"

"Going for a run, ma'am."

"Going for a run?" asked Cindy. "It's hot as blue blazes." She adjusted her tube top.

Reece felt naked in his shorts. "I used to do it all the time. Makes me feel good, works out the tension."

"Are you crazy, boy?" asked Mrs. Sykes. "Does your granny know?"

"Oh yeah. Already got an earful from her. Cindy, want to go with me?"

Cindy laughed. "In my flip-flops? Sure."

"Yeah, right." Reece admired her tanned feet.

"What would your doctor say?" asked Mrs. Sykes.

"I don't really have a doctor. My body needs it, I think. It's only a half mile to the dam. I can walk if I get winded." He wondered what he would do if he had a seizure, squirm on the hot pavement?

"Maybe when I get back and get a shower, we can play cards in the RV?" asked Reece. "It's in the shade."

Cindy smiled. "I don't know, maybe. If you survive your run." She laughed.

Mrs. Sykes frowned. Ringlets of gray hair clung to her sweaty forehead. "Cindy, you know he's engaged, or so I hear."

"I know. He told me so." She adjusted herself in the hammock.

"Okay. I'm off! To the dam!" He folded his arms across his chest, already sweating, and turned back to the road.

"Break a leg, or don't!" said Cindy.

"He's crazy," said Mrs. Sykes.

"Just a little," said Cindy.

Reece walked at first and then developed a slow trot. His shoelaces were too tight, and he experimented with letting his feet fall one way and then another. The first bend in the road led to a steep hill, and Reece determined to make it to the top. Right away, he felt his heart pounding, and he felt short of breath, but damned if you do and damned if you don't.

The incline steepened on the narrow two-lane, and Reece seemed almost to be climbing stairs. He tried breathing through his nose and gave that up right away, sucking for air. He took the hill, going from a mailbox to a tree to a dead animal plastered into the pavement, breaking up his run into short increments. The hill curved, leveled for twenty feet, and then rose again. Sweat streamed down his back and trickled down his face. He felt alive and focused on the next mailbox, imagining that a rope was pulling him there.

"Hell."

As he neared the top of the hill, the lake opened up to his left, and he took it in, almost forgetting that he was running. He lunged, gasping for breath, arteries in his head pounding. He'd just talked to Emma, and his thoughts turned to her.

After losing the connection, Emma rejoined Guthrie and the Ashberrys. No further talk of her attackers emerged. After an hour of idle chat, Emma and Guthrie drove back to his house and bedded down for the night, but Emma couldn't sleep. Why had the damn line gone dead and stayed dead when it did? She made fists. Maybe she should read her Bible, but she had left it in Godo, maybe do her devotional, pray. She fumbled in her travel bag for *My Utmost for His Highest* and picked a random entry.

"...how much more will your Father who is in heaven give good things to those who ask Him!" —Matthew 7:11.

She wondered if there was an exclamation point there and tossed the book onto the bureau, crowded with mementos of Guthrie's son: a generic trophy, a pill bottle of pebbles, a certificate for demonstrating excellent telephone etiquette. Should she ask Him for safe passage? Should she ask Him to kill her attackers? Should she ask Him that Reece and Kristin split up? Why didn't Jesus ever marry or have a girlfriend? Why was He always wanting the little children to sit on his lap?

She lay on the bed, feeling the cold from outside. She imagined there was no insulation in the walls, and she was right. What to do? She remembered the small packet of generic Valium in her bag. She'd taken one every so often in Godo to help her sleep. There had been 5,000 10-milligram tablets in the can, and a few missing wouldn't hurt. She remembered the young girl, only twelve, who had married an old man. He bothered her night and day for sex, and she looked haggard, like an old woman. She had given the girl a handful of the tablets and told her to take one at night, that and some vitamins. What else could she do for her? She hadn't come back for more and had most likely sold them, according to Afewerki. Emma dry swallowed a pill.

She imagined Afewerki in his little house, the white hen roosting above his bed in the rafters. She wondered if she had really promised to sponsor him to come to the States, and she had, and she supposed that it would take care of itself. She would love to help him, to help all of them and wondered if he had asked the same thing of the Icelandic nurses. She shivered and wanted to crawl under the covers, but the dim light was on. She imagined it was the only heat in the room, and it was. Her mind drifted back two years to a party she'd attended, a buddy from nursing school, Celeste, with huge breasts. There had been alcohol and cocaine, and she'd awoken on the floor of the kitchen, her pants askew. She was pretty sure she'd been violated in some manner, but couldn't tell for sure. There had been several guys there, all hitting on her.

"Dammit."

She turned to her side, feeling the bruises on her shoulder and thighs, and doubted her qualifications to serve others, to work in God's name. After the party incident, she'd quit drinking, thrown herself into church, and started dating a Christian guy named Matt. He was the one who had shown her the ads in the Alabama Baptist, calling for volunteer nurses in Ethiopia. She wouldn't have known that Ethiopia was in Africa had it not been for Band-Aid and "Do They Know It's Christmas?" They had discussed her leaving one Sunday evening after church at a Wendy's, eating chocolate Frosties. She remembered the surge of passion she'd felt, the tripwire of excitement building in her to be a part of something so large and grand. Matt had been completely taken by surprise at her enthusiasm and quit talking to her for a week. He wanted kids and more church, solid right there in Alabama. She wanted excitement wherever it might take her, children and church be damned. He had taken her to the airport, but only dropped her off in front.

"Idiot."

Why had Reece wanted to come? She'd never had the opportunity to learn why, and she made fists again. How long had he been there before he was shot, a month and a half, two months? She imagined having dinner with him, maybe visiting Gulf Shores with him, where her sister worked as the manager of the State Park restaurant. She thought about her desire to become a certified SCUBA diver and knew in her heart that he would take lessons with her. His hands on her breasts.

She flopped onto her stomach, the bed squeaking, and pulled a pillow over her head. She wanted to scream. She wanted to call Reece again, but it was too late.

A few minutes passed, her arms getting tingly from being over her head. She remembered working at UAB Hospitals. The noise and confusion, the patients sitting up in bed and dying a few minutes later. The clinic in Godo had been hell at times, but she was in control, although just barely, it seemed. She loved the people and the work, especially when Reece was there.

She rolled to her back and sat up, her feet above the

floor. The mattress was firm but soft. There was a toilet and a hot shower just down the hall. All those things would be hers again when she returned. One hot tear. She stood and walked to the wall switch, turning off the light and crawling beneath the quilts and sheets that smelled of Omo detergent. Her thoughts turned to the zoo in Birmingham, the sad polar bear with yellow fur, and the old orangutan who seemed so lonely. Maybe she would fight to set them free. Perhaps she and Reece could undertake a grand task together and do good things back in the heartland. She massaged her buttock where the penicillin had gone in. Her hands had been shaking, and she was sure that she had closed her eyes.

"Those dirty bastards."

In the dark, she could hear the vague roar of an airplane and imagined being on it, flying away from this place. The plane would probably fly straight to Rome or maybe to Amsterdam. There would be no more Amharic, no more tapeworms. How would she act? Was she a different person? She felt that she could rule the world one second and that she was a broken twig the next.

What were Reece's grandparents like? She imagined them as solid old people, steeped in the same ways as her mother. She would get to know them, love them, share stories with them of how good Reece was in the clinic, of how he had been a godsend.

She curled into a tight ball, trying to hold onto the feeling. Maybe they would grow old together, maybe travel the world, maybe come back one day together to Ethiopia.

Emma realized her eyes were open and closed them. She reached with one hand to make sure they were closed.

She saw streaks of red on black and watched the patterns swirl.

There was a sound of knocking. Emma opened her eyes and realized where she was.

"Emma?" It was Dr. Guthrie.

Emma sat up, wearing her bra and underwear. "Hey!"

"We may have you on a flight today. Tesfaw just called."

Emma looked around for a clock. "What time is it?"

"It's about ten."

"Ten?" She threw back the covers. "Give me a minute."

She stood and put on her socks, and then remembered her shirt and pants. "Holy cow." She hesitated in front of the bureau mirror. She still looked like she was asleep. Was she dreaming? "Hot dog!"

Emma opened the door, "Be right there," and walked to the bathroom. The mauve tile looked fake. The sink was pristine, arranged with two toothbrushes and a plastic container of baking soda for brushing. She turned on the tap and splashed cold water on her face. What had Guthrie said?

She stumbled into the hall and then the spacious living room, windows of light, shafts of pure joy. She saw Guthrie in the doorway to the kitchen, Livvie just beyond him.

"Hey!" said Emma.

"Livvie's got some coffee going," said Guthrie. He touched his buzz cut with both hands.

"Coffee? You said something about a flight?" She stood up straight to hear the news again.

"Yep, leaves at noon, stops in Nairobi, and then to Amsterdam. You'll spend the night there." Guthrie frowned.

"That's good news, right?" asked Emma.

"Hate to lose you is all," said Guthrie.

Emma choked up and recovered. "I don't know what to say. It's all so fast."

"Yeah, well, we better take it while we have it. Not many outgoing seats open up like that. It could take weeks otherwise."

"Thank you." Emma felt chilled, and goosebumps washed her body. "Gosh, what do I need to do? I want to say goodbye to the folks in the compound."

"We have time to do that. Ben and Teresa know you're coming over. You'll need to get your passport from Tesfaw in the office. Do you have any dollars on you?"

"I still have the two hundred I brought over," said Emma.

"That'll get you home. Just have to buy food. Everything else is taken care of."

"I've never been to Amsterdam."

Livvie brought her a cup of coffee. "Gonna miss you, girl."

Emma hugged her, spilling hot coffee on her leg. "Ah!"

"Careful," said Livvie. "You must be thrilled." She handed her the cup, a real cup, not a plastic orange famine cup.

"Holy cow, I don't know what to say."

"We loved having you, Emma," said Guthrie. He let Emma give him a one-armed hug. "Relax a minute and drink your coffee."

"So, will you guys still be here? They're not shutting the whole mission down?"

"We'll be there awhile. The Mission's been here since the late sixties. I've got another six years to retire." He sat.

"Sit down. Enjoy your coffee."

Emma sat on the brown couch, worn in places, but a real-deal American couch. She imagined the plaid couch at her mom's house. She'd made out with more than one guy on that couch.

"What will you do first?" asked Livvie. She never sat down, always moving, cooking, cleaning.

Emma thought. "Well, I think Reece is picking me up from the airport."

Guthrie and Livvie exchanged looks.

"He's worried what his fiancée will think, though. Heck, maybe we'll go to McDonald's, strange as it sounds. I want him to meet my mom."

"You're not the first who's said McDonald's," said Guthrie. "The first thing we like to do when we go back is head to the KFC." He laughed. "Finger lickin' good."

"That and take a long, hot shower with my special shampoo, cucumber soap, and a big, soft towel that smells like Tide," said Emma.

"Well, all we have here is Omo," said Livvie. Did Emma think that her towels were not soft and fluffy?

"Always Omo," said Guthrie. "Well, look. I've got some meetings around town today. Tesfaw is going to drive you to the airport. Not sure if anyone else can go with you. Thomas is up-country and his wife Betsy, well, you know, she doesn't like to leave the house, plus the kids." He looked to Livvie.

"I can go," said Livvie. "That way you'll remember me and not old grumpy Dr. Guthrie here."

"Hey now," said Guthrie. He wagged his finger at Livvie.

"Yeah, that'd be great. Will you make sure that Misrak

gets back to Godo? I hate to leave her in the hospital. She looked rough. And the little girl, too."

Guthrie sighed. "Of course. We'll do our best. You've done your part."

Emma wondered if that was true.

"You probably need to go ahead and get over there, say your goodbyes. You packed?" asked Guthrie.

"Just a couple of things to go. But I'm as ready as ever."

"Good, good. We'll get Tesfaw to pick Livvie up along the way." Guthrie sighed again.

Within fifteen minutes, Guthrie and Emma drove into the Mission's main compound. Ben and Teresa were home, and there were hugs and tears all around, except for Claude, who was a lizard today, darting his tongue in and out, making his eyes into slits. Guthrie walked Emma over to say goodbye to Betsy and her boys and then headed to the office.

Inside, Tesfaw sat at his desk, tapping away at an adding machine. In the back, the printing press clanked. Tesfaw was settling Emma's accounts, her phone bills. With a grim look, he informed her that she owed the Mission 630 birr, a little over 300 dollars.

"Jesus," said Emma.

Guthrie waved his hand. "We'll take care of it, Tesfaw. Just charge it to the Mission. She's earned it."

"Yes," said Tesfaw. He looked a little sour and handed Emma her passport.

Emma took it and looked at her photo. Her hair was wonky, and she had a big smile. She remembered having the photo taken, seeming like yesterday. "Thank you. I can't thank you enough." The tears were back, and she just let them fall one at a time.

Guthrie checked his watch. "We have to get you there ASAP. Do you have your reconciliation form that you got when you arrived, declaring how much cash you brought in? You'll need that."

"Gee, I don't think so. Oh, it was in my Bible. I left it in Godo."

Tesfaw looked alarmed. "They will not let you go, but there is a way."

Guthrie nodded. "They'll take you into a little curtained room and ask for it. Just put twenty birr on the table and everything should be fine. No need to explain anything. Just say that you lost it. You have twenty birr?"

"No. I gave all of my birr to Afewerki to give to Misrak's family."

Guthrie nodded. "Tesfaw?"

Tesfaw was frowning again. He leaned over to a small safe and withdrew a pouch. Emma took the twenty. "Thank you."

"Okay, you're ready to go," said Guthrie. His face flushed red as he gave her one last hug. "You take care. When we come back on furlough, I'll set up a speaking date at your church."

"You'll make your money back, twice over," said Emma.

"I wasn't thinking about that," said Guthrie. "It all balances out in the end. Now go, go. Tesfaw, let's get this girl on a plane. Stop over and get Livvie."

"Ishi," said Tesfaw. He grabbed his crutches and stood, wearing his baggy blue suit.

Guthrie held the door for them, and soon Emma was in the van looking over her shoulder as they pulled onto the road—a knot of emotion that seemed impossible to unravel.

Reece plunged downhill, hardly able to hold back from the momentum. The run up had nearly paralyzed his butt muscles, and now the run down was cramping his thighs. He slowed to almost a walk. Emma was coming home. She wanted him to pick her up at the airport. He imagined her walking through the gate, tan and fit, wearing that half smile that made his heart skip a beat.

Before he knew it, he was at the concrete dam, a thin film of water pouring over to the next small lake below. He took the wooden walkway across to the earthen part of the dam, looking down into the greeny water at the stringy moss and rocks. A turtle slid into the water with a bloop. He decided to go all the way around.

Reece plodded along the long, straight road until it hit the steep, short hill up to the other side. He got halfway up and had to stop and catch his breath. He walked to the top and bore left, a bit wobbly. The next long section of road was hilly, with the lake off to his left. He heard the dog and then saw him, a big white muscle with a clipped tail. The dog growled and circled behind him, closing in fast. Reece veered to the runoff ditch and picked up a jagged rock. He turned, and walking backward, cocked his arm. The dog stopped, lurched away, and kept up its deep-throated growl. He threw the rock over the dog into the woods and turned back, barely able to keep up with his breathing.

The dips in the road gave him the strength to struggle up the small hills. He thought about the steep and rocky paths in Godo, how everything was either up or down, how the women walked stooped over, noses nearly to the ground, with heavy loads of firewood or water. He tried to quicken his pace but couldn't.

He remembered he was supposed to go to the hospital and fill out an application to be rehired. There was the open 11-7 position in the ICU at Carraway. Was that the best option? He'd always wanted to work at UAB Hospitals, where Emma had worked. He wondered how that might play out. Kristin would be livid, and he let the thought go. A car passed, and he waved. Sweat streamed down his face and back. He drifted to that morning in the boathouse with Cindy and let out a huge sigh. She would probably still be there when he finished the run, just under five miles around the lake, and he had the Drambuie in the truck. Thinking about the alcohol kind of made him sick, and he wished he hadn't spent his money on it. What the hell did he want? He felt like kicking himself. Maybe God had punished him for being such a wishy-washy fool.

The road dipped to just above lake level. Across the water, he could see his grandparents' house, the pier, perhaps half a mile away. Where would he be without them? They had taken him in after his parents were killed inside Luby's in Texas. He'd finished out his junior year and then his senior year at the high school nearby, and that had suited him just fine. He loved the lake. He loved his grandparents, maybe even more than his parents.

His parents' funeral had been a boondoggle. When his grandparents found out that his dad had bought a cemetery plot for himself and Reece's mom in Texas, they freaked. Why the hell did they want to be buried in Texas, so far away from home? It had been his mom's idea. He knew it. She had always disliked his dad's parents and resented their attention to him.

When he was born, his mom had gone nuts, shamed at having to breastfeed him and suffering a severe case of depression and psychosis. She had, at one point in her misery, thrown Reece against the wall of their tiny trailer. His dad's parents had stepped in and taken Reece back to Alabama from the Army base in Georgia to care for him the first six months of his life. He'd bonded with Horace and Dora, and that was that. He recalled a night in Birmingham when he was only four or five. He'd been crying to visit his grandparents, who lived about a mile away. His dad was away in Vietnam. His mom had stormed through the house screaming and packed him a suitcase, dressed him in a Sunday suit with a matching hat, put him outside on the porch, and slammed the door.

Reece shook his head and couldn't remember running the last quarter mile. He heaved for breath, heading uphill. Sweat stained his shorts. He'd just stood on the porch, looking out to the dimly lit street, and had begun crying, hitting the door with his fists for what seemed like hours until she let him in. Reece picked up his pace, feeling as angry as he was sorry for his mother. She was possibly the most miserable person he had ever met, and his father had followed close behind.

At the other end of the lake, the road began a series of lefts and rights, working its way up a mild grade to the main road through the area. He recalled the funeral. Both caskets had been closed. He'd wept, but mostly because he felt guilty at being left behind. At the time, he'd wished that he'd been shot in the head as well. Better late than never. The solo of "Amazing Grace" had left everyone crying, and then they were buried in the flat ground near Killeen, Texas. And then he'd moved to Alabama to be with his grandparents. They had saved his life again.

On the main road, Reece ran against traffic, fenced pasture to either side. There was no median, just a white stripe with about six inches of pavement. When a car passed, he looked down and watched his feet, staying outside the line. The dry yellow grass grew three feet tall in the ditch, a huge hill of red ants, a watermelon someone had thrown out, beer cans. He wasn't running anymore as he was fast walking. Every step seemed like a leap, and his body ached from the strain.

Finally, houses again, but a steep, short hill ensued. He couldn't keep the sweat from his eyes, which burned with the salt. He couldn't do it and had to slow to a painful walk to get up the hill. His thoughts went to his mom's parents, the other grandparents. That grandfather had never really liked him, and the grandmother had been a kind of shadow figure, living in fear of her temperamental husband. Reece felt sorry for her and had never really bonded with her. She just cooked and slept in a beat-up recliner that sat in the dining room in front of the farmhouse's lone air conditioner.

One last downhill before the turn to the lake, and Reece held back to keep from pitching forward head over heels. A moat of cattails. More houses. A curve. The community swimming pool, closed for the year, and then a straight shot to the house on the right. He stopped about a block away and walked with his hands on his hips, feeling desperate for air and water or maybe a bottle of Coke.

He could see Horace in the garden, wearing his straw hat. Cindy's car was still next door, but she wasn't outside.

"Boy, you'll kill yourself."

Reece jumped. "Sheesh." Dora was sitting on the metal swing, shelling lima beans.

"Man, that felt so good." Reece bent over and took deep breaths.

"Looks like you've been to the swimming hole. My, you're sweaty. Sit here and cool down in the shade." She ran her thumb up the spine of a butterbean, pushing out the speckled coins into a plastic bowl.

"Yeah, sounds lovely." He plopped into a folding chair and wiped sweat from his face for the hundredth time. "I'll be sore tomorrow." He could hear the beans dropping into the pan, a wind through the tops of the pines.

"Let me ask you something," said Dora.

"Yeah."

"Your granddaddy went to the truck and found a bottle in a paper bag. Said it was something called Rambo…"

Reece coughed. "Rambo?" He laughed, and then laughed some more.

"What's so funny, boy?"

Reece felt his breath leave him as he laughed. He sat up and then doubled over. Rambo. He laughed for a good minute before he could speak.

"You done gone crazy," said Dora. "He said it was forty percent alcohol. That Rambo or whatever it is. That's dangerous, and you don't need to be fooling with stuff such as that."

"Rambo? It's something called Drambuie. I like Rambo better, though." His face felt tired from laughing. "I don't know why I bought it. I just did."

"Well, whatever it's called, you don't need it. You hear me? Tomorrow we're cutting corn, and I want you to help. We don't need a drunk laying around."

"So, where's the bottle?" asked Reece.

"I guess it's still in the truck. I don't want to see it. You just get rid of it, you hear?"

Reece stifled a laugh. "Yeah, okay. You're a real peach."

"Oh, don't try to sweet-talk me. I'm serious."

"I know. I know. No worries. I won't show up at church drunk."

"Better not. Get on inside and get yourself a shower. Plus, you're half naked. My mama would've never let one of her sons run around without a shirt."

"Yeah, I'll get all the housewives worked up and anxious." He laughed and stood. "Taking your advice to get a shower." He wondered if he should get the bottle out of the truck, being so hot outside, but decided another half hour wouldn't hurt. For some reason, he wanted to have a drink with Cindy. He felt like he owed her something.

Bole Road to the airport seemed to hold twice as many vehicles as possible. Tesfaw inched the van along, glancing at his watch. Emma was in danger of missing her flight. He blared his horn along with everyone else, muttering under his breath. Emma and Livvie sat behind him, chatting off and on.

"Is slow." Tesfaw looked in the rearview to search their eyes for sympathy. His withered legs ached.

The flight left at 12:20, and she still had to pick up her ticket. A man named Ben was to meet her with the ticket and itinerary. She wasn't exactly sure where she would meet him.

"What time is it again?"

"Eleven," said Livvie.

"Heaven help us," said Emma.

A Lada taxi tried to squeeze by on the right, half on the road, and Tesfaw cursed and hit the horn.

"We might have to try that, Tesfaw," said Livvie. "We can't miss this flight."

He needed a drink, some tejj to calm his nerves and relax his legs. "We will see," he said. He beeped the horn, hoping for a miracle.

"Did I give you the recipe for the homemade crackers?" asked Livvie. "I know you asked me."

"I wrote it down somewhere. I'll let you know when I get back. I wrote Mom about those crackers."

A man with no legs was making his way between the cars, sitting on a wooden skate with grocery-cart wheels.

He pushed himself with blocks of wood like ski poles. He paused beside the van and knocked on Tesfaw's door. Emma watched Tesfaw open his door and hand the man a birr. The man smiled and pressed his fingers to his lips, showing his single white tooth.

"Good man, Tesfaw," said Emma. She had to pee and bad.

"He will be crush-ed by the trucks," said Tesfaw as if he wanted to spit.

"Maybe not. I see him all the time," said Livvie. "I guess he's what you call a trooper."

"If you looked in the dictionary, you'd probably see his picture," said Emma. A feeling of sadness overcame her. Who would help these people? There were too many of them and not enough helpers. She worried that she was skipping out, that she was betraying the cause. "Life is strange and stranger."

"So, you said earlier that Reece would pick you up at the airport?"

Emma blushed. "I hope. I'll have to call him and let him know the details. I guess he'll have to get his fiancée's permission, though." She bit her lip.

The van lurched. Tesfaw had seen an opening and was on the median, speeding along as fast as possible, flashing his lights, blowing the horn. The airport parking lot was just ahead, but it seemed to be closed, with a military truck with a cargo of soldiers guarding it. Tesfaw assessed the situation, and there was only one thing to do.

"You must run," he said. "With your bag, you must run. There is something here, I don't know." He made eye contact with Emma.

"Dear Lord," said Livvie. "Tesfaw, are you sure?"

He was already stopped. "Open the door. Emma, you must go. It is the only way."

Without missing a beat, Emma slid the van door open and jumped out. Diesel and burning rubber. "I'm outta here. Take care, everyone." She slammed the door and threaded her way through four lanes of traffic toward the parking lot. She had to pass the truck with soldiers, some of whom were jeering at her. She felt like lead, but moved her feet. Without looking up, she stormed past the truck, feeling a hand on her arm that she shrugged away. Someone was yelling at her, and she kept going, headed toward the main entrance.

Two soldiers had followed, and one ran in front of her, trying to block her way. He ordered her to stop, but she shouldered him aside and then broke into a run. All sounds disappeared. A plane was airborne, and she stumbled over a loose shoelace. "Dammit."

In front of the entrance, perhaps a hundred people formed a mob, blocking her way. She pushed into them like a knife through butter, easing her way to an open door. "Aznallo, aznallo," she said, and then she was inside a large, vaulted room that looked like a gymnasium. It was less crowded, and she steered for the ticket counter, wondering how in the world she would find this Ben who had her ticket. Ethiopian Airlines, and the line was fifty deep. Desperate, she looked around. Was Ben an Ethiopian, a ferenj? Would he have a sign with her name on it?

She felt a hand on her shoulder and shrugged it away, determined to move forward.

"Mrs. Smith!"

Emma turned and faced a very short man. He had a British accent and held an envelope.

"Ben?" A flood of anticipation.

"Yes, yes. I need to see your passport." He wore a rumpled long-sleeve shirt and a loose paisley tie.

"Yeah, yeah." She pulled her passport from her front pocket and opened it for him. "Emma Smith."

"I'm glad I found you in this melee. Here is your ticket. You'll still need a boarding pass, I'm afraid."

"Thank you, thank you," said Emma. She hugged him and felt a pair of glasses in his shirt pocket. "Do I owe you anything?"

"No, the Mission will pay. They have an account. You are fortunate today."

"Great, thanks again," and she turned away to get in line, going sideways with her bag.

"Happy travels!" said Ben.

Emma came up short, pressing into a tall, handsome man in front of her. He turned and frowned, but had a watch.

"I'm sorry," said Emma. "Can you tell me the time?"

The man thrust out his arm and let her look at his watch, of which he was very proud.

"How could it be so late?" she said, but she could only wait.

"You are flying to Nairobi, no?" asked the man. He wore a floral perfume.

"I think so. Leaves at 12:20. I can't miss this flight."

The man laughed. "You have a ticket, no?"

"Yeah."

"No problem then."

"But there's not enough time. I think I'm supposed to be an hour early or they won't let me through."

The man had one tooth outlined in gold. His black suit was crisp, but the legs seemed large for him.

"This flight will be delayed. Do not worry. Perhaps one hour, two, maybe three. Who knows?" He laughed. "It is always the same. The pilots stay out late at the disco and cannot rise."

"Really?" said Emma. She wanted to believe him and settled in as the line inched forward.

For the next half hour, she chatted with the man. He was a coffee exporter and was on his way to Rome. His name was Leo, and he was married and had four children, all grown, one studying in London. Finally, it was her turn at the counter. She waved as Leo passed into the fray.

"Passport and ticket, please," said the clerk, all smiles, as if she and Emma were the only two people in the world.

Emma checked her front pockets and panicked, then felt her passport in her back pocket. "My flight leaves in twenty minutes."

"No, no," said the clerk. "This flight will leave at 4:30." She checked her in and handed her two boarding passes. "You are checking this bag?"

"I'll carry it," said Emma. A flood of calm overpowered her. "Thank you."

"Yiqirta," said the clerk. Her nametag said Abebe, another flower Emma was leaving behind.

"Amenseganolo," said Emma. "Which way?" and Abebe pointed. Emma nodded and was on her way to boarding. It seemed within reach, her leaving, and a surge passed through her as the crowd jostled her.

She came to another long line, where luggage was being searched. She was ready to give up her bag if necessary and rocked back and forth on her heels until it was her turn. A soldier in fatigues pointed to her bag and then the table. Emma placed her bag on the table. It said Jeep on the side. The man hesitated, and she realized he wanted her to open it, which she did. A dirty pair of underwear was on top, and Emma blushed as he poked through the contents: a pair of shorts, a tee-shirt, a blouse, a bra, one pair of maroon socks, a bundle of letters, and the rolled painting. She'd left her devotional behind at the Guthrie's. The man nodded okay, and Emma was on her way down the narrow hall to her gate, a soldier with an AK-47 every fifty feet or so.

She arrived at the gate ten minutes later, and it seemed the whole world was there to fly with her. There were no empty chairs, and she pushed her way to a beige wall, putting her bag between her feet. She had made it, or had she? She remembered she was supposed to show her cash declaration form to reconcile any money she had changed into birr. She was to bribe the person, leaving behind the twenty-birr note. A knot rose in her chest, and she looked around for another line, but there didn't seem to be one. One last hurdle, and she was free. She hoped.

Reece showered, shaved, and combed his hair. Vaguely, he expected the phone to ring. Would it be Emma? Or maybe Kristin? He felt dizzy, and wished that he didn't. Wearing clean shorts and a Gold's Gym muscle shirt, he stood in front of the air conditioner as it whummed.

Dora drowsed in her recliner, not quite taking a nap but almost. "What you up to now? You've had enough excitement for today, don't you think?"

"Nothing. I really should be working. I feel like a lazy bum."

"None of that booze, you hear? I told Horace to pour it out."

Reece laughed. "Want me to take Horace a glass of water? Awful hot out there."

"Do that, son. He'll appreciate it. I make him drink water."

"Yep, needs to stay hydrated, and you do, too." He went to the sink and fixed her an amber tumbler of water. "No ice for you. Too expensive. Here."

Dora took the glass and set it on a coaster. "I'll get to it."

"Let me check you out." He reached down, took her hand, and pinched the skin there. The skin took a couple of seconds to regain its shape. "You, my dear, are dehydrated. The proof is in the pudding. Drink."

Dora moaned and took a big swallow. "There, that good enough for you?"

"Nope, drink it all. That's one reason your heart flutters."

She took the glass and drank it down. "Now I'll wet myself."

"Ha," said Reece. "Bathroom's right there."

"You're a good boy."

"I hope so." He took a handful of ice from the freezer and made Horace's ice water.

"Don't you get in no trouble," said Dora.

Reece nodded and was out the back door, headed to the garden. Horace and Mr. Sykes were sitting beneath the black walnut tree.

"Hey now," said Reece. "Hey there, Mr. Sykes." He handed the glass to Horace.

"Well, thank you, son," said Horace. "But you should've brought two straws."

Mr. Sykes laughed his deep, throaty laugh. "I drink lake water, so don't worry about me. Cindy said you was running around the lake like a crazy man."

Reece had already checked the driveway, and she was still there. "It's my exercise, kind of like dialysis of the skin."

"I reckon," said Mr. Sykes. "What you know about this new Supreme Court judge? Think he goes by Anthony Onion. Some kind of Catholic name. Horace here thinks old Reagan made a good choice. Sounds like a foreigner to me, though."

Nothing could have been further from Reece's mind. He hated watching the news because it always left him angry. "Well, remember, I just woke up about a month ago, so I couldn't say. Seems, though, that with the balance of powers, you can have a few crazies, but they get evened out by the dull ones." He could feel a hum in the air, the sounds of life, the lake, red-winged blackbirds, a killdee in the distance. He folded his arms and checked out his biceps.

"I think his name is Scallion. Born up north, a Republican for sure. So that's not altogether a bad thing, except he is a Yankee." Horace's hands were folded in his lap, thumbs twiddling.

Reece remembered that he was supposed to call Kristin when he made it home. "Heck, gotta go make a phone call."

"Don't run off on account of politics," said Mr. Sykes.

"No, just have to call Kristin. I'll be back." Reece trotted to the road and through the yard, touching the pine trunks along the way. Cicadas trilled in the tops, groaning up and down. Inside, Dora snored with her mouth open. He went to the phone by the table and dialed. It took a minute for Kristin to get to the phone.

"Hey! You made it. Why did it take you so long to call? I'm about ready to get off work."

Should he mention the liquor store? "Well, I just forgot, to be honest. I apologize." Should he mention Cindy? Hell no. "You want to come over for dinner and hang out tonight?"

"Well, since you're having seizures, I guess that's best. Look, I need to go. Eudora's waving at me. I think I've got a stat to do on Mrs. Dunlop. Her breathing is labored."

"Yeah, go. I like her from what you've said. Go take care of her, and I'll see you when I see you." He drummed his fingers on the plain tablemat. He took a toothpick and rolled it between his fingers.

"Bye," and she hung up. She took the chart from Eudora

and read the order, an arterial blood gas. She hated to hurt poor old Mrs. Dunlop, but orders were orders. "Thanks," and she headed to the drug cart for a syringe and needle. A group of doctors passed her, and she recognized two of them from the party at Dr. Joiner's. They seemed not to notice her, and she was glad. But then there was Brad. He'd ordered the blood gas on Dunlop and stood in her room. She grabbed two alcohol wipes. He was such a little boy, cute but dangerous.

Mrs. Dunlop lay in bed, her head raised to 45 degrees. Usually, she was busy with her hands, trying to free them from the restraints, running the credit card receipts at Loveman's. Sweat clung to her hairline, and she looked just a faint shade of blue, but her respirations were regular, twenty-four per minute. Her eyes latched onto Kristin.

"Hey, Mrs. Dunlop. You okay, sweetie?" She took a wet rag and wiped her face and forehead. "Are you hot?"

"I'm in the garden," said Mrs. Dunlop. "It's very hot in the...garden."

Kristin checked her core temp readout from the cardiac catheter. She looked at Brad, and he had seen it. "Got a little fever."

"I'm going to order some blood cultures, too," said Brad. "You look mighty fresh to have worked all day."

"Feel real fresh," said Kristin. "Mrs. Dunlop, I'm going to draw some blood, sweetie. It's gonna hurt just a bit. Okay?" She untied her right wrist and raised the bed. She palpated the radial artery, swabbed it, and in went the needle with a magnificent spurt back into the syringe. Mrs. Dunlop let out a low moan, as if she were lost in a cave. "Oh, I'm so sorry. Here, Brad, put pressure on this, will you?"

"Asking me for favors, are you? You're cute when you give orders."

"Shush," said Kristin. She capped the syringe and jammed it into a waiting cup of ice. "All done, Mrs. Dunlop." She would draw the blood cultures straight from the catheter that snaked its way into her heart. "Tie her hand back, please. I'll run this down to the lab."

"Sure thing, Toots," said Brad.

"Toots? Get real. And hold pressure for five minutes, but you know that, right?"

Brad tapped his head. "It's all up here." He laughed.

Kristin grumbled, not sure she could trust him to do the job. She didn't want Mrs. Dunlop bleeding all over the bed. She swiped a sticker with Mrs. Dunlop's name and patient number and wrapped it around the tube before she headed into the quiet hall. The lab was on one, and she took the stairs, enjoying the break from the buzz of the unit. She wondered what Dora was cooking for supper and hoped it wasn't fried green tomatoes.

To kill time, Reece washed the banged-up F-150. A year's worth of grime clung to the paint. He remembered his first date with Kristin. He'd had a red Firebird, but had sold it before he left for Ethiopia. She had looked so pretty sitting in the bucket seat, his Blaupunkt stereo blasting Christian rock. But it seemed not like yesterday but like a former life. He dragged the hose onto the driveway and filled an old bucket with soapy water.

They had gone to a Japanese restaurant, supposedly the most authentic one in Birmingham. What that had meant, he didn't know. He'd been eight years old before he'd even heard of a taco. His parents had never gone out to eat at restaurants, and he had felt daring that night, ready for anything. When his appetizer turned out to be finger-sized fish with the heads on, he kept a straight face and managed two of them with a fork, leaving the heads. He took the old t-shirt and washed the roof, the front windshield, and then the hood. Right away, his bucket of water went from clear to brown.

After the meal, he'd had to work a night shift and had taken her home around ten. The day had been hot and the evening warm, just this side of sweating. He'd practiced what he was going to say, had practiced how he would move in for a kiss, but that went out the window when he pulled into her steep driveway. It was a chore just to get out of the car.

The porch light was on. He walked her up the stairs to the door and froze, standing there saying something, but what he wasn't sure. He just wanted to be alone with her, but he had to get to work. Without missing a beat, she had pulled him close and put her face close to his. On autopilot, he kissed her, and she kissed him back. He put his arm around her waist, then pulled away, said he was sorry that he had to go. Did she laugh? He wasn't sure, but he'd felt like a million dollars and drove away, not knowing where he was going.

"Washing the truck?"

Reece snapped out of his reverie. "Yeah, hey. Washing the truck." It was Cindy in her tube top and bare feet, except she had pulled on a long t-shirt with the arms cut out. The shirt was airbrushed "Florida!"

"Looks like you were daydreaming." Cindy held a beer in a coozy from the car dealership.

"I guess I was. Need a bath?" He wondered why he said that and mentally spanked himself. He felt that he was digging himself into a bottomless hole.

"Do you know how fucking weird you are?" She grinned at him and folded her arms. "When does your honey get off work?"

Reece tackled the side of the truck, washing in big circles. "Three thirty or so once she reports off. She's coming out for supper." He put muscle into the grime.

"I'd like to meet this wonder woman. I mean, you saw my tits and didn't even flinch."

"Yeah." Reece considered how many lost opportunities he'd had in his short life. What it came down to was that he was plain scared of pretty girls. They intimidated him, wracked his nerves, plus all of the Baptist Bible…He entertained the word bullshit. He could stare at her tits forever and a day. They were etched into his mind. All he could think of was how soft they'd looked, the nipples. He screamed inside.

"You're a man of steel. Not like anybody I've ever met. I thought maybe I'd give you a treat, reward you for getting shot in the head." She picked up the hose. "Want me to spray?"

Spray. "Do what? Oh, yeah, spray the truck." He stepped back.

She sprayed his legs, laughing, and then the truck, the soap sliding down to the driveway. He thought about the Drambuie, but didn't mention it. He had decided to spring it on Kristin. If she could drink vodka with a bunch of doctors, she could down some Rambo with him in the RV. He wondered what it tasted like.

The back screen door slammed, and it was Dora with her broom. "Hey there, Cindy." She made a feeble attempt to pretend like she wanted to sweep the sidewalk to the driveway.

"Hey, Mrs. Myers," said Cindy. "What you cooking Reece for dinner? He needs to put on a few pounds." A light breeze blew her blonde hair into her eyes.

"Probably pinecones," said Reece. He tackled the side of the truck bed.

Dora chuckled. "You'll be lucky to get a pinecone. But we're having fried green tomatoes and cube steak. I'd invite you, but Reece's fiancée is coming over. You know her?" She swept back and forth.

"No ma'am, but she sounds like a real catch." She winked at Reece. "Anyway, I have to go here in a little while, unless Reece needs some help with the truck."

"Well, you can spray. Just spray the truck, or maybe give Dora a good soaking." He dipped the t-shirt into the dirty bucket water.

"Watch it, boy," said Dora. "I'll tie a knot in your tail." She proceeded to knock down spider webs beneath the eaves of the garage.

Cindy laughed. "I'd like to see that."

"She's a rascal," said Reece. He moved to the back of the truck.

Dora said, "Ha!"

"The hose won't reach back there, Signor Myers," said Cindy. She blew hair from her face and wiped at sweat on her forehead.

"Yeah," said Reece. "Hold on." He opened the truck door, put it in neutral, and pushed. The truck inched forward until the hose could reach. He stuck his leg in and pushed down the parking brake. "There."

"Using those muscles," said Cindy. She rinsed the back and gave Reece a quick shot of cold water.

Dora was frowning, but smiling too.

"Hey now," said Reece. "That shit's cold."

"Boy, watch your language, especially around ladies," said Dora. "There's a little wasp nest." She whacked it with the broom, sending two wasps scrambling. One got after Cindy, and she dropped the hose and ran to the road, screeching.

"Give us some warning," said Reece. "Did it sting you?" He wished it had, so he could put some Clorox on the sting.

"No, almost got me." She punched Reece in the shoulder.

Emma stood for nearly an hour before a seat opened, but then she could only sit still for a few minutes, and then she was standing again. She paced and moved from one side of the gate to the other, feeling the heat rise as the room filled with people. There were no windows, and she had no idea if there was a plane or not. It seemed that the entire country was leaving on this flight.

The lone door opened, and a hum moved through the crowd. A woman smartly dressed in a green uniform emerged, a stewardess. The crowd parted for her as if by magic, and then they began pressing toward the desk there. Emma joined in the crush, feeling her body touching others on all sides. A tall, thin man was in front of her, and she couldn't see. There were only two other white people on the flight that she could tell. She'd managed to glimpse the title of a book one held, *Remembrance of Things Past,* but she'd never read it. Like her, they seemed alone in the world.

Another half hour passed, and a kind of line was forming, and Emma fought her way into it, holding her passport and boarding pass. A short woman in front of her kept stepping back onto her feet, but Emma didn't say anything, just glad to be moving forward. Twenty in front of her, and then ten. She approached the gate clerk with her credentials held forward, as if offering a great sacrifice. The tired man took one look.

"No, no," he said. "You must have the stamp." He looked as if Emma should disappear.

"What?" asked Emma. Her hand trembled.

"You must go back, your declarations stamp." He pointed to the back of the room. "Go quickly."

Emma felt like screaming. Dr. Guthrie had told her, but she hadn't listened. She turned and only saw the tops of heads, sweaters, and shirts. She steeled herself and, like a fish swimming upstream, plowed forward, saying "Excuse me" over and over.

She looked up for a sign. She looked for a line. Back into the narrow hallway, she felt that she had somehow landed on the wrong side of a wide river. But there, down the way, was a desk and then a curtained room. A line of twenty or so, but she broke into it halfway, ignoring the complaints of a man in a white shirt. She assured herself that she was in the right line and strained to hear any announcements regarding her flight, but there were none. Her carry-on bag seemed like three bowling balls, and she pressed forward, bumping into a man wearing a safari hat. He turned and smiled at her. There was a fishing lure pinned to his hat. Usually, she would start a conversation, but that felt ill-conceived at the moment. Five minutes passed, then ten, then fifteen. The line seemed to move like a clotted artery.

"Passport and boarding pass, please." The woman speaking was golden in color with long, straight hair.

Emma thrust her passport forward and then found herself inside the curtained room with an officious man with a bald head. He had a short mustache that reeked of Adolph Hitler. He asked her for the form, which she did not have. What was she supposed to do? She strained to remember and then found the bill in her pocket. She told the man that she had lost the form and placed the bill on a small table there. The man did not change his expression and only said, "No, no, no."

Without pausing, she reached into her other pocket and peeled off $20 US, placing it on the table, which was worth 160 birr on the black market. The man stamped her boarding pass, put his hand on her shoulder, and pushed her through the curtain. With her heart pounding, Emma immersed herself in the crowd and found her way back to the line at the gate. Had the door closed? It had, but there were fifty people in front of her, all of them buzzing like bees. She imagined herself as a barracuda and slid among the mass until she forced her way to the front. The sour man was still there. He took her passport, scrutinized it, and barely glanced at her boarding pass before motioning her ahead. A tiny yip of excitement escaped her throat, and she opened the door herself, and there was a staircase. It had to be down, and she took the stairs three at a time, stumbling at the bottom. She collected herself and walked through an open door onto the vast tarmac, a gleaming 747 within a hundred feet.

She expected a lightning bolt from the heavens to strike her there, and she hurried. There was a face at the top of the boarding stairs, and she focused on that.

"Welcome," said the attractive stewardess.

Emma choked and said, "Thank you," and walked down the aisle to the left. Everyone seemed to have piles of bags and boxes in their laps, between their feet, as if they had all been on shopping sprees. She looked at her boarding pass. There was only one seat open that she could see, and it was hers. The woman next to her had put a package in her seat. Emma looked for overhead storage, but there was no room. She pointed at the package, and the woman looked annoyed, but she took it and shoved it between her legs.

Emma squeezed into her seat, noticing right away the softness. Everything in Ethiopia was hard and had rough edges. She tried to smile at the woman next to her, but she was looking out the window. Next to the woman sat a well-groomed man with a goatee. He did acknowledge Emma's smile with one of his own.

"You must place the bag under the seat in front of you," said a stewardess. Her skin was golden, and she was tall and buxom with a gap between her front teeth.

Emma complied with some difficulty but soon found herself wondering at her situation. She would be home in forty-eight hours. The thought boggled her mind. With her ticket was an itinerary. She would have a layover in Amsterdam and stay at what appeared to be the Hotel Krasnapolsky. Sounded fancy, but she only wondered what they would have to eat there. She was craving something like chicken salad or pimento cheese, and maybe an apple. There seemed to be no apples in Ethiopia. The plane's air conditioning hummed, and Emma felt the power of the mighty 747 that would soon lift above Addis Ababa and turn northwest for Europe.

The small woman next to her piqued her curiosity. Where is she going? What does she do? Emma sat silent for a few minutes and then said, "Tenesteling."

The woman raised her perfect eyebrows. Her eyes were brown, and she wore a knit skirt with a matching top. It seemed to be a uniform of some sort. "Yes?"

Emma smiled. "Where are you flying to?"

"This plane is flying to Amsterdam," said the woman.

"Right," said Emma. She wondered if her name was Abebe. "I'm going home to the United States. I've been here for about two years."

The woman shifted her gaze toward Emma. "What do you do here?"

"I was a nurse. I mean, I am a nurse. I coordinated a feeding program. The famine, you know." Emma felt silly opening up to this stranger, but she felt compelled as well.

"Oh, that is a problem, you know. The people are becoming lazy with free food." The woman didn't blink.

Emma stumbled. "Really? I'm sure that's not true for everyone."

"These feeding programs have made the crisis last longer. It is well known."

"I hadn't thought of it quite like that," said Emma. "I primarily worked in a clinic, though." She wondered if what this woman said was true. "What do you do?"

"I am working for the national bank." The woman pursed her lips and seemed to be finished talking.

"Cool," said Emma. Her whole reason for being had just been shot down, and she found herself squeezing her knees.

It took another half hour of sitting in silence, but then the plane began to move backward and was soon barreling down the runway, pushing Emma back in her seat. She cringed and gripped an armrest until the plane was banking and climbing at a steady pace. Her ears popped. How would history judge her work in Ethiopia? It all seemed so vague and dismal now. But, what about Misrak? She was receiving care that she would not have been able to afford otherwise. Emma burned to tell the woman about Misrak, about the little girl burned by kerosene. And what about the Hyena? Surely the woman would sympathize with her, but maybe not. She felt just a tiny bit sick, and a great thirst for water consumed her. She licked her lips.

Once at cruising altitude, the flight attendants passed out headphones for the music channels. Emma pressed the button on her armrest until she hit American music. It was Van Halen with Sammy Hagar, and she was mesmerized by the sound, so familiar that it made her a bit weepy. She turned up the volume all the way, but it was still just audible, but it was there.

Her first food out of Ethiopia turned out to be a sandwich with some kind of sliced meat. She wasn't sure what it was, but ate every bite and washed it down with a cup of water and a full Coke. The plane flew and flew and just kept flying, as the Earth rotated beneath the plane. She would call Reece once she was at the hotel. What would he say? Would Kristin forbid him to pick her up? That seemed entirely likely, and in that case, she would call her sister Sally. She imagined the look on her mother's face. No one knew she was coming home, except for Reece, and she soon passed into that half-sleep one endures on a long flight.

The woman next to her was crawling over her to go to the bathroom, and Emma opened her eyes and turned sideways. Outside, it seemed to be dark. She felt greasy and touched her face, the oil there on her nose. Out the window, she could see clouds, but there were a million lights beneath them. She had to pee. Standing, she wobbled and arched her back, making her way to the back of the plane, looking down into laps and onto the tops of heads. There was extreme quiet, just a whooshing, and she imagined the plane tumbling from the sky and bursting into flames when it hit the ground.

More hours passed, and then an announcement. A few passengers were clapping, and then the English version of the upcoming landing. Emma worried about getting to the hotel and wondered if it was even worth the brief layover. She could just sit in the airport for the six hours, but she imagined a hot shower, a soft mattress, and restaurants with steak and watermelon. The thrill returned, but the woman's chastisement of her time in Ethiopia plagued her. Maybe she had just taken a costly and dangerous vacation. She wanted to tell the woman that she'd had dengue fever and amoebiasis, that she'd been attacked, raped for God's sake. How would that change her tune?

The plane bounced once on landing, and more applause broke out as the aircraft reversed its engines and slowed, throwing everyone forward. Was it true about the little boy sticking his thumb in the dike?

Like a robot, Emma soon found herself in the crowded aisle, working her way onto the walkway and then into the bright and airy environs of the Schiphol. She had no idea what time it was and didn't care. She wondered what the time difference was between Amsterdam and Birmingham. It appeared to be two a.m. Was Reece awake? She did the math.

Ultimately, Reece was glad he hadn't invited Cindy to stay for dinner or help him imbibe the Drambuie. He felt he had passed a crossroads and admired Kristin sitting in the chair next to the paneled wall. With four, the table had to be pulled out.

"So, what did you do today?" asked Kristin.

Dora raised her eyebrows and looked at Reece.

"Washed the truck." He cut his fried cube steak with his fork. "Yum, yum. Want some fried green tomatoes?"

"I'll pass," said Kristin. She worked a piece of cube steak and mashed potato onto her fork. "It's really good."

"Nobody goes hungry in my house," said Horace. "Potatoes straight from the garden, tomatoes too."

"Reece?" asked Dora. "What about Cindy?"

"Cindy, yeah. She came by for a visit." He looked up at the ceiling light, trying to sneeze.

"Cindy?" asked Kristin.

"She's the Sykes' granddaughter I told you about. I used to hang out with her brother in the summer."

"So, what did you do?" asked Kristin, her fork halfway to her mouth. She was still in her scrub top but with jeans.

"Just for a little while. Talked on the pier. She's the receptionist at the Honda place. An old friend, I guess." He chewed his cube steak. "This is so good, Granny."

"Better than real steak," said Horace. "That Cindy is a real pretty girl."

"What did y'all talk about?" asked Kristin. She was all ears.

"Oh Lord, just stuff, work, getting shot in the head."

Kristin frowned. "Did she keep her clothes on this time?"

"That's what I was thinking," said Dora.

Reece wanted to change the subject. "Swept the driveway, washed the truck."

"Bought some liquor," said Dora. "But he's gonna pour it out."

At that, Kristin laughed. "Really? To drink?"

Reece pondered his options. At least the subject had changed. "Yeah, I was going to get Cindy drunk, if that's what you mean."

Dora shook her head no.

"Reece!" said Kristin.

"Just kidding, just kidding. I'm a one-woman man." And he was, or he thought he was. He waited for Dora's next revelation.

"Well, and that Emma called him today from Africa."

Reece shriveled.

"You're kidding me? Reece?"

"Yes, she called me. I sure as heck didn't call her."

Horace looked thoughtful and salted his entire plate, scattering salt everywhere.

"Good Lord, Emma and this Cindy," said Kristin. "Is there something I need to know? Why did she call?"

Reece wanted to defend himself, but gave up on that approach. "She's coming home, back to Alabama. Something bad happened." He toyed with a cornmeal-crusted slice of green tomato. "It had to happen sooner or later."

Kristin put down her fork. "Well, what is that supposed to mean?"

"It means she's coming home. You don't think she'd stay there forever, do you?" He knew his face was red.

"I'm sure she's a nice girl," said Dora.

Kristin resumed eating, and a silence lingered for a full minute.

"What do you say we go out in the boat?" asked Reece. "Paddle around like we used to." He remembered the one night they had drifted into the cattails, talking nonstop for over four hours, her body tucked into his, time standing still.

"Do you want to invite Cindy and maybe Emma, too?" She made eye contact with Dora, gathering what sympathy she could.

"Nice evening for a boat ride," said Horace. "We got any more of that rice pudding? I'm hankering for something sweet."

"Sure do," said Dora. "But let's finish eating. I'm not through."

"Ugh," said Reece. "Just us, okay, paddle around, let the wind push us."

"Don't be so fickle. You can't blame me, can you?" asked Kristin.

"No one's to blame here for anything that I can think of," said Reece. "Does the rice pudding have raisins in it?"

Dora laughed. "Yes, but you can pick them out."

"Well, what about Brad? The doctor? What about him? I haven't told them about that little incident."

Kristin scowled. "Reece, please."

"Who's the doctor?" asked Dora.

"He's got a crush on Kristin. He works at Carraway, and he drives a fancy sports car with a lame-ass license plate.

Dr2Be. Jesus, who freakin' cares? Maybe his mother."

"I'm glad you're jealous, but I'm not attracted to him. He constantly bothers me at work, wanting to go out, but I keep telling him that I'm engaged." Kristin flushed.

"Went to his party, though." Reece looked to Dora for support, and then to Horace, who wasn't listening. He'd pushed his chair to the fridge and opened the door, looking for the rice pudding.

"Did he have a nice party?" asked Dora. "I guess life is just more exciting away from the lake."

"It was a nice party for sure," said Reece.

"Reece, don't." Kristin nudged him under the table. She felt something on the underside, a piece of gum, probably from Reece when he was a kid.

Reece paused. "Okay, but the lake is calling. Unless you want rice pudding with raisins. Oh, what the hell? Why am I afraid of little raisins?"

Dora stood to fetch a big spoon, and Horace set the white Corningware bowl on the table.

"Horace, no!" said Dora. "Use the serving spoon, not that little spoon. It's like living with a child."

Horace grinned. "It's like living with a mama." His hearing aid squealed, and he made a face.

"Brother," said Reece. "When it rains, it pours." He laughed.

"I guess I'll have a little," said Kristin. "Since everyone else is."

"Best damn pudding in the world," said Reece.

"Hush up, boy," said Dora. "Just eat."

Everyone cleared a place on their plate for the pudding.

"Mmm. This is good," said Kristin. "Raisins and all. Reece, I didn't know you didn't like raisins. Why the change of heart?"

"Probably getting shot in the head. What's a few raisins after that? In fact, I want your raisins."

"Stop bringing that up," said Kristin. "I can see your scars without you reminding me."

"She's right, son," said Horace. He finished his pudding first and patted his belly. "Kinda late. I guess I'll read." His false teeth flopped for a second, and he pushed his uppers back in place with his tongue. "Your teeth and your ears go first."

"Watch him," said Reece. "He'll grab that *National Geographic.*"

Horace sat in his recliner, pushed back, and grabbed a *National Geographic* from the bookshelf.

"Told ya." Reece picked out a raisin and ate it. "Best damn raisin I ever ate."

"Reece, if you don't watch your language..." Dora moved to gather dishes.

"Well, okay, Mr. Foul Mouth," said Kristin. "I guess I'm ready for the boat ride. Sounds like fun. I'm so ready to relax. I'll tell you about what's going on with Mrs. Dunlop. I'm worried about her. She hasn't had a single visitor the whole time."

"Sad," said Reece. He stood to let her out. "Thanks for the meal, Granny."

"Can I help with the dishes?" asked Kristin.

"No, you two go on. It's my job, I guess. I don't mind. Maybe scrape your plate into the garbage, that's all."

Reece followed Kristin to the back door. The light outside was dim and inviting. The phone rang, and he paused.

"What?" asked Kristin. She passed through the door, holding it for him.

"Reece! For you!"

Reece froze, his feet unable to move.

"If it's that Cindy, I'll kill you," said Kristin.

"Uh, just let me check. Who knows? Could be a job offer."

"Do you need your privacy?"

"Of course not. Just let me get it, though." He worked his way back to the kitchen, and Dora was holding the phone to her chest and shaking her head.

Emma sat scrunched into the tiny phone cubicle, pressing the phone to her ear with a finger in the other. She'd had to call collect. Dora had answered, and she heard the operator ask if she would accept the call. It seemed like minutes passed. Emma felt her heart beating as if on its last legs. It was probably seven in Alabama, maybe eight.

"Hello?"

"Reece! Oh my god, you're there. It's me, Emma." She felt like a glacier melting.

"Hey! Where are you? You okay?"

"I'm in Amsterdam. Holland. The Netherlands. I just landed and have to get a taxi to the hotel. I feel like a zombie."

"Wow, cool. Um, hold on..."

Emma could hear talking in the background. "Reece?" Emma switched the phone to her other ear. It seemed as if Reece was on the other side of the wall.

"Here," said Reece. "Um, Kristin is here. We had a nice dinner. I bet you're starving."

Emma laughed. "Come to think of it, I am. Can you talk? Should I call back later?"

"I can talk for a minute or two. Was just heading out. But I can't believe you're in Amsterdam, out of Ethiopia. What happened?"

"Dr. Guthrie and Tesfaw got me a flight, and I had to leave right away. Otherwise, it could have been weeks. Just got lucky. Is Kristin mad?"

"Yeah, sort of. So, when will you get home? To Alabama?"

"My flight leaves at eight in the morning. Flying to JFK and then to Birmingham. Won't get in till midnight."

"Hold on..." said Reece.

Emma could hear another voice and guessed that it was Kristin.

"Reece, I can call you in the morning if that works better. I don't mean to intrude. I just had to call. I haven't even called my mother yet. I want to surprise her. Can you... pick me up? No problem if you can't."

"Wow," said Reece. He so badly wanted to talk with her, to find out what had happened, to hear more about Godo. "Sure. I can do that. No problem."

Emma's eyes watered. "Oh, thank you! I've got so much to tell you. Some good and some really bad. Everyone said to say hello."

"I can imagine...But I should probably go for now. I'll be there, but you can call again if you need to." His voice sounded strained.

"You sure? Oh my God, Reece. It's just a ride. Tell Kristin that, okay? Heck, she can even come with you."

"I doubt that, but I'll ask. Okay, take care, okay?"

"Yeah, I will. Goodbye, Reece."

"Bye," and the line went dead.

Emma sat there with the phone glued to her ear, mulling over every word. Reece would pick her up. He had survived the gunshot and the tornado. He was walking and talking. Her mom. Her mom would probably have a heart attack when she saw her, but the two of them together could do CPR on her. She wiped a tear from her eye and laughed, realizing it was very late and that she had to get to the hotel quick. She only had six hours till her flight left, but she needed to sleep in a real bed.

With a bit of trouble, she found the taxi line and waited for just a few minutes before a gray Mercedes-Benz pulled up. *Will he take dollars?* An elderly gentleman with long, neatly trimmed sideburns got out and walked around to open her door and take her bag. In English, he asked her where she was going, shutting the trunk.

Emma dug in her back pocket for her itinerary. "Hotel Krasnapolsky."

The man's face brightened. "Ah, yes, the best hotel in Amsterdam."

"Really?" said Emma. Everything had seemed so difficult in Ethiopia. Often, she'd had to wait days for a jeep or fight her way onto a crowded bus. "Do you take dollars?"

"Of course," said the driver. He motioned for her to take the back seat, and she slid in like a hand into a glove. The taxi smelled clean, like aftershave.

The man did not speak as he navigated the nearly empty streets. There seemed to be more bicycles than cars. The buildings and the lit streets amazed her. She relaxed for what seemed the first time in years and let this charming man drive her. It took twenty minutes, and Emma imagined it would cost her a fortune, and then they rolled up to the brightly lit hotel. There were a few stairs and a long, covered walkway.

Emma handed the driver a twenty, not sure what she owed.

"I do not have American change, just guilders. I give my apologies." His face was smooth but worn, and his eyes twinkled in the artificial light.

"Chicorilla," said Emma. "I mean, no, that's fine and

thank you so much." He had exited the car, and she waited for him to open her door.

"You have had a long journey. I can see it in your eyes," said the driver.

Emma took her bag. "You're right. I have."

Walking nearly in her sleep, she entered the hotel door. It had not seemed so grand from the outside, but the interior took her breath away. Red carpet and a chandelier. No, she didn't need help with her bag. Dreaming, she checked in and struggled to remember the directions to her room. She turned back to the receptionist, who pointed her in the right direction to the elevator. She stumbled out of the elevator, found her room, and opened the door. The light was already on. The ceiling seemed so far away, and thick floor-to-ceiling curtains called to her. On the bed was a plush white comforter and four feather pillows, but she needed a wake-up call, perhaps two or three. She felt that she could sleep for a month of Sundays and worried that she should go ahead and take a shower, but the bed was waiting. She dialed, arranged the wake-up call, and dropped into a deep sleep as peaceful as a freshly mowed lawn.

In her dream, a phone was ringing, but the shelf was very high. She fetched a small stepstool, stepped up, and the phone moved higher. What to do? She realized she was naked and that if she put on high heels, she might be able to reach it. The phone kept ringing...Emma awoke with a start. She felt wicked tired, like a hundred-pound chicken. The phone. Her wake-up call! She picked up the receiver and dropped it onto the cradle. The pillow sang to her.

She was so warm and imagined she could sleep just a few more minutes, but she needed to shower. Exerting the will of heaven and all things good, she sat up, pushed her legs over. She noticed the floor was made of beautiful wood. She had to pee.

The bathroom was huge and white with a claw-foot tub in the middle. A shower curtain circled it. She prayed for the water to be hot, and she knew it would be. She took a white towel, a heavy towel, an inch thick, and tossed it over the shower bar. Soon, the hot water poured over her body in torrents. She imagined a bee larva wriggling free into sunshine. She moaned and groaned, letting the water flow over her head. She remembered she had to pee and just let it go there in the tub. She felt alive and free, but she had to hurry, and as she slipped, she nearly fell, grabbing at the shower curtain. "Damn!"

She dressed, only changing her shirt, underwear, and socks. Her t-shirt said, "Awash National Park" with images of a lion and giraffe. It was a bit tight and showed off her curves. She was hungry, so hungry, and hurried downstairs to the breakfast buffet that the receptionist had promised. It took a minute, but she stepped into the buffet, a huge atrium with a black-and-white tile floor. The ceiling soared, and the central buffet seemed to spread for a city block. The sight took her back, and she just stared, walking toward the food. "My God."

The toast alone! There must have been two dozen different kinds of toast, various butters, and a selection of fruits, including pineapple, slices of grapefruit, and cherries. She piled her plate with goodies, put it down on a small table against the wall, and nearly ran to draw down a cup of coffee in a giant mug and a tall glass of ice-cold orange juice. She checked her watch, and it was ten past six. A rush of fear that she would miss her flight. She so wanted to relax and enjoy her food. Reece was picking her up at midnight. She had to get there on time.

Within fifteen minutes, she had brushed her teeth and checked out, standing in front of the hotel, waiting for a taxi. There was a pilot in front of her dressed in black with a white shirt. He asked Emma in a slight accent if she was headed to the Schiphol and offered to share the cab. His name badge said Captain Faircloth.

"I would love to," said Emma. "My plane leaves at eight. Do we just split the fare?"

Captain Faircloth smiled. "Of course," and another Mercedes, this one beige, pulled up. They sat in the back seat and were both headed to the same KLM terminal.

"Have you been visiting Amsterdam?" asked Faircloth. There were four buttons on his coat sleeve.

"No," said Emma. "I've been working in Ethiopia for the past couple of years. Just stopping over."

"You were working with the famine, no? Are you a doctor?"

Emma laughed. "No, a nurse, and yeah, the famine. I worked in a rural clinic, helped to run a feeding program."

"Very nice," said Faircloth. "You are from the American South? I've been to Atlanta many times. The accent is very distinct."

"Wow, you're good." For the first time in a long while, she realized she was from a unique place, that she had been a stranger in a strange land for the past two years. She wondered if the breakfast buffet had seemed as grand to him as it had to her. "Where are you from?"

"I am from Gibraltar. Do you know it?" His nails were long and clean.

"Wow, is that a country or a city? I'm not sure." She could feel a bit of redness in her cheeks.

"A country, very small, at the entrance to the Mediterranean. A British territory."

"Wow." Emma's attention was drawn to the cyclists they were passing. She saw a woman wearing a dress and a brimmed hat. "Maybe I'll visit one day."

"So, how is the famine? Have you put a stop to it?" asked Faircloth.

"Well, the famine has let up. The rains have returned, and the people seem to be okay, except there is a shortage of healthcare in the countryside. It makes me sad to leave. The people were so nice." A lump in her throat.

"You helped many people," said Faircloth.

"I hope so," said Emma. The inside of the taxi was very quiet, a smooth ride, unlike the scarred roads in Addis. She felt as if floating inside a marshmallow, and the silence continued in reverence for those who had suffered and died. Stately shops, somewhat square. A long building of red brick with two towers and ornate windows rounded at their tops. The steep roof seemed a dark blue.

The taxi wended its way to the airport and passed into a maze of lanes, soon arriving at the drop point for KLM. The captain paid the fare and refused to take one of Emma's twenties.

"Are you sure? You're so kind," said Emma. She wanted to hug him.

"It's for the beautiful people you helped. It's my pleasure." He tipped his hat and was off before she could say more.

Emma's walk to her gate kicked in, but first, she paused and looked up at the sky. There were no clouds, but it was a solid white, like an ethereal white bulb of light. She nodded to the driver and, overwhelmed, passed into the spacious and airy terminal.

Reece hung up the phone and, with a pained expression, looked to Kristin for some understanding. She had taken over washing dishes for Dora and was scrubbing the skillet, rinsing it, and putting it into the drying rack. Spoons and forks clanged amid her fury of activity. Dora had taken her recliner next to Horace, picking at her hair with a comb. Just the noise of Kristin washing the dishes.

Reece stood and sidled up beside her. "Can I help? I can dry."

"Yeah, sure," said Kristin. She dropped a clean plate into the rack.

Reece retrieved the plate and dried it with a dish towel. What could he say?

"So, she's coming back," said Kristin. "And then what? You picking her up?"

"Well, she said—"

"What about her mom or her dad?"

Reece could tell she was fighting back tears. "Well, her mom's old. I don't know. Probably doesn't drive at night. Her dad, well, he abused her, so that's out."

"Abused her? You must have had some long conversations with her over there."

"Talking is about all there was to do, other than work." He took another plate from her. "Still want to go out in the boat?"

"I don't know. Wouldn't you rather be in the boat with her?" She plunged clean forks and knives into the rack.

Reece winced. "No, just you." He wanted to put his arm

around her, but held off.

"Whatever. I have to be at work, though, in the morning." She handed him the last plate.

"Y'all go on and I'll finish up," said Dora. She stood. "Get outside and enjoy yourselves. I wish I was as young as you are."

Reece looked thankful. He saw Horace peep over his *National Geographic* and wink at him.

"All right, let's do it," said Kristin. She draped the washcloth over the spigot and walked to the back door, not looking back to see if Reece was following her, but he was.

Outside, night had fallen, but a cool light covered the valley and lake. Cicadas rasped in the pines.

"Let me get something. Make this more interesting. Follow me." He walked to the RV and stepped inside, retrieving the bottle of Drambuie.

"Reece? Is that the liquor you bought?" She stood in the night's single shadow, her skin aglow.

"Yeah. I think it's sweet. Come on." He took her hand and walked her through the pines and across the road, past the garden to the pier. They seemed to be alone in the world. Reece imagined a 747 with Emma on it, hanging over the Atlantic like a toy.

At the pier, he handed the bottle to Kristin and flipped over the flat-bottomed boat. "We'll just float, like we used to." It had only been a few months, but it seemed to him like ages. He grabbed the paddle, threw it into the boat, and pushed it into the shallow water through the cattails. "You get in. I'll hold it."

Kristin stepped in, sending out small waves. Reece stepped in, and the boat was stuck. He motioned her to the back and joined her on the metal seat, pushing backward with the paddle until they were free. He paddled to the end of the pier and then let the boat go where it may. Tiny ripples rubbed against the hull.

"It's still so warm," said Reece. "Here." He slid into the boat bottom, and she joined him there, his arm around her. "This is nice." He looked up at the press of fluffy clouds, a purple sky holding them together.

"Reece?"

"Yes?"

"Why do you like this Emma so much? I mean, we're engaged, but it's like you have a crush on her or something."

"I think if you got to know her, you'd like her too."

"Answer the question."

Reece fumbled with the foil wrap on the bottle's neck. "Being in Godo was stressful. She just needed a friend, that's all. We clicked, like a team, like a working team."

"That doesn't make me feel any better. Should I just give up on us? I mean, we click, right?"

"Yes, we do. We're...romantically involved. If that makes sense."

"Yeah, but we worked together in CCU before you left. Didn't you feel like we were a team at times, that we clicked?"

"Yeah, of course." He pulled out the stopper from the bottle. "Want me to try it first?"

"Why do you keep changing the subject? I really shouldn't. Alcohol doesn't seem to like me."

"Here. I'll take a sip, then you." He put the bottle to his lips. "Ooh, tastes like honey and flowers. Try it."

"You're like the devil, just like Mom says."

"What? She says that?" He watched Kristin taste.

"Weird and sweet. What's in this? It doesn't taste like alcohol."

"Yeah, not bad," and he took the bottle. "I never sat in a boat and drank booze with Emma. Just you."

"Well, that's helpful," said Kristin. She took the bottle. "Here goes nothing."

Reece laughed. "If only Granny could see us now. She'd have a fit."

"Do they like me, your grandparents? They're awful nice, but I can't tell sometimes."

"Of course they do. They think you're pretty and smart, just like I do."

"Not brilliant and gorgeous?"

"Yes, if those are the right words. Gorgeous...and brilliant."

"When I saw Emma in Ethiopia, she looked pretty hot in her tight jeans, and she was hovering over you like a mother hen."

"I have no real recollection of being in the hospital there, just kind of a dark dream."

"I could see it in her eyes. She was there to take care of you in a serious way. Like her life depended on it. I had dinner with her and the Guthries, and all she could talk about was you."

"I think she was just so stressed and lonely in Godo by herself. She was just grateful, that's all."

"Maybe," said Emma. "I can feel this stuff. I cannot get drunk. I have to drive home, you know."

"Maybe you could take a sick day. We could go to the

zoo or something."

"Reece, no. And I thought you didn't like the zoo." She took another swig.

"Yeah, you're right. I don't. Maybe we could go to this French restaurant in Mountain Brook. I've always wanted to go there and have some French onion soup. Did I ever tell you about this guy named Craig? He was completely hairless, and he told me that his wife made the best French onion soup. It sounds delicious. Lots of onions and cheese. We could get a bottle of wine. You know I've never even tasted real wine?"

Kristin laughed. "Hairless, for real?"

"Yeah, he was an engineer, built roads and bridges. A nice guy, but as smooth as an eight ball."

"Huh, sounds like a character. Did he love his wife, or did he hang around with the single women?"

"Oh, spare me," said Reece. "He loved her, and I love you." He squeezed her thigh and looked around to see how they were drifting, but the boat seemed to be lodged against the pier. He grabbed the oar and pushed off, splashing Kristin.

"Hey, bucko!"

"Sorry."

The boat drifted in front of the pier, and they drank from the bottle.

"So," said Kristin. "We've never talked about kids. I want two."

Reece stumbled in his head. He'd never really considered kids. He was getting buzzed. "Why not twenty?"

"Get serious," said Kristin. "You never had a sibling. Wouldn't you have liked to have a little brother?"

"It would have been nice, all the moving. I hated moving all the time."

"You could have had someone to bitch with, like my sister."

"Maybe I needed a…sister." He felt he was slurring his words and reached for the bottle.

"Slow down and save some for me." She giggled and turned to face him, her hair in his face. "Where are you? Kiss me."

"Gladly." He kissed her and felt her mouth relax, his lips sliding over hers.

"Baby," said Kristin. She opened her mouth and let his tongue inside. "God, I want you so bad."

"Shh." Reece set the bottle on the seat behind him. Her mouth was sweet and wet. He turned to his side and cradled her, his hand on her stomach, stroking her there through her scrub top, which was loose.

They kissed, going deeper, and the two fumbled for a comfortable position. Soon she straddled him, his back pressed into the hard metal seat. He ignored the pain and pulled her close, running his hands up her back beneath her top. She sat up for a moment and looked him in the eyes. Reece waited, but then she arched back and pressed her hips into his. He parted his legs and let her fall between them.

"God," he said. "You feel so good." His hands played over her bra strap.

"You lucky devil." She sat up and looked into the darkness. She pulled off her top and lowered her breasts to his face.

Reece groaned. He fumbled with her bra, releasing the

strap, and closed his eyes, then opened them. The bra was hanging on her nipples, and she narrowed her shoulders, letting it fall forward. "Oh, God."

"Stop saying that." She let the bra fall and bent down, letting his mouth seek her nipples.

Like a convict released from twenty years of confinement, he pulled her nipple into his mouth, rolling his tongue. She was digging her nails into his back and breathing into his ear.

"I think...this is it," she said. "Oh, Reece. Is this it?"

"I hope so." He slouched until his neck was hitting the back of the seat. He reached for her jeans, the button and zipper there.

Kristin was taking deep breaths, and she helped him undo her pants. He was trying to pull them down. She shifted, and he tried to sit up but couldn't. Finally, she stood in the boat, rocking it from side to side, and pulled them down to her ankles. Her white panties blinded him in the moonlight.

Emma popped into the restroom and then out, headed to her gate, D-85. The throngs of people calmed her, but were in the freaking way as she hustled to make her flight to JFK. She passed a stand for frozen yogurt, wanting to stop, but pressed forward. Wading through security had taken at least ten minutes.

She passed a large lounge and arrived at her gate with five minutes to spare. She was super thirsty and decided to risk it, popping into a souvenir shop with a cold drink case. The bottle of water cost two US dollars, and she received her change in guilders. So many faces, and it took another twenty minutes, but soon she was safe in her seat next to the window, looking out over the massive wing. She'd heard that wing seats were the safest. She was still hungry and looked forward to the in-flight food.

She wondered at the handsome steward, his eyes a deep blue, his short blond hair in a kind of pompadour. He was tall, like most of the Dutch women, who she noted, were pretty as well. The stewardess greeting them at the entrance had seemed like a supermodel, her shoulder-length brown hair flipped at the ends and shining like glass. Emma dug in her bag for the gummy bears she'd bought with her water. The taste somewhat thrilled her, and she ate them all.

A black woman smiled at her and took the seat beside her. She wore a sweater with a fat collar. And then a large white man with his arm in a sling joined their row. His buzz cut reminded her of Dr. Guthrie. No one spoke, all regarding the space as somewhat sacred and secure from standard rules of etiquette.

The steward with the blue eyes moved down the aisle, passing out pillows and blankets, and Emma took one of each. She was wearing her sweater, but the inside of the plane was very cool, almost cold. She tried to fiddle with her air nozzle, but it was off. Without warning, a deep weariness came over her. She'd had barely four hours of sleep at the hotel, but it had been a grand sleep in the nicest bed and room she'd ever been in. She couldn't wait to tell Reece about the endless breakfast buffet. With her fancy toast, she'd had smoked salmon, pineapple, and cantaloupe. The meal seemed distant now, as if it had never happened, and her stomach growled. She thought about the Israelites wandering in the wilderness for forty years, eating manna. Her head bobbed and snapped. Her eyes seemed like rolls of pennies.

An image of Misrak troubled Emma. The sutured wound where Misrak's breast had been, heavy stitches and drains, her arm swollen twice the normal size. She said a quick prayer for her and the little girl burned with the kerosene, and her mind drifted to the others who needed prayer, and the images collided in her head like bowling pins. She let out a low guttural moan, surprising herself. The women in the shelter and their children. She thought about Atakabura reusing needles in the government clinic, and then she drifted to the Hyena. From this distance, he seemed a frail creature, friendless and fierce in his addictions to alcohol and qat. What about the blind woman who said she had been raped? Her groin squirmed, remembering the soldier on top of her, pushing her into the rocks and dirt. She clenched her fists, and her lower back ached thinking about it. But she had injected herself twice with penicillin, so she should be okay. The idea of becoming pregnant had occurred to her, but she couldn't bear to entertain the thought. The plane was moving backward, announcements over the intercom. She felt crazy and confused, sleep calling to her. She wondered if she looked crazy and tried to put on a regular face, her head leaning into the thin pillow against the window.

The plane lumbered in jerks, and Emma's eyes closed… and then she startled awake, the plane lifting into the white sky. For a moment, she imagined she was at her home church, sitting on a padded pew, waiting to be called forward to share her experiences in Ethiopia with the faithful. She felt like melting ice cream, like her feet were dipped in warm water. She wanted to explain to the woman next to her that all was well, but was it? No, it wasn't, and that unsettled her. Had her time in Ethiopia been a complete waste? Had she helped anyone? Was it her fault that Reece had been shot, and she imagined it was true. The pillow was so thin, and the cabin so cold.

Emma removed the tiny, dark-blue blanket from its plastic and covered her upper body. Beneath it, her hands gripped one another. She wondered if alcohol would be served and decided to try a glass of wine. Her eyes fluttered, her neck relaxed, and she fell into a deep sleep.

Emma opened her eyes. How long had she slept? Were they landing? The woman was tapping on her shoulder. "Oh," she said. The steward and another stewardess were there, passing out Dutch crackers and peanuts with drinks. She tried to fathom words and finally said "crackers." She forgot to order wine and asked only for a cup of water, but she was handed a bottle. "Thank you."

She opened her crackers and put the water between her thighs. The crackers were sweet and delicious, and she wanted more. She thought about Livvie's homemade crackers, how she was going to give the recipe to her mother. She hiccupped, and then again. Would she ever taste enjera again? Had she promised Afewerki that she would help him study in the States? She missed him and thought about his Exxon ballcap, how he always said, "What a hell," and then she smiled. The woman next to her was saying something.

"What?" asked Emma. "I'm sorry."

"Where are you traveling?" the woman asked. Her sweater made her seem as if she didn't have a neck.

Emma thought of all the women in Godo who had goiters, some as big as footballs. "Oh." She had to remind herself that she was headed home. "To Alabama. Birmingham. I've been away for a while. How about you?" Her words seemed empty, as if she would have to learn how to speak again.

"I am visiting my sister in Chicago." She had an accent that Emma couldn't place.

"Is that your home?" asked Emma.

"No, no. I am from Ghana. She has been living there for many years." The woman's brilliant white teeth reminded her of the women in Godo, pearly white up front but rotten in the back.

"Ghana," said Emma. "I've been in Ethiopia."

"Why have you been there? It is a troubled place."

"I'm a nurse..." Emma felt a surge of tears coming on

and braced herself, covering her emotions with a cough. "The famine."

"Yes, I have heard. You are very brave...I could never go there."

"It's a beautiful country, but I'm sure Ghana is too."

"Of course," said the woman. She introduced herself as Diana.

"Nice to meet you. I'm Emma."

"A pretty name."

"Thank you." Emma wanted to pour her heart out to this unlikely Diana, to tell her that good people were suffering, that good people were dying, that being good seemed to have nothing to do with doing good. Her nose seemed stuffy, her throat dry, and she swigged her water. "Diana, like the princess."

"Yes," and the woman laughed.

And that was that, each returning to their private worlds.

Once again, Emma was startled awake by Diana. She felt that she was standing at the end of a diving board and mentally almost stood to simulate taking a dive. A meal was being served. They had already passed by with drinks, but Emma had slept through that. The choice was chicken piccata or vegetarian, and she chose chicken. Emma examined her little portioned tray. With the chicken was a vegetable medley and a brownie. She almost said "Yum" and dug in with her fork and knife. Right away, she wanted two trays, but one would have to do. She'd lost twenty-five pounds in the last two years. To be amid famine, there had always been plenty of food, but it didn't stick to her bones. She now felt that her thighs were too fat and decided to eat only half of the brownie.

Emma looked at Diana's tray. She was still eating, and Emma felt she had wolfed down her food. There was a mint, and she popped it into her mouth, eyeing the remaining brownie on her tray. She sighed and ate it in small bites. Her feet felt swollen in her tennis shoes, and a vague headache seemed to be coming. She hadn't had to pee, which was good, being by the window, but she knew she was dehydrated, feeling her heart beating faster than it probably should due to her mitral valve prolapse. Often in Godo, while walking, she'd felt short of breath, but had attributed it to the altitude. She imagined slipping into heart failure, being placed on a waiting list for a new heart. She scolded herself and shook her head.

The plane flew on. A movie played, *Three Amigos,* with Steve Martin, but she didn't bother to wear her headphones, satisfied with just the images. Diana seemed to be enjoying the film, laughing and laughing. The man next to Diana was snoring with his chin to his chest. Emma drifted in and out, suddenly worried about her luggage, but then she remembered she had only the carry-on bag. The staff glided in the aisles again with trays of yogurt parfaits. Emma took hers, topped with strawberries and nuts, and held it like a precious stone. "Yum." She laughed at herself and glanced to see if Diana had heard her, but she was eating her own parfait.

There was another movie, *Pretty in Pink,* and much to Emma's delight, a sandwich roll with little chocolate-chip cookies. She finally had to pee, and both Diana and the man had to stand to let her out.

"I'm sorry," said Emma. The man nodded and gave her

the once-over as if he'd never seen her before. *Take a picture. It'll last longer.* She faced the sea of heads in their seats and smiled at her humor.

The steward with the blue eyes and pompadour stood in the back galley beyond the bathrooms. He greeted her as she waited in line and asked her name.

Surprised, she said, "Emma." Was her name Emma? It was.

"I am Cees." He pronounced it Case. "You seem very interesting, that you have an interesting life, no?" He was making coffee. "You are, how to say, rugged? Maybe it is not the right word."

Emma blushed. Cees towered over her. "Well, interesting is nice, but maybe not rugged."

Cees laughed. "Where have you been? Your eyes seem to want to tell a story."

The bathroom door opened, but Emma stayed put and moved closer to the galley to let the person behind her go. "Ethiopia. I was a nurse, working in a clinic, in the countryside."

"Yes, that explains it," said Cees. "It takes a special person, right?" His smile was a beautiful thing to behold.

Emma was transfixed, a thousand stories on the tip of her tongue, but with no words to follow. "I suppose so. The people, most of the people, were so nice. It was hard, though, and I needed to come home."

"You should write a book, no?" He held a pot of coffee.

"I could, I suppose. A very long book." Emma imagined his breath smelled of roses and worried that she had not brushed her teeth, that her hair was a mess from sleeping. She wanted to say that she'd been raped, and a flush of helplessness rose in her chest. She felt a covey of quail inside, trying to burst out and fly away. "You are Dutch?" She wondered what Reece was doing.

"Yes, you can tell? Because of the airline?" he asked, the plane coasting high above the earth.

Emma blushed. Why was she flirting with this guy? "Just your look, and you're so tall." The bathroom door opened, and she turned, but a short, fat woman with strings of beads beat her to it.

"I'm keeping you," said Cees. "I should be working, but you are not rugged as you say, but I would say now, striking. Is that correct?" He put the coffee on top of the cart.

"Gosh. Thank you." She looked into his blue eyes as if for the last time and turned away to take her place at the head of the line.

Tangled in the bottom of the boat, darkness darkening, Reece looked awkward lying there with his pants and underwear around his ankles. His hand was still caressing her breast. Kristin was pulling up her underwear, though, and so he did the same, and then his pants.

"Reece, say something," said Kristin. "What did we do?"

Reece laughed. "I think we had sex."

"Was it okay? I mean you'd never had sex, right, like me, with another person?"

"God, that felt so good, like a rocket going off inside of me. We should do that more often."

"Reece, but I was going to wait until we were married. I'm bleeding. I feel like I've sinned."

"I thought I would, too. Look at the bats. They were watching us."

"Maybe it was the booze? Did you plan it like this, to get me drunk and have sex?"

"Heck no," said Reece. "Here, sit up." He pulled her close. He felt a little sick from the Drambuie, like eating too much apple pie. "What about you? Maybe you seduced me."

"Oh, stop. But it was perfect, right? I can feel your stuff inside me like I'm all gushy. You were inside of me."

"It's my new favorite thing, for sure," said Reece. But he was feeling depressed, worried that he'd done something wrong. He'd been raised to think of sex as a bad thing, but he felt a renewed commitment to Kristin, an obligation to take care of her.

"What if I'd had sex with Brad? I was drunk then, too. But we didn't. I wish he would just give up and leave me alone." She snuggled her chin to his neck, gentle waves slapping the boat, a rhythm.

He struggled for words. "Well, you're not engaged to him, right? But to me." He felt tired and wanted to be in his bed, alone, and felt guilty. Should they do it again? Didn't people usually have sex several times? "Want to do it again? Maybe in the RV?"

"What? No, not really. Just hold me...It kind of hurt. My mother told me one time that I'd walk funny if I had sex and that everyone would know."

"I doubt that," said Reece. "I'm sorry it hurt. I was out of control. My body just took over."

"Yeah, me too. You think your grandparents know what we're doing? I don't want them to think I'm a slut, or you, for that matter." She outlined his nose with her finger, smoothed down his eyebrows.

"Stop. They're probably in bed by now."

"It is getting late. Maybe I should go. I wish you could drive me home. I feel like I've been transported, landed in a new country. Weird."

"Yeah, I could follow you..."

"Oh, would you? You could stay for a little, while I get a shower, and then kiss me goodnight on the porch."

"Uh, okay. I can do that. But now I'm worried that your parents will know what we've been up to and start asking questions. I kind of feel like I've peed in the pool and everyone knows."

"What? Like I'm the pool?" She tapped him on the head. "That wasn't very nice."

"I didn't mean it that way. You know what I mean. No one knows except us, and the bats."

He waited for her to break away so he could stand, but she didn't move. "Here, let me help you up." He stood in the boat, rocking it next to the cattails, and pulled on them to bring the boat next to the pier. She reached up. "Careful," and she lifted herself onto the weathered boards.

Reece got out with the short rope and pulled the boat onto land, and flipped it over. The night was so clear, the half-moon showing, lighting the ground with a luminous shadow. Frogs croaked, a breeze blew, and they walked hand in hand toward the house, Reece swinging the half-empty bottle.

"Am I walking funny?" asked Kristin. She laughed and put his arm over her shoulder.

"I can't tell. We're hip to hip. Maybe we're both walking funny."

They crossed the road and then passed through the tall pines that cast long shadows.

"Do you still feel tipsy?" asked Reece. "Can you drive?"

Kristin leaned against her Toyota. "It's strange, but the sex made the woozy feeling go away, like I've been cleansed."

"Yeah, me too. Let's finish the bottle then."

"No, I've had enough. Mom'll smell it on me."

"What about your dad?"

"He never gets out of his recliner except to go to bed."

"Let me go inside and see if they're still up, tell them I'm following you home." He pushed against her and brought his mouth to hers, lingering.

"Mmm. You're a good kisser."

"You're a good kissee."

"I'm glad we did it. It hurt, but felt really good. You're the only one, you know. You lucky boy."

"We could do it again, standing up, right here."

"No, I don't think so, buster. Your granny would be out here in a heartbeat with a broom. She protects you. You better put that bottle away."

"Yeah. She's omniscient, like God." He pulled back. "I shall return. Hold on. I'll put it in the truck."

Inside the house, he eased the screen door shut and peeped around the corner into the den. Horace was in bed, it seemed, but Dora sat in her recliner, sewing up a hole in a pair of pants.

"Hey, boy. Was getting worried about you two. Where's Kristin?"

"She's swimming...across the lake." He monitored his footsteps and focused on not slurring his words.

"You're joking," said Dora.

"Yeah. Ha. She's outside. I'm going to follow her home, maybe stay there for a bit, and then come back." He went as far as the dining room table.

"You okay? You look tired. You sure you don't need to just let her go on? She has to get up early."

"I'm fine. She wants me to. You know." He squeezed the back of a chair, worried he would stumble. "I'll lock the door. Don't wait up." He could hear Horace snoring in the back bedroom. The screen door opened and closed.

"Reece?" said Kristin. She bumped into the doorframe. "Hey, Mrs. Myers." She lingered in the doorway, bracing herself. She was blushing.

"What've you two been up to?" Dora sewed without

looking up.

"Just, oh nothing," said Reece. "Well, we need to go, right?" He turned and tripped over the chair. "Oops."

Dora just stared at them. "You two be careful."

Reece just knew she knew that they'd been drinking and having sex. "Okay, safety first, right?"

Kristin tried to laugh, but only coughed. "I'll, I'll send him home, Mrs. Myers."

Outside, Reece took a deep breath. "Brother, she knows."

Kristin laughed. "She does not. Let's go, okay?"

"Yeah." He hopped into the truck and sat on the bottle. "Dammit." He let Kristin back out and then fell in behind her. He couldn't believe he'd had sex and replayed it in his mind. She had been so wet, and then he'd come, making everything warm and liquid. He imagined he could smell his sperm and felt his crotch, hoping no stains were there.

It took twenty minutes, and they pulled into the steep driveway. Reece cranked down the parking brake and put the truck into first, just in case. He was amazed that he could drive after drinking so much, but maybe it wasn't as much as he'd thought. He chastised himself for knowing so little about the pleasures of life and sidled up to Kristin, hugging her from behind. She could feel him down there.

"Reece, for Pete's sake. Get rid of that thing before we go in." She kissed him at the edge of the yellowish porch light.

"Baby, let me think about that tornado for a minute. That should do it." But his mind drifted instead to being shot, to lying in bed unable to speak or move.

The front door opened. It was Gert.

Reece scrambled and put Kristin in front of him. They stood there like wooden soldiers about to face a firing squad.

"Kristin? It's getting late," said Gert. She ignored Reece, shading her eyes against the porch light.

"Be right in. Reece just followed me home."

"Well, okay," and she let the storm door close, leaving the door ajar.

"God, I feel like a little kid," said Reece. "I think we both need to move out and get our own places."

"When we get married," said Kristin. "Right? It wouldn't make sense to get our own places and then have to move again." She folded herself into his arms. A whippoorwill called from nearby.

"I guess you're right."

"We need to set the date. I figured we would have done that by now, but your accident threw everything off."

"Some accident."

"Reece, you know what I mean. Are you okay down there?" She ran her hand across his crotch.

"Yikes."

"Sensitive little boy. I wish you could tuck me in. But come in anyway. We can talk about the wedding date. I'm sure Dad's asleep if that's worrying you."

"I think they're both probably still mad about us leaving the service during the grand excommunication ceremony. That still rots my gut."

"Reece, get over it. The man was cheating on his wife. Come on in, please?"

"All right, but just for a bit." He followed her through the door and to the den. She left him to go to the bathroom. Edwin was still up, reading his Bible. Reece's stomach fell. "Oh, hey."

"Well, hello there, young man." Edwin peered over his reading glasses. "Have a seat."

"Yeah, sure." Reece sat in a hurry and crossed his legs. He had just deflowered this man's virgin daughter. He felt that his manhood would burst through his pants and confess all.

"I'm reading the Book of Job," said Edwin. "It makes you respect God's power in our lives."

"Is that for Sunday School?" asked Reece. He imagined that Edwin could smell the wetness in his underwear.

"No, just my own Bible Study. Do you do your own Bible study? I mean you are, or were, a missionary."

"Well, usually." He didn't want to say that he'd lost his appetite for scripture, that he was in the process of reevaluating God's plan for his life, for the planet, for the entire frickin' universe. "The last thing I read was the Book of James. How it's useless to preach to a hungry person."

"Well, that's certainly appropriate for what you were doing in Nigeria." He took his reading glasses, seemingly ready for a lengthy discussion with his future son-in-law.

"Yeah, well, I was in Ethiopia. But it's true. Feed the hungry man first. I would even say just leave him alone after that. If he's touched or moved, then he can take the next step."

"So, I don't quite understand. I thought that some of what you were doing over there was teaching them to pray, to find salvation through Christ." Edwin closed his Bible, holding his place with a finger.

Reece thought. Where was Kristin? What was taking

her so long? Was she taking a shower? Had her mother figured things out? "I was just there as a nurse. They already know how to pray. That part of Ethiopia has been Christian, Orthodox, for nearly fifteen hundred years. They have the Bible just like we do, but in their language."

Edwin raised his eyebrows. "Well, I did not know that. So why are the Baptists over there?"

"Well, it goes back to what James said, right? I was just meeting basic needs for healthcare and food. The Mission printed plenty of Bibles in Amharic. The people are more into the Old Testament, though, and they have books in their Bible that we don't have." Reece twiddled his thumbs, ready for the next question.

"I suppose," said Edwin. "Did having the experience you had make you believe less?"

"Do you mean getting shot in the head? I've had lots to think about. The people there didn't invite me over, the Baptists did."

"Sometimes God's will is hard to understand. Am I right?"

Kristin popped into the room, wearing long flannel pajamas. "What you talking about?"

"God's will," said Reece. "I guess it was God's will for me to get shot."

"Reece," said Kristin. She gave him a warning look.

"No, honey, it's all right. I think Reece needs to talk through what happened."

"I'm not a fan of counseling, if that's what you mean," said Reece.

"We never finished our pre-marital counseling," said Kristin. "I was hoping—"

Edwin interrupted. "I think it would be very wise to finish that commitment, honey."

Reece grumbled, crossed his legs the other way, then went back to uncrossed. He looked at the popcorn ceiling. Edwin's lamp cast an oblong oval shadow there.

"Reece?" asked Kristin. "I wanted to bring that up, but know you didn't care for it." She sat beside him, curled her legs under, and leaned into him.

"The counselor made it all seem so silly." He could hear Gert puttering in the kitchen, rearranging the pots and pans, no doubt wanting to chime in.

"It's a lifetime commitment, a sacred bond," said Edwin. His eyes seemed to grow.

"We were talking about setting a date for the wedding," said Kristin. "We'll have plenty of time to finish up the counseling, right?"

Reece wanted to be on a rocket to the moon. "I guess. So, what about next spring, maybe March or April?"

Kristin brightened. "That's exactly what I was thinking." She punched him in the arm.

Edwin looked surprised. "Gert? Did you hear that?"

Gert peeped around the corner as if she hadn't heard. "What's that?"

"Mom, we might have a spring wedding, just like you wanted."

Gert emerged into the gap between the den and the dining room with her hands on her hips. "That sounds like fun. Our friend, Mrs. Evans, from church, offered to let us use her house for the ceremony. She lives in Mountain Brook."

"In somebody's house?" asked Reece. "I guess that's

better than a hotel. I hadn't thought of where." His mind spun. How would they pay for it? Would he invite Emma?

"Well, it's a big house, in Mountain Brook," said Gert.

Reece knew that all of the rich people lived in Mountain Brook, but didn't care.

"She's so nice to offer," said Kristin, looking Reece in the eyes. She pinched him.

"Ow," said Reece. "So, spring it is. I guess we'll need a calendar to sort out the actual day."

"A Saturday would be perfect," said Gert. "What about the honeymoon? Where will you go? This is so exciting."

"Where would you recommend?" asked Reece. He rolled his eyes and watched Gert's face fall.

"Reece," said Kristin in a warning tone.

"I think the beach is a good idea," said Edwin. "Maybe you could go to Gulf Shores."

"Well," said Reece. "We've just about settled everything except who the preacher will be."

"We don't mean to butt in," said Gert. "She's just our baby. I always thought Robyn would get married first, being the oldest."

Reece relaxed and unclenched his jaw. "Just a lot to consider. I still have to get a job." He wished he were a tumbleweed blowing across the desert.

"It's a lot all right," said Edwin. "But you have six or seven months to figure it out. We're just here to help, is all."

"And we'll do the counseling, Dad. I promise, and Reece, you too, right?" Kristin tousled his hair.

"Yes, for you. I guess I did promise." He needed to pee. "I need to powder my nose."

Kristin laughed and watched him disappear into the hallway.

Disembarking into JFK, Emma felt the grime. The ceilings were so low, and the place jam-packed. Again, she worried about her luggage, but then remembered she only had the carry-on. Passing through customs, she placed her bag on a stainless-steel table while a uniformed man asked her to open it. He gazed into the small bag, wearing latex gloves, and pulled out the painting that had been rolled and secured by a rubber band.

"What's this?" He removed the rubber band. "Animal skin?"

Emma searched for words. Her throat felt dry. "It's a church painting on a piece of goatskin." It was the one souvenir from Ethiopia that she had brought, which she could fit into her small bag. The burly man with a thick mustache held the painting up to the fluorescent light.

"Got blood on it," he said. "See, on the edges."

Emma looked. "Maybe it's paint."

"No ma'am. Looks like blood. Can't let this pass through." He was already looking for the next person in line.

"You're kidding," said Emma. "What's it gonna hurt?"

"It's illegal, ma'am, with this blood on it. That's all I know. We can talk about it all day, but that's what it is."

"What're you going to do with it? That's kind of mean, don't you think? There's probably people smuggling dope through left and right."

He was placing the painting into a large plastic bag. "Be destroyed. Not much I can do, ma'am. You're clear otherwise."

Emma zipped the bag and walked away. Her connecting flight was an hour off, and she found a bathroom where she peed, thoroughly washed her face and hands, and did her best to make her hair look halfway decent.

The Delta flight touched down in Charlotte, and Emma changed planes for the last time, headed to Birmingham. She'd missed her chance for wine on the KLM flight, but drank a miniature bottle of white wine as she finally headed home. She compared the dry Chardonnay to the sweet Awash wine she'd had in Ethiopia. She preferred the sweet wine. In just about an hour, the half-full flight began its descent. Emma peered out the window, wondering at the lights below. She was about to see Reece, and her stomach fluttered.

Reece awoke early, dizzy from a dream about a tidal wave from the lake. The water had risen, wiping out the entire valley. Only a mud flat remained, pocked with pools of water and flopping fish. He remembered that Emma was flying in, that he would see her at midnight. His first instinct was to take a shower, but despite his sore legs, he decided to run around the lake again. The run would cleanse him of the Drambuie, which he felt in his gut and his head. He would have to lie to Dora and tell her that he'd poured it out.

What had happened the night before? He'd had sex with Kristin, but it seemed like a dream. He tried to reconcile his eagerness to see Emma with his lust for Kristin's body. They had settled on spring for the wedding and would probably go to the beach for their honeymoon. He remembered that he'd promised to finish the counseling sessions with Kristin and flipped onto his stomach, the pillow over his head. He could hear the "Country Boy Eddie Show" on TV, so that meant it was early, maybe seven? He tried to go back to sleep, but he felt like a lion just released from its cage. Which way to turn? Run? Venture out? Lay there and die? He said a quick prayer.

An hour later, he forced himself out of bed, remembering that he needed to put in his application for a job at Carraway. He dressed in running shorts and a lumber company t-shirt and made his morning appearance. He could smell biscuits, the kind from a cardboard tube, which suited him just fine.

"Hey, son," said Horace. He was drinking a cup of instant coffee and reading the paper. He snapped it and folded it.

"Morning." Reece wondered if he looked like he'd had sex. He would get a shower, but he was going to run first. Dora was at the sink, washing dishes. He rubbed his head and belly.

"You're a sight for sore eyes. You're keeping that girl up too late."

"Heck, she's keeping me up too late." He went to the fridge, then poured a small glass of orange juice.

"Biscuits in the oven," said Dora. "I didn't make you any eggs, since you were still asleep." She slapped him on the butt with the dish towel.

"Hey." Reece did a little dance. *Make a little love.* He grabbed the ancient pie tin with the biscuits from the oven and placed it on the table. Where was Emma? Over the Atlantic? In New York City?

"You and Kristin must have had a lot to talk about last night," said Dora. She gave him a wary look.

Reece tried to remember what they'd talked about. "Yeah, she wants to get married in the spring." He took a perfect half-circle bite of biscuit.

"Well, that would be nice," said Dora. "You sure you're doing the right thing?" She attacked the stove with a scouring pad. Horace snapped and folded his paper.

"I suppose. Just have to get a job first. I think I'll go in today after I run and put in the application." He peeled the biscuit apart, separating the layers.

"Want some syrup with that?" asked Dora.

"No, thanks." He ate a second biscuit, eating the crispy bottom last. Dora always oiled the pan.

"What about that girl in Africa? What's her name again?" She stood over him as if he might float away.

"Emma. She's supposed to get in at midnight."

"And you're picking her up? That worries me, boy. Does Kristin know about it?"

"Sort of, but I'll talk to her later today." He pulled another biscuit apart and covered his plate with thin layers.

"What's that?" asked Horace from his recliner. He adjusted the volume on his hearing aid, making it squeal.

"Reece is picking that girl up from Africa at the airport tonight. She's coming home. I'm not too sure he's not sweet on her. I'll strangle him if he winds up hurting Kristin."

Horace cleared his throat. "Don't get yourself in a pickle, son. Kristin's a sweet young lady."

"Jesus," said Reece. "She saved my life, right? Emma did. The least I can do is pick her up at the airport."

"Maybe explain it that way to Kristin," said Dora.

"Makes sense. I'd like to meet Emma and thank her for what she did."

Reece brightened and finished his last biscuit. "Yeah, that makes perfect sense." He nodded his head in approval, stood, and fixed himself a glass of tap water. "You know the women in Godo had to walk for forty-five minutes downhill to a spring to get water and then walk back uphill with it on their backs in these heavy clay pots."

"God bless 'em," said Dora. "We used to have a well."

Reece drank a second glass of water, hydrating for his run.

"Don't drown yourself," said Dora.

"Trying to set an example. You need a glass too."

"There you go again. I had my coffee and juice."

"It's not enough," said Reece. He took down a clean glass and filled it.

Dora took the glass and sipped. "There, you satisfied?"

"No, drink it."

"I'll pee myself."

"Well, at least you'll be hydrated." He fixed another glass for Horace and walked it to him. "Here you go."

"Don't want it just yet. I'll take it to the garden." He smiled at Reece.

Reece nodded and put the glass on the lamp table. "I may not be a doctor, but I am a master hydrator." He spread his arms wide as if receiving the Holy Ghost. "Worship me!"

"You're crazy," said Horace. "I could hire you out to the circus. Get rich."

"Crazy but hydrated, the heart beating, the lungs like a bellows, plus I'm good looking and smart to boot."

"Hey, call Kristin like you said you would," said Dora. "And dang it, I have to pee."

Reece laughed. "Let me drink some coffee first to get my nerve up. I'm still afraid of what she'll say."

He put a pan of water on to boil and heaped some instant coffee into a mug, then walked outside for a minute to check the weather. The sun lurked behind some low clouds, no doubt shining on the other side. The warm air stirred just ever so slight, and he could feel the humidity. It would rain for sure, and the grass needed mowing. He looked down at the lake, and it was perfectly still like dark green glass. Once he had swum across, and panicked when he ran into one of the giant carp that had been introduced to eat the algae. He had never swum so fast, hyperventilating the entire way. He remembered the Drambuie bottle and decided to put it in the trash.

When he walked back in, Dora had removed the boiling water from the stove and poured it into his mug. "Thanks." He sat beside Horace in the pink recliner. Horace's was blue. He gazed at the phone and recited the number of the CCU to himself. He watched Dora at the sink, finishing up the dishes. He wondered that she didn't wear a hole in the linoleum. Horace snapped the paper and let it fall to the carpet. He always made a mess of the paper. Reece took a slurp of coffee, oddly happy that everything was as it should be, except he needed a job, and he needed to call Kristin. Having Horace and Dora there gave him courage, and he dialed the number.

Kristin checked on Chastity, the young woman with chest trauma and recurrent ventricular tachycardia. "How was breakfast? You ate it all, right?"

"Ugh, no. I ate the boiled egg. Can you maybe have them send down a sandwich of some sort, like turkey with lots of mayonnaise?" She pushed a button and raised her head to forty-five degrees.

"I will if you promise to keep a regular heart rhythm. We need to get you onto a floor where you can walk. Just staying in bed and the chair isn't good for you." Kristin tidied up the little bedstand on wheels, still wondering if her walk was any different.

"I promise," said Chastity, "but I can't guarantee anything. At least I can get to the bathroom by myself. I hate that damn bedpan with a passion."

The intercom came on. It was Eudora. "Hey, you have a call. It's Reece."

"Oh, thanks!"

"That your boyfriend?" asked Chastity. "Go ahead."

"My fiancée. I'll get the sandwich ordered." She hurried out.

"The blinking line," said Eudora.

"Can you order number seven a turkey with extra mayonnaise?" Without waiting for a reply, she stepped to the central desk. "Hey, Reece. You okay?"

"Yeah, very fine. And you?"

"Gosh, we need to talk about last night. I'm still breathless." She waited for Reece to respond. "Reece?"

"Oh yeah. Did you sleep okay? I slept like a log."

Kristin thought. "I had trouble sleeping, thinking about it. You're a naughty boy, you know." She gazed around the unit, at the busyness of it all.

"That's me," said Reece. "Yeah, want me to come over

when you get off work? I'm coming in after lunch to put in the application."

"That would be super, and I think you'll get the job, no problem, with you knowing Sheila and all."

"I hope. Hey, I need to tell you something. You know Emma's coming back, getting in tonight—"

"Reece, no." She held the phone with two hands.

"Wait, let me explain."

"No. She wants you to meet her, doesn't she? I can't believe her nerve. Reece?"

"Yeah, she does. I mean, she saved my life. I wouldn't be here otherwise. That's a big deal, right? I mean—"

"That's all well and good, but I don't trust her. She's got her eyes on you. I just know it."

Reece fumbled for words. "Just, well. I promise just to take her home. That's all. She's a good friend. I think you'd like hanging out with her. You're both nurses."

"Reece, we had such a connection last night. I'm convinced more than ever that we're meant to be together. Is it worth it?" She glanced into number twelve, Mrs. Dunlop's room. She wasn't doing well, becoming more and more short of breath, even with the nasal oxygen.

"I promised her."

"So, you can unpromise her. Did she call you again? I guess she must have."

"No, not again, just the call from Amsterdam. If I don't show up, she'll have to take a taxi home. Her mom doesn't even know. She wants to surprise her."

"Well, she should call her mother. That's just not fair to me. Right? Reece?"

"Oh brother," said Reece. "Look, I'm coming over after

you get off work. We can talk about it some more. We decided last night that we were getting married in the spring. Right?"

"And that takes you out of circulation. Reece, please don't do this." Kristin imagined his warm chest on top of hers, him beside her in the boat.

"Okay, okay. For now, let's say I'm not going to, and then we'll talk about it later today. Maybe I'll pop in when I drop off the application."

"It's so busy. I won't have time to talk. In fact, I need to go. I need to check on Mrs. Dunlop. She's not running the credit cards at Loveman's anymore. I'm afraid she won't make it."

"That's sad. Sorry to hear that."

"I can't talk anymore. Okay. Have to go, and don't forget to come over tonight. You did that one time."

"Yeah, yeah, I promise. No worries."

"Okay, bye." Kristin hung up the beige phone.

She walked into Mrs. Dunlop's room. She wasn't a DNR because there was no family to consult, and she was never in her right mind. She had no idea she was even in the hospital. Kristin checked her oxygen, four liters per minute. Her face was an off shade of blue and her respirations at thirty-two per minute. Kristin checked her IV, which was dripping dopamine to help maintain her blood pressure.

Mrs. Massey coughed, and thick phlegm crowded her mouth. Kristin grabbed the suction wand and sucked out the mess. "Mrs. Dunlop? Can you get your breath?" She squeezed her clammy hand, which was no longer restrained.

Mrs. Dunlop just stared at the ceiling, unmoving. "I

want to…"

Kristin leaned in closer. "What do you need? Just tell me." She could hear the phlegm rattling in her chest.

"I want to…" Her words took forever to form. "…to ride the white horse."

Kristin said, "Damn." She checked her blood pressure, 90 over 50. "Let's hold off on the white horse, Mrs. Dunlop. Let me get your arms and legs moving. You'll feel better."

Kristin pulled the sheet up above her knees and bent her left leg up and down in a slow rhythm, then her right leg, repeating twenty times. She took her left arm and put it through a range of motion exercise, moved to the other side of the bed, and worked the right arm for twenty reps. "Cough for me and get some of that mucus out for me, okay?"

Mrs. Dunlop just stared at the ceiling, her eyes barely moving at the command. Kristin took a cool washcloth and bathed her face and neck. Why would Reece even ask if it was okay for him to pick up this Emma? He was getting to be impossible, and it all revolved around Emma. It could have been anybody who saved his life that night. What if it had been another guy nurse working there? What had she done anyway to save his life? Had she given him CPR? Lots of people knew how to give CPR. She needed to sit down. "I'll be back, Mrs. Dunlop, okay? Tell the white horse to go away. Okay?"

"I want to ride the white horse."

Kristin was about to step out of the room, and Leslie, the monitor tech, yelled out, "Check twelve! Flat line!" Kristin looked at the room monitor, nothing. Mrs. Dunlop had gone from vaguely blue to white in a matter of seconds.

"Code in twelve!" she yelled, and within seconds, the room was crowded. Kristin hit the emergency lever on the bed, laying it flat. Dunlop wasn't breathing. Kristin dived in, gave her two quick breaths, then ten chest compressions. She didn't want to hurt her, but went into the two and ten rhythm. "We just need to let her go," she said to the room.

An attending physician barked orders for an ET tube and the paddles. Kirksy pushed the crash cart into the room, scrambling for the supplies and charging the defibrillator.

An intern pulled down Dunlop's gown, exposing her flat and flabby breasts. The paddles went down on top of gel pads.

"Clear!" and Dunlop's torso jumped with the charge. He shouted for epinephrine.

Kristin kept up the chest compressions.

"Clear!" The charge sounded like a muffled .22 being shot.

The attending moved in with the scope and an ET tube. Kristin pulled off the head of the bed so that he could maneuver behind Dunlop. With dexterity, he forced in the tube. "Tape!" He jammed an ambu bag onto the tube and forced air into her lungs.

Kirksy was injecting the epinephrine. Kristin had resumed compressions. Nothing.

"Epi down the tube," said the attending. He took the syringe and squirted it into the tube, then resumed the Ambu bag. Nothing.

"Let's just stop," said Kristin. She felt that she was

breaking Mrs. Dunlop's ribs.

With the tube taped down and Michael now manning the Ambu bag, the attending physician picked up the paddles again. "Clear!" Dunlop's torso flopped.

Kristin looked at the monitor, just a flat line and a high-pitched tone. She stopped compressions.

"What are you doing?" asked the attending. "Keep going."

"No, sir," said Kristin. "She deserves better."

He looked at her in wonder, checked the monitor, and backed off. "Are you kidding me? That's an order."

"She's dead. She's riding the white horse. She said it just before she coded."

The attending ordered Michael to resume compressions, and he handed the Ambu bag to Kirksy.

Frowning, Michael and Kirksy did as told, looking sheepish.

"Intracardiac epi," said the attending. "Last shot." He pointed at Kristin. He wanted to inject epinephrine directly into Mrs. Dunlop's heart with a six-inch needle.

Kristin said nothing and did nothing. All went quiet in the room except for the alarm announcing that Mrs. Dunlop had mounted the white horse galloping off to brighter pastures, wherever that might be.

Reece pulled into the driveway behind Edwin's sedan and jacked the parking brake. He was still in the slacks and short-sleeved dress shirt that he'd worn to drop off his application. The door squeaked open, and he pushed out onto the steep driveway. Kristin had called, bawling into the phone. He was ready for anything.

Silent, Gert met him at the door and let him pass up the short flight of stairs. In the den, Edwin was watching the evening news, while Kristin sat on the couch, holding Walter in her lap and rubbing his long, floppy ears.

"Hey." He stood over Kristin, waiting for her to ask him to sit, but she didn't.

"Hey. Walter misses you. Right, buddy?" asked Kristin.

Reece sat down, nodding to Edwin.

"She's had a rough day," said Edwin. He turned the volume down just a bit.

"I gather," said Reece. He put his arm behind her.

"It was awful," said Kristin. "And I'm in big trouble with the attending, Dr. Carpaccio."

"You really liked Mrs. Dunlop. I think you did the right thing," said Reece.

"I wish you'd been there. He was such an...an asshole. She knew she was going to die." Tears wet her eyes.

Reece squeezed her shoulder. "Idiot. I hate that."

"Oh, thank you. I mean, really. You would have loved her. She was so quirky and weird, and she deserved to die in peace, not be some kind of lesson in life saving."

Reece scratched Walter's ear. "But he listened to you in

the end, right? He stopped."

"Yeah, but he'll try to get me fired. I know it. He was so mad."

Edwin spoke. "You have to be careful, honey." He held the TV remote like a burrito.

"Careful? What's that supposed to mean? She went from sinus rhythm to asystole. It was quick and easy, except for...Oh, Reece, it makes me so mad."

"Me too," said Reece. "I think Walter is mad, too."

Kristin laughed. "Thank you for being so understanding. That helps. He's going to write me up, though. I just know it."

"Well, there's no head nurse for now. Who's he going to tell?" The head nurse of CCU, Michelle, had drowned on her honeymoon to Cancun a month prior, and she hadn't been replaced.

"Maybe the witch supervisor. You know her. She calls out nurses who wear colored socks. Remember?"

Reece laughed. He'd worn blue socks one day and been lectured. "Yeah, she's a hard-nose. Maybe he'll just let it go. He's got better things to do than make enemies with the nurses."

"Well, he is the doctor," said Edwin. He kept pointing the remote as if he would change the channel.

"Dad, don't," said Kristin.

"He could cause you trouble."

"Who cares? Let him try," said Kristin.

"Just have to see. I think he'll see the light. You may have taught him something. Who knows?" Reece wondered when the issue of Emma would come up. Edwin would side with her on that one. Reece could smell the tuna casserole Gert was making.

"Yeah, I'll see him tomorrow, and I dread it." She scooped up Walter and handed him to Reece. "Here, pet your son." She smiled.

Reece took Walter, but he fidgeted and jumped down. "My son doesn't like me." He wanted to add that his future father-in-law didn't like him either.

"No, he loves you," said Kristin. She reached and patted him on the rump. "I wish they hadn't cut off his tail. Just a little nub."

Wallace, the cat, sauntered through, cautious of Walter.

Reece liked cats better than dogs. "Hey, buddy." He reached down and scratched Wallace's back. Wallace arched, came closer, and Reece pulled him onto his lap. "Good boy." He scratched his ears, Wallace purring like an old refrigerator.

"You're so good with animals," said Kristin.

"Maybe," said Reece. "I don't like spiders, though."

Kristin poked him in the ribs. "Who does?"

"My mother hated spiders," said Reece.

"You never talk about your parents," said Kristin. "You should do that more."

Reece just shook his head. "Hard to do." He remembered that day in Killeen, Texas. Just any other day, except for the mass murder at Luby's.

"Well, you've got your grandparents," said Kristin.

"I do," said Reece. He felt hot inside and let Wallace jump down.

"Y'all," said Gert from the kitchen. "Dinner is about ready if you want to wash up."

Reece followed Kristin to the hall bathroom that

smelled of lemon soap. They lathered their hands and rinsed together beneath the tap, splashing water on each other.

"Hey!" said Kristin.

"Hey, yourself," said Reece. He gazed at her in the large mirror. Maybe she wouldn't even bring it up.

They sat next to each other at the table. Reece put his red cloth napkin on his lap. Gert put the tuna casserole in the center of the table, a big spoon on top.

"You first," said Reece.

"Daddy first," said Kristin. She handed the spoon to Edwin.

Soon, they were all eating, but in silence. It seemed like a game, who would be the first to speak.

Kristin cleared her throat and drank some sweet tea. "Reece's girlfriend from Africa is coming home tonight." She ate another bite of casserole.

Reece coughed. "Geez, she's not my girlfriend."

"Is that the nurse?" asked Gert.

"Yeah," said Reece. He wiped his mouth. "She saved my life the night I got shot."

"There you go," said Kristin. "That's his excuse."

"Excuse for what?" asked Edwin.

"I'm supposed to pick her up from the airport tonight." Reece felt cornered and wracked his brain for something more solid.

"Really?" asked Edwin. "She doesn't have family here?"

"She wants to surprise her mother, or so Reece says."

"Kristin, I promised her. It's just a ride, nothing more."

"Well then, can I go?" She pointed her fork at him.

"That would be awkward," said Gert.

"If you want to, sure. Why not?" said Reece. Hell, maybe they would just have a threesome.

Kristin looked surprised. She toyed with a noodle and brushed off the small bit of mushroom. "I didn't expect you to say that."

"Heck, it's hard to know what to say. I mean, we're engaged. She's just a good friend who happened to really and truly save my life." He wanted to say that Kristin should be grateful, but that seemed to be pushing it.

"So, I should be grateful. Is that what you're saying? Yeah, I'm grateful that you're alive, and maybe she had something to do with that, but she's after you, Reece. Can't you see that?"

"Jesus, she's not after me. She's just, I don't know."

Edwin folded his hands in his lap. "Well, if she knows you're engaged, she shouldn't mind Kristin coming with you, right?"

"But she does have to go to work in the morning," said Gert.

Reece said, "Well?"

"What about the option that you don't pick her up? She can call somebody. You said she had a bunch of sisters." Kristin sighed.

"What if it were you, flying back at midnight? Wouldn't you want someone there to meet you, to take you home?"

"Maybe, but not somebody's fiancée. Oh God, I give up. Just take her home, for God's sake, and get it over with. I trust you, okay?"

Reece puzzled her response. "You sure? I mean, you can go with me. Not a problem. You two know each other from the hospital, right? I'm sure she wouldn't bat an eye."

"No, I trust you. I have no desire to ever see her again. You can pick her up, but that's it. Agreed?"

Reece pondered his options. "Okay, agreed."

"Good, that's settled," said Kristin.

"Sounds like a good compromise," said Gert. "I've got vanilla ice cream for dessert."

"I'll have a bowl with some of those sprinkles," said Edwin.

Emma's Delta flight landed and roared to a near stop, then cruised to the end of the runway. Emma felt warm from the wine, and she struggled to get her ears to pop. Would Reece be at the gate? Would he be in the waiting area? Would he be at the luggage carousel? She ran her fingers through her hair, feeling the weight of the trip there. She needed some serious sleep and yawned. Her eyes felt like lead, and she imagined she could smell her feet.

She waited for the line to start moving before she stood, stooped beneath the overhead bin. Her kidneys felt like waterlogged pinecones, and she stretched, letting go a short moan. She inched forward with the line and soon said goodbye to the stewardess and pilot. She glanced into the cockpit, and it seemed like wall-to-wall clocks. She passed into the walkway to the gate and moved her bag to her shoulder, looking down at the tight carpet.

The door loomed ahead as a rectangle, and she passed into the quiet terminal. It seemed as if the airport was closed. Reece was standing to the side, beyond a velvet rope. She didn't see him. A knot in his stomach untangled.

"Emma!"

As if shot, Emma stopped and turned. "Reece?" She almost didn't recognize him. His hair had begun to grow. He had gained some weight, and his face was tanned from running in the hot sun.

Reece paralleled her as she walked to the end of the barrier. He was searching for words, and then they were hugging.

"Reece, it's so good to see you. I thought you were going to die or at least be in a coma for the rest of your life. You look so healthy. It's crazy." She hugged him again.

"Wow, good to see you too. It seems like yesterday we were working in the clinic together. You look great, tired but great." He wanted to kiss her, and right away, he knew he was in trouble. "Let me carry your bag."

She let him. "It's the only luggage I have." She gazed at the airport walls, the restaurant shuttered for the night. She walked very slow, taking in the vague smell. "I need to visit the ladies' room, if you don't mind."

"Sure, me too."

They met up by the water fountain and walked past security toward the main escalator down.

"How was your flight, or flights?" Reece could feel his heart beating in his ears.

"Fine," said Emma. "It was a shock for sure, being used to jeeps and vans. Amsterdam was amazing, but like a dream. They had the best breakfast buffet I've ever seen in my life. I thought I would die."

They stood side by side on the escalator, each fathoming the energy of the other.

"Ha, I didn't get to see too many sights on my way back. Being shot in the head and all." He laughed. "You saved my life that night."

"Shush. You would have done the same for me. You're a tough little cookie. I mean, look at you, as if nothing happened. Although, I can see the scars. Can I touch them?"

"My stigmata. Sure."

She stopped, reached up, and traced the pinkish indentations. "Looks like someone pressed their finger there. I guess there is a God."

"Well, that's up for debate. I may have left my religion in Godo." He let her go first through the spacious revolving door, exiting into the still night. Mercury lamps hummed overhead, moths banging there. It had rained off and on, and a smell of baked cement hung in the air. "I'm in the deck, on two, I think."

"You hungry?" asked Emma. "I keep thinking about McDonald's."

They took the stairs up.

"Not sure one is open. We can go to the Waffle House with all the late-night drunks."

"You're driving me home, right? I mean, just to make sure."

"Of course. I said I would."

"Yeah, we could go to Waffle House in Hueytown, not too far from the house. That sounds great."

"Maybe we'll have an adventure there," said Reece. "Can I put the bag in the back?"

"Yeah, sure. This your ride?"

"Well, sort of. It's Horace's old truck. I like it, pretty beat up, just like me."

"Suits me." She tried to open her door.

"Have to do it from the inside. Hold on."

She hopped onto the red vinyl seat. "Pretty spacious, not like the jeeps."

"Did you get to fly out of Godo, or did you ride?"

"Flew out with Dr. Guthrie. It all happened so fast. My head is still there to be truthful. This girl fell into a fire.... Misrak's in the hospital with breast cancer."

"Wow, that's too bad. She was a great cook."

"Yep. I hope she makes it back home."

Reece turned the ignition, and nothing happened. He tried it again and then again. "Well, hell. Or what was it that Afewerki always said?"

"'What a hell,'" said Emma. She smiled. "You're the only person I can have a conversation with, you know."

"Suits me. Yeah, I want to know what happened after I left. Let me pop the hood." He popped it and hopped out, checked the battery, and a lead was loose. He walked around to Emma's side of the truck. "Need the pliers out of the glove box."

He tightened the lead and hopped back in. "Here goes nothing." The truck roared to life. "Yes!"

Emma cheered him. "Good work, Mr. Bush Mechanic."

Reece laughed and blushed and began the winding path out of the deck.

"So, what happened after I was shot? Did you have to do CPR?"

"God, there was so much blood. I yelled for IV fluids, and Afewerki ran to the clinic. I started an IV on you. No CPR. You were breathing ragged, though, which made me think I might have to."

Reece pulled out of the deck into the clear night, paid at the gate, and eased onto Airport Road. The entrance to I-59 was just ahead.

"Did you fly me in?"

"We had to wait till the next day. I was up all night, along with everybody else. Put you in my bed, and you bled on my pillow. I left it there, though, in case you wanted it as a souvenir."

Reece floored it and pulled from the ramp into the

sparse interstate traffic.

"And then Terry flew me in from there? To the Polish airfield?"

"No, to the main airport, no, wait, yeah, the main airport. We flew Misrak into the old airport. Getting you two mixed up."

"Hey, you're not buckled," said Reece.

"Oh," and she buckled.

"And then I was in the hospital, and then I flew back on the Med-Jet."

"Yep," said Emma. "Your fiancée came over. We talked, but she wasn't too thrilled with me. I could tell."

"Yeah."

"Does she know you're picking me up?"

"Yeah, we went back and forth, but she said okay. I mean, you freakin' saved my life, right? She wasn't happy about it, though." He wanted to tell her that he'd had sex with Kristin, but that seemed wrong.

"Do you guys have a date? I'd always thought that it was kind of just up in the air."

"We talked about that yesterday. Looks like some time in the spring. Kind of scary to think about it."

"Well, you're awful young still, right?"

"Twenty-two. Let me know when we get to the exit." He drove with one hand, doing the speed limit.

"We're the same age."

Reece felt a lump in his throat. "Yeah, like a team. Working in that clinic with you was a ton of work, but I loved it. I wonder how we'll do going back to the hospital?"

"Not sure that I'll do that. I might do home health care for a change."

"Really? I figured you'd wind up back at UAB. I put my application in at Carraway today." He passed a big rig that was doing fifty.

"Huh, really? In CCU with Kristin?"

"No, in ICU next door. The head nurse, Sheila, knows me."

"I guess Kristin wants to keep you close by."

Reece felt a sting. "It was my choice. We could ride in together, eventually, but the job is for 11 to 7."

"Night shift. That sucks."

"No, it'll be fine. Kind of like I'm starting over."

A silence of a few minutes passed as the truck hummed down the interstate, passing through pools of light and then darkness.

"What happened after I left?" asked Reece. "On the phone, you said that something bad happened."

Emma tensed. "Well, it's why I left so soon. It was time for me to go after that, even though they're shutting down the clinic and the feeding program."

Thirty seconds passed. Reece glanced at her, and she seemed to be so far away.

"I was attacked by some soldiers, driving to AK from Addis. They followed us and stopped when we did to pee. Craig was driving. They had a gun. I think I told you that on the phone."

"Yeah, Craig, the hairless guy."

"Yeah. They held him at gunpoint and..." She bowed her head and let a tear drip.

"Oh shit," said Reece.

She just went ahead and said it. "They raped me, two of them, on the ground. I gave myself big doses of penicillin, though, and I'm not pregnant that I can tell."

"Oh God," said Reece. "That's worse than getting shot."

"Yeah, maybe." She fought back a tide of emotion.

They rode in silence for a minute.

"Are you okay? I mean, did they hurt you?"

"They didn't beat me if that's what you mean. I guess they could have shot us as well, but that didn't happen." She wondered if she should tell him about jumping from the helicopter.

"Hold on, are we close to the exit?"

"I'm sorry. We passed it. My bad."

"No worries. I can exit up here and turn around."

"And they'll get away with it just like the Hyena got away with shooting you. Makes me so mad I could scream. But there you go."

Reece exited and crossed over the bridge. "Is it the next exit once we're back on?"

"Yeah. Exit and then left. The roads, though, seem so strange. Sorry to burden you."

"Hush about that. My God, that sucks so bad. God, I wish I had been with you. That would have never happened. I guarantee it." He gripped the wheel with both hands.

"I thought about that," said Emma. "But you weren't, so there. This exit."

Reece steered onto the ramp, stopped, and took the left, squealing his tires. "Damn."

"I can't tell you how depressed I've been since then. Just helpless. I was helpless."

"How in the hell can people do shit like that and live with themselves? I can't understand it."

"Me neither, except there's evil in the world, even right here, everywhere."

"God almighty," said Reece. He could see the Waffle House sign up ahead.

They pulled into the lot that held three other cars. A chorus of cicadas from a patch of woods nearby greeted them. The sky was clear, but there were too many lights to see the stars.

Reece pulled open the door and held it for Emma. Despite her long flight, she looked good in her jeans and blouse. Disco music on a boom box played "Funky Town," and a waitress was dancing with a large patron wearing overalls and combat boots.

"Looks like a party," said Reece. He made eye contact with the grill chef behind the counter. He wondered if they should stay, if something bad would happen. "You okay with this?"

"Reminds me of the tejj house in Godo. Just different music."

"Sit anywhere you like, but the counter's your best bet!" said the waitress. Her nametag said Wanda. She twirled and stumbled as if she'd been drinking.

"Counter or booth?" asked Reece, but Emma was headed to a booth by the counter. They faced each other.

Wanda kept dancing, but the cook came over to take their order. "What'll it be? Menu's right there."

"I know what I want," said Emma. "A patty melt with bacon and cheese, extra mayo." She smiled at Reece, nodding her head to the music.

"Heck, I'll have the same," said Reece.

"Hashbrowns?" asked the cook.

Reece and Emma said "Yes" at the same time.

"Gotta have the hash browns, right?" asked Emma. "Do I just look like a beast? I feel like I look like a zombie. I feel like a zombie." She gave him that half smile.

"Heck no," said Reece. He felt a little thrill in his spine. The next song was "Pop Music," and there was no sign of the dancing letting up. Reece watched the fat farmer dancing with the waitress. She looked to be thirty, rode hard and put away wet, as Horace would say. "Welcome to America."

Emma laughed. "It's just crazy wherever we go, right? Hueytown, Godo, Addis Ababa." She wanted to reach over, grab his t-shirt, and kiss him on the mouth.

"I guess you're right. But crazy is good, right?"

"Want to dance?" asked Emma.

Reece looked over at the cook, grilling their patty melts. He thought about all the hours and days he'd spent in the church, the hours and hours of prayer, the Bible studies. He'd never had alcohol until Ethiopia, and he'd had sex for the first time just last night.

"Let's do it," said Reece. He slid out.

Emma looked surprised, and with her deadly smile, she slipped out. Wanda yelled "Yippee!" and motioned for them to join in. Soon, the four of them were dancing together. Reece had never danced before and just moved his hips and hands, smiling like a clown at the circus.

Next up was Salt-N-Pepa with "Push It." Wanda gave out a yell and threw her arms around the farmer. He had a green-ink tattoo of a mermaid on his forearm, and sweat poured from his hairline. Emma grabbed Reece and only wanted to slow dance. Together they moved, holding hands, jumping in on the chorus with Wanda.

"Order up!" said the cook. He looked like he was fifty going on eighty. "Wanda! Girl!"

A young couple entered but then turned and left.

"Wanda!" The cook was beyond his limits. He reached over and punched off the boom box.

"Larry!" said Wanda. "What's your goddamn problem?"

Larry put the two patty melts on the table. Reece realized the situation, and his inner brakes took over. He motioned Emma back to the booth.

"That was fun," said Emma. "Oh Lord, that looks delicious." She took a bite of her patty melt and moaned. "How's yours?"

"Good," said Reece. "Need a drink, though." He caught Wanda's eye and motioned her over.

"Y'all are the bomb!" said Wanda. "What'cha need? Oh, Lord, did Larry not get you any drinks? Larry, shame on you!" The farmer had taken a seat at the counter, wiping sweat with tiny napkins.

"Sweet tea for me," said Emma.

"Same here," said Reece. "Thanks." He took another bite and squirted some ketchup on his hash browns. "Well, welcome home."

"Couldn't be any better," said Emma. "I wonder what my mom will do when she sees me?"

"She doesn't have a weak heart, does she?"

"Not that I know of. Maybe I should call her first. She'll be asleep, though." She imagined making out with Reece on the couch.

"Heck, let's just give her the thrill of a lifetime. Plus, we both know CPR, right?"

Emma laughed. "Right, pretty much experts, I would say. Jeez, this burger is tasty. Nice and greasy."

They ate in silence, and a loud threesome entered, two white guys with crushed velvet coats and a black lady in a long red satin dress that barely contained her breasts.

"That's weird," said Emma.

"She's got to be a stripper," said Reece. "That dress is something else."

"The one guy is wearing sunglasses." Emma looked over her shoulder. They had squeezed into a booth against the far window.

The woman in the red dress laughed out loud and then said, "Stop right there, home boy!" They both had their arms around her, crowding her, pinching her, poking her breasts.

"Freakin' idiots," said Reece. He watched Wanda take them menus and caught the gaze of the cook, who looked worried. The farmer was getting his eye full and laughing.

"Just drunk," said Emma.

"Watch it, motherfucker!" said the woman. She was fending them off with her elbows.

Wanda went over. "Y'all need to simmer down, or Larry'll have to ask you to leave. Damn, y'all get off her, give her some breathing room."

"Thank you, sister," said the woman. But then she laughed at something being whispered in her ear.

Reece was glued to the scene, his hand and patty melt halfway to his mouth. "They remind me of the two wild and crazy guys on *Saturday Night Live*."

"At least they were funny," said Emma.

Reece took a bite and chewed, his thoughts returning

to Emma. "So, those soldiers. Any chance at all that they could be charged, punished? I know you said no. Those two numb nuts are practically raping that woman in the booth." He felt his heart beating in his throat.

"Oh, let it go. They're just drunk. They'll settle down. Heck, I'll tell them to—"

"Just..." The two guys were high-fiving each other. Reece could tell they weren't locals, that they had an accent. "So, about those soldiers."

"Dr. Guthrie said it would be nearly impossible to find them, let alone charge them. They'll pay, though, somehow, some way." She scooped hash browns to go with her last bite of patty melt. "Dang, that's good." She was eyeing the pie on a big glassed-over plate. Looked like chocolate meringue.

"Y'all doing okay?" asked Wanda. "Need more tea?"

They both said, "Yes, thank you."

"You ever see those jokers before?" asked Reece.

"No, but see all kinds, especially this time of night. I'll sic Larry on 'em if they get out of hand. The lady looks familiar, and we got a camera up in the corner there and one outside too."

Reece couldn't focus on Emma. Suddenly, a flash of Cindy sitting topless on the pier. The Drambuie and Kristin. Her naked body beneath his. She had smelled like hot iron, and they hadn't used protection. An image of Kristin and Emma both pregnant loomed in his mind.

"Don't do anything, hon. They'll settle once they get some food in their bellies," said Wanda. "I might turn that music back on and see what happens."

"Reece?" said Emma. "Reece. You're in a trance. Oh,

Wanda, I'll have a piece of pie. Reece?"

"Uh, no," said Reece. He took his last bite, soaked in ketchup, and wiped his mouth with a napkin.

Wanda went to get the pie, putting her arm around the farmer who was sitting just there. Larry was busy fixing up three breakfasts with all the trimmings for the wild and crazy guys and the lady in red. He smacked the grill with his spatula, flipping eggs and pressing bacon flat. He had Reece's attention, admiring his short-order handiwork.

Angry words bubbled up from the trio. The lady in red had slapped the older of the two guys. He had a thick mustache.

"Here we go," said Reece. He grabbed his knees and squeezed.

"Reece, don't do anything. Wanda can handle them, or the cook. He can call the cops if need be."

"That's right, sister. Enjoy your pie. Y'all want coffee?" asked Wanda.

"I'm good," said Emma. "Reece?"

"Yeah, sure. Not used to being up so late. I still get really tired, not like I was before."

"How did you recover like you did? You must have had some good nurses working you over," said Emma.

"Well, they were good with me. I had this one nurse's aide, Debbie Dee. She dragged me out of bed and sat me in the chair. She always had cold sores in the corners of her mouth. But then I was at Kristin's house and decided to walk on my own. Crawled at first, went right up the stairs, and scared the bejesus out of her mom." He wanted to laugh, but was still preoccupied with the two guys and the lady in red.

"Wow," said Emma. "You're a tough nut."

"No, I think you're the tougher nut. I was only in Ethiopia for a couple of months, and you were there for two years. I wish I'd come earlier or stayed later. But I feel like I've known you all of my life." He caught himself off guard and held back what could become a sob. "God…I'm just so damn emotional these days."

"Aww. Well, you left in high style. No regrets there. Sometimes I wish that it had been me who was shot. Feel guilty, like I caused it."

Reece watched as one of the guys was groping the woman. She was laughing, sort of. A scenario played in his head. He went back to the day his parents were shot. The guy had yelled something about women being the cause of his rampage.

"Reece, hey, over here," said Emma. "This pie is delish."

"Hey, I'm sorry. This should be all about you." Reece sipped his coffee and spilled some on the table.

"Are you glad I'm back? I couldn't stop thinking about this night, crazy as it sounds. From one crazy place back to another." She gave him the lopsided smile.

"Of course," said Reece. "Kristin almost didn't let me come, but I'd made up my mind to come anyway. You deserve it." He wanted to say something about the bond he had with her. He felt they would be friends for life, regardless.

"At least she didn't follow you. I had a guy who latched onto me and followed me everywhere, even to class. He'd wait outside. Creeped me out."

"I don't think she'd ever do that. I hadn't even considered it."

"Fucking motherfuckers!" The lady in red struggled to

get out of the booth. Reece stood, fists clenched.

"Reece, no!" said Emma.

Wanda jumped into high gear and hit the play button. Reece paused. It was "My Sharona," one of his favorite tunes. Wanda and the farmer were back at it right away. The lady in red had forced her way out of the booth, and the two guys tried to corral her, dancing to the music. Reece walked that way in a daze, not noticing Emma behind him.

"Reece! Dance!"

Reece watched as the two guys and the woman grooved to the music, moving toward them. He felt Emma's hand on his shoulder and let out a tremendous sigh. He shuffled his feet and swayed to the beat. Soon, they were a group, dancing, or at least what could be called "sort of dancing." Emma was smiling, beaming at him, and he felt his heart melt. His entire attention shifted to her.

When the song ended, a collective cheer went up. Reece couldn't believe he was dancing with Emma at a Waffle House, dancing with two guys and probably a stripper, plus the waitress and a farmer in his overalls. The next song started off low, and everyone slowed, waiting. It was "I Feel Love" by Donna Summer. High fives. The music was hypnotic. Hips swayed, and the group congealed. For nearly six minutes, they danced, ending with a rousing round of applause.

"That was great," said Emma. She was sweating. Reece was sweating.

"Let's get out of here while we're still ahead," said Reece. He high-fived the guy wearing a velvet coat.

"You are good dancers!" he said.

"Hey, will twenty-five cover us?" asked Reece.

"Well, thank you," said Wanda. Her hair net was askew, and she was sweating too. "This was great. Y'all come back anytime."

Reece put the cash on the table. "Ready?" He held out his arm for Emma to take, and she took it.

In the truck, they stared at each other. Reece wanted to kiss her. He knew it was there, within reach. He turned the key, and the truck roared to life. "Gotta get you home." A kind of blank pain hugged his kidneys.

"Gonna see Mom," said Emma, so far away from Reece in the truck. She wanted to sit next to him, lean into him, and she just did it, scooted over and buckled the lap belt there. "This okay?"

"Sure," said Reece. His heart was in his mouth. "Which way?" He felt confused.

"We can get there from here, without the interstate. Take a right." Her shoulder nudged his, and she felt Reece's hand squeeze her knee once.

They rode in silence, the truck humming. The sound of the blinkers was deafening. Five minutes passed.

"Take a left at the light, and then about a mile. Gosh, I don't want this to end."

What to say? "I almost didn't recognize you when you came off the plane. You look so different somehow, like you've been transformed."

"I feel transformed...Mom's gonna have a fit. She'll like you. I know it."

Reece thought about how Edwin and Gert felt he was a bad influence, that God had no doubt punished him for some unspoken sin, and maybe it was true.

"Right up here at the mailbox, take a left into the drive-way."

Reece pulled in. The carport light was on, but the house looked dark.

"I hope she doesn't shoot us," said Emma.

"She have a gun?"

"Yeah, more than one. She's still afraid of my dad."

Reece cut the engine. "Here we are." There was that silence again, a sense of longing tearing at his heart. He wanted to kick himself. Kristin would want to know every detail.

Emma opened the door and stretched. Reece hopped out and followed her to the side door. "Here we go," said Emma. She rang the doorbell and then knocked.

For thirty seconds, there was nothing, and Emma rang again and knocked. She tried the knob, and it was locked. "A light came on."

The doorknob was turning, and the door opened very slow.

"Mom, it's me, Emma! Open the door!"

The door swung open, and then the screen door pushed out. Reece stepped back, nearly falling. A woman with a nightcap emerged into the light.

"Emma!" Her mom wrapped Emma in a bear hug and then stood back. "Oh, my Lord! Emma!" She gasped.

"Mom, I'm home," and she gripped her, rubbing her back. "It's me, your little girl."

"For land's sake, Emma. Where did you come from? Why didn't you call me? Jesus, my heart!"

Emma was laughing and crying. "I wanted...to surprise you." She pulled her in for another hug.

"Who's this with you? Did you fly in? Oh, Emma…"

"Mom, this is Reece. He was in Ethiopia with me. I wrote you about him. He picked me up at the airport. We stopped at Waffle House, and they had disco. We danced with a bunch of strangers…Oh, Mom, I'm so glad to be home." They hugged some more.

"Well, come in. The AC is on. No need to dawdle out here with the mosquitoes. Come in, come in."

Emma turned and beamed at Reece, and they followed her into the kitchen."

"Are you hungry? Lord, girl, you look so skinny." She wiped tears from her eyes.

"No, we ate at the Waffle House. Best hamburger I've ever had. Mom, you look so good." They hugged again. "Reece, this is my mom."

"Good to meet you." He held out his hand.

"Come here." She moved in and gave him a big hug. "Are you that boy who was shot?"

"Yeah, that's me. Emma saved my life." He stood there, dangling his arms.

"Well, for Pete's sake. You don't look any worse for the wear. And Emma, you need some of Momma's cooking. I've got to sit down." She sat at the kitchen table and grabbed a pack of cigarettes.

"She's a smoker," said Emma.

"No problem," said Reece. "Maybe we should have one too."

"You want one, here." She held out the pack. Her face was thin, her neck wrinkled, her poofy hair a graying black.

"No ma'am, just kidding. Maybe later." He looked

around the small kitchen, kind of square with green appliances and dark cabinets. Magnets and photos covered the refrigerator. A long fluorescent light hummed and flickered.

"Don't call me ma'am, just call me Sarah." She lit up with a cheap lighter from the corner store. "Y'all sit down. Grab yourself a Coke from the fridge. Hell, do what you want to! I'm so happy. I have been so worried about you, baby girl."

"I'm so happy too," said Emma. She fixed herself a glass of water. "Dehydrated from flying."

They all sat at the table, looking back and forth at faces, smiling. Reece cleared his throat.

"So, you just got in? Just flew in?" asked Sarah.

"Got in at midnight. Flew in on Delta from New York City. I left Amsterdam early this morning, or was it yesterday morning? I've lost track. Anyway, here I am." She reached and patted her mother's hand.

"Your sisters are gonna have a fit when they find out, especially Debbie and Sally." Sarah took a long drag and blew the smoke straight up.

"Dang, I missed them," said Emma. "Debbie still with that plumber? What's his name?"

"Hell yes. I think they're glued together. It's Duane. Duane the plumber. But he pays the bills. Only drinks on the weekends."

Emma laughed. "Reece here is an only child."

"Straight up," said Reece. He was feeling the country in Sarah.

"Well, that's sad, ain't it? Just the one. No brothers or sisters to fight with." She laughed a coarse smoker's laugh, phlegm rattling in her chest.

"Overall, a sad life," said Reece with a straight face.

"Is he joking or serious? I can't tell," said Sarah. She tapped some ash into a Coke can.

"He's hard to read sometimes. I learned that in the clinic. He'd be joking, but I thought he was serious. Can't say anything bad, though. He was a real help in the clinic."

"It was my pleasure," said Reece. "She's one hard-working individual. I could barely keep up, seriously."

"Yeah, she's the go-getter in the family," said Sarah.

Reece looked through the kitchen door to a large, open living space beyond, a stairwell with the light on. He leaned his elbows on the table and could tell that Sarah was looking at the scars on his head.

"It's awful late," said Sarah. "You live in Birmingham, Reece? I like that name."

"North of the city, out on a lake near Palmerdale, with my grandparents."

"Being so late, why don't you just sleep on the couch till the morning? I'll fix you two a big breakfast."

"He probably can't do that," said Emma. She stood to get another glass. "I love this Alabama water."

"Well, why not? Let him answer for himself, darling."

"My grandparents would be worried. I'll need to be moving along pretty soon. Just wanted to make sure Emma got home and had a chance to surprise you. She talked about you a lot."

Emma sat. "He's engaged. His fiancée would have a fit."

"Oh," said Sarah. "Well, that's that, I suppose." She finished the cigarette and dropped it into a Coke can. Reece watched the blue veins roll on the tops of her hands. The skin looked tan but thin, with age spots. He guessed she was in her sixties, and he was right.

"Just gets complicated. Yeah, I'd take you up on your offer otherwise. Takes about an hour to get back from here."

"She'd never know unless you told her," said Emma. She kicked him under the table.

"She'd find out. Dora would tell her for sure."

"Who's Dora?" asked Sarah. "Your granny?" She lit another cigarette.

"Oh yeah," said Reece. "She keeps me honest."

"How long you been engaged?"

"Well, about a month before I went over to Ethiopia, so that makes about five months."

"I hate to say it, but you two are like peas in a pod," said Sarah. "Both just plain damn crazy is what I say." She laughed. "I'd never get myself mixed up over there like you two did. I guess I just don't have the guts."

"It's a beautiful country, hard around the edges, though. The people are dirt poor, but nice as pie. I wouldn't mind going back."

"Reece, really?" said Emma. "But I guess I understand. If it hadn't been for recent events, I'd probably still be there." She stared at the wood-veneer table, the potholder with the salt and pepper on it.

Reece cleared his throat. "Mind if I get a glass of water?"

"Shucks, no, boy," said Sarah. "Help yourself. Get you a Coke for the caffeine."

Reece did just that.

Sarah looked Emma in the eyes. "Recent events?"

Emma drummed her fingers on the table. "Well, a few days ago...a couple of soldiers...attacked me."

Sarah turned a kind of pale and her hand trembled. "No, don't tell me, baby girl. Did they hurt you? Soldiers? Oh, my Lord."

"Yeah, they did. In the worst kind of way." Emma sighed and felt her mother's hand on her own.

"No," said Sarah. "I don't believe it. How could anyone hurt you like that? Are you saying...they raped you?"

Reece waited to open his can of Coke.

"Yeah, Mom, that's what happened. One of them had a pistol. They had followed us out in the middle of nowhere."

"Oh Lord. God help us. Was somebody with you? You weren't traveling by yourself, were you?"

"No, another guy from the Mission, but one of them held a gun on him the whole time."

Sarah scooted and put her arm around Emma. "Baby girl. I can't believe it."

Emma could feel the love in her mother's arm, her voice, the familiar smell of the cigarette. She remembered the rocks pressing into her back, and tears came.

"Let it out, baby girl. Let it out."

Soon, Emma was sobbing, the dam breaking inside her soul. Tears ran into her mouth, and she let her mother comfort her. Reece sat silent, his head down, his face hard. Emma's chest heaved as she cried. She felt broken and that she could sleep for an eternity. They just let her cry.

It took a few minutes for Emma to compose herself. She looked haggard and worn to Reece, on the edge of being destroyed, but with an inner strength that resonated. He popped the top off his Coke.

Emma put her chin in her hands, elbows on the table. She looked at Reece and smiled. "If Reece had been there...maybe..."

"Honey, but they had a gun. They could have killed you. Oh, I just can't bear to think about it."

"I would have just kept driving," said Reece, "until we were in a safer place." He felt bad about second-guessing Craig. He had no real idea what he would have done.

"See," said Emma. "He would have had a plan." She kicked him under the table again.

"Water over the dam," said Sarah. "Did you see a doctor?"

Emma laughed. "No, there was no doctor to see, plus there was no reason to. I took some serious penicillin, though. In the butt."

"She's a survivor," said Reece.

"What about you?" asked Emma. "Shot in the head."

"Well, that's different," said Reece. "Not so personal. I'd plug them into the ground." He tapped his fist on the table.

Emma smiled.

"Well, look, you want to sleep with me tonight, baby girl? You know you can."

Emma tried to laugh. "No, Mom, but thanks." She wiped tears. "I guess I should be getting to bed. I'm exhausted."

"Yeah, don't let me keep you up," said Reece. "I'll...give you a call tomorrow, see how you're doing. You probably want to talk with your mom here in private." He scooted his chair back.

"Let me say goodbye outside, okay?"

"You two do what you need to do," said Sarah. "I'll go

and make sure your bed is ready. Got clean sheets on it."
She stood. "Reece, it's a pleasure meeting you. I understand if I don't see more of you. But I appreciate you being
there for my baby girl. Sounds like you came along at a
good time."

"Great to meet you too," said Reece. He stood and
hugged her bony shoulders.

Emma stood, stretched, and yawned. She pushed
through the screen door onto the covered carport. Moths
banged at the light. Reece followed her to the driveway and
the truck. Above were stars, but not as many as in Godo.
He wanted to take Emma into his arms and just hold her,
just feel her next to him.

"Well, she was surprised for sure," said Reece.

Emma laughed. "Yeah, thanks to you. Thank you for
picking me up...and dancing at the Waffle House. I don't
think I'll ever forget that."

"There's a first time for everything, I suppose." He
leaned against the hood of the truck, waiting for something to happen, somewhat sick at the thought of having
to tell Kristin about Emma's homecoming.

Emma leaned beside him and looked up at the stars.
"You're a swell guy, Reece Myers. Remember when I
thought your name was Rice? Afewerki told me your
name was Rice."

Reece laughed. "Yeah, I get that sometimes." He remembered the first time he saw Emma, struck by her face,
figure, and can-do attitude. That crushing half-smile.

"We were just starting to make out when you were shot.
Do you remember that?" asked Emma.

Reece turned toward her. "Some of it." He felt energy

running from his thighs to his head, a giddy kind of sick feeling. "That guy with the rotten leg. I gave him my bed. I was supposed to sleep on the floor of your place." He had the distinct memory of his hands slipping down inside her scrub top, but that was it.

"Most people wouldn't give up their bed like that. I think the other guys thought you were crazy." She turned, and they were facing one another, her eyes right at his chest. "Can you kiss me goodnight? I mean, you know..."

Reece felt like he was on a rocket to the moon. What to do? "I'd love to, but..."

Emma pulled his waist toward hers and tilted her head up. Reece, completely breathless, felt his mouth meeting hers, and they kissed long and slow, their hearts drumming. He felt he would fall over and pulled away.

"I...I've probably got to go. Not that I want to, but that I should." He pulled her in for a full-body hug.

"Oh, Reece. I missed you so much. I'm so glad you're alive. I couldn't wait to see you again, but yeah, I know you need to go. Call me, though, okay?"

Reece let her go. "Okay, I'll call. Get some rest."

She leaned up and kissed him on the cheek and then pinched his side.

"Ow, hey." He laughed. She laughed. "Okay, got to go. Good night."

"Good night, Reece, and thank you again for everything."

"See ya," and he walked around, opened the door, and hopped in. He watched Emma coast to the door, turn, and wave. He waved and then was on his way back to the lake

It was three before Reece got home, and he slept until ten. Horace was knocking on his bedroom door. Reece sat up, groggy and confused.

"Reece, it's the hospital. Get out here and take this call."

Reece was in his underwear and scrambled to find some shorts. He fell against the wall, putting them on. Why was the hospital calling him? Had something happened to Emma? That was crazy. Was it Kristin? He stumbled to the phone.

"Hello?" He didn't recognize the voice on the other end.

"Did you just wake up?"

"Uh, yeah, sorry about that," said Reece.

"You got the job."

Reece puzzled the pieces. "Oh, Sheila, hey. That's great. No interview?"

"We know who you are. We're glad to have you, but it is the 11 to 7 in ICU and not CCU."

"Yeah, not a problem. Baby steps, right?" He gave a thumbs-up to Horace. Dora was outside sweeping the driveway, which was Reece's job.

"Yeah, right," said Sheila. "I'm so excited to see you come back. You'll need to make sure you do your yearly CEUs, and you'll need to do the drug test, but that's just routine. Get your picture taken, too, for the badge. We have a new system where you swipe your badge to clock in."

"Oh, sure. I need a haircut anyway. Do I need to do orientation?"

"No, we can skip that. It's kind of like you just took a

long vacation. We're lucky to have you back."

"That's for sure," said Reece.

"Okay, great. I'll let human resources know, and they'll be in touch, okay?"

"Yeah, super," said Reece.

"Bye."

"Bye." He handed the phone to Horace.

"You get the job, boy?"

"Sure did." He ran his hands through his hair. He imagined himself in white scrubs, back at it, starting IVs and giving bed baths. Things were slowly gelling, getting back to normal, it seemed.

"Go outside and tell your granny. She was worried they wouldn't hire you back." Horace sat back in his recliner with a big smile.

"Yeah, me too, sort of. I would have tried UAB if not. Let me grab a cup of coffee first." He put a pot of water to boil on the small electric stove and then went to the back door. He saw Dora sweeping as if her life depended on it.

"Hey, son."

"Carraway just called. Got the job in ICU." He breathed out a sigh of relief.

"Oh, honey, that's the cat's meow. Here, you finish sweeping, and I'll cook you up some eggs."

Reece laughed. "I've got water on for coffee. Let me do that first. No problem."

Dora grinned and followed him back inside. "Our boy got his old job back!" She slapped him on the waist.

Horace glanced at her, still smiling from behind a *National Geographic.*

Reece dumped in instant coffee, waiting for the water

to boil.

"You gonna call Kristin and let her know?" asked Dora. "She'll be tickled pink."

"Yeah, I need to do that." He watched bubbles form on the bottom of the pot. It had taken so long to boil water in Godo.

"When do you start?" asked Horace.

"I don't know. I should get a call from human resources about that. I'd rather it be the first of next week." He doubted he was ready. What if he had a seizure on the job? Surely Sheila had heard about the incident in the cafeteria.

"What I want to know is why you came in so late last night," said Dora. "Did you get that Emma home?"

Reece smiled, remembering. "Oh yeah, met her mother. Real nice lady."

"You must of talked for a long time," said Horace.

"It does take an hour to get there, so there's that. She was hungry, so we went to Waffle House first."

"I guess she missed our kind of food," said Dora. "Did she look healthy?"

"Well, she was tired from the flying," said Reece. "Especially her arms."

"Her arms?"

Reece laughed. "Just a joke, you know, flying, arms." He cleared his throat and took the boiling water from the stove.

"I doubt if Kristin will find it very funny," said Dora.

Reece sobered a bit, sipped his coffee, and sat at the table. "She gave me permission."

"But you would've gone anyway, is what I'm guessing,"

said Dora. "I just don't have a good feeling about all this. You want two eggs?"

"Sure, two are good." He rubbed his bed hair.

"Just because a chicken can cross the road doesn't mean he has to," said Horace.

"Talking in riddles," said Reece. "Look, she's a decent person. We worked together. Plus, she was attacked just a few days ago. They were going to shut down the clinic anyway, but they fast-tracked it to get her home." She'd also mentioned that something else had happened, but said she would tell him later.

Dora looked worried and shook her head. "Girls don't need to be getting mixed up with trouble like that. Did they hurt her? I hope not, if it's what I'm thinking."

Reece glanced at Horace, and he had his hand cupped to his ear. "Yeah, they hurt her. Bastards."

"Lord, that's bad news. That's just awful. I guess she thought she could talk to you about it." She scrambled the eggs in a bowl and added milk to make them fluffy. "At least she had sense to come home."

Reece played with the placemat on the table. "Yeah, I said I'll call her back today, once she gets some rest."

"There you go," said Dora. "Where will it end? You have to let her go, son. Kristin is depending on you." She dropped a lump of margarine in the skillet.

"Listen to your granny, boy," said Horace. He went back to his magazine, licked a finger, and turned the page.

"I get it," said Reece. "I'll check with Kristin first. How's that?" He folded the placemat and unfolded it.

"Well, that's a start, I suppose," said Dora. She scraped the eggs with a worn spatula, the handle melted.

"I'll make some toast," said Reece. He stood and went for the loaf of white bread.

"Too many women," said Dora. "Too many."

Reece popped in two slices and laughed. "I'll give Kristin a call right now." He wondered what Cindy was doing. Maybe there were too many women. That had never been a problem in the past.

"Smart boy," said Dora. She piled the eggs onto a plate. "Here you go. Want ketchup?"

"No ketchup. That's Randy's thing." Randy was his dad's younger brother. He poked at his eggs, and the toast jumped up. He started to stand, but Dora beat him to it. "Thanks." He ate in silence as Dora attacked the dirty skillet with a scrub pad.

"Don't forget about the driveway," said Dora.

"Yeah, let me finish and then I'll get on it after I call Kristin." Reece ate his eggs, alternating between bites of toast and sips of coffee. "Here, I'm calling." He took the black phone and dialed the unit.

"CCU, Eudora."

"Hey, Eudora, it's Reece. How are you?" He toyed with the phone cord, trying to work out a kink in the line.

"Hey, boy. You want Kristin?"

"Sure," said Reece. He could tell that he'd been put on hold.

"Hey!" said Kristin.

"Hey," said Reece. "Can you talk?"

"Just for a few. Got a new patient that's a handful, a big man, a garbage truck driver on a vent."

Reece imagined a garbage truck driver on a ventilator. "So, just checking in." He waited for Kristin to ask him about Emma.

"Well, are you going to tell me or what?" Brad was on the unit, scribbling in charts, trying to look busy. That morning in the break room, she'd told him about Reece and Emma.

"Yeah, well, she got in around midnight. She was hungry, so we stopped at a Waffle House, then I took her home, met her mother." The phone felt very heavy in his hand. He closed his eyes.

"She didn't try anything, did she?"

Reece nearly choked. "Uh, no, no. We talked for a while with her mom. I think we scared her coming in so late. You know. She had no idea Emma was even in the country."

"I think that's weird, that she didn't let her mom know."

"Well, it happened pretty fast, her leaving and all."

"Not so fast that she couldn't call you, though." Kristin was across from her new admit in twelve, Mrs. Dunlop's old room. X-ray was doing a chest film. The man, the garbage truck driver, had a massive infection in his lower jaw. Surgery had created four slits in his jaw to allow the pus to drain. "Reece?"

"She just needed a ride, is all I can say." Should he tell her about the kiss? He cringed and felt a little sick, like he had eaten too much ice cream too fast.

"What time did you get home?"

Reece wanted to say two. "Oh, three I think—"

"Three? You must have had a lot to talk about."

"Takes an hour to drive there," said Reece. "We were in the Waffle House for probably an hour. They were playing disco music, and the waitress was...dancing with this guy in overalls."

"Dancing? That's even weirder. Are you sure you don't have a crush on her? It just seems like you have an adventure every time you're with her. Reece?"

"No, no. Just relax."

"Relax? How can I relax? With Cindy nosing around and Emma back, I don't know what's going on. You understand, right?"

Reece knew she was right. "I totally understand. Hey, did Sheila tell you I got the job? In ICU."

"What? Really? I haven't seen her this morning. She hangs out in ICU mostly. Oh, that's great. When you get on day shift, we can ride together."

"Yeah, definitely," said Reece. "Not sure when I start." He realized his eyes were closed and opened them.

Kristin watched the tech back out the portable X-ray machine from room twelve. "Look, I'm going to have to go, okay? But you better come see me later, okay? You can give me all the details then."

"Details? Sure." He closed his eyes again, envisioning the garbage truck man as having a huge belly and a scruff of oily beard. "And tell Sheila thanks again for me, okay?"

"Sure, I will, but let me go, okay?"

"Sure, okay...talk to you later today."

"Bye."

"Bye." Reece hung up the phone and felt his heart skip a beat. When should he call Emma? Probably later was better. He made eye contact with Dora. "See, she's okay."

"Just keep doing the right thing is all I can say," said Dora.

"Not a problem," said Reece.

Emma slept like the dead, dreaming and dreaming, but nothing she could remember. She looked at the big alarm clock on her dresser. 12:47. She closed her eyes, turned over, and slept for another two hours. Her mom was vacuuming downstairs. She turned to her back and sat up, looking around. Everything was just as she had left it, two bottles of perfume on her dresser beside a straw hat, the clock. She inhaled, and it was the smell of home, a kind of pleasant, dried oil smell mixed with berries. What was next? Had Reece kissed her last night? He had, but she'd initiated it. Was it just a friendly kiss? Probably not. Her thoughts went to getting a job, and she felt weak at the effort needed to get back in the rat race under the thumb of doctors and supervisors. She shook off the thought, determined to enjoy home again. Hot shower in the hall bathroom! The vacuum cleaner noise went away.

Emma stood, laughing that she was naked. She'd just ripped her clothes off in a frenzy and dived into her clean bed, relishing the smell of Tide and her feather pillows. She stood and looked at herself in the dresser mirror, noticed that her right breast hung just a bit lower than her left. She was the same Emma, it seemed, but her thoughts went to the day of the rape, and a surge of emotion welled in her chest. She dug out clean panties and a bra, went to her closet, and chose a long, light-blue, sleeveless dress. She hadn't worn a dress since she'd left and loved the freedom she felt wearing it.

"Heck." She'd planned on getting a shower first, but

then decided to see what was up downstairs. There were voices now. Who could it be? And she knew it must be her sister. She hurried downstairs barefoot, and there she was. "Sally! You devil."

Sally leapt off the couch and ran to her, giving her a huge hug. "Mom called me. My God, you've lost weight."

"Well, that's the least of my worries," said Emma. "Hey, Mom." She gave her a hug, too. "Best mom in the world."

"I told her what all happened," said Sarah. She looked grim. "I hope that was okay. No secrets in this family."

"Emma, you didn't deserve that. Are you okay? Here, sit down." Sally pulled Emma onto the couch.

"It sucks," said Emma. "I had to leave on a bad note." Tears swelled, and she put her head in her hands. "But... I'm home. That's what matters."

Sally draped over her. "I'd kill them, you know that? God, that makes me so damn angry."

"Yeah, and I would be fine with it. They'll never be charged, though, being soldiers. That's what Dr. Guthrie said."

"So, were you alone?" asked Sally. She had puffy, dark-blonde hair the same color as Emma's and wore hot pants with a Crimson Tide t-shirt.

"I don't want to have to tell the story more than once. But there was a guy, Craig, with me. They held him at gunpoint. Nothing he could do." She wiped her eyes. "So, how's the family, Sammy and Heather?" Sammy was Sally's husband, and Heather their only child.

"Good, good. He's working and Heather's at school, but they're coming over later. We're gonna have a party to end all parties. Right, Mom?"

Sarah frowned and then laughed. "If you say so. I'm all for it. I'm just damn happy to have you back, baby girl." She pushed the vacuum to the wall and sat in the wing-back chair. "Cool enough in here for you all?" She wore her loose jeans and favorite plaid shirt, frayed at the edges.

"Hey, I haven't had air conditioning for two years," said Emma. "Feels fine to me."

"I still can't believe you ran off and did that," said Sally. "I would say God was watching over you, but maybe not."

"Me and God have a lot of talking to do, that's for sure." Emma wondered when she would be able to tell them about her suicidal thoughts, about jumping from the helicopter.

"You want some food?" asked Sarah. She'd called and taken the day off from the barbecue. "Made some chicken salad with those pickles you like."

"That sounds right on," said Emma. "I can fix it, though."

"No, no, just sit there and talk." She went to the kitchen, limping a bit from the arthritis in her hips.

"Are you sure you're okay?" asked Sally. "You might need to go to the doctor."

"No, I'm fine. Nothing to be done now."

"Maybe you know what I'm thinking." Sally folded her hands in her lap. Her eyes were light blue, unlike Emma's greenish brown. "You need to know for sure."

"Yeah, I know what you mean. God couldn't be that cruel, I hope. I can get one of those tests you check your pee with. You look good."

"Well, I haven't been suffering in Africa for God knows how long."

"I didn't suffer. Everyone was welcoming and friendly, except for a select few. I had plenty to eat, although my stomach stayed upset most of the time. The food was delicious but spicy."

"Yeah, you wrote about that. I don't think I could have done it, but you are the crazy one in the bunch." Sally laughed. They were sitting thigh to thigh. "So, what about this guy I'm hearing about, the guy who was shot over there? He brought you home last night? I can't believe you didn't call one of us to pick you up. He must be special. What's his name? Rice?"

Emma laughed. "No, dummy, it's Reece. And I guess he is special. We worked in the clinic together in Godo, until he was shot by this guy who ran the village, the Hyena we called him."

"That's just sad and sadder. But he lived."

"Yeah, and walking and talking too. It's a miracle. He looked entirely dead in the hospital over there. His fiancée came to see him."

"Yep, that's got my curiosity up," said Sally. "He's taken, I gather."

Emma wavered. "Technically, I guess. He'll come over, and you can meet him. He's a friend for life, regardless. Has nice legs and broad shoulders, kinda skinny. Wears glasses."

"Babydoll, I can tell by your voice. Don't get into something that's gonna hurt you, regardless of how nice he is. What about that guy you were dating before you went over there? The one from the church."

"That's over. We never really dated anyway. Too strait-laced for me. Reece is just fun, and smart too."

Sally smoothed back Emma's hair. "You need a shower. Look how oily your hair is. My goodness."

"The last shower I took was in Amsterdam. I was only at the hotel for about six hours, I think. It was heaven. You wouldn't believe the breakfast buffet. I about died."

"God, you've got some stories to tell me, girl. I've never even been farther than Florida. Do the people wear wooden shoes there?"

"Ha," said Emma. "Used to probably. It was beautiful, and lots of people on bicycles. I saw a lady wearing a dress riding one."

"Hey!" said Sarah from the kitchen. "Come in here and get your sandwich. No eating on the couch."

Emma looked at Sally. Sally looked at Emma, and they stood. "You have to tell me more about this Reece character."

Emma sighed.

On the kitchen table were two plates with chicken salad on white bread, sweet tea, and potato chips. Sarah was smoking. "Dig in. I'll make you another one if you like."

Emma seated herself, anticipating the sweet chicken salad with grape halves and mayonnaise. "Looks yummy, Mom. Thanks." She lifted the sandwich, cut on the diagonal, took a bite, and moaned. "Oh, Mom. That's the best thing I ever ate."

Sally nodded in agreement.

"Ooh, and Lay's potato chips, I can tell." She crunched a few and washed them down with the cold, sweet tea. "Better than sex."

"Well, I wouldn't know," said Sarah. She laughed and then coughed her smoker's cough. "You tell Sally more about Reece?"

"Yeah, a little." She took another bite and moaned again.

"Not bad looking, but skinny as a rail," said Sarah. "I think he's sweet on Emma. But then there's the complication."

"Yeah," said Sally. "I smell trouble in the making."

Emma just took another bite, gazing around in wonder at the kitchen, her kitchen, her house, her sister, her mother. "I have no idea about that."

"Come on," said Sally. "There's something you're not telling. Mom, you need to cut back on your smoking. Tell her, Emma."

Emma nodded with her mouth full. "She can do what she wants. Nobody can tell her what to do. You know that. But it is bad for you, Mom."

"I know," said Sarah. She finished and stubbed the butt in an ashtray from Gatlinburg.

"So, is this Reece character sweet on you like Momma says? I can tell you have a thing for him. I know that look, you devil. Just you be careful, though. Does he know what happened to you over there?"

"Yeah, I told him. He kissed me last night." She blushed and drank some tea.

"I knew it," said Sally. "And did you kiss him?"

"I certainly did," said Emma. She laughed.

"Emma, you've got to watch yourself. He's practically a married man," said Sarah. She lit another cigarette with paper matches from the barbecue.

"I get it. I know," said Emma. "I just get this vibe from him that he's in over his head, that maybe he wants out.

His fiancée has no idea what he went through."

"And you do, baby girl?"

"That's it. I do. And he gets me. What can I say?" Emma finished her sandwich, crusts and all.

"Another one?" asked Sarah. "You look about as skinny as Reece."

"Just another half, but I could eat three."

"I can't imagine going without chicken salad," said Sally. "I've got to meet this Reece. You think he'll come back over? What's his fiancée going to say?"

"Maybe she'll come with him," said Emma. "I guess I just don't know."

"That would be some kind of awkward," said Sally.

"It sure would be," said Sarah. She put her sandwich on the table and inhaled.

Standing in the roof gutter, Reece swept pine straw down the incline onto the flat portion over his room. Around him, the tall pines swayed in their tops, and cicadas buzzed like party horns. He looked over the road to the lake glistening below, at Horace sitting beneath the black walnut tree, and felt lucky to be alive, to be back home doing everyday things. One of his favorite jobs had been at Food Giant, where he'd swept and mopped the aisles, front to back. That was during nursing school. He was about to do a Tarzan yell, but changed his mind.

He swept a pile to the edge and pushed it over, then headed up to the ridge to do the other side. Had he kissed Emma? *I did.* Her lips were so soft, but Kristin's were too. He grunted and tried to clear his head, but was perplexed. He reassured himself that he would see Kristin soon and focused on that. He wanted to hear more about the patient who was a garbage man. He'd also found Mrs. Dunlop's obituary in *The Birmingham News* and had cut it out for her, just a mere twenty words.

He started at the end and swept down, going to the other end, turning and continuing until he could sweep it off the edge. He knew that the straw was falling onto Dora's elephant ears and that he would have to brush them off. He laughed. She still came out and checked after he mowed the lawn to make sure he didn't miss anything. He felt like taking a pee off the roof, but worried that the elderly woman, Mrs. Pinkie, up behind them was watching. He imagined two snakes fighting, each swallowing the other until poof! all gone. Soon, he was finished and gazed at the garage just a quick leap over. He'd never made the leap, being a good five feet, and pondered it, but let the idea drop along with the broom to the ground. He mounted the ladder and descended. He imagined it was about three, and it was. Time for a shower.

Reece let the screen door slam behind him and walked into the cool kitchen. Dora drowsed in the recliner, her eyes half open, her jaw slack.

"You get that straw swept?" She opened her eyes all the way.

"Yes, ma'am," said Reece.

"Did you knock the straw off the elephant ears? Looks bad if you don't."

"Ah, you got me there. I'll do it before I see Kristin. Getting a shower."

"Where's your dad? You know I call him your dad."

"In the garden. Where else? I thought he was going to pull corn today?"

"Lord, don't mention that. Not today, anyways. Makes such a mess, and I have to clean it up." She was reclined and talking to the ceiling.

"Yeah, right. Not a problem." He fetched a pair of underwear and disappeared into the bathroom.

It was about four-fifteen when Reece pulled into the steep driveway. The entire front yard was steep as well, making it almost unusable. He'd never seen Edwin mowing it, but it was always cut. He pulled behind Kristin's Toyota.

Kristin met him at the door, holding Wallace the cat. "Hey there, Mr. Popular. Wallace misses you."

Reece rubbed Wallace's head and frowned. "Hey there, buddy." Inside, he could smell the signature aroma of stuffed bell peppers in the oven, Edwin's favorite dish of all time. "Want to go on the deck?"

"Sure. Hey, Daddy. Look who's here. Your future son-in-law."

Edwin put his recliner down so that his feet touched the floor. "Well, I recognize him, honey. How are ya? Kristin said you got the job at Carraway."

"I did indeed," said Reece. "Human resources called, and I can start next Monday. Just have to do the drug test. The only problem is that I can't find my nurse's license. They wanted to make another copy. Not sure why."

"You could be an imposter," said Kristin. She took his arm. "We're going on the almighty deck."

Gert emerged from the kitchen, wiping her hands on her apron. "Congratulations on the job." She cracked a fragile smile.

"Thanks. Got to earn the big bucks. Kristin wants a new boat and a Corvette to pull it with." He kept a straight face.

"What?" asked Gert.

"He's pulling your leg, honey," said Edwin. He turned the TV on with the remote.

"He's a leg puller," said Kristin. "Come on. We got some talking to do."

"Uh oh," said Reece. He followed her onto the squarish deck, stained a dark brown. When the sun was out, it was too hot to stand on in bare feet, except for the shaded part where Harvey the three-legged squirrel lived in the covered baby pool. Reece peered in, and there he was, stretched out and covered with pine shavings.

"Poor old Harvey. He gets lonely out here."

"Where's Walter?" asked Reece.

"Asleep on my bed. He's so cute under the blanket. Here, sit."

Reece sat next to her on the hard bench. "So, how was work? How's the garbage man? I got something for you." He reached for his tiny wallet.

"He's a mess. I feel so sorry for him. His rotten teeth got infected and abscessed. His whole lower jaw is a nightmare, about as nasty as I've ever seen. He's on a vent to keep his airway open." She put her hand on his knee. "Brad asked me out again, to another party at some other resident's place, a pool party this weekend. I said I'd come if I could bring you, and he kind of walked away."

"He's a persistent, pardon my language, son of a bitch."

"You're pardoned, at least for that. So, Mr. Hotshot, tell me more about last night with the princess from far-off Africa. Is she glad to be home?"

"It seems that way."

"I can't believe you got home so late."

"It's a long drive from there and back. Does the garbage man have a name? Any family? I just imagine a garbage man living alone in a little shack. But happy."

"His last name is Odo. No family that I've seen yet. So, you met her mother, too? Did you like her as much as you like Emma?"

"Stop. She was nice enough, older than I expected, but she does have seven kids. Emma's the youngest girl."

"Do you like the younger women? I'm younger than you are. Don't forget that."

"I'm engaged to you for Pete's sake. Is he conscious, Mr.

Odo?"

"Well dang, you'll have to come and see him. He's alert but sedated. He gets agitated. The look in his eyes is pretty wild. I'm pretty sure he's scared out of his mind. But, back to you. How did she look? Emma."

"Tired mostly."

"Oh, you've got more than that. Kiss me." She leaned in, and Reece kissed her on the lips. "You know we did it, right? You can't forget that."

"Are you kidding? But I am worried. You know, no condom and all."

"What? And then you will have to marry me."

"What would your parents say? They would hate me then."

"They don't hate you. Maybe they just don't trust you, is all. You are a bad boy sometimes."

"Well, I don't go to parties with oddball doctors." He leaned over, elbows on knees, and Kristin rubbed his back. "Yeah, just up a little higher." He scrunched his shoulders.

"Emma never scratched your back, did she? I know that's your favorite thing. But dang it, tell me what you guys did last night."

"Keep scratching, over to the spine, on the spine." He moaned for effect.

"You little hussy. I will not until you talk."

"Okay, okay," said Reece. The sun felt good on his back. "We went to the Waffle House. The waitress was playing disco. This black lady in a red dress came in with these two characters. Before I knew it, we were dancing in the restaurant—"

"You and Emma?"

"No, everybody, except for the cook. He was cooking and looked petrified half the time. It was weird but strangely... appropriate. I mean getting shot in the head and all, everything together."

"That sounds bad, Reece. You like her."

"It's just what happened. That's all." He sighed and sat up, giving up on the back scratch. "And then I took her home and met her mother. We talked for a while."

"What did you talk about?"

"She was attacked before she left. Raped by two soldiers..."

"What? You're kidding?"

"No, just a day or two before she left. That's why she came home as quick as she did. They were shutting the clinic down anyway, but..." A pang of guilt drove through his body like an old riding lawnmower.

"Jesus, Reece, that's horrible. But she was putting herself in harm's way, right?"

Reece coughed. "That's probably a bit judgmental, wouldn't you say?" He picked up a piece of pine straw and studied the gray, papery cap holding the three needles together. "I guess I put myself in harm's way. It's like saying it was my fault that I got shot, that she was raped."

"No, you know that's not what I mean? I mean, it's not surprising that something nasty happened over there, to both of you. And that's got me worried even more."

"What?"

"Well, you both were attacked. You can bond over things like that. It's not rocket science. I need to check Harvey's water bowl." She stood and peered into the tiny pool. The bowl was half full.

"Harvey lost a leg, so I guess we've bonded, too," said Reece. "I guess I can bond with anyone with one leg. What about Mr. Odo, the garbage man? I guess we're pals too." He leaned back against the deck and crossed his legs.

"Oh, you make me a little bit mad sometimes." She stared into the pool, watching Harvey cleaning his face. "I just need to know what's going on inside your head."

"Will you always need to know? I mean that's a lot to ask someone, to empty their head on demand." He folded his arms, then rubbed the back of his neck where the sun was hitting.

She folded her arms. "Reece, you have to be honest with me, always. How can I trust you otherwise?"

"Maybe you have to develop the gift of trust. It can't just hinge on me. How did we get on this subject anyway? So, are you going to Brad's party? You never said."

"That's clever. Should I? Maybe I'll go and say I didn't. How would you feel?"

"I wouldn't know, so I guess I'd feel fine." He put his arm on the deck rail and turned to look out over the yard.

The back door opened. It was Gert letting out Walter. "Go, go on."

"Come here, baby," said Kristin, and Walter scuttled onto the porch, wagging his entire backside, his tail nub switching. "Who's Mommy's little boy?" She scratched his ears, and he slobbered on her hand.

"Walter, Walter," said Reece. "Mr. Walter."

Just silence.

"Okay, I'll be the big person here," said Kristin. "I'm sorry that Emma was attacked. It's horrible." She sat down beside him and turned his face toward hers. "Your turn."

Reece pondered his options. Should he run scream-ing through the street? He felt like it. "They were soldiers, one with a gun. She was with this guy, Craig. It was on the way to AK. How's that?" He could feel his heart beat-ing. He imagined Kristin telling the story to her mom, the shocked look on her face.

"Better, but you're not being very nice. Please be nice. Reece, I love you. I want the best for us. You want that too, right? We have to talk about these things, right?"

Reece was fine with never uttering another single sylla-ble. "Yeah, yeah, you're right, I suppose."

"Suppose? Reece, that's not good enough. Put your arm around me like you care."

Reece did as he was told. A jet roared high overhead. He imagined the pilots looking down at the postage-stamp houses, laughing at a dirty joke. He remembered having sex with Kristin and loosened up. How was it that he'd gone twenty-two years without having sex? The church and the Bible. His parents. He felt like an idiot who had a million dollars but couldn't afford to buy soap.

"There, that's better," said Kristin. "We had sex."

"Yeah, I was thinking about that." He pulled her closer. "There is one thing I didn't tell you, maybe two or three." He felt like a balloon was coming out of his mouth.

Emma spent a good deal of the afternoon on the phone with her other sisters, not mentioning the rape. Her brother lived in Austin, working in a bar, but practically unreachable. She said bye to her sister, Mindy, in Gulf Shores and placed the plastic phone on its base. Sally had left to pick up her daughter, Heather, from school, but she was coming back with Emma's favorite dessert, a pecan pie, and a pregnancy test.

The living room was quiet, her mom outside puttering in the flowers. Emma just soaked it in, feeling safe for the first time in a long while. She loved the homey smell, the tan walls, the brown carpet, the beat-up couch covered in a rose pattern. The TV sat there looking at her, and she realized she could watch it if she wanted to. She turned it on to a fuzzy Channel 42. It was a talk show she'd never seen before with an attractive black woman as the host. She turned it off and headed to the kitchen.

She searched and found a box of Frosted Mini Wheats, one of her favorites. Just the sight of the box sent a thrill through her. She took a handful and pushed out through the screen door onto the cool cement carport. Warm air washed over her face. Her mom was bent over a giant Hosta, pulling off dead leaves.

"Hey, Mom." She crunched the cereal and sat in a folding chair not unlike those in the dining hut back in Godo. Had it been a dream? She remembered her promise to Afewerki and wondered how that would play out.

"Hey, baby girl," said Sarah. She stood and arched her

back. "You planted this, remember?"

"Yeah, I guess I did. It's huge. You going back to work tomorrow?"

"Well, they need me. I don't trust that bunch of girls. Too scatterbrained for my liking." She laughed and wiped sweat from her brow. Beyond the deep lot, cars passed on the road.

"Come sit by me, Momma. Gosh, I missed you."

"I missed you, too, baby girl. God, I'm glad you're home. You got some catching up to do." She took a folding chair and pulled it close. "Whew, I'm winded."

"It's those dang cigarettes," said Emma.

"Now, don't you start." She coughed. "I sure hope to God you're not pregnant. Sally told me what she's bringing." She looked around for her lighter.

"It's on the back of the car," said Emma. "I'll get it."

"What would you do?" She took the disposable lighter and fished the hard pack of Marlboro Lights from her pants pocket.

"Jesus, I'm not pregnant. Don't you think I'd know?" Emma knew that sounded silly.

"Well, God willing," said Sarah. "That would turn your world upside down. Believe me, I know."

Emma wondered what Reece would do if the test were positive. "Well, you'll make a good granny, right?" She wanted to laugh but couldn't.

"You're taking this pretty good, baby girl. You sure you're okay?"

"Not okay. But what can I do? I mean, I do need to get back to work." She watched Sarah inhale and blow smoke. "You want me to smoke one with you?"

"What? Are you crazy?"

"A little," said Emma. "Maybe a lot. Gimme one."

"No, I won't. You'll get addicted like I did."

"I'll take one then." Laughing, she grabbed the pack off the chair. Sarah grabbed but missed. Emma took one and put it to her lips. "Need the lighter. How do I look?"

"Plumb silly, if you ask me. Here. Suit yourself. If you want to cough like I do, then go right ahead."

Emma lit up, pulled smoke into her mouth. "Not bad. I already want another one and another one. I'm gonna smoke the whole damn pack." She laughed.

"Yeah, you are a little crazy," said Sarah. "Seeing you smoke makes me want to quit. You beat all. You know that?"

"You know, I never saw one person smoking in Ethiopia. Lots of drinking but no tobacco."

"Probably too expensive, don't you think?" She dropped her stub on the cement and stepped on it.

"Here comes trouble."

Sally pulled into the long driveway with Heather, who jumped out and ran. "Emma!" She stopped. "You're smoking?"

Emma laughed. "Get over here!"

They hugged and danced around, Emma dropping her cigarette.

"Holy cow!" said Emma. "You've grown a foot, girl!" She watched Sally, who was holding a paper grocery sack.

"And you've lost weight," said Heather. "Hey, Nanna." She gave Sarah a side hug.

"I've got the goods," said Sally. She rattled the paper sack.

"Pecan pie?" asked Emma.

"Yep, and something extra special just for you." Her words came out strained.

"Emma?" asked Heather. "Mom told me what happened. I wish you hadn't gone over there." She wore faded, torn jeans and a football jersey with baggy sleeves. Her hair was black like her daddy's.

Emma frowned. She supposed everyone knew by now, maybe even her dad, who lived less than half a mile away. "I'm okay, though, right?" In the ensuing silence, a dread came over her, and she fought back a sob.

"Emma," said Sally. She put the sack on the back of the car and hugged her. "Cry if you need to. We're here for you. We'll protect you, us girls. Right, Heather?"

"Hell yes," said Heather.

Sarah watched from her chair, an airy, lost feeling in her chest.

Emma stifled the upwelling and put her hands in her dress pockets. She wiped at a lone tear clinging to the inside of her eye.

"Well, hey, let's eat some pie. Your favorite, Emma."

Everyone headed into the cool kitchen. Sarah took down a pack of paper plates and fished out four forks and a case knife from the silverware drawer. Soon, everyone had an oozy slice.

Emma was first to dig in. She chewed slow and then took another bite. "Oh my god, that's good."

"Lady at the bakery said it's made with Karo syrup and lots of butter," said Sally. "It is mighty fine."

Sarah picked at her piece. "Y'all know I don't care for sweets, but it is good. Expensive too...about six dollars?"

Sally nodded. "I don't care if it costs a hundred." She laughed and punched Emma in the arm. "You owe me, sister."

"Ow." Emma slowed down, saving the chewy crust for last. "If Reece comes over, we'll get one of these. His favorite pie is pecan, too."

"Well, here comes Reece out of nowhere," said Sally. "First, you feed him, and then you pull back and set the hook. Right?"

"Who's Reece?" asked Heather. She spun her plate with her finger.

"He worked with me in Godo, in Ethiopia. He's a nurse, the one who was shot and lived to tell about it."

"Mom told me." She looked alarmed. "Is he nice?"

"He's real nice," said Sarah. "He brought Emma home from the airport."

"I didn't tell you about the disco music at the Waffle House, did I?"

Sally nodded, and Emma told the story of how they were all dancing to Donna Summer.

"He must be a little crazy like you," said Heather. "I'd like to meet him. I've never met anyone who was shot before."

"Well, we'll see," said Emma. "I'll ask him. Maybe tomorrow or Friday."

"If he can swing it with his fiancée," said Sally. She laughed. What Emma wanted, Emma usually got.

"Fiance?" asked Heather. She was only thirteen but worldly-wise.

"We're just good friends, I suppose," said Emma. "No harm in him coming over. Don't go blabbing to the preacher on me." She savored her last bite of pie. "Anybody else want a glass of water?" Sarah did, and Emma fixed two glasses.

Everyone soon lapsed into gossip, catching Emma up on neighborhood news and personal matters. Sally told her about finding a *Hustler* in Sammy's pickup truck toolbox. How they'd looked at it together and then had sex on the floor.

"Mom!" Heather plugged her ears and frowned.

Emma laughed and lost her breath, waiting for the next bit of hilarity, which Sarah volunteered. She had answered the door in her bra a while back, surprising the mailman.

"He wanted you, Momma," said Sally.

"Well, he's got a pot belly and a tattoo. Maybe I'll pass." She lit a cigarette.

They talked for a few more minutes, but Sally couldn't wait any longer. "Emma, I got the test. You need to know." Everyone went silent.

"It could be too soon," said Emma. A little color drained from her face. "Maybe tomorrow."

"But we won't be around. You need us with you. But do it for yourself, okay?"

A horn blew in the driveway.

"That's Sammy," said Sally. "Come to join the party." Sammy worked at the stone quarry and got off at five.

Everyone fidgeted and watched for the storm door to open. Sammy waltzed in with a daisy that he'd picked in the yard. "Emma! Your worst nightmare is here!"

Emma stood and let Sammy squeeze the life out of her. "Hey, brother-in-law! My, you look tan and fit." She gave him a squeeze back. "Get a chair. We were just talking about you."

Sammy pulled over a barstool from the counter. "Is that pecan pie? I'm absolutely starving. I thought maybe you'd have a big spread to celebrate with." He helped himself to a slice and licked his lips. "Should've washed my hands. Oh well." He looked around, waiting to be included in the conversation.

"Yeah, what's for dinner?" asked Emma. "I don't see any steaks on the grill. I have been away for a year and a half."

"Well," said Sarah. "I thought we'd go to the Seafood Box. What you think?"

"Yum," said Heather.

"Oh, that's perfect," said Sally.

"Suits me," said Sammy.

"Did we invite you?" asked Emma. She laughed.

"You can't get rid of me," said Sammy. "Like an old dog that you feed."

Emma smiled and yawned. She felt like she was being cared for, that there was a busy machine holding her up and cheering her on. "Can I get a quick shower? I'm filthy. I've been meaning to take one all day."

"Sure, baby girl, go ahead," said Sarah. "We ain't in no hurry." She coughed, and her chest rattled with phlegm.

"No talking while I'm gone, okay?" Emma stood and walked into the living room.

"I can't get over how she looks so different," said Sally. "Like she's some kind of foreigner. You notice that?"

Heather agreed. "Lost that weight too."

"I think she looks good," said Sarah. "Travel will change a person."

"But she's the same old Emma," said Sammy. "I didn't

realize how much I missed her till now." He finished his pie and went for a cup of coffee from the pot on the counter. It was cold, but he didn't care.

"Sammy, something bad happened to her over there. I've already told Heather," said Sally. Her face went serious.

Sammy looked worried. "What? What happened?"

Sally looked at Sarah. Sarah nodded. "She was raped by soldiers, two of them, over there, right before she came home." She took a deep breath.

Sammy looked sick. "Oh, hell no. I had no idea from the way she acted."

Sarah coughed.

"We were about to have her do a test, but you came rolling in."

"A test? You mean…"

"Yeah, that," said Sally.

"Jesus fucking Christ," said Sammy. He sipped his cold coffee.

"Mom, don't talk about it," said Heather. "It makes me sick."

"Me too," said Sarah.

"She needs us to talk to about it. She can't get all bottled up. That would be worse." She thought about her father, touching her all those years ago, and shivered.

"That's true," said Sammy.

They also talked more about Emma and Reece, wondering what would become of them. Sammy said he couldn't be a bad guy, being a volunteer and being shot like that. He said he wanted to meet him and thank him for being with Emma over there.

In the shower, Emma soaped her hair with Prell and cried into the hot water. She knew they were talking about her, that Sally was telling Sammy about the rape. She recovered, toweled off, and put her blue dress back on. She combed her wet hair straight back and gazed at herself in the fogged mirror, wiping a clear spot there. She wondered if Reece had told Kristin yet about picking her up, about Waffle House, and then the kiss on the carport.

"There she is!" said Sammy. They were still gathered at the kitchen table. "You ready? Let's take two cars so we can scoot home after dinner."

"Well, y'all have to take both of your cars, and I can drive Mom," said Emma.

"No way!" said Sally. "We're piling into Mom's car, all together." She had the test kit in her purse.

"I'll have to move my truck," said Sammy. He knew that Sally was serious. "I'll drive, and Emma's got shotgun."

"Damn straight," said Sally. "All for one, and one for all!"

Emma smiled, feeling lucky beyond lucky.

They piled into the big Buick, and Sammy backed out of the driveway, turning around in the yard.

"Don't hit the yellowbells," said Sarah. She was squeezed between Sally and Heather.

It took just five minutes, and Sammy pulled into the Seafood Box, a hole-in-the-wall café that only served fried white fish, hushpuppies, fried dill pickles, and creamy slaw. They had to wait a few minutes for a booth to clear.

"Y'all look like a happy bunch," said the waitress. Her name was Emma, too. She took their orders and sashayed to get their drinks, sweet teas all around.

"I dreamed about this place once while I was over there," said Emma. "I swear I did."

"So, tell us what you ate over there, baby girl. I know you wrote me about it."

Emma brightened. "Mostly enjera, this big flat pancake made from teff, a kind of black grain. It was sour, fermented, but was so good. There were little stews called wots that you ate with it. Super spicy. Goat, sheep, chicken, beans."

"Did your stomach stay upset? I know you got sick," said Sally.

"Pretty much all the time. I got amoebiasis twice, burping rotten eggs. I don't want to talk about that, though. Yuck. Diarrhea to kill a horse."

Sammy laughed. Emma, the waitress, put two baskets of mini fried hushpuppies on the table with three dipping sauces. "Y'all enjoy."

"Aunt Emma," said Heather. "What did you drink?"

"Water mostly, but you could buy Cokes and Fanta in the city. At night, I would make tea. They had teahouses that made really sweet spiced teas, and the coffee was yummy, although I'm not a big coffee drinker. Sammy, they had some good beer you would have liked, the bottled kind. There was a homemade brew that tasted like smoke, called talla. Kind of made me gag."

"Sounds pretty damn normal. Fanta and beer." He put his arm around her and squeezed. He joked with Sally that he would have married Emma if Sally had said no.

They continued with small talk until the food arrived, big red plastic baskets lined with wax paper and filled with fried fish, fries, and little tubs of slaw and tartar sauce. Emma, the waitress, put two bottles of ketchup on the table. "Y'all good?"

"Good enough," said Sammy.

"Thank you," said Emma.

"She just got back from Africa," said Sarah, nodding toward Emma.

Emma, the waitress, put her hands on her hips. "Well, ain't that something. I declare. You just never know." She hurried back to the kitchen, pushing through the heavy gray door.

Emma laughed. She knew that it was pointless to try to explain her trip in a few words. Better to just keep quiet.

"Well," said Sally, "while we're waiting for the fish to cool down, maybe us girls should hit the powder room." She tried to kick Emma under the table, and kicked Sammy instead.

"Hey now. Just eat, for God's sake. It'll get cold," said Sammy.

Emma knew what Sally was up to. She didn't want to do a pregnancy test at the Seafood Box. "Let's just eat, sister dear." She winked at Sally.

Sarah coughed. She needed a cigarette. "Just hold your horses, but go if you need to." She listened as Sally whispered into her ear. "Here? You crazy?"

"You need to know, and the sooner the better," said Sally. "Just trying to be the big sister is all."

Emma ate a French fry dipped in tartar sauce. "No, not right now. Wait till we get home, okay?" She felt pale and sick at the thought of a positive test. What the hell would she do?

Sally rolled her eyes and folded her arms. "Two minutes?"

"Sally," said Sarah. "Let her be. She's eating. I'm eating. You've got the patience of a two-year-old."

Heather laughed. "The bathroom's tiny. We can't all fit in there anyway."

"Hush and eat," said Sally. She took a bite of fish.

"Dang, this is good," said Emma. She could feel the air conditioning blowing her hair. She gazed around the small space, which had three booths and five tables, all full. A cute little girl sat in an old-fashioned highchair with a metal tray, her face a mess of ketchup and grease. Emma smiled and realized her body was capable of creating such a thing.

They ate and ate until the baskets sat empty, save the wax paper. The clock on the wall said 6:25.

Sammy picked up the tab, shelling out three twenties. "Y'all ready?"

"Sammy, you go outside. Us girls are going to the bathroom. No buts about it. Emma?" Sally stood with her hands on her hips.

"Sally!" said Sarah. "Don't be so pushy. Emma, you do what you want."

Emma felt like she was about to get on a roller coaster. A mantle of dread settled over her, and Sally was holding her hand, and they were walking to the bathroom with Heather and Sarah in tow.

The door was locked, and they waited for what seemed an eternity before a large woman with strings of beads emerged. She looked embarrassed, fanning her face.

Sally took charge, hustling everyone inside and closing the door. They stood shoulder to shoulder in the tiny room, which held a sink and one toilet, with a heavy-duty plunger beside it.

"Ugh, wall-to-wall stink," said Emma. The bathroom felt dirty and forbidding. "So, what next?"

"Sit on the commode," said Sally. She had opened the box and withdrawn the blue and white stick. "Says it'll show blue for positive and pink for negative." Her hand shook.

"For Pete's sake," said Sarah. "This is crazy."

Sally was in control. "Now, Emma, you pee, and I'll hold this in the stream." She jostled for elbow room. "Y'all stand back."

Emma looked up at the most important women in her life. She thought about Misrak and the women in the shelter, the soldiers pressing her into the dirt and rocks, the little girl who had been burned. Nothing would come, and then she closed her eyes.

"Turn the water on in the sink!" said Sally.

Sarah turned the squeaky knob, and water whistled from the tap.

Emma imagined squatting in the shintabet back in Godo, over the toilet seat cemented into the floor. If she could pee there, she could pee here, surrounded by her crazy family.

"That's a girl," said Sally. She dipped the instrument into the flow of urine and pulled it back, dripping. She stood, afraid to look. The test took two minutes to percolate.

Emma finished peeing, her head in her hands, and just sat there staring at her tennis shoes, the floor made of tiny white square tiles. The grout had gone black in places.

A quiet settled in the room, the toilet flushing. There was a knock at the door, and someone was rattling the knob.